FRITZ LEIBER

THE DEFINITIVE
CHANGE WAR COLLECTION

Creative Minority Productions
Montrose, CA

FIRST EDITION, 2016

Creative Minority web site:
http://www.creativeminorityproductions.com

ISBN:
978-1-944327-03-3 (Library Binding)
978-1-944327-02-6 (Paperback)
978-1-944327-04-0 (Ebook)

This book was created using the LaTeX typesetting system. The body text is set in the font Palatino, created by Hermann Zaph.

Cover by Kevin A. Straight

"Try and Change the Past" first published in *Astounding Science Fiction*, 1958; "The Big Time" first published in *Galaxy*, 1958; "A Deskful of Girls" first published in *The Magazine of Fantasy and Science Fiction*, 1958; "Damnation Morning" first published in *Fantastic*, 1959; "The Oldest Soldier" first published in *The Magazine of Fantasy and Science Fiction*, 1960; "No Great Magic" first published in *Galaxy*, 1960; "When the Change Winds Blow" first published in *The Magazine of Fantasy and Science Fiction*, 1964; "Knight to Move" first published in *Broadside*, 1965.

Snakes & Spiders:
The Definitive Change War Collection

Contents

CONTENTS

Introduction

Time travel is one of the classic themes in science fiction, inspiring untold thousands of stories. Every author treats the mechanics differently, from the epic but linear depiction in H.G. Wells' *The Time Machine*, to the fragile time continuum in Ray Bradbury's *A Sound of Thunder*, in which the death of a single prehistoric butterfly is enough to change the entire course of history, to the many permutations of Robert Heinlein's systems of interconnected alternate timelines[1]. Fritz Leiber's concept, as set forth in the Change War stories, is notable in several ways. Firstly, Leiber sees the timeline as unitary. That is, everyone is on one single timeline; changes in the past change the future for the whole universe. This is in contrast to the Heinleinian idea that a change in the timeline at any point creates a divergence point, spawning an alternate reality[2], and that a character might be able to travel between these realities. In the Change War universe there is only one reality which leads different factions to try and change the past deliberately for their own benefit. At the same time, temporally aware individuals—"doublegangers"—are able to retain memories of the former timeline even after changes are made, a necessary device since it allows them to plot temporal strategy and be aware of the actions of their enemies.

The time stream in Leiber's world, however, is far from fragile,

> Change one event in the past and you get a brand new future? Erase the conquests of Alexander by nudging a Neolithic pebble? Extirpate America by pulling up a shoot of Sumerian grain? Brother, that isn't the way it works at all! The space-time continuum's built of stubborn stuff and change is anything but a chain-reaction. Change the past and

---

[1] Interestingly, Heinlein was one of Leiber's favorite contemporary authors and is the only one of the so-called "Big Three", Heinlein, Asimov, and Clark, to whose work he periodically alludes in his stories and essays.

[2] Modern physics, at least at the time I write, seems to be leaning towards the "many alternate realities" theory.

you start a wave of changes moving futurewards, but it damps out mighty fast[3].

The "Law of Conservation of Reality", propounded in *Try and Change the Past* and *The Big Time*, states that the universe resists changes in the way things should happen. This means that it is *hard* to change the timeline; it requires careful planning and coordinated effort. An individual time traveler accidentally killing a butterfly—or even deliberately assassinating a historical individual—is unlikely to change anything; it requires concerted effort by a large, well-equipped covert organization.

Perhaps the dominant characteristic of Leiber's time travel stories, however, is that most of them aren't really about time travel. While time travel provides the setting, the stories are about people—their weaknesses, foibles, and capacity to deal with change. In contrast to many "hard" sci-fi writers, who are more interested in exploring the abstract effects of their time travel mechanics, Leiber explores the personal and interpersonal conflicts created by people dealing with their own, often petty, problems while caught up in a struggle they don't really understand between organizations in which they are only minor players.

Many critics have attempted to cast the Change War as a metaphor for the social struggles of the twentieth century, or for mankind's response to the rapidly increasing pace of change in modern life, the so called "accelerative thrust[4]." Others have pointed out the importance of the theme of the individual versus the organization or society. Certainly, all these messages are characteristic of Leiber's work and are present in force in the Change War. But too much focus on these themes risks missing the universal nature of these stories. These characters could live in any society, with or without time travel. These situations could arise in any war.

Why publish another Fritz Leiber anthology? Leiber is already one of the most anthologized writers of the twentieth century, and at least three previous books have collected substantial portions of his Change War series. That being the case, I feel obliged, as an editor, to explain why this edition is special.

The most important reason is to offer the stories to a new generation of readers. All three of the previous Change War anthologies are currently out of print—and these stories are too good not to be readily available. And because this edition will be offered in both e-book and print on demand (POD) versions, these stories will never go out of print again.

A second reason is a desire to create a *definitive* edition. Neither Ace's *The Mind Spider and Other Stories* (1961) nor Gregg's *The Change War*

---

[3] *Try and Change The Past*
[4] As Alvin Toffler calls it in his bestselling book *Future Shock*.

(1978), nor Ace's *Changewar* (1983) include the novelette *The Big Time* which is, in many ways, the keystone story of the canon. While it is true that Ace also published a double edition of *The Mind Spider* and *The Big Time,* that book is now nearly impossible to find. Additionally, previous anthologies included other Fritz Leiber stories which, while wonderful in their own way, were not actually about the Change War[5]. This book is intended to provide all the Change War stories, and only the Change War stories, in a handsome, readable, easily available format.

Fritz Leiber is one for the greatest names in speculative fiction. His work spanned the genres of hard science fiction, social science fiction, horror, and sword and sorcery and often mixed elements from each. A "writer's writer", he won nearly every award his peers could bestow and is listed as a major influence by countless contemporary authors. As a horror writer he is the undisputed link between the older work of H.P. Lovecraft and Edgar Allan Poe and that of modern writers such as Stephen King and Neil Gaiman. He has been credited with more or less single-handedly reanimating the genre of Gothic horror in America. In fantasy his Fafhrd and Grey Mouser cycle is probably the most famous sword and sorcery series of all time[6].

Leiber was born in Chicago in 1910 to famous Shakespearean actors Fritz Leiber Sr. and Virginia Bronson Leiber. The influence of the theater, first imparted by his parents and then reinforced by his own short but modestly successful acting career, was one of the most important formative factors on his writing. Both his dramatic sensibilities and his comfort with period dialog suffuse his work, giving it a dramatic and linguistic depth which few other writers have obtained.

As a young man "Fritzie" Leiber briefly toured with his parents' acting company before attending The University of Chicago, then in one of its golden ages. He graduated into the height of the Great Depression. An Episcopalian priest friend talked him in to studying for the ministry, since a clergical career would provide steady and comfortable employment. Although Leiber found the academic side of the seminary relatively easy after the University of Chicago, and his acting background and personal charisma made him well suited to preaching, he decided that he had no genuine call to the priesthood.

He left the seminary after a year and returned to the University of Chicago to attend graduate school on a scholarship, studying philosophy. While there he met his future wife Jonquil Stevens. During this period he also wrote some of his first short stories and poetry.

---

[5]See the appendix "List of Change War Apocrypha."

[6]The other candidate would be Robert E. Howards *Conan* but, while *Conan* enjoys greater name recognition, largely as a result of the movies, Leiber's series has stayed in print for a larger proportion of its history and sold more total copies.

After school Leiber acted again, doing another tour with his parents. Their final shows were on the west coast, where Fritz Leiber Sr. disbanded the company and settled in Hollywood to focus on his film acting career. Fritzie stayed with his parents for a few months, playing small roles in movies, until he was offered a job back in Chicago writing scientific articles for an encyclopedia. In his free time he kept working on fiction projects, finally selling *Two Sought Adventure*, his first Fafhrd and Grey Mouser story, in 1939. As yet, however, fiction writing provided only a tiny fraction of his income. In 1941 the Leibers moved back to California, where he took a position at Occidental College as a teacher of speech and drama. Fritz had fun teaching plays he had acted in with his parents and directing college productions, but he had trouble fitting into academic life; department politics bored him and he felt that his new colleagues took themselves much too seriously. When Pearl Harbor brought the US into World War II he quickly overcame his pacifist scruples and took a job at Douglas Aircraft in Santa Monica as a quality inspector on DC-3 aircraft—as much to get away from Occidental as to help with the war effort. After the war the Leibers returned to Chicago and Fritz went back to his old encyclopedia job at *Science Digest,* this time as editor.

Fritz Leiber had always been a heavy drinker and by the 1950's he was showing signs of full-blown alcoholism. His lifetime of struggle with that disease provided another major influence on his fiction. He reached a personal bottom between 1954 and 1956, spending his off-work hours too drunk to write at all. In 1957, with the help of Alcoholics Anonymous, he became sober. Soon after he wrote his first three Change War stories: *The Big Time, Try and Change the Past,* and *A Deskful of Girls,* selling all three in the same month to different magazines . The success of these and other stories that he sold that year gave him the confidence to move back to California and begin writing fiction full time in a borrowed studio overlooking the coastal valleys of Los Angeles.

Jonquil's death in 1969 radically changed Leiber's life. He moved north to San Francisco and entered another dark alcoholic period. He spent the lonely years of the 1970's living and working in tiny apartment, poor, and troubled with alcohol and barbiturate abuse.

Things looked up in the 1980's as Leiber began to be an active participant in the emerging science fiction convention scene, where he was able to connect with other writers and fans. When the gaming company TSR licensed his Fafhrd and the Grey Mouser mythos for their Dungeons and Dragons game he found himself with a regular income for the first time in years. In 1992 Leiber, now an elder statesman figure in the sci-fi community and (mostly) sober, married his long-time friend Margo Skinner. A few months later he collapsed on the way home from a convention and died in a few weeks at the age of eighty-two.

INTRODUCTION

All of the stories which make up the Change War cannon were written and published over a seven year period beginning in 1957, but Leiber lived another 34 years and kept writing science fiction up to the week he died. Why did he stop writing Change War stories?

One explanation is financial. For most of his life Leiber was a poor man. Although he seemed satisfied with a fairly simple life, especially after his wife's death, he periodically felt poverty's bite. The Change War was never a huge money maker; the original stories were sold to magazines at the going word rate, and the novelization of *The Big Time* and reprints of the stories in various anthologies, while popular with fans, provided only modest royalties spread over many years. It was the proceeds of a Fafhrd and The Grey Mouser story that gave him the confidence to start writing seriously and it was the money from licensing the Fafhrd and The Grey Mouser which provided him with a comfortable lifestyle in his old age. Given finite resources of time and creative energy, it is natural that he would focus on the series which was more likely to pay his rent.

This mercenary explanation seems inadequate, however. Leiber was already playing with the ideas which would later become the Change War while he was still in graduate school and seems never to have stopped thinking about them. It seems incredible that in the large corpus of short stories he wrote between 1964 and 1992 he never revisited his second most popular franchise. A deeper explanation requires an understanding of Leiber's philosophy of speculative fiction, particularly the role of the mysterious. In his one-page forward to *The Mind Spider and Other Stories* he writes, "...I sometimes think the powers that created the universe were chiefly interested in maximizing its mystery. That's why I write science fiction." Fritz Leiber didn't believe in answering all the questions. Mystery for him was one of the defining elements of the genres in which he wrote, and his best fiction always leaves the reader with a sense of ambiguity. One of the central tropes of *The Change War* is that none of the characters ever knows what is going on outside their own limited viewpoint.

Had he continued to write more Change War stories, Leiber would have been forced to start filling in the blanks and connecting larger plot arcs. In the Fafhrd and Grey Mouser stories, once he had established the mythos, his later stories fleshed out the chronology of the characters' lives and expanded the details of their world. Had he applied such an approach to the Change War universe it would have destroyed the same sense of the unknown which he had worked so hard to create. He was simply too great an artist to do that.

Except that he was working on a new Change War story when he died. His son Justin found it among his father's effects and has written that it involved the character Sidney Lessingham (whom you will meet in *The Big Time* and *No Great Magic*) with stop-overs in contemporary San Francisco and the Roman Republic of the Gracchi brothers. Such scant details are maddening for *Change War* fans. Leiber was finally ready to come back to the Change War. Had he lived a few more years, this anthology might have been twice as long.

We will never get to read that final story. Justin Leiber could have completed it: he is a multiply published science fiction writer in his own right, an expert on his father's writings, and (in his academic life) frequently writes philosophical essays on the theory of time. It is hard to imagine a writer better qualified to pick up where Fritz left off. In recent decades we have seen other second generation writers like Christopher Tolkein, Todd McCaffrey, and Brian Herbert continuing their parents' work. But Justin decided not to finish his father's last story or write new ones. I am as desperate as anyone to know what Lessingham was doing in Rome, but I can respect his decision. No matter how fine a job he had done, the result would have been a Justin Leiber story, not a Fritz Leiber one.

The final section of an introduction is where most editors take a few pages to introduce each story and put it in context, but I'm not going to do that. For one thing, it is almost impossible to do without introducing spoilers or at least biasing the readers reception of the story with the editor's own preconceptions. If you have read these stories before, then they don't need an introduction from me. If this is your first experience with the Change War, or you have never read Leiber at all, then I want to try and give you the experience of wonder you would have had if you had come across them in a golden age pulp magazine, as they were intended to be discovered.

I do, however, feel that a brief note is in order regarding the order in which the stories appear. Because these are time travel stories in a reality that is constantly shifting, there is no way to establish an internal chronology. Additionally, only a few characters appear in more than one story. One solution would have been to print the stories in publication order, on the theory that this was the order in which Leiber expected them to be read. In my opinion, however, this is not the best presentation from a standpoint of dramatic pacing. Instead, after considerable thought, I have arranged them in an order that I feel gives the most logical and entertaining introduction to the Change War universe.

And so, welcome to the Change War.

Kevin A. Straight
February 2016

Selected Bibliography

Leiber, Fritz. (1961). "Forward" in *The Mind Spider and Other Stories*. New York, NY: Ace Books.

Leiber, Fritz. (1984). "Not So Much Disorder and Not So Early Sex" in *The Ghost Light*. New Work, NY: Berkley Publishing Corporation.

Leiber, Justin. (2008). "But Time and Chance Happeneth to them All: The Genesis and Applications of Fritz Leiber's Theory of Time" in *Fritz Leiber: Critical Essays*. Jefferson, NC: McFarland & Co., Inc., Publishers.

Staicar, Tom. (1983). *Fritz Leiber*. New York, NY: Frederick Unger Publishing Co.

Silversack, John. (1978). "Introduction" in *The Change War*. Boston, MA: Gregg Press.

The Oldest Soldier

The one we called the Leutnant took a long swallow of his dark Lowenbrau. He'd just been describing a battle of infantry rockets on the Eastern Front, the German and Russian positions erupting bundles of flame.

Max swished his paler beer in its green bottle and his eyes got a faraway look and he said, "When the rockets killed their thousands in Copenhagen, they laced the sky with fire and lit up the steeples in the city and the masts and bare spars of the British ships like a field of crosses."

"I didn't know there were any landings in Denmark," someone remarked with an expectant casualness.

"This was in the Napoleonic wars," Max explained. "The British bombarded the city and captured the Danish fleet. Back in 1807."

"Vas you dere, Maxie?" Woody asked, and the gang around the counter chuckled and beamed. Drinking at a liquor store is a pretty dull occupation and one is grateful for small vaudeville acts.

"Why bare spars?" someone asked.

"So there'd be less chance of the rockets setting the launching ships afire," Max came back at him. "Sails burn fast and wooden ships are tinder anyway–that's why ships firing red-hot shot never worked out. Rockets and bare spars were bad enough. Yes, and it was Congreve rockets made the "red glare" at Fort McHenry, he continued unruffled, "while the 'bombs bursting in air' were about the earliest precision artillery shells, fired from mortars on bomb-ketches. There's a condensed history of arms in the American anthem." He looked around smiling.

"Yes, I was there, Woody—just as I was with the South Martians when they stormed Copernicus in the Second Colonial War. And just as I'll be in a foxhole outside Copeybawa a billion years from now while the blast waves from the battling Venusian spaceships shake the soil and roil the mud and give me some more digging to do."

This time the gang really snorted its happy laughter and Woody was slowly shaking his head and repeating, "Copenhagen and Copernicus and—what was the third? Oh, what a mind he's got," and the Leutnant was saying, "Yah, you vas there—in books," and I was thinking, *Thank*

[1]

God for all the screwballs, especially the brave ones who never flinch, who never lose their tempers or drop the act, so that you never do quite find out whether its just a gag or their solemnest belief. There's only one person here takes Max even one percent seriously, but they all love him because he won't ever drop his guard...

"The only point I was trying to make," Max continued when he could easily make himself heard, "was the way styles in weapons keep moving in cycles."

"Did the Romans use rockets?" asked the same light voice as had remarked about the landings in Denmark and the bare spars. I saw now it was Sol from behind the counter.

Max shook his head. "Not so you'd notice. Catapults were their specialty." He squinted his eyes, "Though now you mention it, I recall a dogfoot telling me Archimedes faked up some rockets powdered with Greek fire to touch off the sails of the Roman ships at Syracuse—and none of this romance about a giant burning glass."

"You mean," said Woody, "that there are other gazebos besides yourself in this fighting-all-over-the-universe-and-to-the-end-of-time racket?" His deep whiskey voice was at its solemnest and most wondering.

"Naturally," Max told him earnestly. "How else do you suppose wars ever get really fought and refought?"

"Why should wars ever be refought?" Sol asked lightly. "Once ought to be enough."

"Do you suppose anybody could time-travel and keep his hands off wars?" Max countered.

I put in my two cents' worth. "Then that would make Archimedes' rockets the earliest liquid-fuel rockets by a long shot."

Max looked straight at me, a special quirk in his smile. "Yes, I guess so," he said after a couple of seconds. "On this planet, that is."

The laughter had been falling off, but that brought it back and while Woody was saying loudly to himself, "I like that refighting part—that's what we're all so good at," the Leutnant asked Max with only a moderate accent that fit North Chicago, "And zo you aggshually have fought on Mars?"

"Yes, I have," Max agreed after a bit. "Though that ruckus I mentioned happened on our moon—expeditionary forces from the Red Planet."

"Ach, yes. And now let me ask you something—"

I really mean that about screwballs, you know. I don't care whether they're saucer addicts or extrasensory perception bugs or religious or musical maniacs or crackpot philosophers or psychologists or merely guys with a strange dream or gag like Max—for my money they are the ones who are keeping individuality alive in this age of conformity. They are the ones who are resisting the encroachments of the mass media and motivation research and the mass man. The only really bad thing about crack pottery and screwballistics (as with dope and prostitution) is the coldblooded people who prey on it for money. So I say to all screwballs: Go it on your own. Don't take any wooden nickels or give out any silver dimes. Be wise and brave—like Max.

He and the Leutnant were working up a discussion of the problems of artillery in airless space and low gravity that was a little too technical to keep the laughter alive. So Woody up and remarked, "Say, Maximillian, if you got to be in all these wars all over hell and gone, you must have a pretty tight schedule. How come you got time to be drinking with us bums?"

"I often ask myself that," Max cracked back at him. "Fact is, I'm on a sort of unscheduled furlough, result of a transportation slip-up. I'm due to be picked up and returned to my outfit any day now—that is, if the enemy underground doesn't get to me first."

It was just then, as Max said that bit about enemy underground, and as the laughter came, a little diminished, and as Woody was chortling "Enemy underground now. How do you like that?" and as I was thinking how much Max had given me in these couple of weeks—a guy with an almost poetic flare for vivid historical reconstruction, but with more than that...it was just then that I saw the two red eyes low down in the dusty plate glass window looking in from the dark street.

Everything in modern America has to have a big plate glass display window, everything from suburban mansions, general managers' offices and skyscraper apartments to barber shops and beauty parlors and gin mills—there are even gymnasium swimming pools with plate glass windows twenty feet high opening on busy boulevards—and Sol's dingy liquor store was no exception; in fact I believe there's a law that it's got to be that way. But I was the only one of the gang who happened to be looking out of this particular window at the moment. It was a dark windy night outside and it's a dark untidy street at best and across from Sol's are more plate glass windows that sometimes give off very odd reflections, so when I got a glimpse of this black formless head with the two eyes like red coals peering in past the brown pyramid of empty whiskey bottles, I don't suppose it was a half second before I realized it must be something like a couple of cigarette butts kept alive by the wind, or more likely a freak reflection of tail lights from some car turning a corner down street, and in another half second it was gone, the car having finished turning the comer or the wind blowing the cigarette butts away altogether. Still, for a moment it gave me a very goosey feeling, coming right on top of that remark about an enemy underground.

And I must have shown my reaction in some way, for Woody, who is very observant, called out, "Hey, Fred, has that soda pop you drink started to rot your nerves—or are even Max's friends getting sick at the outrageous lies he's been telling us?"

Max looked at me sharply and perhaps he saw something too. At any rate he finished his beer and said, "I guess I'll be taking off." He didn't say it to me particularly, but he kept looking at me. I nodded and put down on the counter my small green bottle, still one-third full of the lemon pop I find overly sweet, though it was the sourest Sol stocked. Max and I zipped up our wind-breakers. He opened the door and a little of the wind came in and troubled the tanbark around the sill. The Leutnant said to Max, "Tomorrow night we design a better space gun;" Sol routinely advised the two of us, "Keep your noses clean;" and Woody called, "So long space soldiers." (And I could imagine him saying as the door closed, "That Max is nuttier than a fruitcake and Freddy isn't much better. Drinking soda pop—ugh!")

And then Max and I were outside leaning into the wind, our eyes slitted against the blown dust, for the three-block trudge to Max's pad—a name his tiny apartment merits without any attempt to force the language.

There weren't any large black shaggy dogs with red eyes slinking about and I hadn't quite expected there would be.

Why Max and his soldier-of-history gag and our outwardly small comradeship meant so much to me is something that goes way back into my childhood. I was a lonely timid child, with no brothers and sisters to spar around with in preparation for the battles of life, and I never went through the usual stages of boyhood gangs either. In line with those things I grew up into a very devout liberal and "hated war" with a mystical fervor during the intermission between 1918 and 1939—so much so that I made a point of avoiding military service in the second conflict, though merely by working in the nearest war plant, not by the arduously heroic route of out-and-out pacifism.

But then the inevitable reaction set in, sparked by the liberal curse of being able, however, belatedly, to see both sides of any question. I began to be curious about and cautiously admiring of soldiering and soldiers. Unwillingly at first, I came to see the necessity and romance of the spearmen—those guardians, often lonely as myself, of the perilous camps of civilization and brotherhood in a black hostile universe...necessary guardians, for all the truth in the indictments that war caters to irrationality and sadism and serves the munition makers and reaction.

I commenced to see my own hatred of war as in part only a mask for cowardice, and I started to look for some way to do honor in my life to the other half of the truth. Though it's anything but easy to give yourself a feeling of being brave just because you suddenly want that feeling. Obvious opportunities to be obviously brave come very seldom in our largely civilized culture, in fact they're clean contrary to safety drives and so-called normal adjustment and good peacetime citizenship and all the rest, and they come mostly in the earliest part of a man's life. So that for the person who belatedly wants to be brave it's generally a matter of waiting for an opportunity for six months and then getting a tiny one and muffing it in six seconds.

But however uncomfortable it was, I had this reaction to my devout early pacifism, as I say. At first I took it out only in reading. I devoured war books, current and historical, fact and fiction. I tried to soak up the military aspects and jargon of all ages, the organization and weapons, the strategy and tactics. Characters like Tros of Samothrace and Horatio Hornblower became my new secret heroes, along with Heinlein's space cadets and Bullard and other brave rangers of the spaceways.

But after a while reading wasn't enough. I had to have some real soldiers and I finally found them in the little gang that gathered nightly at Sol's liquor store. It's funny but liquor stores that serve drinks have a clientele with more character and comradeship than the clienteles of most bars—perhaps it is the absence of jukeboxes, chromium plate, bowling machines, trouble-hunting, drink-cadging women, and—along with those—men in search of fights and forgetfulness. At any rate, it was at Sol's liquor store that I found Woody and the Leutnant and Bert and Mike and Pierre and Sol himself. The casual customer would hardly have guessed that they were anything but quiet souses, certainly not soldiers, but I got a clue or two and I started to hang around, making myself inconspicuous and drinking my rather symbolic soda pop, and pretty soon they started to open up and yarn about North Africa and Stalingrad and Anzio and Korea and such and I was pretty happy in a partial sort of way.

And then about a month ago Max had turned up and he was the man I'd really been looking for. A genuine soldier with my historical slant on things—only he knew a lot more than I did, I was a rank amateur by comparison—and he had this crazy appealing gag too, and besides that he actually cottoned to me and invited me on to his place a few times, so that with him I was more than a tavern hanger-on. Max was good for me, though I still hadn't the faintest idea of who he really was or what he did.

Naturally Max hadn't opened up the first couple of nights with the gang, he'd just bought his beer and kept quiet and felt his way much as I had. Yet he looked and felt so much the soldier that I think the gang was inclined to accept him from the start—a quick stocky man with big hands and a leathery face and smiling tired eyes that seemed to have seen everything at one time or another. And then on the third or fourth night Bert told something about the Battle of the Bulge and

Max chimed in with some things he'd seen there, and I could tell from the looks Bert and the Leutnant exchanged that Max had "passed"—he was now the accepted seventh member of the gang, with me still as the tolerated clerical-type hanger-on, for I'd never made any secret of my complete lack of military experience.

Not long afterwards—it couldn't have been more than one or two nights—Woody told some tall tales and Max started matching him and that was the beginning of the time-and-space-soldier gag. It was funny about the gag. I suppose we just should have assumed that Max was a history nut and liked to parade his bookish hobby in a picturesque way—and maybe some of the gang did assume just that—but he was so vivid yet so casual in his descriptions of other times and places that you felt there had to be something more and sometimes he'd get such a lost, nostalgic look on his face talking of things fifty million miles or five hundred years away that Woody would almost die laughing, which was really the sincerest sort of tribute to Max's convincingness.

Max even kept up the gag when he and I were alone together, walking or at his place—he'd never come to mine—though he kept it up in a minor-key sort of way, so that it sometimes seemed that what he was trying to get across was not that he was the Soldier of a Power that was fighting across all of time to change history, but simply that we men were creatures with imaginations and it was our highest duty to try to feel what it was really like to live in other times and places and bodies. Once he said to me, "The growth of consciousness is everything, Fred—the seed of awareness sending its roots across space and time. But it can grow in so many ways, spinning its web from mind to mind like the spider or burrowing into the unconscious darkness like the snake. The biggest wars are the wars of thought."

But whatever he was trying to get across, I went along with his gag—which seems to me the proper way to behave with any other man, screwball or not, so long as you can do it without violating your own personality. Another man brings a little life and excitement into the world, why try to kill it? It is simply a matter of politeness and style.

I'd come to think a lot about style since knowing Max. It doesn't matter so much what you do in life, he once said to me—soldiering or clerking, preaching or picking pockets—so long as you do it with style. Better to fail in a grand style than to succeed in a mean one—you won't enjoy the successes you get the second way.

Max seemed to understand my own special problems without my having to confess them. He pointed out to me that the soldier is trained for bravery. The whole object of military discipline is to make sure that when the six seconds of testing come every six months or so, you do the brave thing without thinking, by drilled second nature. It's not a matter of the soldier having some special virtue or virility the civilian lacks. And then about fear. All men are afraid, Max said, except a few psychopathic or suicidal types and they merely haven't fear at the conscious level. But the better you know yourself and the men around you and the situation you're up against (though you can never know all of the last and sometimes you have only a glimmering), then the better you are prepared to prevent fear from mastering you.

Generally speaking, if you prepare yourself by the daily self-discipline of looking squarely at life, if you imagine realistically the troubles and opportunities that may come, then the chances are you won't fail in the testing. Well, of course I'd heard and read all those things before, but coming from Max they seemed to mean a lot more to me. As I say, Max was good for me.

So on this night when Max had talked about Copenhagen and Copernicus and Copeybawa and I'd imagined I'd seen a big black dog with red eyes and we were walking the lonely streets hunched in our jackets and I was listening to the big clock over at the University tolling eleven...well, on this night I wasn't thinking anything special except that I was with my screwball buddy and pretty soon we'd be at his place and having a nightcap. I'd make mine coffee.

I certainly wasn't expecting anything.

Until, at the windy corner just before his place, Max suddenly stopped.

Max's junky front room-and-a-half was in a smoky brick building two flights up over some run-down stores. There is a rust-flaked fire-escape on the front of it, running past the old-fashioned jutting bay windows, its lowest flight a counter-balanced one that only swings down when somebody walks out onto it—that is, if a person ever had occasion to.

When Max stopped suddenly, I stopped too of course. He was looking up at his window. His window was dark and I couldn't see anything in particular, except that he or somebody else had apparently left a big black bundle of something out on the fire-escape and—it wouldn't be the first time I'd seen that space used for storage and drying wash and what not, against all fire regulations, I'm sure.

But Max stayed stopped and kept on looking.

"Say, Fred," he said softly then, "how about going over to your place for a change? Is the standing invitation still out?"

"Sure Max, why not," I replied instantly, matching my voice to his. "I've been asking you all along."

My place was just two blocks away. We'd only have to turn the corner we were standing on and we'd be headed straight for it.

"Okay, then," Max said. "Lets get going." There was a touch of sharp impatience in his voice that I'd never heard there before. He suddenly seemed very eager that we should get around that corner. He took hold of my arm.

He was no longer looking up at the fire-escape, but I was. The wind had abruptly died and it was very still. As we went around the corner—to be exact as Max pulled me around it—the big bundle of something lifted up and looked down at me with eyes like two red coals.

I didn't let out a gasp or say anything. I don't think Max realized then that I'd seen anything, but I was shaken. This time I couldn't lay it to cigarette butts or reflected tail lights, they were too difficult to place on a third-story fire escape. This time my mind would have to rationalize a lot more inventively to find an explanation, and until it did I would have to believe that something...well, alien...was at large in this part of Chicago.

Big cities have their natural menaces—hold-up artists, hopped-up kids, sick-headed sadists, that sort of thing—and you're more or less prepared for them. You're not prepared for something...alien. If you hear a scuttling in the basement you assume it's rats and although you know rats can be dangerous, you're not particularly frightened and you may even go down to investigate. You don't expect to find bird-catching Amazonian spiders.

The wind hadn't resumed yet. We'd gone about a third of the way down the first block when I heard behind us, faintly but distinctly, a rusty creaking ending in a metallic jar that didn't fit anything but the first flight of the fire escape swinging down to the sidewalk.

I just kept walking then, but my mind split in two—half of it listening and straining back over my shoulder, the other half darting off to investigate the weirdest notions, such as that Max was a refugee from some unimaginable concentration camp on the other side of the stars. If there were such concentration camps, I told myself in my cold hysteria, run by some sort of supernatural SS men, they'd have dogs just like the one I'd thought I'd seen...and, to be honest, thought I'd see padding along if I looked over my shoulder now.

It was hard to hang on and just walk, not run, with this insanity or whatever it was hovering over my mind, and the fact that Max didn't say a word didn't help either.

Finally, as we were starting the second block, I got hold of myself and I quietly reported to Max exactly what I thought I'd seen. His response surprised me.

"What's the layout of your apartment, Fred? Third floor, isn't it?"

"Yes. Well..."

"Begin at the door we'll be going in," he directed me.

"That's the living room, then there's a tiny short open hall, then the kitchen. It's like an hour-glass, with the living room and kitchen the

[8]

ends, and the hall the wasp waist. Two doors open from the hall: the one to your right (figuring from the living room) opens into the bathroom; the one to your left, into a small bedroom."

"Windows?"

"Two in the living room, side by side," I told him. "None in the bathroom. One in the bedroom, onto an air shaft. Two in the kitchen, apart."

"Back door in the kitchen?" he asked.

"Yes. To the back porch. Has glass in the top half of it. I hadn't thought about that. That makes three windows in the kitchen."

"Are the shades in the windows pulled down now?"

"No."

Questions and answers had been rapid-fire, without time for me to think, done while we walked a quarter of a block. Now after the briefest pause Max said, "Look, Fred, I'm not asking you or anyone to believe in all the things I've been telling as if for kicks at Sol's—that's too much for all of a sudden—but you do believe in that black dog, don't you? He touched my arm warningly. "No, don't look behind you!"

I swallowed. "I believe in him right now," I said.

"Okay. Keep on walking. I'm sorry I got you into this, Fred, but now I've got to try to get both of us out. Your best chance is to disregard the thing, pretend you're not aware of anything strange happened—then the beast won't know whether I've told you anything, it'll be hesitant to disturb you, it'll try to get at me without troubling you, and it'll even hold off a while if it thinks it will get me that way. But it won't hold off forever—it's only imperfectly disciplined. My best chance is to get in touch with headquarters—something I've been putting off—and have them pull me out. I should be able to do it in an hour, maybe less. You can give me that time, Fred."

"How?" I asked him. I was mounting the steps to the vestibule. I thought I could hear, very faintly, a light pad-padding behind us. I didn't look back.

Max stepped through the door I held open and we started up the stairs.

"As soon as we get in your apartment," he said, "you turn on all the lights in the living room and kitchen. Leave the shades up. Then start doing whatever you might be doing if you were staying up at this time of night. Reading or typing, say. Or having a bite of food, if you can manage it. Play it as naturally as you can. If you hear things, if you feel things, try to take no notice. Above all, don't open the windows or doors, or look out of them to see anything, or go to them if you can help it— you'll probably feel drawn to do just that. Just play it naturally. If you can hold them...it...off that way for half an hour or so—until midnight,

[9]

say—if you can give me that much time, I should be able to handle my end of it. And remember, it's the best chance for you as well as for me. Once I'm out of here, you're safe."

"But you—" I said, digging for my key, "—what will you—?"

"As soon as we get inside," Max said, "I'll duck in your bedroom and shut the door. Pay no attention. Don't come after me, whatever you hear. Is there a plug-in in your bedroom? I'll need juice."

"Yes," I told him, turning the key. "But the lights have been going off a lot lately. Someone has been blowing the fuses."

"That's great," he growled, following me inside.

I turned on the lights and went in the kitchen, did the same there and came back. Max was still in the living room, bent over the table beside my typewriter. He had a sheet of light-green paper. He must have brought it with him. He was scrawling something at the top and bottom of it. He straightened up and gave it to me.

"Fold it up and put it in your pocket and keep it on you the next few days," he said.

It was just a blank sheet of cracklingly thin light-green paper with "Dear Fred" scribbled at the top and "Your friend, Max Bournemann" at the bottom and nothing in between.

"But what—?" I began, looking up at him.

"Do as I say!" He snapped at me. Then, as I almost flinched away from him, he grinned—a great big comradely grin.

"Okay, lets get working," he said, and he went into the bedroom and shut the door behind him.

I folded the sheet of paper three times and unzipped my windbreaker and tucked it inside the breast pocket. Then I went to the bookcase and pulled at random a volume out of the top shelf—my psychology shelf, I remembered the next moment—and sat down and opened the book and looked at a page without seeing the print.

And now there was time for me to think. Since I'd spoken of the red eyes to Max there had been no time for anything but to listen and to remember and to act. Now there was time for me to think.

My first thoughts were: *This is ridiculous! I saw something strange and frightening, sure, but it was in the dark, I couldn't see anything clearly, there must be some simple natural explanation for whatever it was on the fire escape. I saw something strange and Max sensed I was frightened and when I told him about it he decided to play a practical joke on me in line with that eternal gag he lives by. I'll bet right now he's lying on my bed and chuckling, wondering how long it'll be before...*

The window beside me rattled as if the wind has suddenly risen again. The rattling grew more violent—and then it abruptly stopped without

[10]

dying away, stopped with a feeling of tension, as if the wind or something more material were still pressing against the pane.

And I did not turn my head to look at it, although (or perhaps because) I knew there was no fire escape or other support outside. I simply endured that sense of a presence at my elbow and stared unseeingly at the book in my hands, while my heart pounded and my skin froze and flushed.

I realized fully then that my first skeptical thoughts had been the sheerest automatic escapism and that, just as I'd told Max, I believed with my whole mind in the black dog. I believed in the whole business insofar as I could imagine it. I believed that there are undreamed of powers warring in this universe. I believed that Max was a stranded time-traveller and that in my bedroom he was now frantically operating some unearthly device to signal for help from some unknown headquarters. I believed that the impossible and the deadly was loose in Chicago.

But my thoughts couldn't carry further than that. They kept repeating themselves, faster and faster. My mind felt like an engine that is shaking itself to pieces. And the impulse to turn my head and look out the window came to me and grew.

I forced myself to focus on the middle of the page where I had the book open and start reading.

> Jung's archetype transgress the barriers of time and space. More than that: they are capable of breaking the shackles of the laws of causality. They are endowed with frankly mystical "prospective faculties." The soul itself, according to Jung, is the reaction of the personality to the unconscious and includes in every person both male and female elements, the animus and anima, as well as the persona or the persons reaction to the outside world...

I think I read that last sentence a dozen times, swiftly at first, then word by word, until it was a meaningless jumble and I could no longer force my gaze across it.

Then the glass in the window beside me creaked.

I laid down the book and stood up, eyes front, and went into the kitchen and grabbed a handful of crackers and opened the refrigerator.

The rattling that muted itself in hungry pressure followed. I heard it first in one kitchen window, then the other, then in the glass in the top of the door. I didn't look.

I went back in the living room, hesitated a moment beside my typewriter, which had a blank sheet of yellow paper in it, then sat down again in the armchair beside the window, putting the crackers and the half carton of milk on the little table beside me. I picked up the book I'd tried to read and put it on my knees.

The rattling returned with me—at once and peremptorily, as if something were growing impatient.

I couldn't focus on the print any more. I picked up a cracker and put it down. I touched the cold milk carton and my throat constricted and I drew my fingers away.

I looked at my typewriter and then I thought of the blank sheet of green paper and the explanation for Max's strange act suddenly seemed clear to me. Whatever happened to him tonight, he wanted me to be able to type a message over his signature that would exonerate me. A suicide note, say. Whatever happened to him...

The window beside me shook violently, as if at a terrific gust.

It occurred to me that while I must not look out the window as if expecting to see something (that would be the sort of give-away against which Max warned me) I could safely let my gaze slide across it—say, if I turned to look at the clock behind me. Only, I told myself, I mustn't pause or react if I saw anything.

I nerved myself. After all, I told myself, there was the blessed possibility that I would see nothing outside the taut pane but darkness.

I turned my head to look at the clock.

I saw it twice, going and coming back, and although my gaze did not pause or falter, my blood and my thoughts started to pound as if my heart and mind would burst.

It was about two feet outside the window—a face or mask or muzzle of a more gleaming black than the darkness around it. The face was at the same time the face of a hound, a panther, a giant bat, and a man—in between those four. A pitiless, hopeless man-animal face alive with knowledge but dead with a monstrous melancholy and a monstrous malice. There was the sheen of needlelike white teeth against black lips or dewlaps. There was the dull pulsing glow of eyes like red coals.

My gaze didn't pause or falter or go back—yes—and my heart and mind didn't burst, but I stood up then and stepped jerkily to the typewriter and sat down at it and started to pound the keys. After a while my gaze stopped blurring and I started to see what I was typing.

The first thing I'd typed was:

the quick red fox jumped over the crazy black dog...

I kept on typing. It was better than reading. Typing I was doing something, I could discharge. I typed a flood of fragments: "Now is

[12]

the time for all good men—, the first words of the Declaration of Independence and the Constitution, the Winston Commercial, six lines of Hamlet's "To be or not to be," without punctuation, Newton's Third Law of Motion, "Mary had a big black—

In the middle of it all the face of the electric clock that I'd looked at sprang into my mind. My mental image of it had been blanked out until then. The hands were at quarter to twelve.

Whipping in a fresh yellow sheet, I typed the first stanza of Poe's "Raven," the Oath of Allegiance to the American Flag, the lost-ghost lines from Thomas Wolfe, the Creed and the Lords prayer, "Beauty is truth; truth, blackness—"

The rattling made a swift circuit of the windows—though I heard nothing from the bedroom, nothing at all—and finally the rattling settled on the kitchen door. There was a creaking of wood and metal under pressure.

I thought: *You are standing guard. You are standing guard for yourself and for Max. And then the second thought came: If you open the door, you welcome it in, you open the kitchen door and then the bedroom door, it will spare you, it will not hurt you.*

Over and over again I fought down that second thought and the urge that went with it. It didn't seem to be coming from my mind, but from the outside. I typed Ford, Buick, the names of all the automobiles I could remember, *Overland Moon*, I typed all the four-letter words, I typed the alphabet, lower case and capitals. I typed the numerals and punctuation marks, I typed the keys of the keyboard in order from left to right, top to bottom, then in from each side alternately. I filled the last yellow sheet I was on and it fell out and I kept pounding mechanically, making shiny black marks on the dull black platen.

But then the urge became something I could not resist. I stood up and in the sudden silence I walked through the hall to the back door, looking down at the floor and resisting, dragging each step as much as I could.

My hands touched the knob and the long-handled key in the lock. My body pressed the door, which seemed to surge against me, so that I felt it was only my counter-pressure that kept it from bursting open in a shower of splintered glass and wood.

Far off, as if it were something happening in another universe, I heard the University clock tolling. One...two...

And then, because I could resist no longer, I turned the key and the knob.

The lights all went out.

In the darkness the door pushed open against me and something came in past me like a gust of cold black wind with streaks of heat in it.

[13]

I heard the bedroom door swing open.

The clock completed its strokes. Eleven...twelve...

And then...

Nothing...nothing at all. All pressures lifted from me. I was aware only of being alone, utterly alone. I knew it, deep down.

After some...minutes, I think, I shut and locked the door and I went over and opened a drawer and rummaged out a candle, lit it, and went through the apartment and into the bedroom.

Max wasn't there. I'd known he wouldn't be. I didn't know how badly I'd failed him. I lay down on the bed and after a while I began to sob and, after another while, I slept.

Next day I told the janitor about the lights. He gave me a funny look.

"I know," he said. "I just put in a new fuse this morning. I never saw one blown like that before. The window in the fuse was gone and there was a metal sprayed all over the inside of the box."

That afternoon I got Max's message. I'd gone for a walk in the park and was sitting on a bench beside the lagoon, watching the water ripple in the breeze when I felt something burning against my chest.

For a moment I thought Id dropped my cigarette butt inside my windbreaker. I reached in and touched something hot in my pocket and jerked it out. It was the sheet of green paper Max had given me.

Tiny threads of smoke were rising from it.

I flipped it open and read, in a scrawl that smoked and grew blacker instant by instant:

> Thought you'd like to know I got through okay. Just in time. I'm back with my outfit. It's not too bad. Thanks for the rearguard action.

The handwriting (thought-writing?) of the blackening scrawl was identical with the salutation above and the signature below.

And then the sheet burst into flame. I flipped it away from me. Two boys launching a model sailboat looked at the paper flaming, blackening, whitening, disintegrating...

I know enough chemistry to know that paper smeared with wet white phosphorus will burst into flame when it dries completely. And I know there are kinds of invisible writing that are brought out by heat. There are those general sorts of possibility. Chemical writing.

And then there's thought-writing, which is nothing but a word I've coined. Writing from a distance—a literal telegram.

And there may be a combination of the two—chemical writing activated by thought from a distance...from a great distance.

[14]

I don't know. I simply don't know. When I remember that last night with Max, there are parts of it I doubt. But there's one part I never doubt.

When the gang asks me, "Where's Max?" I just shrug.

But when they get to talking about withdrawals they've covered; rearguard actions they've been in, I remember mine. I've never told them about it, but I never doubt that it took place.

Damnation Morning

Time traveling, which is not quite the good clean boyish fun it's cracked up to be, started for me when this woman with the sigil on her forehead looked in on me from the open doorway of the hotel bedroom where I'd hidden myself and the bottles and asked me,

"Look, Buster, do you want to live?"

It was the sort of question would have suited a religious crackpot of the strong-arm, save-your-soul variety, but she didn't look like one.

And I might very well have answered it—in fact I almost did—with a hangover, one percent humorous, "Good God, no!" Or—a poor second—I could have studied the dark, dust-burnished arabesques of the faded blue carpet for a perversely long time and then countered with a grudging, "Oh, if you insist."

But I didn't, perhaps because there didn't seem to be anything like one percent of humor in the situation. Point One: I have been blacked out the past half hour or so—this woman might just have opened the door or she might have been watching me for ten minutes. Point Two: I was in the fringes of DTs, trying to come off a big drunk. Point Three: I knew for certain that I had just killed someone or left him or her to die, though I hadn't the faintest idea of whom or why.

Let me try to picture my state of mind a little more vividly. My consciousness, the sentient self-aware part of me, was a single quivering point in the center of an endless plane vibrating harshly with misery and menace. I was like a man in a rowboat in the middle of the Pacific—or better, I was like a man in a shellhole in the North-African desert (I served under Montgomery and any region adjoining the DTs is certainly a No Mans Land). Around me, in every direction—this is my consciousness I'm describing, remember—miles of flat burning sand, nothing more. Way beyond the horizon were two divorced wives, some estranged children, assorted jobs, and other unexceptional wreckage. Much closer, but still beyond the horizon, were State Hospital (twice) and Psycho (four times). Shallowly buried very near at hand, or perhaps blackening in the open just behind me in the shellhole, was the person I had killed.

But remember that I knew I had killed a real person. That wasn't anything allegorical.

Now for a little more detail on this "Look, Buster," woman. To begin with, she didn't resemble any part of the DTs or its outlying kingdoms, though an amateur might have thought differently—especially if he had given too much weight to the sigil on her forehead. But I was no amateur.

She seemed about my age—forty-five—but I couldn't be sure. Her body looked younger than that, her face older; both were trim and had seen a lot of use, I got the impression. She was wearing black sandals and a black unbelted tunic with just a hint of the sack dress to it, yet she seemed dressed for the street. It occurred to me even then (off-track ideas can come to you very swiftly and sharply in the DT outskirts) that it was a costume that, except perhaps for the color, would have fitted into any number of historical eras: old Egypt, Greece, maybe the Directoire, World War I, Burma, Yucatan, to name some. (Should I ask her if she spoke Mayathan? I didn't, but I don't think the question would have fazed her; she seemed altogether sophisticated, a real cosmopolite—she pronounced "Buster" as if it were part of a curious, somewhat ridiculous jargon she was using for shock purposes.)

From her left arm hung a black handbag that closed with a drawstring and from which protruded the tip of silvery object about which I found myself apprehensively curious.

Her right arm was raised and bent, the elbow touching the door frame, the hand brushing back the very dark bangs from her forehead to show me the sigil, as if that had a bearing on her question.

The sigil was an eight-limbed asterisk made of fine dark lines and about as big as a silver dollar. An X superimposed on a plus sign. It looked permanent.

Except for the bangs she wore her hair pinned up. Her ears were flat, thin-edged, and nicely shaped, with the long lobes that in Chinese art mark the philosopher. Small square silver flats with rounded corners ornamented them.

Her face might have been painted by Toulouse-Lautrec or Degas. The skin was webbed with very fine lines; the eyes were darkly shadowed and there was a touch of green on the lids (Egyptian?—I asked myself); her mouth was wide, tolerant, but realistic. Yes, beyond all else, she seemed realistic.

And as I've indicated, I was ready for realism, so when she asked, "Do you want to live?" I somehow managed not to let slip any of the flippant answers that came flocking into my mouth, I realized that this was the one time in a million when a big question is really meant and your answer really counts and there are no second chances, I realized that the line of my life had come to one of those points where there is a kink in

[18]

it and the wrong (or maybe the right) tug can break it and that as far as I was concerned at the present moment, she knew all about everything.

So I thought for a bit, not long, and I answered, "Yes."

She nodded—not as if she approved my decision, or disapproved it for that matter, but merely as if she accepted it as a basis for negotiations—and she let her bangs fall back across her forehead. Then she gave me a quick dry smile and she said, "In that case you and I have got to get out of here and do some talking."

For me that smile was the first break in the shell—the shell around my rancid consciousness or perhaps the dark, star-pricked shell around the space-time continuum.

"Come on," she said. "No, just as you are. Don't stop for anything and—" (She caught the direction of my immediate natural movement) "—don't look behind you if you meant that about wanting to live."

Ordinarily being told not to look behind you is a remarkably silly piece of advice, it makes you think of those "pursuing fiend" horror stories that scare children, and you look around automatically—if only to prove you're no child. Also in this present case there was my very real and dreadful curiosity: I wanted terribly (yes, terribly) to know whom it was I had just killed—a forgotten third wife? a stray woman? a jealous husband or boyfriend? (though I seemed too cracked up for love affairs) the hotel clerk? a fellow derelict?

But somehow, as with her "want to live" question, I had the sense to realize that this was one of those times when the usually silly statement is dead serious, that she meant her warning quite literally.

If I looked behind me, I would die.

I looked straight ahead as I stepped past the scattered brown empty bottles and the thin fume mounting from the tiny crater in the carpet where I'd dropped a live cigarette.

As I followed her through the door I caught, from the window behind me, the distant note of a police siren.

Before we reached the elevator the siren was nearer and it sounded as if the fire department had been called out too.

I saw a silvery flicker ahead. There was a big mirror facing the elevators.

"What I told you about not looking behind you goes for mirrors too," my conductress informed me. "Until I tell you differently."

The instant she said that, I knew that I had forgotten what I looked like; I simply could not visualize that dreadful witness (generally inhabiting a smeary bathroom mirror) of so many foggy mornings: my own face. One glance in the mirror...

But I told myself: realism. I saw a blur of brown shoes and black sandals in the big mirror, nothing more.

[19]

The cage of the right-hand elevator, dark and empty, was stopped at this floor. A cross-wise wooden bar held the door open. My conductress removed the bar and we stepped inside. The door closed and she touched the controls. I wondered, "Which way will it go? Sideways?"

It began to sink normally. I started to touch my face, but didn't. I started to try to remember my name, but stopped. It would be bad tactics, I thought, to let myself become aware of any more gaps in my knowledge. I knew I was alive. I would stick with that for a while.

The cage sank two and a half floors and stopped, its doorway blocked by the drab purple wall of the shaft. My conductress switched on the tiny dome light and turned to me.

"Well?" she said.

I put my last thought into words.

"I'm alive," I said, "and I'm in your hands."

She laughed lightly. "You find it a compromising situation? But you're quite correct. You accepted life from me, or through me, rather. Does that suggest anything to you?"

My memory may have been lousy, but another, long unused section of my mind was clicking. "When you get anything," I said, "you have to pay for it and sometimes money isn't enough, though I've only once or twice been in situations where money didn't help."

"Three times now," she said. "Here is how it stacks up: You've bought your way with something other than money, into an organization of which I am an agent. Or perhaps you'd rather go back to the room where I recruited you? We might just be able to manage it."

Through the walls of the cage and shaft I could hear the sirens going full blast, underlining her words.

I shook my head. I said, "I think I knew that—I mean, that I was joining an organization—when I answered your first question."

"It's a very big organization," she went on, as if warning me. "Call it an empire or a power if you like. So far as you are concerned, it has always existed and always will exist. It has agents everywhere, literally. Space and time are no barriers to it. Its purpose, so far as you will ever be able to know it, is to change, for its own aggrandizement, not only the present and future, but also the past. It is a ruthlessly competitive organization and is merciless to its employees."

"I. G. Farben?" I asked grabbing nervously and clumsily at humor.

She didn't rebuke my flippancy, but said, "And it isn't the Communist Party or the Ku Klux Klan, or the Avenging Angels or the Black Hand, either, though its enemies give it a nastier name."

"Which is?" I asked.

"The Spiders," she said.

That word gave me the shudders, coming so suddenly. I expected the sigil to step off her forehead and scuttle down her face and leap at me—something like that.

She watched me. "You might call it the Double Cross," she suggested, "if that seems better."

"Well, at least you don't try to prettify your organization," was all I could think to say.

She shook her head. "With the really big ones you don't have to. You never know if the side into which you are born or reborn is 'right' or 'good'—you only know that it's your side and you try to learn about it and form an opinion as you live and serve."

"You talk about sides," I said. "Is there another?"

"We won't go into that now," she said, "but if you ever meet someone with an S on his forehead, he's not a friend, no matter what else he may be to you. That S stands for Snakes."

I don't know why that word coming just then, gave me so much worse a scare—crystallized all my fears, as it were—but it did. Maybe it was only some little thing, like Snakes meaning DTs. Whatever it was, I felt myself turning to mush.

"Maybe we'd better go back to the room where you found me," I heard myself saying. I don't think I meant it, though I surely felt it.

The sirens had stopped, but I could hear a lot of general hubbub, outside the hotel and inside it too, I thought—noise from the other elevator shaft and it seemed to me, from the floor we'd just left—hurrying footsteps, taut voices, something being dragged. I knew terror here, in this stalled elevator, but that *loudness* outside would be worse.

"It's too late now," my conductress informed me. She slitted her eyes at me. "You see, Buster," she said, "you're still back in that room. You might be able to handle the problem of rejoining yourself if you went back alone, but not with other people around."

"What did you do to me?" I said very softly.

"I'm a Resurrectionist," she said as quietly. "I dig bodies out of the space-time continuum and give them the freedom of the fourth dimension. When I Resurrected you, I cut you out of your lifeline close to the point that you think of as the Now."

"My lifeline?" I interrupted. "Something in my palm?"

"All of you from your birth to your death," she said. "A you-shaped rope embedded in the space-time continuum—I cut you out of it. Or I made a fork in your lifeline, if you want to think of it that way, and you're in the free branch. But the other you, the buried you, the one people think of as the real you, is back in your room with the other Zombies going through the motions."

[21]

"But how can you cut people out of their lifelines?" I asked. "As a bull-session theory, perhaps. But to actually do it—"

"You can if you have the proper tool," she said flatly swinging her handbag. "Any number of agents might have done it. A Snake might have done it as easily as a Spider. Might still—but we won't go into that."

"But if you've cut me out of my lifeline," I said, "and given me the freedom of the fourth dimension, why are we in the same old space-time? That is, if this elevator still is—"

"It is," she assured me. "We're still in the same space-time because I haven't led us out of it. We're moving through it at the same temporal speed as the you we left behind, keeping pace with his Now. But we both have an added mode of freedom, at present imperceptible and inoperative. Don't worry, I'll make a Door and get us out of here soon enough—if you pass the test."

I stopped trying to understand her metaphysics. Maybe I was between floors with a maniac. Maybe I was a maniac myself. No matter—I would just go on clinging to what felt like reality. "Look," I said, that person I murdered, or left to die, is he back in the room too? Did you see him—or her?"

She looked at me and then nodded. She said carefully, "The person you killed or doomed is still in the room."

An aching impulse twisted me a little. "Maybe I should try to go back,—" I began. "Try to go back and unite the selves..."

"It's too late now," she repeated.

"But I want to," I persisted. "There's something pulling at me, like a chain hooked to my chest."

She smiled unpleasantly. "Of course there is," she said. "It's the vampire in you—the same thing that drew me to your room or would draw any Spider or Snake. The blood scent of the person you killed or doomed."

I drew back from her. "Why do you keep saying 'or'?" I blustered. "I didn't look but you must have seen. You must know. Whom did I kill? And what is the Zombie me doing back there in that room with the body?"

"There's no time for that now," she said, spreading the mouth of her handbag. Later you can go back and find out, if you pass the test."

She drew from her handbag a pale gray gleaming implement that looked by quick turns to me like a knife, a gun, a slim scepter, and a delicate branding iron—especially when its tip sprouted an eight-limbed star of silver wire.

"The test?" I faltered, staring at the thing.

[22]

"Yes, to determine whether you can live in the fourth dimension or only die in it."

The star began to spin, slowly at first, then faster and faster. Then it held still, but something that was part of it or created by it went on spinning like a Helmholtz color wheel—a fugitive, flashing rainbow spiral. It looked like the brain's own circular scanning pattern become visible and that frightened me because that is what you see at the onset of alcoholic hallucinations.

"Close your eyes," she said.

I wanted to. jerk away, I wanted to lunge at her, but I didn't dare. Something might shake loose in my brain if I did. The spiral flashed through the wiry fringe of my eyebrows as she moved it closer. I closed my eyes.

Something stung my forehead icily, like ether, and I instantly felt that I was moving forward with an easy rise and fall, as if I were riding a very gentle roller coaster. There was a low pulsing roar in my ears.

I snapped my eyes open. The illusion vanished. I was standing stock still in the elevator and the only sounds were the continuing hubbub that had succeeded the sirens. My conductress was smiling at me, encouragingly.

I closed my eyes again. Instantly I was surging forward through the dark on the gentle roller coaster and the hubbub was an almost musical roar that rose and fell. Smoky lights showed ahead. I glided through a cobblestoned alleyway where cloaked and broad-hatted bravoes with rapiers swinging at their sides turned their heads to stare at me knowingly, while women in gaudy dresses that swept the dirt leered in a way that was half inviting, half contemptuous.

Darkness swallowed them. An iron gate clanged behind me. Bluer, cleaner lights sprang up. I passed a field studded with tall silver ships. Tall, slender-limbed men and women in blue and silver smocks broke off their tasks or games to watch me—evenly but a little sadly, I thought. They drifted out of sight behind me and another gate clanged. For a moment the pulsing sound shaped itself into words:

"There's a road to travel. It's a road that's wide..."

I opened my eyes again. I was back in the stalled elevator, hearing the muted hubbub, facing my smiling conductress. It was very strange—an illusion that could be turned on or off by lowering or raising the eyelids. I remembered fleetingly that the brains alpha rhythm, which may be the rhythm of its scanning pattern idling, vanishes when you open your eyes and I wondered if the roller coaster was the alpha rhythm.

When I closed my eyes this time I plunged deeper into the illusion. I burst through many scenes: a street of flashing swords, the central aisle of a dark cavernous factory filled with unknown untended machines,

[23]

a Chinese pavilion, a Harlem nightclub, a square filled with brightly-painted statues and noisy white-togaed men, a humped road across which a ragged muddy-footed throng fled in terror from a porticoed temple which showed only as wide bars of light rising in a mist from behind a low hill.

And always the half-music pulsed without cease. From time to time I heard the "Road to Travel" song repeated with two endings, now one, now another: "It leads around the cosmos to the other side," and "It leads to insanity or suicide."

I could have whichever ending I chose, it seemed to me—I needed only to will it.

And then it burst on me that I could go wherever I wanted, see whatever I wanted, just by willing it. I was traveling along that dark mysterious avenue, swaying and undulating in every dimension of freedom, that leads to every hidden vista of the unconscious mind, to any and every spot in space and time—the avenue of the adventurer freed from all limitations.

I grudgingly opened my eyes again to the stalled elevator. "This is the test?" I asked my conductress quickly. She nodded, watching me speculatively, no longer smiling. I dove eagerly back into the darkness.

In the exultation of my newly realized power I skimmed a universe of sensation, darting like a bird or bee from scene to scene: a battle, a banquet, a pyramid a-building, a tatter-sailed ship in a storm, beasts of all descriptions, a torture chamber, a death ward, a dance, an orgy, a leprosary, a satellite launching, a stop at a dead star between galaxies, a newly-created android rising from a silver vat, a witch-burning, a cave birth, a crucifixion...

Suddenly I was afraid. I had gone so far, seen so much, so many gates had clanged behind me, and there was no sign of my free flight stopping or even slowing down. I could control where I went but not whether I went—I had to keep on going. And going. And going.

My mind was tired. When your mind is tired and you want to sleep you close your eyes. But if, whenever you close your eyes, you start going again, you start traveling the road...

I opened mine. "How do I ever sleep?" I asked the woman. My voice had gone hoarse.

She didn't answer. Her expression told me nothing. Suddenly I was very frightened. But at the same time I was horribly tired, mind and body. I closed my eyes...

I was standing on a narrow ledge that gritted under the soles of my shoes whenever I inched a step one way or another to ease the cramps in my leg muscles. My hands and the back of my head were flattened against a gritty wall. Sweat stung my eyes and trickled inside my collar. There was a medley of voices I was trying not to hear. Voices far below.

I looked down at the toes of my shoes, which jutted out a little over the edge of the ledge. The brown leather was dusty and dull. I studied each gash in it, each rolled or loose peeling of tanning surface, each pale shallow pit.

Around the toes of my shoes a crowd of people clustered, but small, very small—tiny oval faces mounted crosswise on oval bodies that were scarcely larger—navy beans each mounted on a kidney bean. Among them were red and black rectangles, proportionately small—police cars and fire trucks. Between the toes of my shoes was an empty gray space.

In spirit or actuality, I was back in the body I had left in the hotel bedroom, the body that had climbed through the window and was threatening to jump.

I could see from the corner of my eye that someone in black was standing beside me, in spirit or actuality. I tried to turn my head and see who it was, but that instant the invisible roller coaster seized me and I surged forward and—this time down.

The faces started to swell. Slowly.

A great scream puffed up at me from them. I tried to ride it but it wouldn't hold me. I plunged on down, face first.

The faces below continued to swell. Faster. Much faster, and then...

One of them looked all matted hair except for the forehead, which had an S on it.

My fall took me past that horror face and then checked three feet from the gray pavement (I could see fine, dust-drifted cracks and a trodden wad of chewing gum) and without pause I shot upward again, like a high diver who fetches bottom, or as if I'd hit an invisible sponge-rubber cushion yards thick.

I soared upward in a great curve, losing speed all the time, and landed without a jar on the ledge from which I'd just fallen.

Beside me stood the woman in black. A gust of wind ruffled her bangs and I saw the eight-limbed sigil on her forehead.

I felt a surge of desire and I put my arms around her and pulled her face toward mine.

She smiled but she dipped her head so that our foreheads touched instead of our lips...

Ether ice shocked my brain. I closed my eyes for an instant.

When I opened them we were back in the stalled elevator and she was drawing away from me with a smile and I felt a wonderful strength and freshness and power, as if all avenues were open to me now without compulsion, as if all space and time were my private preserve.

[25]

I closed my eyes and there was only blackness quiet as the grave and close as a caress. No roller coaster, no scanning pattern digging movement and faces from the dark, no realms of the DT fringes. I laughed and I opened my eyes.

My conductress was at the controls of the elevator and we were dropping smoothly and her smile was sardonic but comradely now, as if we were fellow professionals.

The elevator stopped and the door slid open on the crowded lobby and we stepped out arm in arm. My partner checked a moment in her stride and I saw her lift an "Out of Order" sign off the door and drop it behind the sand vase.

We strode toward the entrance. I knew what Zombies were now—the people around me, hotel folk, public, cops, firemen. They were all staring toward the entrance, where the revolving doors were pinned open, as if they were waiting (an eternity, if necessary) for something to happen. They didn't see us at all—except that one or two trembled uneasily, like folk touched by nightmares, as we brushed past them.

As we went through the doorway my partner said to me rapidly, "When we get outside do whatever you have to, but when I touch your shoulder come with me. There'll be a Door behind you."

Once more she drew the gray implement from her handbag and there was a silver spinning beside me. I did not look at it.

I walked out into empty sidewalk and a scream that came from dozens of throats. Hot sunlight struck my face. We were the only souls for ten yards around, then came a line of policemen and the screaming mob. Everyone of them was looking straight up, except for a man in dirty shirtsleeves who was pushing his way, head down, between two cops.

You know the sound when a butcher slams a chunk of beef down on the chopping block? I heard that now, only much bigger. I blinked my eyes and there was a body on its back in the middle of the empty space and the finest spray of blood was misting down on the gray sidewalk.

I sprang forward and knelt beside the body, vaguely aware that the man who had pushed between the cops was doing the same from the other side. I studied the face of the man who had leaped to his death.

The face was unmarred, though it was rather closer to the sidewalk than it would have been if the back of the head had been intact. It was a face with a week's beard on it that rose higher than the cheekbones—the big forehead was the only sizable space on it clear of hair. It was the tormented face of a drunk, but now at peace. It was a face I knew, in fact had always known. It was simply the face my conductress had not let me see, the face of the person I had doomed to die: myself.

I lifted my hand and this time I let it touch the week's growth of beard matting my face. Well, I thought. I had given the crowd an exciting half hour.

I lifted my eyes and there on the other side of the body was the dirty-sleeved man. It was the same beard-matted face as that on the ground between us, the same beard matted face as my own.

On the forehead was a black S that looked permanent. He was staring at my face—and then at my forehead—with a surprise, and then a horror, that I knew my own features were registering too as I stared at him. A hand touched my shoulder.

My conductress had told me that you never know whether the side into which you are reborn is "right" or "good." Now, as I turned and saw the shimmering silver man-high Door behind me, and her hand vanishing into it, and as I stepped through, past a rim of velvet blackness and stars, I clung to that memory, for I knew that I would be fighting on both sides forever.

The Big Time

I. ENTER THREE HUSSARS

When shall we three meet again
In thunder, lightning, or in rain?

When the hurlyburly's done.
When the battle's lost and won.

–Macbeth

My name is Greta Forzane. Twenty-nine and a party girl would describe me. I was born in Chicago, of Scandinavian parents, but now I operate chiefly outside space and time—not in Heaven or Hell, if there are such places, but not in the cosmos or universe you know either.

I am not as romantically entrancing as the immortal film star who also bears my first name, but I have a rough-and-ready charm of my own. I need it, for my job is to nurse back to health and kid back to sanity Soldiers badly roughed up in the biggest war going. This war is the Change War, a war of time travelers—in fact, our private name for being in this war is being on the Big Time. Our Soldiers fight by going back to change the past, or even ahead to change the future, in ways to help our side win the final victory a billion or more years from now. A long killing business, believe me.

You don't know about the Change War, but it's influencing your lives all the time and maybe you've had hints of it without realizing.

Have you ever worried about your memory, because it doesn't seem to be bringing you exactly the same picture of the past from one day to the next? Have you ever been afraid that your personality was changing because of forces beyond your knowledge or control? Have you ever felt sure that sudden death was about to jump you from nowhere? Have you ever been scared of Ghosts—not the story-book kind, but the billions of beings who were once so real and strong it's hard to believe they'll just sleep harmlessly forever? Have you ever wondered about those things you may call devils or Demons—spirits able to range through all time and space, through the hot hearts of stars and the cold skeleton of space between the galaxies? Have you ever thought that the whole universe might be a crazy, mixed-up dream? If you have, you've had hints of the Change War.

How I got recruited into the Change War, how it's conducted, what the two sides are, why you don't consciously know about it, what I really think about it—you'll learn in due course.

The place outside the cosmos where I and my pals do our nursing job I simply call the Place. A lot of my nursing consists of amusing and humanizing Soldiers fresh back from raids into time. In fact, my formal title is Entertainer and I've got my silly side, as you'll find out.

My pals are two other gals and three guys from quite an assortment of times and places. We're a pretty good team, and with Sid bossing, we run a pretty good Recuperation Station, though we have our family troubles. But most of our troubles come slamming into the Place with the beat-up Soldiers, who've generally just been going through hell and want to raise some of their own. As a matter of fact, it was three newly arrived Soldiers who started this thing I'm going to tell you about, this thing that showed me so much about myself and everything.

When it started, I had been on the Big Time for a thousand sleeps and two thousand nightmares, and working in the Place for five hundred-one thousand. This two-nightmares routine every time you lay down your dizzy little head is rough, but you pretend to get used to it because being on the Big Time is supposed to be worth it.

The Place is midway in size and atmosphere between a large nightclub where the Entertainers sleep in and a small Zeppelin hangar decorated for a party, though a Zeppelin is one thing we haven't had yet. You go out of the Place, but not often if you have any sense and if you are an Entertainer like me, into the cold light of a morning filled with anything from the earlier dinosaurs to the later spacemen, who look strangely similar except for size.

Solely on doctor's orders, I have been on cosmic leave six times since coming to work at the Place, meaning I have had six brief vacations, if you care to call them that, for believe me they are busman's holidays, considering what goes on in the Place all the time. The last one I spent in Renaissance Rome, where I got a crush on Cesare Borgia, but I got over it. Vacations are for the birds, anyway, because they have to be fitted by the Spiders into serious operations of the Change War, and you can imagine how restful that makes them.

"See those Soldiers changing the past? You stick along with them. Don't go too far up front, though, but don't wander off either. Relax and enjoy yourself."

Ha! Now the kind of recuperation Soldiers get when they come to the Place is a horse of a far brighter color, simply dazzling by comparison. Entertainment is our business and we give them a bang-up time and send them staggering happily back into action, though once in a great while something may happen to throw a wee shadow on the party.

I am dead in some ways, but don't let that bother you—I am lively enough in others. If you met me in the cosmos, you would be more apt to yak with me or try to pick me up than to ask a cop to do same or a father to douse me with holy water, unless you are one of those hard-boiled reformer types. But you are not likely to meet me in the cosmos, because (bar Basin Street and the Prater) 15th Century Italy and Augustan Rome—until they spoiled it—are my favorite (Ha!) vacation spots and, as I have said, I stick as close to the Place as I can. It is really the nicest Place in the whole Change World. (Crisis! I even *think* of it capitalized!)

Anyhoo, when this thing started, I was twiddling my thumbs on the couch nearest the piano and thinking it was too late to do my fingernails and whoever came in probably wouldn't notice them anyway.

The Place was jumpy like it always is on an approach and the gray velvet of the Void around us was curdled with the uneasy lights you see when you close your eyes in the dark.

Sid was tuning the Maintainers for the pick-up and the right shoulder of his gold-worked gray doublet was streaked where he'd been wiping his face on it with quick ducks of his head.

Beauregard was leaning as close as he could over Sid's other shoulder, one white-trousered knee neatly indenting the rose plush of the control divan, and he wasn't missing a single flicker of Sid's old fingers on the dials; Beau's co-pilot besides piano player. Beau's face had that dead blank look it must have had when every double eagle he owned and more he didn't were riding on the next card to be turned in the gambling saloon on one of those wedding-cake Mississippi steamboats.

Doc was soused as usual, sitting at the bar with his top hat pushed back and his knitted shawl pulled around him, his wide eyes seeing whatever horrors a life in Nazi-occupied Czarist Russia can add to being a drunk Demon in the Change World.

Maud, who is the Old Girl, and Lili—the New Girl, of course—were telling the big beads of their identical pearl necklaces.

You might say that all us Entertainers were a bit edgy; being Demons doesn't automatically make us brave.

Then the red telltale on the Major Maintainer went out and the Door began to darken in the Void facing Sid and Beau, and I felt Change Winds blowing hard and my heart missed a couple of beats, and the next thing three Soldiers had stepped out of the cosmos and into the Place, their first three steps hitting the floor hard as they changed times and weights.

They were dressed as officers of hussars, as we'd been advised, and—praise the Bonny Dew!—I saw that the first of them was Erich, my own dear little commandant, the pride of the von Hohenwalds and the Terror of the Snakes. Behind him was some hard-faced Roman or other, and beside Erich and shouldering into him as they stamped forward was a new boy, blond, with a face like a Greek god who's just been touring a Christian hell.

They were uniformed exactly alike in black—shakos, fur-edged pelisses, boots, and so forth—with white skull emblems on the shakos. The only difference between them was that Erich had a Caller on his wrist and the New Boy had a black-gauntleted glove on his left hand and was clenching the mate in it, his right hand being bare like both of Erich's and the Roman's.

"You've made it, lads, hearts of gold," Sid boomed at them, and Beau twitched a smile and murmured something courtly and Maud began to chant, "Shut the Door!" and the New Girl copied her and I joined in because the Change Winds do blow like crazy when the Door is open, even though it can't ever be shut tight enough to keep them from leaking through.

"Shut it before it blows wrinkles in our faces," Maud called in her gamin voice to break the ice, looking like a skinny teen-ager in the tight, knee-length frock she'd copied from the New Girl.

But the three Soldiers weren't paying attention. The Roman—I remembered his name was Mark—was blundering forward stiffly as if there were something wrong with his eyes, while Erich and the New Boy were yelling at each other about a kid and Einstein and a summer palace and a bloody glove and the Snakes having booby-trapped Saint Petersburg. Erich had that taut sadistic smile he gets when he wants to hit me.

The New Boy was in a tearing rage. "Why'd you pull us out so bloody fast? We fair chewed the Nevsky Prospekt to pieces galloping away."

"Didn't you feel their stun guns, *Dummkopf*, when they sprung the trap—too soon, *Gott sei Dank?*" Erich demanded.

"I did," the New Boy told him. "Not enough to numb a cat. Why didn't you show us action?"

"Shut up. I'm your leader. I'll show you action enough."

"You won't. You're a filthy Nazi coward."

"Weibischer Engländer!"

"Bloody Hun!"

"Schlange!"

The blond lad knew enough German to understand that last crack. He threw back his sable-edged pelisse to clear his sword arm and he swung away from Erich, which bumped him into Beau. At the first sign of the quarrel, Beau had raised himself from the divan as quickly and silently as a—no, I won't use that word—and slithered over to them.

"Sirs, you forget yourselves," he said sharply, off balance, supporting himself on the New Boy's upraised arm. "This is Sidney Lessingham's Place of Entertainment and Recuperation. There are ladies—"

With a contemptuous snarl, the New Boy shoved him off and snatched with his bare hand for his saber. Beau reeled against the divan, it caught him in the shins and he fell toward the Maintainers. Sid whisked them out of the way as if they were a couple of beach radios—simply nothing in the Place is nailed down—and had them back on the coffee table before Beau hit the floor. Meanwhile, Erich had his saber out and had parried the New Boy's first wild slash and lunged in return, and I heard the scream of steel and the rutch of his boot on the diamond-studded pavement.

Beau rolled over and came up pulling from the ruffles of his shirt bosom a derringer I knew was some other weapon in disguise—a stun gun or even an Atropos. Besides scaring me damp for Erich and everybody, that brought me up short: us Entertainers' nerves must be getting as naked as the Soldiers', probably starting when the Spiders canceled all cosmic leaves twenty sleeps back.

Sid shot Beau his look of command, rapped out, "I'll handle this, you whoreson firebrand," and turned to the Minor Maintainer. I noticed that the telltale on the Major was glowing a reassuring red again, and I found a moment to thank Mamma Devi that the Door was shut.

Maud was jumping up and down, cheering I don't know which—nor did she, I bet—and the New Girl was white and I saw that the sabers were working more businesslike. Erich's flicked, flicked, flicked again and came away from the blond lad's cheek spilling a couple of red drops. The blond lad lunged fiercely, Erich jumped back, and the next moment they were both floating helplessly in the air, twisting like they had cramps.

I realized quick enough that Sid had shut off gravity in the Door and Stores sectors of the Place, leaving the rest of us firm on our feet in the Refresher and Surgery sectors. The Place has sectional gravity to suit our Extraterrestrial buddies—those crazy ETs sometimes come whooping in for recuperation in very mixed batches.

From his central position, Sid called out, kindly enough but taking no nonsense, "All right, lads, you've had your fun. Now sheathe those swords."

For a second or so, the two black hussars drifted and contorted. Erich laughed harshly and neatly obeyed—the commandant is used to free fall. The blond lad stopped writhing, hesitated while he glared upside down at Erich and managed to get his saber into its scabbard, although he turned a slow somersault doing it. Then Sid switched on their gravity, slow enough so they wouldn't get sprained landing.

Erich laughed, lightly this time, and stepped out briskly toward us. He stopped to clap the New Boy firmly on the shoulder and look him in the face.

"So, now you get a good scar," he said.

The other didn't pull away, but he didn't look up and Erich came on. Sid was hurrying toward the New Boy, and as he passed Erich, he wagged a finger at him and gayly said, "You rogue." Next thing I was giving Erich my "Man, you're home" hug and he was kissing me and cracking my ribs and saying, "*Liebchen! Doppchen!*"—which was fine with me because I do love him and I'm a good lover and as much a Doubleganger as he is.

We had just pulled back from each other to get a breath—his blue eyes looked so sweet in his worn face—when there was a thud behind us. With the snapping of the tension, Doc had fallen off his bar stool and his top hat was over his eyes. As we turned to chuckle at him, Maud squeaked and we saw that the Roman had walked straight up against the Void and was marching along there steadily without gaining a foot, like it does happen, his black uniform melting into that inside-your-head gray.

Maud and Beau rushed over to fish him back, which can be tricky. The thin gambler was all courtly efficiency again. Sid supervised from a distance.

"What's wrong with him?" I asked Erich.

He shrugged. "Overdue for Change Shock. And he was nearest the stun guns. His horse almost threw him. *Mein Gott*, you should have seen Saint Petersburg, *Liebchen*: the Nevsky Prospekt, the canals flying by like reception carpets of blue sky, a cavalry troop in blue and gold that blundered across our escape, fine women in furs and ostrich plumes, a monk with a big tripod and his head under a hood—it gave me the horrors seeing all those Zombies flashing past and staring at me in that sick unawakened way they have, and knowing that some of them, say the photographer, might be Snakes."

Our side in the Change War is the Spiders, the other side is the Snakes, though all of us—Spiders and Snakes alike—are Doublegangers and Demons too, because we're cut out of our lifelines in the cosmos. Your lifeline is all of you from birth to death. We're Doublegangers because we can operate both in the cosmos and outside of it, and Demons because we act reasonably alive while doing so—which the Ghosts don't. Entertainers and Soldiers are all Demon-Doublegangers, whichever side they're on—though they say the Snake Places are simply ghastly. Zombies are dead people whose lifelines lie in the so-called past.

"What were you doing in Saint Petersburg before the ambush?" I asked Erich. "That is, if you can talk about it."

"Why not? We were kidnapping the infant Einstein back from the Snakes in 1883. Yes, the Snakes got him, *Liebchen*, only a few sleeps back, endangering the West's whole victory over Russia—"

"—which gave your dear little Hitler the world on a platter for fifty years and got me loved to death by your sterling troops in the Liberation of Chicago—"

"—but which leads to the ultimate victory of the Spiders and the West over the Snakes and Communism, *Liebchen*, remember that. Anyway, our counter-snatch didn't work. The Snakes had guards posted—most unusual and we weren't warned. The whole thing was a great mess. No wonder Bruce lost his head—not that it excuses him."

"The New Boy?" I asked. Sid hadn't got to him and he was still standing with hooded eyes where Erich had left him, a dark pillar of shame and rage.

"*Ja*, a lieutenant from World War One. An Englishman."

"I gathered that," I told Erich. "Is he really effeminate?"

"*Weibischer?*" He smiled. "I had to call him something when he said I was a coward. He'll make a fine Soldier—only needs a little more shaping."

"You men are so original when you spat." I lowered my voice. "But you shouldn't have gone on and called him a Snake, Erich mine."

"*Schlange?*" The smile got crooked. "Who knows—about any of us? As Saint Petersburg showed me, the Snakes' spies are getting cleverer than ours." The blue eyes didn't look sweet now. "Are you, *Liebchen*, really nothing more than a good loyal Spider?"

"Erich!"

"All right, I went too far—with Bruce and with you too. We're all hacked these days, riding with one leg over the breaking edge."

Maud and Beau were supporting the Roman to a couch, Maud taking most of his weight, with Sid still supervising and the New Boy still sulking by himself. The New Girl should have been with him, of course, but I couldn't see her anywhere and I decided she was probably having a nervous breakdown in the Refresher, the little jerk.

"The Roman looks pretty bad, Erich," I said.

"Ah, Mark's tough. Got virtue, as his people say. And our little starship girl will bring him back to life if anybody can and if..."

"...you call this living," I filled in dutifully.

He was right. Maud had fifty-odd years of psychomedical experience, 23rd Century at that. It should have been Doc's job, but that was fifty drunks back.

"Maud and Mark, that will be an interesting experiment," Erich said. "Reminiscent of Goering's with the frozen men and the naked gypsy girls."

[35]

"You are a filthy Nazi. She'll be using electrophoresis and deep suggestion, if I know anything."

"How will you be able to know anything, *Liebchen*, if she switches on the couch curtains, as I perceive she is preparing to do?"

"Filthy Nazi I said and meant."

"Precisely." He clicked his heels and bowed a millimeter. "Erich Friederich von Hohenwald, *Oberleutnant* in the army of the Third Reich. Fell at Narvik, where he was Recruited by the Spiders. Lifeline lengthened by a Big Change after his first death and at latest report Commandant of Toronto, where he maintains extensive baby farms to provide him with breakfast meat, if you believe the handbills of the *voyageurs* underground. At your service."

"Oh, Erich, it's all so lousy," I said, touching his hand, reminded that he was one of the unfortunates Resurrected from a point in their lifelines well before their deaths—in his case, because the date of his death had been shifted forward by a Big Change after his Resurrection. And as every Demon finds out, if he can't imagine it beforehand, it is pure hell to remember your future, and the shorter the time between your Resurrection and your death back in the cosmos, the better. Mine, bless Bab-ed-Din, was only an action-packed ten minutes on North Clark Street.

Erich put his other hand lightly over mine. "Fortunes of the Change War, *Liebchen*. At least I'm a Soldier and sometimes assigned to future operations—though why we should have this monomania about our future personalities back there, I don't know. Mine is a stupid *Oberst*, thin as paper—and frightfully indignant at the *voyageurs*! But it helps me a little if I see him in perspective and at least I get back to the cosmos pretty regularly, *Gott sei Dank*, so I'm better off than you Entertainers."

I didn't say aloud that a Changing cosmos is worse than none, but I found myself sending a prayer to the Bonny Dew for my father's repose, that the Change Winds would blow lightly across the lifeline of Anton A. Forzane, professor of physiology, born in Norway and buried in Chicago. Woodlawn Cemetery is a nice gray spot.

"That's all right, Erich," I said. "We Entertainers Got Mittens too."

He scowled around at me suspiciously, as if he were wondering whether I had all my buttons on.

"Mittens?" he said. "What do you mean? I'm not wearing any. Are you trying to say something about Bruce's gloves—which incidentally seem to annoy him for some reason. No, seriously, Greta, why do you Entertainers need mittens?"

"Because we get cold feet sometimes. At least I do. Got Mittens, as I say."

A sickly light dawned in his Prussian puss. He muttered, "Got mittens...*Gott mit uns*...God with us," and roared softly, "Greta, I don't know how I put up with you, the way you murder a great language for cheap laughs."

"You've got to take me as I am," I told him, "mittens and all, thank the Bonny Dew—" and hastily explained, "That's French—*le bon Dieu*—the good God—don't hit me. I'm not going to tell you any more of my secrets."

He laughed feebly, like he was dying.

"Cheer up," I said. "I won't be here forever, and there are worse places than the Place."

He nodded grudgingly, looking around. "You know what, Greta, if you'll promise not to make some dreadful joke out of it: on operations, I pretend I'll soon be going backstage to court the world-famous ballerina Greta Forzane."

He was right about the backstage part. The Place is a regular theater-in-the-round with the Void for an audience, the Void's gray hardly disturbed by the screens masking Surgery (Ugh!), Refresher and Stores. Between the last two are the bar and kitchen and Beau's piano. Between Surgery and the sector where the Door usually appears are the shelves and taborets of the Art Gallery. The control divan is stage center. Spaced around at a fair distance are six big low couches—one with its curtains now shooting up into the gray—and a few small tables. It is like a ballet set and the crazy costumes and characters that turn up don't ruin the illusion. By no means. Diaghilev would have hired most of them for the Ballet Russe on first sight, without even asking them whether they could keep time to music.

II. A RIGHT-HAND GLOVE

Last week in Babylon,
Last night in Rome,

–Hodgson

Beau had gone behind the bar and was talking quietly at Doc, but with his eyes elsewhere, looking very sallow and professional in his white, and I thought—Damballa!—I'm in the French Quarter. I couldn't see the New Girl. Sid was at last getting to the New Boy after the fuss about Mark. He threw me a sign and I started over with Erich in tow.

"Welcome, sweet lad. Sidney Lessingham's your host, and a fellow Englishman. Born in King's Lynn, 1564, schooled at Cambridge, but London was the life and death of me, though I outlasted Bessie, Jimmie, Charlie, and Ollie almost. And what a life! By turns a clerk, a spy, a bawd—the two trades are hand in glove—a poet of no account, a beggar, and a peddler of resurrection tracts. Beau Lassiter, our throats are tinder!"

At the word "poet," the New Boy looked up, but resentfully, as if he had been tricked into it.

"And to spare your throat for drinking, sweet gallant, I'll be so bold as to guess and answer one of your questions," Sid rattled on. "Yes, I knew Will Shakespeare—we were of an age—and he was such a modest, mind-your-business rogue that we all wondered whether he really did write those plays. Your pardon, 'faith, but that scratch might be looked to."

Then I saw that the New Girl hadn't lost her head, but gone to Surgery (Ugh!) for a first-aid tray. She reached a swab toward the New Boy's sticky cheek, saying rather shrilly, "If I might..."

Her timing was bad. Sid's last words and Erich's approach had darkened the look in the young Soldier's face and he angrily swept her arm aside without even glancing at her. Erich squeezed my arm. The tray clattered to the floor—and one of the drinks that Beau was bringing almost followed it. Ever since the New Girl's arrival, Beau had been figuring that she was his responsibility, though I don't think the two of them had reached an agreement yet. Beau was especially set on it be-

[38]

cause I was thick with Sid at the time and Maud with Doc, she loving tough cases.

"Easy now, lad, and you love me!" Sid thundered, again shooting Beau the "Hold it" look. "She's just a poor pagan trying to comfort you. Swallow your bile, you black villain, and perchance it will turn to poetry. Ah, did I touch you there? Confess, you are a poet."

There isn't much gets by Sid, though for a second I forgot my psychology and wondered if he knew what he was doing with his insights.

"Yes, I'm a poet, all right," the New Boy roared. "I'm Bruce Marchant, you bloody Zombies. I'm a poet in a world where even the lines of the King James and your precious Will whom you use for laughs aren't safe from Snakes' slime and the Spiders' dirty legs. Changing our history, stealing our certainties, claiming to be so blasted all-knowing and best intentioned and efficient, and what does it lead to? This bloody SI glove!"

He held up his black-gloved left hand which still held the mate and he shook it.

"What's wrong with the Spider Issue gauntlet, heart of gold?" Sid demanded. "And you love us, tell us." While Erich laughed, "Consider yourself lucky, *Kamerad*. Mark and I didn't draw any gloves at all."

"What's wrong with it?" Bruce yelled. "The bloody things are both lefts!" He slammed it down on the floor.

We all howled, we couldn't help it. He turned his back on us and stamped off, though I guessed he would keep out of the Void. Erich squeezed my arm and said between gasps, "*Mein Gott, Liebchen*, what have I always told you about Soldiers? The bigger the gripe, the smaller the cause! It is infallible!"

One of us didn't laugh. Ever since the New Girl heard the name Bruce Marchant, she'd had a look in her eyes like she'd been given the sacrament. I was glad she'd got interested in something, because she'd been pretty much of a snoot and a wet blanket up until now, although she'd come to the Place with the recommendation of having been a real whoopee girl in London and New York in the Twenties. She looked disapprovingly at us as she gathered up the tray and stuff, not forgetting the glove, which she placed on the center of the tray like a holy relic.

Beau cut over and tried to talk to her, but she ghosted past him and once again he couldn't do anything because of the tray in his hands. He came over and got rid of the drinks quick. I took a big gulp right away because I saw the New Girl stepping through the screen into Surgery and I hate to be reminded we have it and I'm glad Doc is too drunk to use it, some of the Arachnoid surgical techniques being very sickening as I know only too well from a personal experience that is number one on my list of things to be forgotten.

By that time, Bruce had come back to us, saying in a carefully hard voice, "Look here, it's not the dashed glove itself, as you very well know, you howling Demons."

"What is it then, noble heart?" Sid asked, his grizzled gold beard heightening the effect of innocent receptivity.

"It's the principle of the thing," Bruce said, looking around sharply, but none of us cracked a smile. "It's this mucking inefficiency and death of the cosmos—and don't tell me that isn't in the cards!—masquerading as benign omniscient authority. The Spiders—and we don't know who they are ultimately; it's just a name; we see only agents like ourselves—the Spiders pluck us from the quiet graves of our lifelines—"

"Is that bad, lad?" Sid murmured, innocently straight-faced.

"—and Resurrect us if they can and then tell us we must fight another time-traveling power called the Snakes—just a name, too—which is bent on perverting and enslaving the whole cosmos, past, present and future."

"And isn't it, lad?"

"Before we're properly awake, we're Recruited into the Big Time and hustled into tunnels and burrows outside our space-time, these miserable closets, gray sacks, puss pockets—no offense to this Place—that the Spiders have created, maybe by gigantic implosions, but no one knows for certain, and then we're sent off on all sorts of missions into the past and future to change history in ways that are supposed to thwart the Snakes."

"True, lad."

"And from then on, the pace is so flaming hot and heavy, the shocks come so fast, our emotions are wrenched in so many directions, our public and private metaphysics distorted so insanely, the deepest thread of reality we cling to tied in such bloody knots, that we never can get things straight."

"We've all felt that way, lad," Sid said soberly; Beau nodded his sleek death's head; "You should have seen me, *Kamerad*, my first fifty sleeps," Erich put in; while I added, "Us girls, too, Bruce."

"Oh, I know I'll get hardened to it, and don't think I can't. It's not that," Bruce said harshly. "And I wouldn't mind the personal confusion, the mess it's made of my spirit, I wouldn't even mind remaking history and destroying priceless, once-called imperishable beauties of the past, if I felt it were for the best. The Spiders assure us that, to thwart the Snakes, it is all-important that the West ultimately defeat the East. But what have they done to achieve this? I'll give you some beautiful examples. To stabilize power in the early Mediterranean world, they have built up Crete at the expense of Greece, making Athens a ghost city, Plato a trivial fabulist, and putting all Greek culture in a minor key."

"You got time for culture?" I heard myself say and I clapped my hand over my mouth in gentle reproof.

"But *you* remember the dialogues, lad," Sid observed. "And rail not at Crete—I have a sweet Keftian friend."

"For how long will I remember Plato's dialogues? And who after me?" Bruce challenged. "Here's another. The Spiders want Rome powerful and, to date, they've helped Rome so much that she collapses in a blaze of German and Parthian invasions a few years after the death of Julius Caesar."

This time it was Beau who butted in. Most everybody in the Place loves these bull sessions. "You omit to mention, sir, that Rome's newest downfall is directly due to the Unholy Triple Alliance the Snakes have fomented between the Eastern Classical World, Mohammedanized Christianity, and Marxist Communism, trying to pass the torch of power futurewards by way of Byzantium and the Eastern Church, without ever letting it pass into the hands of the Spider West. That, sir, is the Snakes' Three-Thousand-Year Plan which we are fighting against, striving to revive Rome's glories."

"Striving is the word for it," Bruce snapped. "Here's yet another example. To beat Russia, the Spiders kept England and America out of World War Two, thereby ensuring a German invasion of the New World and creating a Nazi empire stretching from the salt mines of Siberia to the plantations of Iowa, from Nizhni Novgorod to Kansas City!"

He stopped and my short hairs prickled. Behind me, someone was chanting in a weird spiritless voice, like footsteps in hard snow.

"*Salz, Salz, bringe Salz. Kein' Peitsch', gnädige Herren. Salz, Salz, Salz.*"

I turned and there was Doc waltzing toward us with little tiny steps, bent over so low that the ends of his shawl touched the floor, his head crooked up sideways and looking through us.

I knew then, but Erich translated softly. "'Salt, salt, I bring salt. No whip, merciful sirs.' He is speaking to my countrymen in their language." Doc had spent his last months in a Nazi-operated salt mine.

He saw us and got up, straightening his top hat very carefully. He frowned hard while my heart thumped half a dozen times. Then his face slackened, he shrugged his shoulders and muttered, "*Nichevo.*"

"And it does not matter, sir," Beau translated, but directing his remark at Bruce. "True, great civilizations have been dwarfed or broken by the Change War. But others, once crushed in the bud, have bloomed. In the 1870s, I traveled a Mississippi that had never known Grant's gunboats. I studied piano, languages, and the laws of chance under the greatest European masters at the University of Vicksburg."

"And you think your pipsqueak steamboat culture is compensation for—" Bruce began but, "Prithee none of that, lad," Sid interrupted smartly. "Nations are as equal as so many madmen or drunkards, and

I'll drink dead drunk the man who disputes me. Hear reason: nations are not so puny as to shrivel and vanish at the first tampering with their past, no, nor with the tenth. Nations are monsters, boy, with guts of iron and nerves of brass. Waste not your pity on them."

"True indeed, sir," Beau pressed, cooler and keener for the attack on his Greater South. "Most of us enter the Change World with the false metaphysic that the slightest change in the past—a grain of dust misplaced—will transform the whole future. It is a long while before we accept with our minds as well as our intellects the law of the Conservation of Reality: that when the past is changed, the future changes barely enough to adjust, barely enough to admit the new data. The Change Winds meet maximum resistance always. Otherwise the first operation in Babylonia would have wiped out New Orleans, Sheffield, Stuttgart, and Maud Davies' birthplace on Ganymede!

"Note how the gap left by Rome's collapse was filled by the imperialistic and Christianized Germans. Only an expert Demon historian can tell the difference in most ages between the former Latin and the present Gothic Catholic Church. As you yourself, sir, said of Greece, it is as if an old melody were shifted into a slightly different key. In the wake of a Big Change, cultures and individuals are transposed, it's true, yet in the main they continue much as they were, except for the usual scattering of unfortunate but statistically meaningless accidents."

"All right, you bloody savants—maybe I pushed my point too far," Bruce growled. "But if you want variety, give a thought to the rotten methods we use in our wonderful Change War. Poisoning Churchill and Cleopatra. Kidnapping Einstein when he's a baby."

"The Snakes did it first," I reminded him.

"Yes, and we copied them. How resourceful does that make us?" he retorted, arguing like a woman. "If we need Einstein, why don't we Resurrect him, deal with him as a man?"

Beau said, serving his culture in slightly thicker slices, "*Pardonnez-moi*, but when you have enjoyed your status as Doubleganger a *soupçon* longer, you will understand that great men can rarely be Resurrected. Their beings are too crystallized, sir, their lifelines too tough."

"Pardon me, but I think that's rot. I believe that most great men refuse to make the bargain with the Snakes, or with us Spiders either. They scorn Resurrection at the price demanded."

"Brother, they ain't that great," I whispered, while Beau glided on with, "However that may be, you have accepted Resurrection, sir, and so incurred an obligation which you as a gentleman must honor."

"I accepted Resurrection all right," Bruce said, a glare coming into his eyes. "When they pulled me out of my line at Passchendaele in '17 ten minutes before I died, I grabbed at the offer of life like a drunkard grabs at a drink the morning after. But even then I thought I was also seizing a chance to undo historic wrongs, work for peace." His voice was getting wilder all the time. Just beyond our circle, I noticed the New Girl watching him worshipfully. "But what did I find the Spiders wanted me for? Only to fight more wars, over and over again, make them crueler and stinkinger, cut the swath of death a little wider with each Big Change, work our way a little closer to the death of the cosmos."

Sid touched my wrist and, as Bruce raved on, he whispered to me, "What kind of ball, think you, will please and so quench this fire-brained rogue? And you love me, discover it."

I whispered back without taking my eyes off Bruce either, "I know somebody who'll be happy to put on any kind of ball he wants, if he'll just notice her."

"The New Girl, sweetling? 'Tis well. This rogue speaks like an angry angel. It touches my heart and I like it not."

Bruce was saying hoarsely but loudly, "And so we're sent on operations in the past and from each of those operations the Change Winds blow futurewards, swiftly or slowly according to the opposition they breast, sometimes rippling into each other, and any one of those Winds may shift the date of our own death ahead of the date of our Resurrection, so that in an instant—even here, outside the cosmos—we may molder and rot or crumble to dust and vanish away. The wind with our name in it may leak through the Door."

Faces hardened at that, because it's bad form to mention Change Death, and Erich flared out with, *"Halt's Maul, Kamerad!* There's always another Resurrection."

But Bruce didn't keep his mouth shut. He said, "Is there? I know the Spiders promise it, but even if they do go back and cut another Doubleganger from my lifeline, is he me?" He slapped his chest with his bare hand. "I don't think so. And even if he is me, with unbroken consciousness, why's he been Resurrected again? Just to refight more wars and face more Change Death for the sake of an almighty power—" his voice was rising to a climax—"an almighty power so bloody ineffectual, it can't furnish one poor Soldier pulled out of the mud of Passchendaele, one miserable Change Commando, one Godforsaken Recuperee a proper issue of equipment!"

And he held out his bare right hand toward us, fingers spread a little, as if it were the most amazing object and most deserving of outraged sympathy in the whole world.

The New Girl's timing was perfect. She whisked through us, and before he could so much as wiggle the fingers, she whipped a black gauntleted glove on it and anyone could see that it fitted his hand perfectly.

This time our laughing beat the other. We collapsed and slopped our drinks and pounded each other on the back and then started all over.

"*Ach, der Handschuh, Liebchen!* Where'd she get it?" Erich gasped in my ear.

"Probably just turned the other one inside out—that turns a left into a right—I've done it myself," I wheezed, collapsing again at the idea.

"That would put the lining outside," he objected.

"Then I don't know," I said. "We got all sorts of junk in Stores."

"It doesn't matter, *Liebchen*," he assured me. "*Ach, der Handschuh!*"

All through it, Bruce just stood there admiring the glove, moving the fingers a little now and then, and the New Girl stood watching him as if he were eating a cake she'd baked.

When the hysteria quieted down, he looked up at her with a big smile. "What did you say your name was?"

"Lili," she said, and believe you me, she was Lili to me even in my thoughts from then on, for the way she'd handled that lunatic.

"Lilian Foster," she explained. "I'm English also. Mr. Marchant, I've read *A Young Man's Fancy* I don't know how many times."

"You have? It's wretched stuff. From the Dark Ages—I mean my Cambridge days. In the trenches, I was working up some poems that were rather better."

"I won't hear you say that. But I'd be terribly thrilled to hear the new ones. Oh, Mr. Marchant, it was so strange to hear you call it Passiondale."

"Why, if I may ask?"

"Because that's the way I pronounce it to myself. But I looked it up and it's more like Pas-ken-DA-luh."

"Bless you! All the Tommies called it Passiondale, just as they called Ypres Wipers."

"How interesting. You know, Mr. Marchant, I'll wager we were Recruited in the same operation, summer of 1917. I'd got to France as a Red Cross nurse, but they found out my age and were going to send me back."

"How old were you—are you? Same thing, I mean to say."

"Seventeen."

"Seventeen in '17," Bruce murmured, his blue eyes glassy.

It was real corny dialogue and I couldn't resent the humorous leer Erich gave me as we listened to them, as if to say, "Ain't it nice, *Liebchen*, Bruce has a silly little English schoolgirl to occupy him between operations?"

Just the same, as I watched Lili in her dark bangs and pearl necklace and tight little gray dress that reached barely to her knees, and Bruce hulking over her tenderly in his snazzy hussar's rig, I knew that I was

[44]

seeing the start of something that hadn't been part of me since Dave died fighting Franco years before I got on the Big Time, the sort of thing that almost made me wish there could be children in the Change World. I wondered why I'd never thought of trying to work things so that Dave got Resurrected and I told myself: no, it's all changed, I've changed, better the Change Winds don't disturb Dave or I know about it.

"No, I didn't die in 1917—I was merely Recruited then," Lili was telling Bruce. "I lived all through the Twenties, as you can see from the way I dress. But let's not talk about that, shall we? Oh, Mr. Marchant, do you think you can possibly remember any of those poems you started in the trenches? I can't fancy them bettering your sonnet that concludes with, 'The bough swings in the wind, the night is deep; Look at the stars, poor little ape, and sleep.'"

That one almost made me whoop—what monkeys we are, I thought—though I'd be the first to admit that the best line to use on a poet is one of his own—in fact, as many as possible. I decided I could safely forget our little Britons and devote myself to Erich or whatever needed me.

III. NINE FOR A PARTY

> Hell is the place for me. For to Hell go the fine churchmen,
> and the fine knights, killed in the tourney or in some grand
> war, the brave soldiers and the gallant gentlemen. With them
> will I go. There go also the fair gracious ladies who have
> lovers two or three beside their lord. There go the gold and
> the silver, the sables and ermine. There go the harpers and
> the minstrels and the kings of the earth.
> –Aucassin

I exchanged my drink for a new one from another tray Beau was
bringing around. The gray of the Void was beginning to look real pleasant, like warm thick mist with millions of tiny diamonds floating in it.
Doc was sitting grandly at the bar with a steaming tumbler of tea—a
chaser, I guess, since he was just putting down a shot glass. Sid was
talking to Erich and laughing at the same time and I said to myself it
begins to feel like a party, but something's lacking.

It wasn't anything to do with the Major Maintainer; its telltale was
glowing a steady red like a nice little home fire amid the tight cluster
of dials that included all the controls except the lonely and frightening
Introversion switch that was never touched. Then Maud's couch curtains
winked out and there were she and the Roman sitting quietly side by
side.

He looked down at his shiny boots and the rest of his black duds like
he was just waking up and couldn't believe it all, and he said, "*Omnia
mutantur, nos et mutamur in illis*," and I raised my eyebrows at Beau,
who was taking the tray back, and he did proud by old Vicksburg by
translating: "All things change and we change with them."

Then Mark slowly looked around at us, and I can testify that a Roman
smile is just as warm as any other nationality, and he finally said, "We
are nine, the proper number for a party. The couches, too. It is good."

Maud chuckled proudly and Erich shouted, "Welcome back from the
Void, *Kamerad*," and then, because he's German and thinks all parties
have to be noisy and satirically pompous, he jumped on a couch and announced, "*Herren und Damen*, permit me to introduce the noblest Roman
of them all, Marcus Vipsaius Niger, legate to Nero Claudius (called Ger-
manicus in a former time stream) and who in 763 A.U.C. (Correct, Mark?

[46]

It means 10 A.D., you meatheads!) died bravely fighting the Parthians and the Snakes in the Battle of Alexandria. *Hoch, hoch, hoch!*"

We all swung our glasses and cheered with him and Sid yelled at Erich, "Keep your feet off the furniture, you unschooled rogue," and grinned and boomed at all three hussars, "Take your ease, Recuperees," and Maud and Mark got their drinks, the Roman paining Beau by refusing Falernian wine in favor of scotch and soda, and right away everyone was talking a mile a minute.

We had a lot to catch up on. There was the usual yak about the war—"The Snakes are laying mine fields in the Void," "I don't believe it, how can you mine nothing?"—and the shortages—bourbon, bobby pins, and the stabilitin that would have brought Mark out of it faster—and what had become of people—"Marcia? Oh, she's not around any more," (She'd been caught in a Change Gale and green and stinking in five seconds, but I wasn't going to say that)—and Mark had to be told about Bruce's glove, which convulsed us all over again, and the Roman remembered a legionary who had carried a gripe all the way to Octavius because he'd accidentally been issued the unbelievable luxury item sugar instead of the usual salt, and Erich asked Sid if he had any new Ghostgirls in stock and Sid sucked his beard like the old goat he is. "Dost thou ask me, lusty Allemand? Nay, there are several great beauties, amongst them an Austrian countess from Strauss's Vienna, and if it were not for sweetling here...Mnnnn."

I poked a finger in Erich's chest between two of the bright buttons with their tiny death's heads. "You, my little von Hohenwald, are a menace to us real girls. You have too much of a thing about the unawakened, ghost kind."

He called me his little Demon and hugged me a bit too hard to prove it wasn't so, and then he suggested we show Bruce the Art Gallery. I thought this was a real brilliant idea, but when I tried to argue him out of it, he got stubborn. Bruce and Lili were willing to do anything anyone wanted them to, though not so willing to pay any attention while doing it. The saber cut was just a thin red line on his cheek; she'd washed away all the dried blood.

The Gallery gets you, though. It's a bunch of paintings and sculptures and especially odd knick-knacks, all made by Soldiers recuperating here, and a lot of them telling about the Change War from the stuff they're made of—brass cartridges, flaked flint, bits of ancient pottery glued into futuristic shapes, mashed-up Incan gold rebeaten by a Martian, whorls of beady Lunan wire, a picture in tempera on a crinkle-cracked thick round of quartz that had filled a starship porthole, a Sumerian inscription chiseled into a brick from an atomic oven.

There are a lot of things in the Gallery and I can always find some I haven't ever seen before. It gets you, as I say, thinking about the guys that made them and their thoughts and the far times and places they came from, and sometimes, when I'm feeling low, I'll come and look at them so I'll feel still lower and get inspired to kick myself back into a good temper. It's the only history of the Place there is and it doesn't change a great deal, because the things in it and the feelings that went into them resist the Change Winds better than anything else.

Right now, Erich's witty lecture was bouncing off the big ears I hide under my pageboy bob and I was thinking how awful it is that for us that there's not only change but Change. You don't know from one minute to the next whether a mood or idea you've got is really new or just welling up into you because the past has been altered by the Spiders or Snakes.

Change Winds can blow not only death but anything short of it, down to the featheriest fancy. They blow thousands of times faster than time moves, but no one can say how much faster or how far one of them will travel or what damage it'll do or how soon it'll damp out. The Big Time isn't the little time.

And then, for the Demons, there's the fear that our personality will just fade and someone else climb into the driver's seat and us not even know. Of course, we Demons are supposed to be able to remember through Change and in spite of it; that's why we are Demons and not Ghosts like the other Doublegangers, or merely Zombies or Unborn and nothing more, and as Beau truly said, there aren't any great men among us—and blamed few of the masses, either—we're a rare sort of people and that's why the Spiders have to Recruit us where they find us without caring about our previous knowledge and background, a Foreign Legion of time, a strange kind of folk, bright but always in the background, with built-in nostalgia and cynicism, as adaptable as Centaurian shape-changers but with memories as long as a Lunan's six arms, a kind of Change People, you might say, the cream of the damned.

But sometimes I wonder if our memories are as good as we think they are and if the whole past wasn't once entirely different from anything we remember, and we've forgotten that we forgot.

As I say, the Gallery gets you feeling real low, and so now I said to myself, "Back to your lousy little commandant, kid," and gave myself a stiff boot.

Erich was holding up a green bowl with gold dolphins or spaceships on it and saying, "And, to my mind, this proves that Etruscan art is derived from Egyptian. Don't you agree, Bruce?"

Bruce looked up, all smiles from Lili, and said, "What was that, dear chap?"

Erich's forehead got dark as the Door and I was glad the hussars had parked their sabers along with their shakos, but before he could even get out a Jerry cussword, Doc breezed up in that plateau-state of drunkenness so like hypnotized sobriety, moving as if he were on a dolly, ghosted the bowl out of Erich's hand, said, "A beautiful specimen of Middle Systemic Venusian. When Eightaitch finished it, he told me you couldn't look at it and not feel the waves of the Northern Venusian Shallows rippling around your hoofs. But it might look better inverted. I wonder. Who are you, young officer? *Nichevo*," and he carefully put the bowl back on its shelf and rolled on.

It's a fact that Doc knows the Art Gallery better than any of us, really by heart, he being the oldest inhabitant, though he maybe picked a bad time to show off his knowledge. Erich was going to take out after him, but I said, "Nix, *Kamerad*, remember gloves and sugar," and he contented himself with complaining, "That *nichevo*—it's so gloomy and hopeless, *ungeheuerlich*. I tell you, *Liebchen*, they shouldn't have Russians working for the Spiders, not even as Entertainers."

I grinned at him and squeezed his hand. "Not much entertainment in Doc these days, is there?" I agreed.

He grinned back at me a shade sheepishly and his face smoothed and his blue eyes looked sweet again for a second and he said, "I shouldn't want to claw out at people that way, Greta, but at times I am just a jealous old man," which is not entirely true, as he isn't a day over thirty-three, although his hair is nearly white.

Our lovers had drifted on a few steps until they were almost fading into the Surgery screen. It was the last spot I would have picked for the formal preliminaries to a little British smooching, but Lili probably didn't share my prejudices, though I remembered she'd told me she'd served a brief hitch in an Arachnoid Field Hospital before being transferred to the Place.

But she couldn't have had anything like the experience I'd had during my short and sour career as a Spider nurse, when I'd acquired my best-hated nightmare and flopped completely (jobwise, but on the floor, too) at seeing a doctor flick a switch and a being, badly injured but human, turn into a long cluster of glistening strange fruit—ugh, it always makes me want to toss my cookies and my buttons. And to think that dear old Daddy Anton wanted his Greta chile to be a doctor.

Well, I could see this wasn't getting me anywhere I wanted to go, and after all there was a party going on.

Doc was babbling something at a great rate to Sid—I just hoped Doc wouldn't get inspired to go into his animal imitations, which sound pretty fierce and once seriously offended some recuperating ETs.

Maud was demonstrating to Mark a 23rd Century two-step and Beau sat down at the piano and improvised softly on her rhythm.

[49]

As the deep-thrumming relaxing notes hit us, Erich's face brightened and he dragged me over. Pleasantly soon I had my feet off the diamond-rough floor, which we don't carpet because most of the ETs, the dear boys, like it hard, and I was shouldering back deep into the couch nearest the piano, with cushions all around me and a fresh drink in my hand, while my Nazi boy friend was getting ready to discharge his *Weltschmerz* as song, which didn't alarm me too much, as his baritone is passable.

Things felt real good, like the Maintainer was just idling to keep the Place in existence and moored to the cosmos, not exerting itself at all or at most taking an occasional lazy paddle stroke. At times the Place's loneliness can be happy and comfortable.

Then Beau raised an eyebrow at Erich, who nodded, and next thing they were launched into a song we all know, though I've never found out where it originally came from. This time it made me think of Lili, and I wondered why—and why it's a tradition at Recuperation Stations to call the new girl Lili, though in this case it happened to be her real name.

> *Standing in the Doorway just outside of space,*
> *Winds of Change blow 'round you but don't touch your face;*
> *You smile as you whisper tenderly,*
> *"Please cross to me, Recuperee;*
> *The operation's over, come in and close the Door."*

IV. SOS FROM NOWHERE

De Bailhache, Fresca, Mrs. Cammel, whirled
Beyond the circuit of the shuddering Bear
In fractured atoms.

–Eliot

I realized the piano had deserted Erich and I cranked my head up and saw Beau, Maud and Sid streaking for the control divan. The Major Maintainer was blinking emergency-green and fast, but the code was plain enough for even me to recognize the Spider distress call and for a second I felt just sick. Then Erich blew out his reserve breath in the middle of "Door" and I gave myself another of those helpful mental boots at the base of the spine and we hurried after them toward the center of the Place along with Mark.

The blinks faded as we got there and Sid told us not to move because we were making shadows. He glued an eye to the telltale and we held still as statues as he caressed the dials like he was making love.

One sensitive hand flicked out past the Introversion switch over to the Minor Maintainer and right away the Place was dark as your soul and there was nothing for me but Erich's arm and the knowledge that Sid was nursing a green light I couldn't even see, although my eyes had plenty time to accommodate.

Then the green light finally came back very slowly and I could see the dear reliable old face—the green-gold beard making him look like a merman—and then the telltale flared bright and Sid flicked on the Place lights and I leaned back.

"That nails them, lads, whoever and whenever they may be. Get ready for a pick-up."

Beau, who was closest of course, looked at him sharply. Sid shrugged uneasily. "Meseemed at first it was from our own globe a thousand years before our Lord, but that indication flickered and faded like witchfire. As it is, the call comes from something smaller than the Place and certes adrift from the cosmos. Meseemed too at one point I knew the fist of the caller—an antipodean atomicist named Benson-Carter—but that likewise changed."

Beau said, "We're not in the right phase of the cosmos-places rhythm for a pick-up, are we, sir?"

Sid answered, "Ordinarily not, boy."

Beau continued, "I didn't think we had any pick-ups scheduled. Or stand-by orders."

Sid said, "We haven't."

Mark's eyes glowed. He tapped Erich on the shoulder. "An octavian denarius against ten Reichsmarks it is a Snake trap."

Erich's grin showed his teeth. "Make it first through the Door next operation and I'm on."

It didn't take that to tell me things were serious, or the thought that there's always a first time for bumping into something from really outside the cosmos. The Snakes have broken our code more than once. Maud was quietly serving out weapons and Doc was helping her. Only Bruce and Lili stood off. But they were watching.

The telltale brightened. Sid reached toward the Maintainer, saying, "All right, my hearties. Remember, through this Doorway pass the fishiest finaglers in and out of the cosmos."

The Door appeared to the left and above where it should be and darkened much too fast. There was a gust of stale salt sea wind, if that makes sense, but no stepped-up Change Winds I could tell—and I had been bracing myself against them. The Door got inky and there was a flicker of gray fur whips and a flash of copper flesh and gilt and something dark and a clump of hoofs and Erich was sighting a stun gun across his left forearm, and then the Door had vanished like that and a tentacled silvery Lunan and a Venusian satyr were coming straight toward us.

The Lunan was hugging a pile of clothes and weapons. The satyr was helping a wasp-waisted woman carry a heavy-looking bronze chest. The woman was wearing a short skirt and high-collared bolero jacket of leather so dark brown it was almost black. She had a two-horned *petsofa* hairdress and she was boldly gilded here and there and wore sandals and copper anklets and wristlets—one of them a copper-plated Caller—and from her wide copper belt hung a short-handled double-headed ax. She was dark-complexioned and her forehead and chin receded, but the effect was anything but weak; she had a face like a beautiful arrowhead—and a familiar one, by golly!

But before I could say, "Kabysia Labrys," Maud shrilly beat me to it with, "It's Kaby with two friends. Break out a couple of Ghostgirls."

And then I saw it really was old-home week because I recognized my Lunan boy friend Ilhilihis, and in the midst of all the confusion I got a nice kick out of knowing I was getting so I could tell the personality of one silver-furred muzzle from another.

They reached the control divan and Illy dumped his load and the others let down the chest, and Kaby staggered but shook off the two ETs when they started to support her, and she looked daggers at Sid when he tried to do the same, although she's his "sweet Keftian friend" he'd mentioned to Bruce.

She leaned straight-armed on the divan and took two gasping breaths so deep that the ridges of her spine showed through her brown-skinned waist, and then she threw up her head and commanded, "Wine!"

While Beau was rushing it, Sid tried to take her hand again, saying, "Sweetling, I'd never heard you call before and knew not this pretty little fist," but she ripped out, "Save your comfort for the Lunan," and I looked and saw—Hey, Zeus!—that one of Ilhilihis' six tentacles was lopped off halfway.

That was for me, and, going to him, I fast briefed myself: "Remember, he only weighs fifty pounds for all he's seven feet high; he doesn't like low sounds or to be grabbed; the two legs aren't tentacles and don't act the same; uses them for long walks, tentacles for leaps; uses tentacles for close vision too and for manipulation, of course; extended, they mean he's at ease; retracted, on guard or nervous; sharply retracted, disgusted; greeting—"

Just then, one of them swept across my face like a sweet-smelling feather duster and I said, "Illy, man, it's been a lot of sleeps," and brushed my fingers across his muzzle. It still took a little self-control not to hug him, and I did reach a little cluckingly for his lopped tentacle, but he wafted it away from me and the little voice-box belted to his side squeaked, "Naughty, naughty. Papa will fix his little old self. Greta girl, ever bandaged even a Terra octopus?"

I had, an intelligent one from around a quarter billion A.D., but I didn't tell him so. I stood and let him talk to the palm of my hand with one of his tentacles—I don't savvy feather-talk but it feels good, though I've often wondered who taught him English—and watched him use a couple others to whisk a sort of Lunan band-aid out of his pouch and cap his wound with it.

Meanwhile, the satyr knelt over the bronze chest, which was decorated with little death's heads and crosses with hoops at the top and swastikas, but looking much older than Nazi, and the satyr said to Sid, "Quick thinkin, Gov, when ya saw the Door comin in high 'n soffened up gravty unner it, but cud I hav sum hep now?"

Sid touched the Minor Maintainer and we all got very light and my stomach did a flip-flop while the satyr piled on the chest the clothes and weapons that Illy had been carrying and pranced off with it all and carefully put it down at the end of the bar. I decided the satyr's English instructor must have been quite a character, too. Wish I'd met him—her—it.

Sid thought to ask Illy if he wanted Moon-normal gravity in one sector, but my boy likes to mix, and being such a lightweight, Earth-normal gravity doesn't bother him. As he said to me once, "Would Jovian gravity bother a beetle, Greta girl?"

I asked Illy about the satyr and he squeaked that his name was Sevensee and that he'd never met him before this operation. I knew the satyrs were from a billion years in the future, just as the Loonies were from a billion in the past, and I thought—Kreesed us!—but it must have been a real big or emergency-like operation to have the Spiders using those two for it, with two billion years between them—a time-difference that gives you a feeling of awe for a second, you know.

I started to ask Illy about it, but just then Beau came scampering back from the bar with a big red-and-black earthenware goblet of wine—we try to keep a variety of drinking tools in stock so folks will feel more at home. Kaby grabbed it from him and drained most of it in one swallow and then smashed it on the floor. She does things like that, though Sid's tried to teach her better. Then she stared at what she was thinking about until the whites showed all around her eyes and her lips pulled way back from her teeth and she looked a lot less human than the two ETs, just like a fury. Only a time traveler knows how like the wild murals and engravings of them some of the ancients can look.

My hair stood up at the screech she let out. She smashed a fist into the divan and cried, "Goddess! Must I see Crete destroyed, revived, and now destroyed again? It is too much for your servant."

Personally, I thought she could stand anything.

There was a rush of questions at what she said about Crete—I asked one of them, for the news certainly frightened me—but she shot up her arm straight for silence and took a deep breath and began.

"In the balance hung the battle. Rowing like black centipedes, the Dorian hulls bore down on our outnumbered ships. On the bright beach, masked by rocks, Sevensee and I stood by the needle gun, ready to give the black hulls silent wounds. Beside us was Ilhilihis, suited as a sea monster. But then...then..."

Then I saw she wasn't altogether the iron babe, for her voice broke and she started to shake and to sob rackingly, although her face was still a mask of rage, and she threw up the wine. Sid stepped in and made her stop, which I think he'd been wanting to do all along.

V. SID INSISTS ON GHOSTGIRLS

> Whenever I take up a newspaper and read it, I fancy I see
> ghosts creeping between the lines. There must be ghosts all
> over the world. They must be as countless as the grains of
> the sands, it seems to me.
> –Ibsen

My Elizabethan boy friend put his fists on his hips and laid down the law to us as if we were a lot of nervous children who'd been playing too hard.

"Look you, masters, this is a Recuperation Station and I am running it as such. A plague of all operations! I care not if the frame of things disjoints and the whole Change World goes to ruin, but you, warrior maid, are going to rest and drink more wine slowly before you tell your tale and your colleagues are going to be properly companioned. No questions, anyone. Beau, and you love us, give us a lively tune."

Kaby relaxed a little and let him put his hand carefully against her back in token of support and she said grudgingly, "All right, Fat Belly."

Then, so help me, to the tune of the Muskrat Ramble, which I'd taught Beau, we got girls for those two ETs and everybody properly paired up.

Right here I want to point out that a lot of the things they say in the Change World about Recuperation Stations simply aren't so—and anyway they always leave out nine-tenths of it. The Soldiers that come through the Door are looking for a good time, sure, but they're hurt real bad too, every one of them, deep down in their minds and hearts, if not always in their bodies or so you can see it right away.

Believe me, a temporal operation is no joke, and to start with, there isn't one person in a hundred who can endure to be cut from his lifeline and become a really wide-awake Doubleganger—a Demon, that is—let alone a Soldier. What does a badly hurt and mixed-up creature need who's been fighting hard? *One individual* to look out for him and feel for him and patch him up, and it helps if the one is of the opposite sex—that's something that goes beyond species.

There's your basis for the Place and the wild way it goes about its work, and also for most other Recuperation Stations or Entertainment Spots. The name Entertainer can be misleading, but I like it. She's got

[55]

to be a lot more than a good party girl—or boy—though she's got to be that too. She's got to be a nurse and a psychologist and an actress and a mother and a practical ethnologist and a lot of things with longer names—and a reliable friend.

None of us are all those things perfectly or even near it. We just try. But when the call comes, Entertainers have to forget grudges and gripes and envies and jealousies—and remember, they're lively people with sharp emotions—because there isn't any time then for anything but *help and don't ask who!*

And, deep inside her, a good Entertainer doesn't care who. Take the way it shaped up this time. It was pretty clear to me I ought to shift to Illy, although I wasn't quite easy in my mind about leaving Erich, because the Lunan was a long time from home and, after all, Erich was among anthropoids. Ilhilihis needed someone who was *simpatico.*

I like Illy and not just because he is a sort of tall cross between a spider monkey and a persian cat—though that is a handsome combo when you come to think of it. I like him for himself. So when he came in all lopped and shaky after a mean operation, I was the right person to look out for him. Now I've made my little speech and know-nothings in the Change World can go on making their bum jokes. But I ask you, how could an arrangement between Illy and me be anything but Platonic?

We might have had some octopoid girls and nymphs in stock—Sid couldn't be sure until he checked—but Ilhilihis and Sevensee voted for real people and I knew Sid saw it their way. Maud squeezed Mark's hand and tripped over to Sevensee ("Those are sharp hoofs you got, man"— she's picked up some of my language, like she has everything else), though Beau did frown over his shoulder at Lili from the piano, maybe to argue that she ought to take on the ET, as Mark had been a real casualty and could use live nursing. But it was plain as day to anybody but Beau that Bruce and Lili were a big thing and the last to be disturbed.

Erich acted stiffly hurt at losing me, but I knew he wasn't. He thinks he has a great technique with Ghostgirls and he likes to show it off, and he really is pretty slick at it, if you go for that sort of thing and—yang my yin!—who doesn't at times?

And when Sid formally wafted the Countess out of Stores—a real blonde stunner in a white satin hobble skirt with a white egret swaying up from her tiny hat, way ahead of Maud and Lili and me when it came to looks, though transparent as cigarette smoke—and when Erich clicked his heels and bowed over her hand and proudly conducted her to a couch, black Svengali to her Trilby, and started to German-talk some life into her with much head cocking and toothy smiling and a flow of witty flattery, and when she began to flirt back and the dream look in her eyes sharpened hungrily and focused on him—well, then I knew that Erich was happy and felt he was doing proud by the *Reichswehr*. No, my little commandant wasn't worrying me on that score.

Mark had drawn a Greek hetaera, name of Phryne; I suppose not the one who maybe still does the famous courtroom striptease back in Athens, and he was waking her up with little sips of his scotch and soda, though, from some looks he'd flashed, I got the idea Kaby was the kid he really went for. Sid was coaxing the fighting gal to take some high-energy bread and olives along with the wine, and, for a wonder, Doc seemed to be carrying on an animated and rational conversation with Sevensee and Maud, maybe comparing notes on the Northern Venusian Shallows, and Beau had got on to Panther Rag, and Bruce and Lili were leaning on the piano, smiling very appreciatively, but talking to each other a mile a minute.

Illy turned back from inspecting them all and squeaked, "Animals with clothes are so refreshing, dahling! Like you're all carrying banners!"

Maybe he had something there, though my banners were kind of Ash Wednesday, a charcoal gray sweater and skirt. He looked at my mouth with a tentacle to see how I was smiling and he squeaked softly, "Do I seem dull and commonplace to you, Greta girl, because I haven't got banners? Just another Zombie from a billion years in your past, as gray and lifeless as Luna is today, not as when she was a real dreamy sister planet simply bursting with air and water and feather forests. Or am I as strangely interesting to you as you are to me, girl from a billion years in my future?"

"Illy, you're sweet," I told him, giving him a little pat. I noticed his fur was still vibrating nervously and I decided the heck with Sid's orders, I'm going to pump him about what he was doing with Kaby and the satyr. Couldn't have him a billion years from home and bottled up, too. Besides, I was curious.

VI. CRETE CIRCA 1300 B.C.

> Maiden, Nymph, and Mother are the eternal royal Trinity
> of the island, and the Goddess, who is worshipped there in
> each of these aspects, as New Moon, Full Moon, and Old
> Moon, is the sovereign Deity.
> –Graves

Kaby pushed back at Sid some seconds of bread and olives, and, when he raised his bushy eyebrows, gave him a curt nod that meant she knew what she was doing. She stood up and sort of took a position. All the talk quieted down fast, even Bruce's and Lili's. Kaby's face and voice weren't strained now, but they weren't relaxed either.

"Woe to Spider! Woe to Cretan! Heavy is the news I bring you. Bear it bravely, like strong women. When we got the gun unlimbered, I heard seaweed fry and crackle. We three leaped behind the rock wall, saw our gun grow white as sunlight in a heat-ray of the Serpents! Natch, we feared we were outnumbered and I called upon my Caller."

I don't know how she does it, but she does—in English too. That is, when she figures she's got something important to report, and maybe she needs a little time to get ready.

Beau claims that all the ancients fit their thoughts into measured lines as naturally as we pick a word that will do, but I'm not sure how good the Vicksburg language department is. Though why I should wonder about things like that when I've got Kaby spouting the stuff right in front of me, I don't know.

"But I didn't die there, kiddos. I still hoped to hurt the Greek ships, maybe with the Snake's own heat gun. So I quick tried to outflank them. My two comrades crawled beside me—they are males, but they have courage. Soon we spied the ambush-setters. They were Snakes and they were many, filthily disguised as Cretans."

There was an indignant murmur at this, for our cutthroat Change War has its code, the Soldiers tell me. Being an Entertainer, I don't have to say what I think.

"They had seen us when we saw them," Kaby swept on, "and they loosed a killing volley. Heat- and knife-rays struck about us in a storm of wind and fire, and the Lunan lost a feeler, fighting for Crete's Triple Goddess. So we dodged behind a sand hill, steered our flight back toward the water. It was awful, what we saw there: Crete's brave ships all sunk or sinking, blue sky sullied by their death-smoke. Once again the Greeks had licked us!—aided by the filthy Serpents.

"Round our wrecks, their black ships scurried, like black beetles, filth their diet, yet this day they dine on heroes. On the quiet sunlit beach there, I could feel a Change Gale blowing, working changes deep inside me, aches and pains that were a stranger's. Half my memories were doubled, half my lifeline crooked and twisted, three new moles upon my sword-hand. Goddess, Goddess, Triple Goddess—"

Her voice wavered and Sid reached out a hand, but she straightened her back.

"Triple Goddess, give me courage to tell everything that happened. We ran down into the water, hoping to escape by diving. We had hardly gotten under when the heat-rays hit above us, turning all the cool green surface to a roaring white inferno. But as I believe I told you, I was calling on my Caller, and a Door now opened to us, deep below the deadly steam-clouds. We dived in like frightened minnows and a lot of water with us."

Off Chicago's Gold Coast, Dave once gave me a lesson in skin-diving and, remembering it, I got a flash of Kaby's Door in the dark depths.

"For a moment, all was chaos. Then the Door slammed shut behind us. We'd been picked up in time's nick by—an Express Room of our Spiders!—sloshing two feet deep in water, much more cramped for space than this Place. It was manned by a magician, an old coot named Benson-Carter. He dispelled the water quickly and reported on his Caller. We'd got dry, were feeling human, Illy here had shed his swimsuit, when we looked at the Maintainer. It was glowing, changing, melting! And when Benson-Carter touched it, he fell backward—death was in him. Then the Void began to darken, narrow, shrink and close around us, so I called upon my Caller—without wasting time, let me tell you!

"We can't say for sure what was it slowly squeezed that sweet Express Room, but we fear the dirty Snakes have found a way to find our Places and attack outside the cosmos!—found the Spiderweb that links us in the Void's gray less-than-nothing."

No murmur this time. This reaction was genuine; we'd been hit where we lived and I could see everybody was scared as sick as I was. Except maybe Bruce and Lili, who were still holding hands and beaming gently. I decided they were the kind that love makes brave, which it doesn't do to me. It just gives me two people to worry about.

"I can see you dig our feelings," Kaby continued. "This thing scared the pants off of us. If we could have, we'd have even Introverted the Maintainer, broken all the ties that bind us, chanced it incommunicado. But the little old Maintainer was a seething red-hot puddle filled with bubbles big as handballs. We sat tight and watched the Void close. I kept calling on my Caller."

I squeezed my eyes shut, but that made it easier to see the three of them with the Void shutting down on them. (Was ours still behaving? Yes, Bibi Miriam.) Poetry or no poetry, it got me.

"Benson-Carter, lying dying, also thought the Snakes had done it. And he knew that death was in him, so he whispered me his mission, giving me precise instructions: how to press the seven death's hands, starting lockside counterclockwise, one, three, five, six, two, four, seven, then you have a half an hour; after you have pressed the seven, do not monkey with the buttons—get out fast and don't stop moving."

I wasn't getting this part and I couldn't see that anyone else was, though Bruce was whispering to Lili. I remembered seeing skulls engraved on the bronze chest. I looked at Illy and he nodded a tentacle and spread two to say, I guessed, that yes, Benson-Carter had said something like that, but no, Illy didn't know much about it.

"All these things and more he whispered," Kaby went on, "with the last gasps of his life-force, telling all his secret orders—for he'd not been sent to get us, he was on a separate mission, when he heard my SOSs. Sid, it's you he was to contact, as the first leg of his mission, pick up from you three black hussars, death's-head Demons, daring Soldiers, then to wait until the Places next match rhythm with the cosmos—matter of two mealtimes, barely—and to tune in northern Egypt in the age of the last Caesar, in the year of Rome's swift downfall, there to start an operation in a battle near a city named for Thrace's Alexander, there to change the course of battle, blow sky-high the stinking Serpents, all their agents, all their Zombies!

"Goddess, pardon, now I savvy how you've guided my least footstep, when I thought you'd gone and left me—for I flubbed your three-mole signal. We've found Sid's Place, that's the first leg, and I see the three black hussars, and we've brought with us the weapon and the Parthian disguises, salvaged from the doomed Express Room when your Door appeared in time's nick, and the Room around us closing spewed us through before it vanished with the corpse of Benson-Carter. Triple Goddess, draw the milk now from the womanhood I flaunt here and inject the blackest hatred! Vengeance now upon the Serpents, vengeance sweet in northern Egypt, for your island, Crete, Goddess!—and a victory for the Spiders! Goddess, Goddess, we can swing it!"

The roar that made me try to stop my ears with my shoulders didn't come from Kaby—she'd spoken her piece—but from Sid. The dear boy was purple enough to make me want to remind him you can die of high blood pressure just as easy in the Change World.

"Dump me with ops! 'Sblood, I'll not endure it! Is this a battle post? They'll be mounting operations from field hospitals next. Kabysia Labrys, thou art mad to suggest it. And what's this prattle of locks, clocks, and death's heads, buttons and monkeys? This brabble, this farrago, this hocus-pocus! And where's the weapon you prate of? In that whoreson bronze casket, I suppose."

She nodded, looking blank and almost a little shy as poetic possession faded from her. Her answer came like its faltering last echo.

"It is nothing but a tiny tactical atomic bomb."

VII. TIME TO THINK

>After about 0.1 millisecond (one ten-thousandth part of a second) has elapsed, the radius of the ball of fire is some 45 feet, and the temperature is then in the vicinity of 300,000 degrees Centigrade. At this instant, the luminosity, as observed at a distance of 100,000 yards (5.7 miles), is approximately 100 times that of the sun as seen at the earth's surface...the ball of fire expands very rapidly to its maximum radius of 450 feet within less than a second from the explosion.
>–Los Alamos

Brother, that was all we needed to make everybody but Kaby and the two ETs start yelping at once, me included. It may seem strange that Change People, able to whiz through time and space and roust around outside the cosmos and knowing at least by hearsay of weapons a billion years in the future, like the Mindbomb, should panic at being shut in with a little primitive mid-20th Century gadget. Well, they feel the same as atomic scientists would feel if a Bengal tiger were brought into their laboratory, neither more nor less scared.

I'm a moron at physics, but I do know the Fireball is bigger than the Place. Remember that, besides the bomb, we'd recently been presented with a lot of other fears we hadn't had time to cope with, especially the business of the Snakes having learned how to get at our Places and melt the Maintainers and collapse them. Not to mention the general impression—first Saint Petersburg, then Crete—that the whole Change War was going against the Spiders.

Yet, in a free corner of my mind, I was shocked at how badly we were all panicking. It made me admit what I didn't like to: that we were all in pretty much the same state as Doc, except that the bottle didn't happen to be our out.

And had the rest of us been controlling our drinking so well lately?

Maud yelled, "Jettison it!" and pulled away from the satyr and ran from the bronze chest. Beau, harking back to what they'd thought of doing in the Express Room when it was too late, hissed, "Sirs, we must Introvert," and vaulted over the piano bench and legged it for the control divan. Erich seconded him with a white-faced *"Gott in Himmel, ja!"*

from beside the surly, forgotten Countess, holding, by its slim stem, an empty, rose-stained wine glass.

I felt my mind flinch, because Introverting a Place is several degrees worse than foxholing. It's supposed not only to keep the Door tight shut, but also to lock it so even the Change Winds can't get through—cut the Place loose from the cosmos altogether.

I'd never talked with anyone from a Place that had been Introverted.

Mark dumped Phryne off his lap and ran after Maud. The Greek Ghostgirl, quite solid now, looked around with sleepy fear and fumbled her apple-green chiton together at the throat. She wrenched my attention away from everyone else for a moment, and I couldn't help wondering whether the person or Zombie back in the cosmos, from whose lifeline the Ghost has been taken, doesn't at least have strange dreams or thoughts when something like this happens.

Sid stopped Beau, though he almost got bowled over doing it, and he held the gambler away from the Maintainer in a bear hug and bellowed over his shoulders, "Masters, are you mad? Have you lost your wits? Maud! Mark! Marcus! Magdalene! On your lives, unhand that casket!"

Maud had swept the clothes and bows and quivers and stuff off it and was dragging it out from the bar toward the Door sector, so as to dump it through fast when we got one, I guess, while Mark acted as if he were trying to help her and wrestle it away from her at the same time.

They kept on as if they hadn't heard a word Sid said, with Mark yelling, "Let go, *meretrix*! This holds Rome's answer to Parthia on the Nile."

Kaby watched them as if she wanted to help Mark but scorned to scuffle with a mere—well, Mark had said it in Latin, I guess—call girl.

Then, on the top of the bronze chest, I saw those seven lousy skulls starting at the lock as plain as if they'd been under a magnifying glass, though ordinarily they'd have been a vague circle to my eyes at the distance, and I lost my mind and started to run in the opposite direction, but Illy whipped three tentacles around me, gentle-like, and squeaked, "Easy now, Greta girl, don't you be doing it, too. Hold still or Papa spank. My, my, but you two-leggers can whirl about when you have a mind to."

My stampede had carried his featherweight body a couple of yards, but it stopped me and I got my mind back, partly.

"Unhand it, I say!" Sid repeated without accomplishing anything, and he released Beau, though he kept a hand near the gambler's shoulder.

Then my fat friend from Lynn Regis looked real distraught at the Void and blustered at no one in particular, "'Sdeath, think you I'd mutiny against my masters, desert the Spiders, go to ground like a spent fox and pull my hole in after me? A plague of such cowardice! Who suggests it? Introversion's no mere last-ditch device. Unless ordered, supervised and sanctioned, it means the end. And what if I'd Introverted ere we got Kaby's call for succor, hey?"

His warrior maid nodded with harsh approval and he noticed it and shook his free hand at her and scolded her, "Not that I say yea to your mad plan for that Devil's casket, you half-clad lackwit. And yet to jettison...Oh, ye gods, ye gods—" he wiped his hand across his face—"grant me a minute in which I may think!"

Thinking time wasn't an item even on the strictly limited list at the moment, although Sevensee, squatting dourly on his hairy haunches where Maud had left him, threw in a dead-pan "Thas tellin em, Gov."

Then Doc at the bar stood up tall as Abe Lincoln in his top hat and shawl and 19th Century duds and raised an unwavering arm for silence and said something that sounded like: "Introversh, inversh, glovsh," and then his enunciation switched to better than perfect as he continued, "I know to an absolute certainty what we must do."

It showed me how rabbity we were that the Place got quiet as a church while we all stopped whatever we were doing and waited breathless for a poor drunk to tell us how to save ourselves.

He said something like, "Inversh...bosh..." and held our eyes for a moment longer. Then the light went out of his and he slobbered out a *"Nichevo"* and slid an arm far along the bar for a bottle and started to pour it down his throat without stopping sliding.

Before he completed his collapse to the floor, in the split second while our attention was still focused on the bar, Bruce vaulted up on top of it, so fast it was almost like he'd popped up from nowhere, though I'd seen him start from behind the piano.

"I've a question. Has anyone here triggered that bomb?" he said in a voice that was very clear and just loud enough. "So it can't go off," he went on after just the right pause, his easy grin and brisk manner putting more heart into me all the time. "What's more, if it were to be triggered, we'd still have half an hour. I believe you said it had that long a fuse?"

He stabbed a finger at Kaby. She nodded.

"Right," he said. "It'd have to be that long for whoever plants it in the Parthian camp to get away. There's another safety margin.

"Second question. Is there a locksmith in the house?"

For all Bruce's easiness, he was watching us like a golden eagle and he caught Beau's and Maud's affirmatives before they had a chance to explain or hedge them and said, "That's very good. Under certain circumstances, you two'd be the ones to go to work on the chest. But before we consider that, there's Question Three: Is anyone here an atomics technician?"

That one took a little conversation to straighten out, Illy having to explain that, yes, the Early Lunans had atomic power—hadn't they blasted the life off their planet with it and made all those ghastly craters?—but no, he wasn't a technician exactly, he was a "thinger" (I thought at first his squeakbox was lisping); what was a thinger?—well, a thinger was someone who manipulated things in a way that was truly impossible to describe, but no, you couldn't possibly thing atomics; the idea was quite ridiculous, so he couldn't be an atomics thinger; the term was worse than a contradiction, well, really!—while Sevensee, from his two-thousand-millennia advantage of the Lunan, grunted to the effect that his culture didn't rightly use any kind of power, but just sort of moved satyrs and stuff by wrestling space-time around, "or think em roun ef we hafta. Can't think em in the Void, tho, wus luck. Hafta have—I dunno wut. Dun havvit anyhow."

"So we don't have an A-tech," Bruce summed up, "which makes it worse than useless, downright dangerous, to tamper with the chest. We wouldn't know what to do if we did get inside safely. One more question." He directed it toward Sid. "How long before we can jettison anything?"

Sid, looking a shade jealous, yet mostly grateful for the way Bruce had calmed his chickens, started to explain, but Bruce didn't seem to be taking any chance of losing his audience, and as soon as Sid got to the word "rhythm," he pulled the answer away from him.

"In brief, not until we can effectively tune in on the cosmos again. Thank you, Master Lessingham. That's at least five hours—two mealtimes, as the Cretan officer put it," and he threw Kaby a quick soldierly smile. "So, whether the bomb goes to Egypt or elsewhere, there's not a thing we can do about it for five hours. All right then!"

His smile blinked out like a light and he took a couple of steps up and down the bar, as if measuring the space he had. Two or three cocktail glasses sailed off and popped, but he didn't seem to notice them and we hardly did either. It was creepy the way he kept staring from one to another of us. We had to look up. Behind his face, with the straight golden hair flirting around it, was only the Void.

"All right then," he repeated suddenly. "We're twelve Spiders and two Ghosts, and we've time for a bit of a talk, and we're all in the same bloody boat, fighting the same bloody war, so we'll all know what we're talking about. I raised the subject a while back, but I was steamed up about a glove, and it was a big jest. All right! But now the gloves are off!"

Bruce ripped them out of his belt where they'd been tucked and slammed them down on the bar, to be kicked off the next time he paced back and forth, and it wasn't funny.

[65]

"Because," he went right on, "I've been getting a completely new picture of what this Spiders' war has been doing to each one of us. Oh, it's jolly good sport to slam around in space and time and then have a rugged little party outside both of them when the operation's over. It's sweet to know there's no cranny of reality so narrow, no privacy so intimate or sacred, no wall of was or will be strong enough, that we can't shoulder in. Knowledge is a glamorous thing, sweeter than lust or gluttony or the passion of fighting and including all three, the ultimate insatiable hunger, and it's great to be Faust, even in a pack of other Fausts.

"It's sweet to jigger reality, to twist the whole course of a man's life or a culture's, to ink out his or its past and scribble in a new one, and be the only one to know and gloat over the changes—hah! killing men or carrying off women isn't in it for glutting the sense of power. It's sweet to feel the Change Winds blowing through you and know the pasts that were and the past that is and the pasts that may be. It's sweet to wield the Atropos and cut a Zombie or Unborn out of his lifeline and look the Doubleganger in the face and see the Resurrection-glow in it and Recruit a brother, welcome a newborn fellow Demon into our ranks and decide whether he'll best fit as Soldier, Entertainer, or what.

"Or he can't stand Resurrection, it fries or freezes him, and you've got to decide whether to return him to his lifeline and his Zombie dreams, only they'll be a little grayer and horrider than they were before, or whether, if she's got that tantalizing something, to bring her shell along for a Ghostgirl—that's sweet, too. It's even sweet to have Change Death poised over your neck, to know that the past isn't the precious indestructible thing you've been taught it was, to know that there's no certainty about the future either, whether there'll even be one, to know that no part of reality is holy, that the cosmos itself may wink out like a flicked switch and God be not and nothing left but nothing!"

He threw out his arms against the Void. "And knowing all that, it's doubly sweet to come through the Door into the Place and be out of the worst of the Change Winds and enjoy a well-earned Recuperation and share the memories of all these sweetnesses I've been talking about, and work out all the fascinating feelings you've been accumulating back in the cosmos, layer by black layer, in the company of and with the help of the best bloody little band of fellow Fausts and Faustines going!

"Oh, it's a sweet life, all right, but I'm asking you—" and here his eyes stabbed us again, one by one, fast—"I'm asking you what it's done to us. I've been getting a completely new picture, as I said, of what my life was and what it could have been if there'd been changes of the sort that even we Demons can't make, and what my life is. I've been watching how we've all been responding to things just now, to the news of Saint Petersburg and to what the Cretan officer told beautifully—only it wasn't beautiful what she had to tell—and mostly to that bloody box of bomb. And I'm simply asking each one of you, what's happened to you?"

He stopped his pacing and stuck his thumbs in his belt and seemed to be listening to the wheels turning in at least eleven other heads—only I stopped mine pretty quick, with Dave and Father and the Rape of Chicago coming up out of the dark on the turn and Mother and the Indiana Dunes and Jazz Limited just behind them, followed by the unthinkable thing the Spider doctor had flicked into existence when I flopped as a nurse, because I can't stand that to be done to my mind by anybody but myself.

I stopped them by using the old infallible Entertainers' gimmick, a fast survey of the most interesting topic there is—other people's troubles.

Offhand, Beau looked as if he had most troubles, shamed by his boss and his girl given her heart to a Soldier; he was hugging them to himself very quiet.

I didn't stop for the two ETs—they're too hard to figure—or for Doc; nobody can tell whether a fallen-down drunk's at the black or bright end of his cycle; you just know it's cycling.

Maud ought to be suffering as much as Beau, called names and caught out in a panic, which always hurts her because she's plus three hundred years more future than the rest of us and figures she ought to be that much wiser, which she isn't always—not to mention she's over fifty years old, though her home-century cosmetic science keeps her looking and acting teenage most of the time. She'd backed away from the bronze chest so as not to stand out, and now Lili came from behind the piano and stood beside her.

Lili had the opposite of troubles, a great big glow for Bruce, proud as a promised princess watching her betrothed. Erich frowned when he saw her, for he seemed proud too, proud of the way his *Kamerad* had taken command of us panicky whacks *Führer*-fashion. Sid still looked mostly grateful and inclined to let Bruce keep on talking.

Even Kaby and Mark, those two dragons hot for battle, standing a little in front and to one side of us by the bronze chest, like its guardians, seemed willing to listen. They made me realize one reason Sid had for letting Bruce run on, although the path his talk was leading us down was flashing with danger signals: When it was over, there'd still be the problem of what to do with the bomb, and a real opposition shaping up between Soldiers and Entertainers, and Sid was hoping a solution would turn up in the meantime or at least was willing to put off the evil day.

But beyond all that, and like the rest of us, I could tell from the way Sid was squinting his browy eyes and chewing his beardy lip that he was shaken and moved by what Bruce had said. This New Boy had dipped into our hearts and counted our kicks so beautifully, better than most of us could have done, and then somehow turned them around so that we had to think of what messes and heels and black sheep and lost lambs we were—well, we wanted to keep on listening.

VIII. A PLACE TO STAND

Give me a place to stand, and I will move the world.

–Archimedes

Bruce's voice had a faraway touch and he was looking up left at the Void as he said, "Have you ever really wondered why the two sides of this war are called the Snakes and the Spiders? Snakes may be clear enough—you always call the enemy something dirty. But Spiders—our name for ourselves? Bear with me, Ilhilihis; I know that no being is created dirty or malignant by Nature, but this is a matter of anthropoid feelings and folkways. Yes, Mark, I know that some of your legions have nicknames like the Drunken Lions and the Snails, and that's about as insulting as calling the British Expeditionary Force the Old Contemptibles.

"No, you'd have to go to bands of vicious youths in cities slated for ruin to find a habit of naming like ours, and even they would try to brighten up the black a bit. But simply—Spiders. And Snakes, for that's their name for themselves too, you know. Spiders and Snakes. What are our masters, that we give them names like that?"

It gave me the shivers and set my mind working in a dozen directions and I couldn't stop it, although it made the shivers worse.

Illy beside me now—I'd never given it a thought before, but he did have eight legs of a sort, and I remembered thinking of him as a spider monkey, and hadn't the Lunans had wisdom and atomic power and a billion years in which to get the Change War rolling?

Or suppose, in the far future, Terra's own spiders evolved intelligence and a cruel cannibal culture. They'd be able to keep their existence secret. I had no idea of who or what would be on Earth in Sevensee's day, and wouldn't it be perfect black hairy poisoned spider-mentality to spin webs secretly through the world of thought and all of space and time?

And Beau—wasn't there something real Snaky about him, the way he moved and all?

Spiders and Snakes. *Spinne und Schlange*, as Erich called them. S & S. But SS stood for the Nazi *Schutzstaffel*, the Black Shirts, and what if some of those cruel, crazy Jerries had discovered time travel and—I brought myself up with a jerk and asked myself, "Greta, how nuts can you get?"

From where he was on the floor, the front of the bar his sounding board, Doc shrieked up at Bruce like one of the damned from the pit, "Don't speak against the Spiders! Don't blaspheme! They can hear the Unborn whisper. Others whip only the skin, but they whip the naked brain and heart," and Erich called out, "That's enough, Bruce!"

But Bruce didn't spare him a look and said, "But whatever the Spiders are and no matter how much whip they use, it's plain as the telltale on the Maintainer that the Change War is not only going against them, but getting away from them. Dwell for a bit on the current flurry of stupid slugging and panicky anachronism, when we all know that anachronism is what gets the Change Winds out of control. This punch-drunk pounding on the Cretan-Dorian fracas as if it were the only battle going and the only way to work things. Whisking Constantine from Britain to the Bosporus by rocket, sending a pocket submarine back to sail with the Armada against Drake's woodensides—I'll wager you hadn't heard those! And now, to save Rome, an atomic bomb.

"Ye gods, they could have used Greek fire or even dynamite, but a fission weapon...I leave you to imagine what gaps and scars that will make in what's left of history—the smothering of Greece and the vanishment of Provence and the troubadours and the Papacy's Irish Captivity won't be in it!"

The cut on his cheek had opened again and was oozing a little, but he didn't pay any attention to it, and neither did we, as his lips thinned in irony and he said, "But I'm forgetting that this is a cosmic war and that the Spiders are conducting operations on billions, trillions of planets and inhabited gas clouds through millions of ages and that we're just one little world—one little solar system, Sevensee—and we can hardly expect our inscrutable masters, with all their pressing preoccupations and far-flung responsibilities, to be especially understanding or tender in their treatment of our pet books and centuries, our favorite prophets and periods, or unduly concerned about preserving any of the trifles that we just happen to hold dear.

"Perhaps there are some sentimentalists who would rather die forever than go on living in a world without the *Summa*, the Field Equations, *Process and Reality*, *Hamlet*, Matthew, Keats, and the *Odyssey*, but our masters are practical creatures, ministering to the needs of those rugged souls who want to go on living no matter what."

Erich's "Bruce, I'm telling you that's enough," was lost in the quickening flow of the New Boy's words. "I won't spend much time on the minor signs of our major crack-up—the canceling of leaves, the sharper shortages, the loss of the Express Room, the use of Recuperation Stations

[70]

for ops and all the other frantic patchwork—last operation but one, we were saddled with three Soldiers from outside the Galaxy and, no fault of theirs, they were no earthly use. Such little things might happen at a bad spot in any war and are perhaps only local. But there's a big thing."

He paused again, to let us wonder, I guess. Maud must have worked her way over to me, for I felt her dry little hand on my arm and she whispered out of the side of her mouth, "What do we do now?"

"We listen," I told her the same way. I felt a little impatient with her need to be doing something about things.

She cocked a gold-dusted eyebrow at me and murmured, "You, too?"

I didn't get to ask her me, too, what? Crush on Bruce? Nuts!—because just then Bruce's voice took up again in the faraway range.

"Have you ever asked yourselves how many operations the fabric of history can stand before it's all stitches, whether too much Change won't one day wear out the past? And the present and the future, too, the whole bleeding business. Is the law of the Conservation of Reality any more than a thin hope given a long name, a prayer of theoreticians? Change Death is as certain as Heat Death, and far faster. Every operation leaves reality a bit cruder, a bit uglier, a bit more makeshift, and a whole lot less rich in those details and feelings that are our heritage, like the crude penciled sketch on canvas when you've stripped off the paint.

"If that goes on, won't the cosmos collapse into an outline of itself, then nothing? How much thinning can reality stand, having more and more Doublegangers cut out of it? And there's another thing about every operation—it wakes up the Zombies a little more, and as its Change Winds die, it leaves them a little more disturbed and nightmare-ridden and frazzled. Those of you who have been on operations in heavily worked-over temporal areas will know what I mean—that look they give you out of the sides of their eyes as if to say, 'You again? For Christ's sake, go away. We're the dead. We're the ones who don't want to wake up, who don't want to be Demons and hate to be Ghosts. Stop torturing us.'"

I looked around at the Ghostgirls; I couldn't help it. They'd somehow got together on the control divan, facing us, their backs to the Maintainers. The Countess had dragged along the bottle of wine Erich had fetched her earlier and they were passing it back and forth. The Countess had a big rose splotch across the ruffled white lace of her blouse.

Bruce said, "There'll come a day when all the Zombies and all the Unborn wake up and go crazy together and figuratively come marching at us in their numberless hordes, saying, 'We've had enough.'"

But I didn't turn back to Bruce right away. Phryne's chiton had slipped off one shoulder and she and the Countess were sitting sagged forward, elbows on knees, legs spread—at least, as far as the Countess's hobble skirt would let her—and swayed toward each other a little. They were still surprisingly solid, although they hadn't had any personal attention for a half hour, and they were looking up over my head with half-shut eyes and they seemed, so help me, to be listening to what Bruce was saying and maybe hearing some of it.

"We make a careful distinction between Zombies and Unborn, between those troubled by our operations whose lifelines lie in the past and those whose lifelines lie in the future. But is there any distinction any longer? Can we tell the difference between the past and the future? Can we any longer locate the now, the real now of the cosmos? The Places have their own nows, the now of the Big Time we're on, but that's different and it's not made for real living.

"The Spiders tell us that the real now is somewhere in the last half of the 20th Century, which means that several of us here are also alive in the cosmos, have lifelines along which the now is traveling. But do you swallow that story quite so easily, Ilhilihis, Sevensee? How does it strike the servants of the Triple Goddess? The Spiders of Octavian Rome? The Demons of Good Queen Bess? The gentlemen Zombies of the Greater South? Do the Unborn man the starships, Maud?

"The Spiders also tell us that, although the fog of battle makes the now hard to pin down precisely, it will return with the unconditional surrender of the Snakes and the establishment of cosmic peace, and roll on as majestically toward the future as before, quickening the continuum with its passage. Do you really believe that? Or do you believe, as I do, that we've used up all the future as well as the past, wasted it in premature experience, and that we've had the real now smudged out of existence, stolen from us forever, the precious now of true growth, the child-moment in which all life lies, the moment like a newborn baby that is the only home for hope there is?"

He let that start to sink in, then took a couple of quick steps and went on, his voice rising over Erich's "Bruce, for the last time—" and seeming to pick up a note of hope from the very word he had used, "But although things look terrifyingly black, there remains a chance—the slimmest chance, but still a chance—of saving the cosmos from Change Death and restoring reality's richness and giving the Ghosts good sleep and perhaps even regaining the real now. We have the means right at hand. What if the power of time traveling were used not for war and destruction, but for healing, for the mutual enrichment of the ages, for quiet communication and growth, in brief, to bring a peace message—"

But my little commandant is quite an actor himself and knows a wee bit about the principles of scene-stealing, and he was not going to let Bruce drown him out as if he were just another extra playing a Voice from the Mob. He darted across our front, between us and the bar, took a running leap, and landed bang on the bloody box of bomb.

A bit later, Maud was silently showing me the white ring above her elbow where I'd grabbed her and Illy was teasing a clutch of his tentacles out of my other hand and squeaking reproachfully, "Greta girl, don't ever do that."

Erich was standing on the chest and I noticed that his boots carefully straddled the circle of skulls, and I should have known anyway you could hardly push them in the right order by jumping on them, and he was pointing at Bruce and saying, "—and that means mutiny, my young sir. *Um Gottes willen*, Bruce, listen to me and step down before you say anything worse. I'm older than you, Bruce. Mark's older. Trust in your *Kameraden*. Guide yourself by their knowledge."

He had got my attention, but I had much rather have him black my eye.

"You older than me?" Bruce was grinning. "When your twelve-years' advantage was spent in soaking up the wisdom of a race of sadistic dreamers gone paranoid, in a world whose thought-stream had already been muddied by one total war? Mark older than me? When all his ideas and loyalties are those of a wolf pack of unimaginative sluggers two thousand years younger than I am? Either of you older because you have more of the killing cynicism that is all the wisdom the Change World ever gives you? Don't make me laugh!

"I'm an Englishman, and I come from an epoch when total war was still a desecration and the flowers and buds of thoughts not yet whacked off or blighted. I'm a poet and poets are wiser than anyone because they're the only people who have the guts to think and feel at the same time. Right, Sid? When I talk to all of you about a peace message, I want you to think about it concretely in terms of using the Places to bring help across the mountains of time when help is really needed, not to bring help that's undeserved or knowledge that's premature or contaminating, sometimes not to bring anything at all, but just to check with infinite tenderness and concern that everything's safe and the glories of the universe unfolding as they were intended to—"

"Yes, you are a poet, Bruce," Erich broke in. "You can tootle soulfully on the flute and make us drip tears. You can let out the stops on the big organ pipes and make us tremble as if at Jehovah's footsteps. For the last twenty minutes, you have been giving us some very *charmante* poetry. But what are you? An Entertainer? Or are you a Soldier?"

Right then—I don't know what it was, maybe Sid clearing his throat— I could sense our feelings beginning to turn against Bruce. I got the strangest feeling of reality clamping down and bright colors going dull and dreams vanishing. Yet it was only then I also realized how much Bruce had moved us, maybe some of us to the verge of mutiny, even. I was mad at Erich for what he was doing, but I couldn't help admiring his cockiness.

I was still under the spell of Bruce's words and the more-than-words behind them, but then Erich would shift around a bit and one of his heels would kick near the death's-head pushbuttons and I wanted to stamp with spike heels on every death's-head button on his uniform. I didn't know exactly what I felt yet.

"Yes, I'm a Soldier," Bruce told him, "and I hope you won't ever have to worry about my courage, because it's going to take more courage than any operation we've ever planned, ever dreamed of, to carry the peace message to the other Places and to the wound-spots of the cosmos. Perhaps it will be a fast wicket and we'll be bowled down before we score a single run, but who cares? We may at least see our real masters when they come to smash us, and for me that will be a deep satisfaction. And we may do some smashing of our own."

"So you're a Soldier," Erich said, his smile showing his teeth. "Bruce, I'll admit that the half-dozen operations you've been on were rougher than anything I drew in my first hundred sleeps. For that, I am all honest sympathy. But that you should let them get you into such a state that love and a girl can turn you upside down and start you babbling about peace messages—"

"Yes, by God, love and a girl have changed me!" Bruce shouted at him, and I looked around at Lili and I remembered Dave saying, "I'm going to Spain," and I wondered if anything would ever again make my face flame like that. "Or, rather, they've made me stand up for what I've believed in all along. They've made me—"

"*Wunderbar,*" Erich called and began to do a little sissy dance on the bomb that set my teeth on edge. He bent his wrists and elbows at arty angles and stuck out a hip and ducked his head simperingly and blinked his eyes very fast. "Will you invite me to the wedding, Bruce? You'll have to get another best man, but I will be the flower girl and throw pretty little posies to all the distinguished guests. Here, Mark. Catch, Kaby. One for you, Greta. *Danke schön. Ach, zwei Herzen in dreivierteltakt...ta-ta...ta-ta...ta-ta-ta-ta-ta...*"

"What the hell do you think a woman is?" Bruce raged. "Something to mess around with in your spare time?"

Erich kept on humming "Two Hearts in Waltz Time"—and jigging around to it, damn him—but he slipped in a nod to Bruce and a "Precisely." So I knew where I stood, but it was no news to me.

"Very well," Bruce said, "let's leave this Brown Shirt *maricón* to amuse himself and get down to business. I made all of you a proposal and I don't have to tell you how serious it is or how serious Lili and I are about it. We not only must infiltrate and subvert other Places, which luckily for us are made for infiltration, we also must make contact with the Snakes and establish working relationships with their Demons at our level as one of our first steps."

That stopped Erich's jig and got enough of a gasp from some of us to make it seem to come from practically everybody. Erich used it to work a change of pace.

"Bruce! We've let you carry this foolery further than we should. You seem to have the idea that because anything goes in the Place—dueling, drunkenness, *und so weiter*—you can say what you have and it will all be forgotten with the hangover. Not so. It is true that among such a set of monsters and free spirits as ourselves, and working as secret agents to boot, there cannot be the obvious military discipline that would obtain in a Terran army.

"But let me tell you, Bruce, let me grind it home into you—Sid and Kaby and Mark will bear me out in this, as officers of equivalent rank—that the Spider line of command stretches into and through this Place just as surely as the word of *der Führer* rules Chicago. And as I shouldn't have to emphasize to you, Bruce, the Spiders have punishments that would make my countrymen in Belsen and Buchenwald—well, pale a little. So while there is still a shadow of justification for our interpreting your remarks as utterly tasteless clowning—"

"Babble on," Bruce said, giving him a loose downward wave of his hand without looking. "I made you people a proposal." He paused. "How do you stand, Sidney Lessingham?"

Then I felt my legs getting weak, because Sid didn't answer right away. The old boy swallowed and started to look around at the rest of us. Then the feeling of reality clamping down got something awful, because he didn't look around, but straightened his back a little. Just then, Mark cut in fast.

"It grieves me, Bruce, but I think you are possessed. Erich, he must be confined."

Kaby nodded, almost absently. "Confine or kill the coward, whichever is easier, whip the woman, and let's get on to the Egyptian battle."

"Indeed, yes," Mark said. "I died in it. But now perhaps no longer."

Kaby said to him, "I like you, Roman."

Bruce was smiling, barely, and his eyes were moving and fixing. "You, Ilhilihis?"

Illy's squeak box had never sounded mechanical to me before, but it did as he answered, "I'm a lot deeper into borrowed time than the rest of you, tra-la-la, but Papa still loves living. Include me very much out, Brucie."

"Miss Davies?"

Beside me, Maud said flatly, "Do you think I'm a fool?" Beyond her, I saw Lili and I thought, "My God, I might look as proud if I were in her shoes, but I sure as hell wouldn't look as confident."

Bruce's eyes hadn't quite come to Beau when the gambler spoke up. "I have no cause to like you, sir, rather the opposite. But this Place has come to bore me more than Boston and I have always found it difficult to resist a long shot. A very long one, I fear. I am with you, sir."

There was a pain in my chest and a roaring in my ears and through it I heard Sevensee grunting, "—sicka these lousy Spiders. Deal me in."

And then Doc reared up in front of the bar and he'd lost his hat and his hair was wild and he grabbed an empty fifth by the neck and broke the bottom of it all jagged against the bar and he waved it and screeched, "*Ubivaytye Pauki—i Nyemetzi!*"

And right behind his words, Beau sang out fast the English of it, "Kill the Spiders—and the Germans!"

And Doc didn't collapse then, though I could see he was hanging onto the bar tight with his other hand, and the Place got stiller, inside and out, than I've ever known it, and Bruce's eyes were finally moving back toward Sid.

But the eyes stopped short of Sid and I heard Bruce say, "Miss Forzane?" and I thought, "That's funny," and I started to look around at the Countess, and felt all the eyes and I realized, "Hey, that's me! But this can't happen to me. To the others, yes, but not to me. I just work here. Not to Greta, no, no, no!"

But it had, and the eyes didn't let go, and the silence and the feeling of reality were Godawful, and I said to myself, "Greta, you've got to say something, if only a suitable four-letter word," and then suddenly I knew what the silence was like. It was like that of a big city if there were some way of shutting off all the noise in one second. It was like Erich's singing when the piano had deserted him. It was as if the Change Winds should ever die completely...and I knew beforehand what had happened when I turned my back on them all.

The Ghostgirls were gone. The Major Maintainer hadn't merely been switched to Introvert. It was gone, too.

IX. A LOCKED ROOM

> "We examined the moss between the bricks, and found it undisturbed."
>
> "You looked among D——'s papers, of course, and into the books of the library?"
>
> "Certainly; we opened every package and parcel; we not only opened every book, but we turned over every leaf in each volume..."
>
> –Poe

Three hours later, Sid and I plumped down on the couch nearest the kitchen, though too tired to want to eat for a while yet. A tighter search than I could ever have cooked up had shown that the Maintainer was not in the Place.

Of course it had to be in the Place, as we kept telling each other for the first two hours. It had to be, if circumstances and the theories we lived by in the Change World meant anything. A Maintainer is what maintains a Place. The Minor Maintainer takes care of oxygen, temperature, humidity, gravity, and other little life-cycle and matter-cycle things generally, but it's the Major Maintainer that keeps the walls from buckling and the ceiling from falling in. It is little, but oh my, it does so much.

It doesn't work by wires or radio or anything complicated like that. It just hooks into local space-time.

I have been told that its inside working part is made up of vastly tough, vastly hard giant molecules, each one of which is practically a vest-pocket cosmos in itself. Outside, it looks like a portable radio with a few more dials and some telltales and switches and plug-ins for earphones and a lot of other sensory thingumajigs.

But the Maintainer was gone and the Void hadn't closed in, yet. By this time, I was so fagged, I didn't care much whether it did or not.

One thing for sure, the Maintainer had been switched to Introvert before it was spirited away or else its disappearance automatically produced Introversion, take your choice, because we sure were Introverted—real nasty martinet-schoolmaster grip of reality on my thoughts that I knew, without trying, liquor wouldn't soften, not a breath of Change Wind, absolutely stifling, and the gray of the Void seeming so much inside my head that I think I got a glimmering of what the science boys mean when they explain to me that the Place is a kind of interweaving of the material and the mental—a Giant Monad, one of them called it.

Anyway, I said to myself, "Greta, if this is Introversion, I want no part of it. It is not nice to be cut adrift from the cosmos and know it. A lifeboat in the middle of the Pacific and a starship between galaxies are not in it for loneliness."

I asked myself why the Spiders had ever equipped Maintainers with Introversion switches anyway, when we couldn't drill with them and weren't supposed to use them except in an emergency so tight that it was either Introvert or surrender to the Snakes, and for the first time the obvious explanation came to me:

Introversion must be the same as scuttling, its main purpose to withhold secrets and materiel from the enemy. It put a place into a situation from which even the Spider high command couldn't rescue it, and there was nothing left but to sink down, down (out? up?), down into the Void.

If that was the case, our chances of getting back were about those of my being a kid again playing in the Dunes on the Small Time.

I edged a little closer to Sid and sort of squunched under his shoulder and rubbed my cheek against the smudged, gold-worked gray velvet. He looked down and I said, "A long way to Lynn Regis, eh, Siddy?"

"Sweetling, thou spokest a mouthful," he said. He knows very well what he is doing when he mixes his language that way, the wicked old darling.

"Siddy," I said, "why this gold-work? It'd be a lot smoother without it."

"Marry, men must prick themselves out and, 'faith I know not, but it helps if there's metal in it."

"And girls get scratched." I took a little sniff. "But don't put this doublet through the cleaner yet. Until we get out of the woods, I want as much you around as possible."

"Marry, and why should I?" he asked blankly, and I think he wasn't fooling me. The last thing time travelers find out is how they do or don't smell. Then his face clouded and he looked as though he wanted to squunch under my shoulder. "But 'faith, sweetling, your forest has a few more trees than Sherwood."

"Thou saidst it," I agreed, and wondered about the look. He oughtn't to be interested in my girlishness now. I knew I was a mess, but he had stuck pretty close to me during the hunt and you never can tell. Then I remembered that he was the other one who hadn't declared himself when Bruce was putting it to us, and it probably troubled his male vanity. Not me, though—I was still grateful to the Maintainer for getting me out of that spot, whatever other it had got us all into. It seemed ages ago.

[78]

We'd all jumped to the conclusion that the two Ghostgirls had run away with the Maintainer, I don't know where or why, but it looked so much that way. Maud had started yipping about how she'd never trusted Ghosts and always known that some day they'd start doing things on their own, and Kaby had got it firmly fixed in her head, right between the horns, that Phryne, being a Greek, was the ringleader and was going to wreak havoc on us all.

But when we were checking Stores the first time, I had noticed that the Ghostgirl envelopes looked flat. Ectoplasm doesn't take up much space when it's folded, but I had opened one anyway, then another, and then called for help.

Every last envelope was empty. We had lost over a thousand Ghostgirls, Sid's whole stock.

Well, at least it proved what none of us had ever seen or heard of being demonstrated: that there is a spooky link—a sort of Change Wind contact—between a Ghost and its lifeline; and when that umbilicus, I've heard it called, is cut, the part away from the lifeline dies.

Interesting, but what had bothered me was whether we Demons were going to evaporate too, because we are as much Doublegangers as the Ghosts and our apron strings had been cut just as surely. We're more solid, of course, but that would only mean we'd take a little longer. Very logical.

I remember I had looked up at Lili and Maud—us girls had been checking the envelopes; it's one of the proprieties we frequently maintain and anyway, if men check them, they're apt to trot out that old wheeze about "instant women" which I'm sick to death of hearing, thank you.

Anyway, I had looked up and said, "It's been nice knowing you," and Lili had said, "Twenty-three, skiddoo," and Maud had said, "Here goes nothing," and we had shook hands all around.

We figured that Phryne and the Countess had faded at the same time as the other Ghostgirls, but an idea had been nibbling at me and I said, "Siddy, do you suppose it's just barely possible that, while we were all looking at Bruce, those two Ghostgirls would have been able to work the Maintainer and get a Door and lam out of here with the thing?"

"Thou speakst my thoughts, sweetling. All weighs against it: Imprimis, 'tis well known that Ghosts cannot lay plots or act on them. Secundo, the time forbade getting a Door. Tercio—and here's the real meat of it—the Place folds without the Maintainer. Quadro, 'twere folly to depend on not one of—how many of us? ten, elf—not looking around in all the time it would have taken them—"

"I looked around once, Siddy. They were drinking and they had got to the control divan under their own power. Now when was that? Oh, yes, when Bruce was talking about Zombies."

"Yes, sweetling. And as I was about to cap my argument with quin-quo when you 'gan prattle, I could have sworn none could touch the Maintainer, much less work it and purloin it, without my certain knowledge. Yet..."

"Eftsoons yet," I seconded him."

Somebody must have got a door and walked out with the thing. It certainly wasn't in the Place. The hunt had been a lulu. Something the size of a portable typewriter is not easy to hide and we had been inside everything from Beau's piano to the renewer link of the Refresher.

We had even fluoroscoped everybody, though it had made Illy writhe like a box of worms, as he'd warned us; he said it tickled terribly and I insisted on smoothing his fur for five minutes afterward, although he was a little standoffish toward me.

Some areas, like the bar, kitchen and Stores, took a long while, but we were thorough. Kaby helped Doc check Surgery: since she last made the Place, she has been stationed in a Field Hospital (it turns out the Spiders actually are mounting operations from them) and learned a few nice new wrinkles.

However, Doc put in some honest work on his own, though, of course, every check was observed by at least three people, not including Bruce or Lili. When the Maintainer vanished, Doc had pulled out of his glassy-eyed drunk in a way that would have surprised me if I hadn't seen it happen to him before, but when we finished Surgery and got on to the Art Gallery, he had started to putter and I noticed him hold out his coat and duck his head and whip out a flask and take a swig and by now he was well on his way toward another peak.

The Art Gallery had taken time too, because there's such a jumble of strange stuff, and it broke my heart but Kaby took her ax and split a beautiful blue woodcarving of a Venusian medusa because, although there wasn't a mark in the paw-polished surface, she claimed it was just big enough. Doc cried a little and we left him fitting the pieces together and mooning over the other stuff.

After we'd finished everything else, Mark had insisted on tackling the floor. Beau and Sid both tried to explain to him how this is a one-sided Place, that there is nothing, but nothing, under the floor; it just gets a lot harder than the diamonds crusting it as soon as you get a quarter inch down—that being the solid equivalent of the Void. But Mark was knuckle-headed (like all Romans, Sid assured me on the q.t.) and broke four diamond-plus drills before he was satisfied.

Except for some trick hiding places, that left the Void, and things don't vanish if you throw them at the Void—they half melt and freeze forever unless you can fish them out. Back of the Refresher, at about eye-level, are three Venusian coconuts that a Hittite strongman threw there during a major brawl. I try not to look at them because they are so much like witch heads they give me the woolies. The parts of the Place right up against the Void have strange spatial properties which one of the gadgets in Surgery makes use of in a way that gives me the worse woolies, but that's beside the point.

During the hunt, Kaby and Erich had used their Callers as direction finders to point out the Maintainer, just as they're used in the cosmos to locate the Door—and sometimes in the Big Places, people tell me. But the Callers only went wild—like a compass needle whirling around without stopping—and nobody knew what that meant.

The trick hiding places were the Minor Maintainer, a cute idea, but it is no bigger than the Major and has its own mysterious insides and had obviously kept on doing its own work, so that was out for several reasons, and the bomb chest, though it seemed impossible for anyone to have opened it, granting they knew the secret of its lock, even before Erich jumped on it and put it in the limelight double. But when you've ruled out everything else, the word impossible changes meaning.

Since time travel is our business, a person might think of all sorts of tricks for sending the Maintainer into the past or future, permanently or temporarily. But the Place is strictly on the Big Time and everybody that should know tells me that time traveling *through* the Big Time is out. It's this way: the Big Time is a train, and the Little Time is the countryside and we're on the train, unless we go out a Door, and as Gertie Stein might put it, you can't time travel through the time you time travel in when you time travel.

I'd also played around with the idea of some fantastically obvious hiding place, maybe something that several people could pass back and forth between them, which would mean a conspiracy, and, of course, if you assume a big enough conspiracy, you can explain anything, including the cosmos itself. Still, I'd got a sort of shell-game idea about the Soldiers' three big black shakos and I hadn't been satisfied until I'd got the three together and looked in them all at the same time.

"Wake up, Greta, and take something. I can't stand here forever." Maud had brought us a tray of hearty snacks from then and yon, and I must say they were tempting; she whips up a mean hors d'oeuvre.

I looked them over and said, "Siddy, I want a hot dog."

"And I want a venison pasty! Out upon you, you finical jill, you o'erscrupulous jade, you whimsic and tyrannous poppet!"

I grabbed a handful and snuggled back against him.

"Go on, call me some more, Siddy," I told him. "Real juicy ones."

X. MOTIVES AND OPPORTUNITIES

My thought, whose murder yet is but fantastical,
Shakes so my single state of man that function
Is smother'd in surmise, and nothing is
But what is not.

–Macbeth

My big bad waif from King's Lynn had set the tray on his knees and started to wolf the food down. The others were finishing up. Erich, Mark and Kaby were having a quietly furious argument I couldn't overhear at the end of the bar nearest the bronze chest, and Illy was draped over the piano like a real octopus, listening in.

Beau and Sevensee were pacing up and down near the control divan and throwing each other a word now and then. Beyond them, Bruce and Lili were sitting on the opposite couch from us, talking earnestly about something. Maud had sat down at the other end of the bar and was knitting—it's one of the habits like chess and quiet drinking, or learning to talk by squeak box, that we pick up to pass the time in the Place in the long stretches between parties. Doc was fiddling around the Gallery, picking things up and setting them down, still managing to stay on his feet at any rate.

Lili and Bruce stood up, still gabbing intensely at each other, and Illy began to pick out with one tentacle a little tune in the high keys that didn't sound like anything on God's earth. "Where do they get all the energy?" I wondered.

As soon as I asked myself that, I knew the answer and I began to feel the same way myself. It wasn't energy; it was nerves, pure and simple.

Change is like a drug, I realized—you get used to the facts never staying the same, and one picture of the past and future dissolving into another maybe not very different but still different, and your mind being constantly goosed by strange moods and notions, like nightclub lights of shifting color with weird shadows between shining right on your brain.

The endless swaying and jogging is restful, like riding on a train.

You soon get to like the movement and to need it without knowing, and when it suddenly stops and you're just you and the facts you think

[82]

from and feel from are exactly the same when you go back to them—boy, that's rough, as I found out now.

The instant we got Introverted, everything that ordinarily leaks into the Place, wake or sleep, had stopped coming, and we were nothing but ourselves and what we meant to each other and what we could make of that, an awfully lonely, scratchy situation.

I decided I felt like I'd been dropped into a swimming pool full of cement and held under until it hardened.

I could understand the others bouncing around a bit. It was a wonder they didn't hit the Void. Maud seemed to be standing it the best; maybe she'd got a little preparation from the long watches between stars; and then she is older than all of us, even Sid, though with a small "o" in "older."

The restless work of the search for the Maintainer had masked the feeling, but now it was beginning to come full force. Before the search, Bruce's speech and Erich's interruptions had done a passable masking job too. I tried to remember when I'd first got the feeling and decided it was after Erich had jumped on the bomb, about the time he mentioned poetry. Though I couldn't be sure. Maybe the Maintainer had been Introverted even earlier, when I'd turned to look at the Ghostgirls. I wouldn't have known. Nuts!

Believe me, I could feel that hardened cement on every inch of me. I remembered Bruce's beautiful picture of a universe without Big Change and decided it was about the worst idea going. I went on eating, though I wasn't so sure now it was a good idea to keep myself strong.

"Does the Maintainer have an Introversion telltale? Siddy!"

"'Sdeath, chit, and you love me, speak lower. Of a sudden, I feel not well, as if I'd drunk a butt of Rhenish and slept inside it. Marry yes, blue. In short flashes, saith the manual. Why ask'st thou?"

"No reason. God, Siddy, what I'd give for a breath of Change Wind."

"Thou can'st say that eftsoons," he groaned. I must have looked pretty miserable myself, for he put his arm around my shoulders and whispered gruffly, "Comfort thyself, sweetling, that while we suffer thus sorely, we yet cannot die the Change Death."

"What's that?" I asked him.

I didn't want to bounce around like the others. I had a suspicion I'd carry it too far. So, to keep myself from going batty, I started to rework the business of who had done what to the Maintainer.

During the hunt, there had been some pretty wild suggestions tossed around as to its disappearance or at least its Introversion: a feat of Snake science amounting to sorcery; the Spider high command bunkering the Places from above, perhaps in reaction to the loss of the Express Room, in such a hurry that they hadn't even time to transmit warnings; the hand of the Late Cosmicians, those mysterious hypothetical beings who are supposed to have successfully resisted the extension of the Change War into the future much beyond Sevensee's epoch—unless the Late Cosmicians are the ones fighting the Change War.

One thing these suggestions had steered very clear of was naming any one of us as a suspect, whether acting as Snake spy, Spider political police, agent of—who knows, after Bruce?—a secret Change World Committee of Public Safety or Spider revolutionary underground, or strictly on our own. Just as no one had piped a word, since the Maintainer had been palmed, about the split between Erich's and Bruce's factions.

Good group thinking probably, to sink differences in the emergency, but that didn't apply to what I did with my own thoughts.

Who wanted to escape so bad they'd Introvert the Place, cutting off all possible contact and communication either way with the cosmos and running the very big risk of not getting back to the cosmos at all?

Leaving out what had happened since Bruce had arrived and stirred things up, Doc seemed to me to have the strongest motive. He knew that Sid couldn't keep covering up for him forever and that Spider punishments for derelictions of duty are not just the clink of a firing squad, as Erich had reminded us. But Doc had been flat on the floor in front of the bar from the time Bruce had jumped on top of it, though I certainly hadn't had my eye on him every second.

Beau? Beau had said he was bored with the Place at a time when what he said counted, so he'd hardly lock himself in it maybe forever, not to mention locking Bruce in with himself and the babe he had a yen for.

Sid loves reality, Changing or not, and every least thing in it, people especially, more than any man or woman I've ever known—he's like a big-eyed baby who wants to grab every object and put it in his mouth—and it was hard to imagine him ever cutting himself off from the cosmos.

Maud, Kaby, Mark and the two ETs? None of them had any motive I knew of, though Sevensee's being from the very far future did tie in with that idea about the Late Cosmicians, and there did seem to be something developing between the Cretan and the Roman that could make them want to be Introverted together.

"Stick to the facts, Greta," I reminded myself with a private groan.

That left Erich, Bruce, Lili and myself.

Erich, I thought—now we're getting somewhere. The little commandant has the nervous system of a coyote and the courage of a crazy tomcat, and if he thought it would help him settle his battle with Bruce better to be locked in with him, he'd do it in a second.

But even before Erich had danced on the bomb, he'd been heckling Bruce from the crowd. Still, there would have been time between heckles

[84]

for him to step quietly back from us, Introvert the Maintainer and...well, that was nine-tenths of the problem.

If I was the guilty party, I was nuts and that was the best explanation of all. Gr-r-r!

Bruce's motives seemed so obvious, especially the mortal (or was it immortal?) danger he'd put himself in by inciting mutiny, that it seemed a shame he'd been in full view on the bar so long. Surely, if the Maintainer had been Introverted before he jumped on the bar, we'd all have noticed the flashing blue telltale. For that matter, I'd have noticed it when I looked back at the Ghostgirls—if it worked as Sid claimed, and he said he had never seen it in operation, just read in the manual—oh, 'sdeath!

But Bruce didn't need opportunity, as I'm sure all the males in the Place would have told me right off, because he had Lili to pull the job for him and she had as much opportunity as any of the rest of us. Myself, I have large reservations to this woman-putty-in-the-hands-of-the-man-she-loves-madly theory, but I had to admit there was something to be said for it in this case, and it had seemed quite natural to me when the rest of us had decided, by unspoken agreement, that neither Lili's nor Bruce's checks counted when we were hunting for the Maintainer.

That took care of all of us and left only the mysterious stranger, intruding somehow through a Door (how'd he get it without using our Maintainer?) or from an unimaginable hiding place or straight out of the Void itself. I know that last is impossible—nothing can step out of nothing—but if anything ever looked like it was specially built for something not at all nice to come looming out of, it's the Void—misty, foggily churning, slimy gray...

"Wait a second," I told myself, "and hang onto this, Greta. It should have smacked you in the face at the start."

Whatever came out of the Void, or, more to the point, whoever slipped back from our crowd to the Maintainer, Bruce would have seen them. He was looking at the Maintainer past our heads the whole time, and whatever happened to it, he saw it.

Erich wouldn't have, even after he was on the bomb, because he'd been stagewise enough to face Bruce most of the time to build up his role as tribune of the people.

But Bruce would have—unless he got so caught up in what he was saying...

No, kid, a Demon is always an actor, no matter how much he believes in what he's saying, and there never was an actor yet who wouldn't instantly notice a member of the audience starting to walk out on his big scene.

So Bruce knew, which made him a better actor than I'd have been willing to grant, since it didn't look as if anyone else had thought of what had just occurred to me, or they'd have gone over and put it to him.

Not me, though—I don't work that way. Besides, I didn't feel up to it—Nervy Anna enfold me, I felt like pure hell.

"Maybe," I told myself encouragingly, "the Place is Hell," but added, "Be your age, Greta—be a real rootless, ruleless, ruthless twenty-nine."

XI. THE WESTERN FRONT, 1917

The barrage roars and lifts. Then, clumsily bowed
With bombs and guns and shovels and battle gear,
Men jostle and climb to meet the bristling fire.
Lines of gray, muttering faces, masked with fear,
They leave their trenches, going over the top,
While time ticks blank and busy on their wrists

–Sassoon

"Please don't, Lili."

"I shall, my love."

"Sweetling, wake up! Hast the shakes?"

I opened my eyes a little and lied to Siddy with a smile and locked my hands together tight and watched Bruce and Lili quarrel nobly near the control divan and wished I had a great love to blur my misery and provide me with a passable substitute for Change Winds.

Lili won the argument, judging from the way she threw her head back and stepped away from Bruce's arms while giving him a proud, tender smile. He walked off a few steps; praise be, he didn't shrug his shoulders at us like an old husband, though his nerves were showing and he didn't seem to be standing Introversion well at all, as who of us were?

Lili rested a hand on the head of the control divan and pressed her lips together and looked around at us, mostly with her eyes. She'd wound a gray silk bandeau around her bangs. Her short gray silk dress without a waistline made her look, not so much like a flapper, though she looked like that all right, as like a little girl, except the neckline was scooped low enough to show she wasn't.

Her gaze hesitated and then stopped at me and I got a sunk feeling of what was coming, because women are always picking on me for an audience. Besides, Sid and I were the centrist party of two in our fresh-out-of-the-shell Place politics.

She took a deep breath and stuck out her chin and said in a voice that was even a little higher and Britisher than she usually uses, "We girls have often cried, 'Shut the Door!' But now the Door is jolly well shut for keeps!"

[87]

I knew I'd guessed right and I felt crawly with embarrassment, because I know about this love business of thinking you're the other person and trying to live their life—and grab their glory, though you don't know that—and carry their message for them, and how it can foul things up. Still, I couldn't help admitting what she said wasn't too bad a start—unpleasantly apt to be true, at any rate.

"My fiance believes we may yet be able to open the Door. I do not. He thinks it is a bit premature to discuss the peculiar pickle in which we all find ourselves. I do not."

There was a rasp of laughter from the bar. The militarists were reacting. Erich stepped out, looking very happy. "So now we have to listen to women making speeches," he called. "What is this Place, anyhow? Sidney Lessingham's Saturday Evening Sewing Circle?"

Beau and Sevensee, who'd stopped their pacing halfway between the bar and the control divan, turned toward Erich, and Sevensee looked a little burlier, a little more like half a horse, than satyrs in mythology book illustrations. He stamped—medium hard, I'd say—and said, "Ahh, go flya kite." I'd found out he'd learned English from a Demon who'd been a longshoreman with syndicalist-anarchist sympathies. Erich shut up for a moment and stood there grinning, his hands on his hips.

Lili nodded to the satyr and cleared her throat, looking scared. But she didn't speak; I could see she was thinking and feeling something, and her face got ugly and haggard, as if she were in a Change Wind that hadn't reached me yet, and her mouth went into a snarl to fight tears, but some spurted out, and when she did speak her voice was an octave lower and it wasn't just London talking but New York too.

"I don't know how Resurrection felt to you people, because I'm new and I loathe asking questions, but to me it was pure torture and I wished only I'd had the courage to tell Suzaku, 'I wish to remain a Zombie, if you don't mind. I'd rather the nightmares.' But I accepted Resurrection because I've been taught to be polite and because there is the Demon in me I don't understand that always wishes to live, and I found that I still felt like a Zombie, although I could flit about, and that I still had the nightmares, except they'd grown a deal vivider.

"I was a young girl again, seventeen, and I suppose every woman wishes to be seventeen, but I wasn't seventeen inside my head—I was a woman who had died of Bright's disease in New York in 1929 and also, because a Big Change blew my lifeline into a new drift, a woman who had died of the same disease in Nazi-occupied London in 1955, but rather more slowly because, as you can fancy, the liquor was in far shorter supply. I had to live with both those sets of memories and the Change World didn't blot them out any more than I'm told it does those of any

[88]

Demon, and it didn't even push them into the background as I'd hoped it would.

"When some Change Fellow would say to me, 'Hallo, beautiful, how about a smile?' or 'That's a posh frock, kiddo,' I'd be back at Bellevue looking down at my swollen figure and the light getting like spokes of ice, or in that dreadful gin-steeped Stepney bedroom with Phyllis coughing herself to death beside me, or at best, for a moment, a little girl in Glamorgan looking at the Roman road and wondering about the wonderful life that lay ahead."

I looked at Erich, remembering he had a long nasty future back in the cosmos himself, and at any rate he wasn't smiling, and I thought maybe he's getting a little humility, knowing someone else has two of those futures, but I doubted it.

"Because, you see," Lili kept forcing it out, "all my three lives I'd been a girl who fell in love with a great young poet she'd never met, the voice of the new youth and all youth, and she'd told her first big lie to get in the Red Cross and across to France to be nearer him, and it was all danger and dark magics and a knight in armor, and she pictured how she'd find him wounded but not seriously, with a little bandage around his head, and she'd light a fag for him and smile lightly, never letting him guess what she felt, but only being her best self and watching to see if that made something happen to him...

"And then the Boche machine guns cut him down at Passchendaele and there couldn't ever have been bandages big enough and the girl stayed seventeen inside and messed about and tried to be wicked, though she wasn't very good at that, and to drink, and she had a bit more talent there, though drinking yourself to death is not nearly as easy as it sounds, even with a kidney weakness to help. But she turned the trick.

"Then a cock crows. She wakes with a tearing start from the gray dreams of death that fill her lifeline. It's cold daybreak. There's the smell of a French farm. She feels her ankles and they're not at all like huge rubber boots filled with water. They're not swollen the least bit. They're young legs.

"There's a little window and the tops of a row of trees that may be poplars when there's more light, and what there is shows cots like her own and heads under blankets, and hanging uniforms make large shadows and a girl is snoring. There's a very distant rumble and it moves the window a bit. Then she remembers they're Red Cross girls many, many kilometers from Passchendaele and that Bruce Marchant is going to die at dawn today.

"In a few more minutes, he's going over the top where there's a crop-headed machine-gunner in field gray already looking down the sights and swinging the gun a bit. But she isn't going to die today. She's going to die in 1929 and 1955.

"And just as she's going mad, there's a creaking and out of the shadows tiptoes a Jap with a woman's hairdo and the whitest face and the blackest eyebrows. He's wearing a rose robe and a black sash which belts to his sides two samurai swords, but in his right hand he has a strange silver pistol. And he smiles at her as if they were brother and sister and lovers at the same time and he says, '*Voulez-vous vivre, mademoiselle?*' and she stares and he bobs his head and says, 'Missy wish live, yes, no?'"

Sid's paw closed quietly around my shaking hands. It always gets me to hear about anyone's Resurrection, and although mine was crazier, it also had the Krauts in it. I hoped she wouldn't go through the rest of the formula and she didn't.

"Five minutes later, he's gone down a stairs more like a ladder to wait below and she's dressing in a rush. Her clothes resist a little, as if they were lightly gummed to the hook and the stained wall, and she hates to touch them. It's getting lighter and her cot looks as if someone were still sleeping there, although it's empty, and she couldn't bring herself to put her hand on the place if her new life depended on it.

"She climbs down and her long skirt doesn't bother her because she knows how to swing it. Suzaku conducts her past a sentry who doesn't see them and a puffy-faced farmer in a smock coughing and spitting the night out of his throat. They cross the farmyard and it's filled with rose light and she sees the sun is up and she knows that Bruce Marchant has just bled to death.

"There's an empty open touring car chugging loudly, waiting for someone; it has huge muddy wheels with wooden spokes and a brass radiator that says 'Simplex.' But Suzaku leads her past it to a dunghill and bows apologetically and she steps through a Door."

I heard Erich say to the others at the bar, "How touching! Now shall I tell everyone about my operation?" But he didn't get much of a laugh.

"That's how Lilian Foster came into the Change World with its steel-engraved nightmares and its deadly pace and deadlier lassitudes. I was more alive than I ever had been before, but it was the kind of life a corpse might get from unending electrical shocks and I couldn't summon any purpose or hope and Bruce Marchant seemed farther away than ever.

"Then, not six hours ago, a Soldier in a black uniform came through the Door and I thought, 'It can't be, but it does look like his photographs,' and then I thought I heard someone say the name Bruce, and then he shouted as if to all the world that he was Bruce Marchant, and I knew there was a Resurrection beyond Resurrection, a true resurrection. Oh, Bruce—"

She looked at him and he was crying and smiling and all the young beauty flooded back into her face, and I thought, "It has to be Change Winds, but it can't be. Face it without slobbering, Greta—there's something that works bigger miracles than Change."

And she went on, "And then the Change Winds died when the Snakes vaporized the Maintainer or the Ghostgirls Introverted it and all three of them vanished so swiftly and silently that even Bruce didn't notice—those are the best explanations I can summon and I fancy one of them is true. At all events, the Change Winds died and my past and even my futures became something I could bear lightly, because I have someone to bear them with me, and because at last I have a true future stretching out ahead of me, an unknown future which I shall create by living. Oh, don't you see that all of us have it now, this big opportunity?"

"*Hussa* for Sidney's suffragettes and the W.C.T.U.!" Erich cheered. "Beau, will you play us a medley of 'Hearts and Flowers' and 'Onward, Christian Soldiers'? I'm deeply moved, Lili. Where do the rest of us queue up for the Great Love Affair of the Century?"

XII. A BIG OPPORTUNITY

> Now is a bearable burden. What buckles the back is the
> added weight of the past's mistakes and the future's fears.
> I had to learn to close the front door to tomorrow and the
> back door to yesterday and settle down to here and now.
> –Anonymous

Nobody laughed at Erich's screwball sarcasms and still I thought, "Yes, perish his hysterical little gray head, but he's half right—Lili's got the big thing now and she wants to serve it up to the rest of us on a platter, only love doesn't cook and cut that way."

Those weren't bad ideas she had about the Maintainer, though, especially the one about the Ghostgirls doing the Introverting—it would explain why there couldn't be Introversion drill, the manual stuff about blue flashes being window-dressing, and something disappearing without movement or transition is the sort of thing that might not catch the attention—and I guess they gave the others something to think about too, for there wasn't any follow-up to Erich's frantic sniping.

But I honestly didn't see where there was this big opportunity being stuck away in a gray sack in the Void and I began to wonder and I got the strangest feeling and I said to myself, "Hang onto your hat, Greta. It's hope."

"The dreadful thing about being a Demon is that you have all time to range through," Lili was saying with a smile. "You can never shut the back door to yesterday or the front door to tomorrow and simply live in the present. But now that's been done for us: the Door is shut, we need never again rehash the past or the future. The Spiders and Snakes can never find us, for who ever heard of a Place that was truly lost being rescued? And as those in the know have told me, Introversion is the end as far as those outside are concerned. So we're safe from the Spiders and Snakes, we need never be slaves or enemies again, and we have a Place in which to live our new lives, the Place prepared for us from the beginning."

She paused. "Surely you understand what I mean? Sidney and Beauregard and Dr. Pyeshkov are the ones who explained it to me. The Place is a balanced aquarium, just like the cosmos. No one knows how many ages of Big Time it has been in use, without a bit of new material being brought in—only luxuries and people—and not a bit of waste cast off. No one knows how many more ages it may not sustain life. I never heard of Minor Maintainers wearing out. We have all the future, all the security, anyone can hope for. We have a Place to live together."

You know, she was dead right and I realized that all the time I'd had the conviction in the back of my mind that we were going to suffocate or something if we didn't get a Door open pretty quick. I should have known differently, if anybody should, because I'd once been in the Place without a Door for as long as a hundred sleeps during a foxhole stretch of the Change War and we'd had to start cycling our food and it had been okay.

And then, because it is also the way my mind works, I started to picture in a flash the consequences of our living together all by ourselves like Lili said.

I began to pair people off; I couldn't help it. Let's see, four women, six men, two ETs.

"Greta," I said, "you're going to be Miss Polly Andry for sure. We'll have a daily newspaper and folk-dancing classes, we'll shut the bar except evenings, Bruce'll keep a rhymed history of the Place."

I even thought, though I knew this part was strictly silly, about schools and children. I wondered what Siddy's would look like, or my little commandant's. "Don't go near the Void, dears." Of course that would be specially hard on the two ETs, but Sevensee at least wasn't so different and the genetics boys had made some wonderful advances and Maud ought to know about them and there were some amazing gadgets in Surgery when Doc sobered up. The patter of little hoofs...

"My fiance spoke to you about carrying a peace message to the rest of the cosmos," Lili added, "and bringing an end to the Big Change, and healing all the wounds that have been made in the Little Time."

I looked at Bruce. His face was set and strained, as will happen to the best of them when a girl starts talking about her man's business, and I don't know why, but I said to myself, "She's crucifying him, she's nailing him to his purpose as a woman will, even when there's not much point to it, as now."

And Lili went on, "It was a wonderful thought, but now we cannot carry or send any message and I believe it is too late in any event for a peace message to do any good. The cosmos is too raveled by change, too far gone. It will dissolve, fade, 'leave not a rack behind.' We're the survivors. The torch of existence has been put in our hands.

"We may already be all that's left in the cosmos, for have you thought that the Change Winds may have died at their source? We may never reach another cosmos, we may drift forever in the Void, but who of us has been Introverted before and who knows what we can or cannot do?

We're a seed for a new future to grow from. Perhaps all doomed universes cast off seeds like this Place. It's a seed, it's an embryo, let it grow."

She looked swiftly at Bruce and then at Sid and she quoted, "'Come, my friends, 'tis not too late to seek a newer world'."

I squeezed Sid's hand and I started to say something to him, but he didn't know I was there; he was listening to Lili quote Tennyson with his eyes entranced and his mouth open, as if he were imagining new things to put into it—oh, Siddy!

And then I saw the others were looking at her the same way. Ilhilihis was seeing finer feather forests than long-dead Luna's grow. The greenhouse child Maud ap-Ares Davies was stowing away on a starship bound for another galaxy, or thinking how different her life might have been, the children she might have had, if she'd stayed on the planets and out of the Change World. Even Erich looked as though he might be blitzing new universes, and Mark subduing them, for an eight-legged *Führer-imperator*. Beau was throbbing up a wider Mississippi in a bigger-than-life sidewheeler.

Even I—well, I wasn't dreaming of a Greater Chicago. "Let's not go hog-wild on this sort of thing," I told myself, but I did look up at the Void and I got a shiver because I imagined it drawing away and the whole Place starting to grow.

"I truly meant what I said about a seed," Lili went on slowly. "I know, as you all do, that there are no children in the Change World, that there cannot be, that we all become instantly sterile, that what they call a curse is lifted from us girls and we are no longer in bondage to the moon."

She was right, all right—if there's one thing that's been proved a million times in the Change World, it's that.

"But we are no longer in the Change World," Lili said softly, "and its limitations should no longer apply to us, including that one. I feel deeply certain of it, but—" she looked around slowly—"we are four women here and I thought one of us might have a surer indication."

My eyes followed hers around like anybody's would. In fact, everybody was looking around except Maud, and she had the silliest look of surprise on her face and it stayed there, and then, very carefully, she got down from the bar stool with her knitting. She looked at the half-finished pink bra with the long white needles stuck in it and her eyes bugged bigger yet, as if she were expecting it to turn into a baby sweater right then and there. Then she walked across the Place to Lili and stood beside her. While she was walking, the look of surprise changed to a quiet smile. The only other thing she did was throw her shoulders back a little.

I was jealous of her for a second, but it was a double miracle for her, considering her age, and I couldn't grudge her that. And to tell the truth,

I was a little frightened, too. Even with Dave, I'd been bothered about this business of having babies.

Yet I stood up with Siddy—I couldn't stop myself and I guess he couldn't either—and hand in hand we walked to the control divan. Beau and Sevensee were there and Bruce, of course, and then, so help me, those Soldiers to the death, Kaby and Mark, started over from the bar and I couldn't see anything in their eyes about the greater glory of Crete and Rome, but something, I think, about each other, and after a moment Illy slowly detached himself from the piano and followed, lightly trailing his tentacles on the floor.

I couldn't exactly see him hoping for little Illies in this company, unless it was true what the jokes said about Lunans, but maybe he was being really disinterested and maybe he wasn't; maybe he was simply figuring that Illy ought to be on the side with the biggest battalions.

I heard dragging footsteps behind us and here came Doc from the Gallery, carrying in his folded arms an abstract sculpture as big as a newborn baby. It was an agglomeration of perfect shiny gray spheres the size of golf balls, shaping up to something like a large brain, but with holes showing through here and there. He held it out to us like an infant to be admired and worked his lips and tongue as if he were trying very hard to say something, though not a word came out that you could understand, and I thought, "Maxey Aleksevich may be speechless drunk and have all sorts of holes in his head, but he's got the right instincts, bless his soulful little Russian heart."

We were all crowded around the control divan like a football team huddling. The Peace Packers, it came to me. Sevensee would be fullback or center and Illy left end—what a receiver! The right number, too. Erich was alone at the bar, but now even he—"Oh, no, this can't be," I thought—even he came toward us. Then I saw that his face was working the worst ever. He stopped halfway and managed to force a smile, but it was the worst, too. "That's my little commandant," I thought, "no team spirit."

"So now Lili and Bruce—yes, and *Grossmutterchen* Maud—have their little nest," he said, and he wouldn't have had to push his voice very hard to get a screech. "But what are the rest of us supposed to be—cowbirds?"

He crooked his neck and flapped his hands and croaked, "Cuc-koo! Cuc-koo!" And I said to myself, "I often thought you were crazy, boy, but now I know."

"*Teufelsdreck!*—yes, Devil's dirt!—but you all seem to be infected with this dream of children. Can't you see that the Change World is the natural and proper end of evolution?—a period of enjoyment and measuring, an ultimate working out of things, which women call destruction—

[95]

'Help, I'm being raped!' 'Oh, what are they doing to my children?'—but which men know as fulfillment.

"You're given good parts in *Götterdämmerung* and you go up to the author and tap him on the shoulder and say, 'Excuse me, Herr Wagner, but this Twilight of the Gods is just a bit morbid. Why don't you write an opera for me about the little ones, the dear little blue-eyed curly-tops? A plot? Oh, boy meets girl and they settle down to breed, something like that.'

"Devil's dirt doubled and damned! Have you thought what life will be like without a Door to go out of to find freedom and adventure, to measure your courage and keenness? Do you want to grow long gray beards hobbling around this asteroid turned inside out? Putter around indoors to the end of your days, mooning about little baby cosmoses?—incidentally, with a live bomb for company. The cave, the womb, the little gray home in the nest—is that what you want? It'll grow? Oh, yes, like the city engulfing the wild wood, a proliferation of *Kinder, Kirche, Küche*—I should live so long!

"Women!—how I hate their bright eyes as they look at me from the fireside, bent-shouldered, rocking, deeply happy to be old, and say, 'He's getting weak, he's giving out, soon I'll have to put him to bed and do the simplest things for him.' Your filthy Triple Goddess, Kaby, the birther, bride, and burier of man! Woman, the enfeebler, the fetterer, the crippler! Woman!—and the curly-headed little cancers she wants!"

He lurched toward us, pointing at Lili. "I never knew one who didn't want to cripple a man if you gave her the chance. Cripple him, swaddle him, clip his wings, grind him to sausage to mold another man, hers, a doll man. You hid the Maintainer, you little smother-hen, so you could have your nest and your Brucie!"

He stopped, gasping, and I expected someone to bop him one on the schnozzle, and I think he did, too. I turned to Bruce and he was looking, I don't know how, sorry, guilty, anxious, angry, shaken, inspired, all at once, and I wished people sometimes had simple suburban reactions like magazine stories.

Then Erich made the mistake, if it was one, of turning toward Bruce and slowly staggering toward him, pawing the air with his hands as if he were going to collapse into his arms, and saying, "Don't let them get you, Bruce. Don't let them tie you down. Don't let them clip you—your words or your deeds. You're a Soldier. Even when you talked about a peace message, you talked about doing some smashing of your own. No matter what you think and feel, Bruce, no matter how much lying you do and how much you hide, you're really not on their side."

That did it.

It didn't come soon enough or, I think, in the right spirit to please me, but I will say it for Bruce that he didn't muck it up by tipping or softening his punch. He took one step forward and his shoulders spun and his fist connected sweet and clean.

As he did it, he said only one word, "Loki!" and darn if that didn't switch me back to a campfire in the Indiana Dunes and my mother telling me out of the Elder Saga about the malicious, sneering, all-spoiling Norse god and how, when the other gods came to trap him in his hideaway by the river, he was on the point of finishing knotting a mysterious net big enough, I had imagined, to snare the whole universe, and that if they'd come a minute later, he would have.

Erich was stretched on the floor, his head hitched up, rubbing his jaw and glaring at Bruce. Mark, who was standing beside me, moved a little and I thought he was going to do something, maybe even clobber Bruce in the old spirit of you can't do that to my buddy, but he just shook his head and said, "*Omnia vincit amor.*" I nudged him and said, "Meaning?" and he said, "Love licks everything."

I'd never have expected it from a Roman, but he was half right at any rate. Lili had her victory: Bruce clearing the field for the marriage by laying out the woman-hating boy friend who would be trying to get him to go out nights. At that moment, I think Bruce wanted Lili and a life with her more than he wanted to reform the Change World. Sure, us women have our little victories—until the legions come or the Little Corporal draws up his artillery or the Panzers roar down the road.

Erich scrambled to his feet and stood there in a half-slump, half-crouch, still rubbing his jaw and glaring at Bruce over his hand, but making no move to continue the fight, and I studied his face and said to myself, "If he can get a gun, he's going to shoot himself, I know."

Bruce started to say something and hesitated, like I would have in his shoes, and just then Doc got one of his unpredictable inspirations and went weaving out toward Erich, holding out the sculpture and making deaf-and-dumb noises like he had to us. Erich looked at him as if he were going to kill him, and then grabbed the sculpture and swung it up over his head and smashed it down on the floor, and for a wonder, it didn't shatter. It just skidded along in one piece and stopped inches from my feet.

That thing not breaking must have been the last straw for Erich. I swear I could see the red surge up through his eyes toward his brain. He swung around into the Stores sector and ran the few steps between him and the bronze bomb chest.

Everything got very slow motion for me, though I didn't do any moving. Almost every man started out after Erich. Bruce didn't, though, and Siddy turned back after the first surge forward, while Illy squunched down for a leap, and it was between Sevensee's hairy shanks and Beau's scissoring white pants that I saw that under-the-microscope circle of death's heads and watched Erich's finger go down on them in the order Kaby had given: one, three, five, six, two, four, seven. I was able to pray seven distinct times that he'd make a mistake.

He straightened up. Illy landed by the box like a huge silver spider and his tentacles whipped futilely across its top. The others surged to a frightened halt around them.

Erich's chest was heaving, but his voice was cool and collected as he said, "You mentioned something about our having a future, Miss Foster. Now you can make that more specific. Unless we get back to the cosmos and dump this box, or find a Spider A-tech, or manage to call headquarters for guidance on disarming the bomb, we have a future exactly thirty minutes long."

XIII. THE TIGER IS LOOSE

> But whence he was, or of what wombe ybore,
> Of beasts, or of the earth, I have not red:
> But certes was with milke of wolves and tygres fed.

–Spenser

I guess when they really push the button or throw the switch or spring the trap or focus the beam or what have you, you don't faint or go crazy or anything else convenient. I didn't. Everything, everybody, every move that was made, every word that was spoken, was painfully real to me, like a hand twisting and squeezing things deep inside me, and I saw every least detail spotlighted and magnified like I had the seven skulls.

Erich was standing beyond the bomb chest; little smiles were ruffling his lips. I'd never seen him look so sharp. Illy was beside him, but not on his side, you understand. Mark, Sevensee and Beau were around the chest to the nearer side. Beau had dropped to a knee and was scanning the chest minutely, terror-under-control making him bend his head a little closer than he needed to for clear vision, but with his hands locked together behind his back, I guess to restrain the impulse to push any and everything that looked like a disarming button.

Doc was sprawled face down on the nearest couch, out like a light, I suppose.

Us four girls were still by the control divan. With Kaby, that surprised me, because she didn't look scared or frozen, but almost as intensely alive as Erich.

Sid had turned back, as I'd said, and had one hand stretched out toward but not touching the Minor Maintainer, and a look on his beardy face as if he were calling down death and destruction on every boozy rogue who had ever gone up from King's Lynn to Cambridge and London, and I realized why: if he'd thought of the Minor Maintainer a second sooner, he could have pinned Erich down with heavy gravity before he could touch the buttons.

Bruce was resting one hand on the head of the control divan and was looking toward the group around the chest, toward Erich, I think, as if Erich had done something rather wonderful for him, though I can't

imagine myself being tickled at being included in anybody's suicide surprise party. Bruce looked altogether too dreamy, Brahma blast him, for
someone who must have the same steel-spiked thought in his head that
I know darn well the rest of us had: that in twenty-nine minutes or so,
the Place would be a sun in a bag.

Erich was the first to get down to business, as I'd have laid any odds
he would be. He had the jump on us and he wasn't going to lose it.

"Well, when are you going to start getting Lili to tell us where she
hid the Maintainer? It has to be her—she was too certain it was gone
forever when she talked. And Bruce must have seen from the bar who
took the Maintainer, and who would he cover up for but his girl?"

There he was plagiarizing my ideas, but I guess I was willing to sign
them over to him in full if he got us the right pail of water for that
time-bomb.

He glanced at his wrist. "According to my Caller, you have twenty-
nine and a half minutes, including the time it will take to get a Door or
contact headquarters. When are you going to get busy on the girl?"

Bruce laughed a little—deprecatingly, so help me—and started toward him. "Look here, old man," he said, "there's no need to trouble
Lili, or to fuss with headquarters, even if you could. Really not at all.
Not to mention that your surmises are quite unfounded, old chap, and
I'm a bit surprised at your advancing them. But that's quite all right
because, as it happens, I'm an atomics technician and I even worked on
that very bomb. To disarm it, you just have to fiddle a bit with some of
the ankhs, those hoopy little crosses. Here, let me—"

Allah il allah, but it must have struck everybody as it did me as being
just too incredible an assertion, too bloody British a bare-faced bluff, for
Erich didn't have to say a word; Mark and Sevensee grabbed Bruce by
the arms, one on each side, as he stooped toward the bronze chest, and
they weren't gentle about it. Then Erich spoke.

"Oh, no, Bruce. Very sporting of you to try to cover up for your
girl friend, but we aren't going to let ourselves be blown to stripped
atoms twenty-eight minutes too soon while you monkey with the buttons,
the very thing Benson-Carter warned against, and pray for a guesswork
miracle. It's too thin, Bruce, when you come from 1917 and haven't
been on the Big Time for a hundred sleeps and were calling for an A-tech
yourself a few hours ago. Much too thin. Bruce, something is going to
happen that I'm afraid you won't like, but you're going to have to put
up with it. That is, unless Miss Foster decides to be cooperative."

"I say, you fellows, let me go," Bruce demanded, struggling experimentally. "I know it's a bit thick to swallow and I did give you the wrong
impression calling for an A-tech, but I just wanted to capture your attention then; I didn't want to have to work on the bomb. Really, Erich,

would they have ordered Benson-Carter to pick us up unless one of us were an A-tech? They'd be sure to include one in the bally operation."

"When they're using patchwork tactics?" Erich grinningly quoted back at him.

Kaby spoke up beside me and said, "Benson-Carter was a magician of matter and he was going on the operation disguised as an old woman. We have the cloak and hood with the other garments," and I wondered how this cold fish of a she-officer could be the same girl who was giving Mark slurpy looks not ten minutes ago.

"Well?" Erich asked, glancing at his Caller and then swinging his eyes around at us as if there must be some of the old *Wehrmacht* iron somewhere. We all found ourselves looking at Lili and she was looking so sharp herself, so ready to jump and so at bay, that it was all *I* needed, at any rate, to make Erich's theory about the Maintainer a rock-bottom certainty.

Bruce must have realized the way our minds were working, for he started to struggle in earnest and at the same time called, "For God's sake, don't do anything to Lili! Let me loose, you idiots! Everything's true I told you—I can save you from that bomb. Sevensee, you took my side against the Spiders; you've nothing to lose. Sid, you're an Englishman. Beau, you're a gentleman and you love her, too—for God's sake, stop them!"

Beau glanced up over his shoulder at Bruce and the others surging around close to his ankles and he had on his poker face. Sid I could tell was once more going through the purgatory of decision. Beau reached his own decision first and I'll say it for him that he acted on it fast and intelligently. Right from his kneeling position and before he'd even turned his head quite back, he jumped Erich.

But other things in this cosmos besides Man can pick sides and act fast. Illy landed on Beau midway and whipped his tentacles around him tight and they went wobbling around like a drunken white-and-silver barber pole. Beau got his hands each around a tentacle, and at the same time his face began to get purple, and I winced at what they were both going through.

Maybe Sevensee had a hoof in Sid's purgatory, because Bruce shook loose from the satyr and tried to knock out Mark, but the Roman twisted his arm and kept him from getting in a good punch.

Erich didn't make a move to mix into either fight, which is my little commandant all over. Using his fists on anybody but me is beneath him.

Then Sid made his choice, but there was no way for me to tell what it was, for, as he reached for the Minor Maintainer, Kaby contemptuously snatched it away from his hands and gave him a knee in the belly that doubled me up in sympathy and sent him sprawling on his knees toward the fighters. On the return, Kaby gave Lili, who'd started to grab too, an effortless backhand smash that set her down on the divan.

Erich's face lit up like an electric sign and he kept his eyes fixed on Kaby.

She crouched a little, carrying her weight on the balls of her feet and firmly cradling the Minor Maintainer in her left arm, like a basketball captain planning an offensive. Then she waved her free hand decisively to the right. I didn't get it, but Erich did and Mark too, for Erich jumped for the Refresher sector and Mark let go of Bruce and followed him, ducking around Sevensee's arms, who was coming back into the fight on which side I don't know. Illy un-whipped from Beau and copied Erich and Mark with one big spring.

Then Kaby twisted a dial as far as it would go and Bruce, Beau, Sevensee and poor Siddy were slammed down and pinned to the floor by about eight gravities.

It should have been lighter near us—I hoped it was, but you couldn't tell from watching Siddy; he went flat on his face, spread-eagled, one hand stretched toward me so close, I could have touched it (but not let go!), and his mouth was open against the floor and he was gasping through a corner of it and I could see his spine trying to sink through his belly. Bruce just managed to get his head and one shoulder up a bit, and they all made me think of a Dore illustration of the *Inferno* where the cream of the damned are frozen up to their necks in ice in the innermost circle of Hell.

The gravity didn't catch me, although I could feel it in my left arm. I was mostly in the Refresher sector, but I dropped down flat too, partly out of a crazy compassion I have, but mostly because I didn't want to take a chance of having Kaby knock me down.

Erich, Mark and Illy had got clear and they headed toward us. Maud picked the moment to make her play; she hadn't much choice of times, if she wanted to make one. The Old Girl was looking it for once, but I guess the thought of her miracle must have survived alongside the fear of sacked sun and must have meant a lot to her, for she launched out fast, all set to straight-arm Kaby into the heavy gravity and grab the Minor Maintainer with the other hand.

XIV. "NOW WILL YOU TALK?"

Like diamonds, we are cut with our own dust.

–Webster

Cretans have eyes under their back hair, or let's face it, Entertainers aren't Soldiers. Kaby weaved to one side and flicked a helpful hand and poor old Maud went where she'd been going to send Kaby. It sickened me to see the gravity take hold and yank her down.

I could have jumped up and made it four in a row for Kaby, but I'm not a bit brave when things like my life are at stake.

Lili was starting to get up, acting a little dazed. Kaby gently pushed her down again and quietly said, "Where is it?" and then hauled off and slapped her across the face. What got me was the matter-of-fact way Kaby did it. I can understand somebody getting mad and socking someone, or even deliberately working up a rage so as to be able to do something nasty, but this cold-blooded way turns my stomach.

Lili looked as if half her face were about to start bleeding, but she didn't look dazed any more and her jaw set. Kaby grabbed Lili's pearl necklace and twisted it around her neck and it broke and the pearls went bouncing around like ping-pong balls, so Kaby yanked down Lili's gray silk bandeau until it was around the neck and tightened that. Lili started to choke through her tight-pressed lips. Erich, Mark and Illy had come up and crowded around, but they seemed to be content with the job Kaby was doing.

"Listen, slut," she said, "we have no time. You have a healing room in this place. I can work the things."

"Here it comes," I thought, wishing I could faint. On top of everything, on top of death even, they had to drag in the nightmare personally stylized for me, the horror with my name on it. I wasn't going to be allowed to blow up peacefully. They weren't satisfied with an A-bomb. They had to write my private hell into the script.

"There is a thing called an Invertor," Kaby said exactly as I'd known she would, but as I didn't really hear it just then—a mental split I'll explain in a moment. "It opens you up so they can cure your insides without cutting your skin or making you bleed anywhere. It turns the big parts of you inside out, but not the blood tubes. All your skin—your eyes, ears, nose, toes, all of it—becoming the lining of a little hole that's half-filled with your hair.

"Meantime, your insides are exposed for whatever the healer wants to do to them. You live for a while on the air inside the hole. First the healer gives you an air that makes you sleep, or you go mad in about fifty heartbeats. We'll see what ten heartbeats do to you without the sleepy air. Now will you talk?"

I hadn't been listening to her, though, not the real me, or I'd have gone mad without getting the treatment. I once heard Doc say your liver is more mysterious and farther away from you than the stars, because although you live with your liver all your life, you never see it or learn to point to it instinctively, and the thought of someone messing around with that intimate yet unknown part of you is just too awful.

I knew I had to do something quick. Hell, at the first hint of Introversion, before Kaby had even named it, Illy had winced so that his tentacles were all drawn up like fat feather-sausages. Erich had looked at him questioningly, but that lousy Looney had un-endeared himself to me by squeaking, "Don't mind me, I'm just sensitive. Get on with the girl. Make her tell."

Yes, I knew I had to do something, and here on the floor that meant thinking hard and in high gear about something else. The screwball sculpture Erich had tried to smash was a foot from my nose and I saw a faint trail of white stuff where it had skidded. I reached out and touched the trail; it was finely gritty, like powdered glass. I tipped up the sculpture and the part on which it had skidded wasn't marred at all, not even dulled; the gray spheres were as glisteningly bright as ever. So I knew the trail was diamond dust rubbed off the diamonds in the floor by something even harder.

That told me the sculpture was something special and maybe Doc had had a real idea in his pickled brain when he'd been pushing the thing at all of us and trying to tell us something. He hadn't managed to say anything then, but he had earlier when he'd been going to tell us what to do about the bomb, and maybe there was a connection.

I twisted my memory hard and let it spring back and I got "Inversh... bosh..." Bosh, indeed! Bosh and inverse bosh to all boozers, Russki or otherwise.

So I quick tried the memory trick again and this time I got "glovsh" and then I grasped and almost sneezed on diamond dust as I watched the pieces fit themselves together in my mind like a speeded-up movie reel.

It all hung on that black right-hand hussar's glove Lili had produced for Bruce. Only she couldn't have found it in Stores, because we'd searched every fractional pigeonhole later on and there hadn't been any gloves there, not even the left-hand mate there would have been.

Also, Bruce had had two left-hand gloves to start with, and we had been through the whole Place with a fine-tooth comb, and there had been only the two black gloves on the floor where Bruce had kicked them off the bar—those two and those two only, the left-hand glove he'd brought from outside and the right-hand glove Lili had produced for him.

So a left-hand glove had disappeared—the last I'd seen of it, Lili had been putting it on her tray—and a right-hand glove had appeared. Which could only add up to one thing: Lili had turned the left-hand glove into an identical right. She couldn't have done it by turning it inside out the ordinary way, because the lining was different.

But as I knew only too sickeningly well, there was an extraordinary way to turn things inside out, things like human beings. You merely had to put them on the Invertor in Surgery and flick the switch for full Inversion.

Or you could flick it for partial Inversion and turn something into a perfect three-dimensional mirror image of itself, just what a right-hand glove is of a left. Rotation through the fourth dimension, the science boys call it; I've heard of it being used in surgery on the highly asymmetric Martians, and even to give a socially impeccable right hand to a man who'd lost one, by turning an amputated right arm into an amputated left.

Ordinarily, nothing but live things are ever Inverted in Surgery and you wouldn't think of doing it to an inanimate object, especially in a Place where the Doc's a drunk and the Surgery hasn't been used for hundreds of sleeps.

But when you've just fallen in love, you think of wonderful crazy things to do for people. Drunk with love, Lili had taken Bruce's extra left-hand glove into Surgery, partially Inverted it, and got a right-hand glove to give him.

What Doc had been trying to say with his "Inversh...bosh..." was "Invert the box," meaning we should put the bronze chest through full Inversion to get at the bomb inside to disarm it. Doc too had got the idea from Lili's trick with the glove. What an inside-out tactical atomic bomb would look like, I could not imagine and did not particularly care to see. I might have to, though, I realized.

But the fast-motion film was still running in my head. Later on, Lili had decided like I had that her lover was going to lose out in his plea for mutiny unless she could give him a really captive audience—and maybe, even then, she had been figuring on creating the nest for Bruce's chicks and...all those other things we'd believed in for a while. So she'd taken the Major Maintainer and remembered the glove, and not many seconds later, she had set down on a shelf of the Art Gallery an object that no one would think of questioning—except someone who knew the Gallery by heart.

I looked at the abstract sculpture a foot from my nose, at the clustered gray spheres the size of golf balls. I had known that the inside of the Maintainer was made up of vastly tough, vastly hard giant molecules, but I hadn't realized they were quite *that* big.

I said to myself, "Greta, this is going to give you a major psychosis, but you're the one who has to do it, because no one is going to listen to your deductions when they're all practically living on negative time already."

I got up as quietly as if I were getting out of a bed I shouldn't have been in—there are some things Entertainers are good at—and Kaby was just saying "you go mad in about fifty heartbeats." Everybody on their feet was looking at Lili. Sid seemed to have moved, but I had no time for him except to hope he hadn't done anything that might attract attention to me.

I stepped out of my shoes and walked rapidly to Surgery—there's one good thing about this hardest floor anywhere, it doesn't creak. I walked through the Surgery screen that is like a wall of opaque, odorless cigarette smoke and I concentrated on remembering my snafued nurse's training, and before I had time to panic, I had the sculpture positioned on the gleaming table of the Invertor.

I froze for a moment when I reached for the Inversion switch, thinking of the other time and trying to remember what it had been that bothered me so much about an inside-out brain being bigger and not having eyes, but then I either thumbed my nose at my nightmare or kissed my sanity good-by, I don't know which, and twisted the switch all the way over, and there was the Major Maintainer winking blue about three times a second as nice as you could want it.

It must have been working as sweet and steady as ever, all the time it was Inverted, except that, being inside out, it had hocused the direction finders.

XV. LORD SPIDER

black legged spiders
with red hearts of hell

—marquis

"Jesu!" I turned and Sid's face was sticking through the screen like a tinted bas-relief hanging on a gray wall and I got the impression he had peered unexpectedly through a slit in an arras into Queen Elizabeth's bedroom.

He didn't have any time to linger on the sensation, even if he'd wanted to, for an elbow with a copper band thrust through the screen and dug his ribs and Kaby marched Lili in by the neck. Erich, Mark and Illy were right behind. They caught the blue flashes and stopped dead, staring at the long-lost. Erich spared me one look which seemed to say, so you did it, not that it matters. Then he stepped forward and picked it up and held it solidly to his left side in the double right-angle made by fingers, forearm and chest, and reached for the Introversion switch with a look on his face as if he were opening a fifth of whisky.

The blue light died and Change Winds hit me like a stiff drink that had been a long, long time in coming, like a hot trumpet note out of nowhere.

I felt the changing pasts blowing through me, and the uncertainties whistling past, and ice-stiff reality softening with all its duties and necessities, and the little memories shredding away and dancing off like autumn leaves, leaving maybe not even ghosts behind, and all the crazy moods like Mardi Gras dancers pouring down an evening street, and something inside me had the nerve to say it didn't care whether Greta Forzane's death was riding in those Winds because they felt so good.

I could tell it was hitting the others the same way. Even battered, tight-lipped Lili seemed to be saying, you're making me drink the stuff and I hate you for it, but I do love it. I guess we'd all had the worry that even finding and Extroverting the Maintainer wouldn't put us back in touch with the cosmos and give us those Winds we hate and love.

The thing that cut through to us as we stood there glowing was not the thought of the bomb, though that would have come in a few seconds more, but Sid's voice. He was still standing in the screen, except that

[107]

now his face was out the other side and we could just see parts of his gray-doubleted back, but, of course, his "Jesu!" came through the screen as if it weren't there.

At first I couldn't figure out who he could be talking to, but I swear I never heard his voice so courtly obsequious before, so strong and yet so filled with awe and an under-note of, yes, sheer terror.

"Lord, I am filled from top to toe with confusion that you should so honor my poor Place," he said. "Poor say I and mine, when I mean that I have ever busked it faithfully for you, not dreaming that you would ever condescend...yet knowing that your eye was certes ever upon me... though I am but as a poor pinch of dust adrift between the suns...I abase myself. Prithee, how may I serve thee, sir? I know not e'en how most suitably to address thee, Lord...King...Emperor Spider!"

I felt like I was getting very small, but not a bit less visible, worse luck, and even with the Change Winds inside me to give me courage, I thought this was really too much, coming on top of everything else; it was simply unfair.

At the same time, I realized it was to be expected that the big bosses would have been watching us with their unblinking beady black eyes ever since we had Introverted waiting to pounce if we should ever come out of it. I tried to picture what was on the other side of the screen and I didn't like the assignment.

But in spite of being petrified, I had a hard time not giggling, like the zany at graduation exercises, at the way the other ones in Surgery were taking it.

I mean the Soldiers. They each stiffened up like they had the old ramrod inside them, and their faces got that important look, and they glanced at each other and the floor without lowering their heads, as if they were measuring the distance between their feet and mentally chalking alternate sets of footprints to step into. The way Erich and Kaby held the Major and Minor Maintainers became formal; the way they checked their Callers and nodded reassuringly was positively esoteric. Even Illy somehow managed to look as if he were on parade.

Then from beyond the screen came what was, under the circumstances, the worst noise I've ever heard, a seemingly wordless distant-sounding howling and wailing, with a note of menace that made me shake, although it also had a nasty familiarity about it I couldn't place. Sid's voice broke into it, loud, fast and frightened.

"Your pardon, Lord, I did not think...certes, the gravity...I'll attend to it on the instant." He whipped a hand and half a head back through the screen, but without looking back and snapped his fingers, and before I could blink, Kaby had put the Minor Maintainer in his hand.

[108]

Sid went completely out of sight then and the howling stopped, and I thought that if that was the way a Lord Spider expressed his annoyance at being subjected to incorrect gravity, I hoped the bosses wouldn't start any conversations with me.

Erich pursed his lips and threw the other Soldiers a nod and the four of them marched through the screen as if they'd drilled a lifetime for this moment. I had the wild idea that Erich might give me his arm, but he strode past me as if I were...an Entertainer.

I hesitated a moment then, but I had to see what was happening outside, even if I got eaten up for it. Besides, I had a bit of the thought that if these formalities went on much longer, even a Lord Spider was going to discover just how immune he was to confined atomic blast.

I walked through the screen with Lili beside me.

The Soldiers had stopped a few feet in front of it. I looked around ahead for whatever it was going to turn out to be, prepared to drop a curtsy or whatever else, bar nothing, that seemed expected of me.

I had a hard time spotting the beast. Some of the others seemed to be having trouble too. I saw Doc weaving around foolishly by the control divan, and Bruce and Beau and Sevensee and Maud on their feet beyond it, and I wondered whether we were dealing with an invisible monster; ought to be easy enough for the bosses to turn a simple trick like invisibility.

Then I looked sharply left where everyone else, even glassy-eyed Doc, was coming to look, into the Door sector, only there wasn't any monster there or even a Door, but just Siddy holding the Minor Maintainer and grinning like when he is threatening to tickle me, only more fiendishly.

"Not a move, masters," he cried, his eyes dancing, "or I'll pin the pack of you down, marry and amen I will. It is my firm purpose to see the Place blasted before I let this instrument out of my hands again."

My first thought was, "'Sblood but Siddy is a real actor! I don't care if he didn't study under anyone later than Burbage, that just proves how good Burbage is."

Sid had convinced us not only that the real Spiders had arrived, but earlier that the gravity in the edge of Stores had been a lot heavier than it actually was. He completely fooled all those Soldiers, including my swelled-headed victorious little commandant, and I kind of filed away the timing of that business of reaching out the hand and snapping the fingers without looking, it was so good.

"Beauregard!" Sid called. "Get to the Major Maintainer and call headquarters. But don't come through Door, marry go by Refresher. I'll not trust a single Demon of you in this sector with me until much more has been shown and settled."

[109]

"Siddy, you're wonderful," I said, starting toward him. "As soon as I got the Maintainer unsnarled and looked around and saw your sweet old face—"

"Back, tricksy trull! Not the breadth of one scarlet toenail nearer me, you Queen of Sleights and High Priestess of Deception!" he bellowed. "You least of all do I trust. Why you hid the Maintainer, I know not, 'faith, but later you'll discover the truth to me or I'll have your gizzard."

I could see there was going to have to be a little explaining.

Doc, touched off, I guess, by Sid waving his hand at me, threw back his head and let off one of those shuddery Siberian wolf-howls he does so blamed well. Sid waved toward him sharply and he shut up, beaming toothily, but at least I knew who was responsible for the Spider wail of displeasure that Sid had either called for or more likely got as a gift of the gods and used in his act.

Beau came circling around fast and Erich shoved the Major Maintainer into his hands without making any fuss. The four Soldiers were looking pretty glum after losing their grand review.

Beau dumped some junk off one of the Art Gallery's sturdy taborets and set the Major Maintainer on it carefully but fast, and quickly knelt in front of it and whipped on some earphones and started to tune. The way he did it snatched away from me my inward glory at my big Inversion brainwave so fast, I might never have had it, and there was nothing in my mind again but the bronze bomb chest.

I wondered if I should suggest Inverting the thing, but I said to myself, "Uh-uh, Greta, you got no diploma to show them and there probably isn't time to try two things, anyway."

Then Erich for once did something I wanted him to, though I didn't care for its effect on my nerves, by looking at his Caller and saying quietly, "Nine minutes to go, if Place time and cosmic time are synching."

Beau was steady as a rock and working adjustments so fine that I couldn't even see his fingers move.

Then, at the other end of the Place, Bruce took a few steps toward us. Sevensee and Maud followed a bit behind him. I remembered Bruce was another of our nuts with a private program for blowing up the place.

"Sidney," he called, and then, when he'd got Sid's attention, "Remember, Sidney, you and I both came down to London from Peterhouse."

I didn't get it. Then Bruce looked toward Erich with a devil-may-care challenge and toward Lili as if he were asking her forgiveness for something. I couldn't read her expression; the bruises were blue on her throat and her cheek was puffy.

Then Bruce once more shot Erich that look of challenge and he spun and grabbed Sevensee by a wrist and stuck out a foot—even half-horses aren't too sharp about infighting, I guess, and the satyr had every right to feel at least as confused as I felt—and sent him stumbling into Maud, and the two of them tumbled to the floor in a jumble of hairy legs and pearl-gray frock. Bruce raced to the bomb chest.

Most of us yelled, "Stop him, Sid, pin him down," or something like that—I know I did because I was suddenly sure that he'd been asking Lili's pardon for blowing the two of them up—and all the rest of us too, the love-blinded stinker.

Sid had been watching him all the time and now he lifted his hand to the Minor Maintainer, but then he didn't touch any of the dials, just watched and waited, and I thought, "Shaitan shave us! Does Siddy want in on death, too? Ain't he satisfied with all he knows about life?"

Bruce had knelt and was twisting some things on the front of the chest, and it was all as bright as if he were under a bank of Klieg lights, and I was telling myself I wouldn't know anything when the fireball fired, and not believing it, and Sevensee and Maud had got unscrambled and were starting for Bruce, and the rest of us were yelling at Sid, except that Erich was just looking at Bruce very happily, and Sid was still not doing anything, and it was unbearable except just then I felt the little arteries start to burst in my brain like a string of fire-crackers and the old aorta pop, and for good measure, a couple of valves come unhinged in my ticker, and I was thinking, "Well, now I know what it's like to die of heart failure and high blood pressure," and having a last quiet smile at having cheated the bomb, when Bruce jumped up and back from the chest.

"That does it!" he announced cheerily. "She's as safe as the Bank of England."

Sevensee and Maud stopped themselves just short of knocking him down and I said to myself, "Hey, let's get a move on! I thought heart attacks were fast."

Before anyone else could speak, Beau did. He had turned around from the Major Maintainer and pulled aside one of the earphones.

"I got headquarters," he said crisply. "They told me how to disarm the bomb—I merely said I thought we ought to know. What did you do, sir?" he called to Bruce.

"There's a row of four ankhs just below the lock. The first to your left you give a quarter turn to the right, the second a quarter turn to the left, same for the fourth, and you don't touch the third."

"That is it, sir," Beau confirmed.

The long silence was too much for me; I guess I must have the shortest span for unspoken relief going. I drew some nourishment out of my restored arteries into my brain cells and yelled, "Siddy, I know I'm a tricksy trull and the High Vixen of all Foxes, but what the Hell is Peterhouse?"

"The oldest college at Cambridge," he told me rather coolly.

XVI. THE POSSIBILITY-BINDERS

"Familiar with infinite universe sheafs and open-ended postulate systems?—the notion that everything is possible— and I mean everything—and everything has happened. *Everything.*"

–Heinlein

An hour later, I was nursing a weak highball and a black eye in the sleepy-time darkness on the couch farthest from the piano, half watching the highlighted party going on around it and the bar, while the Place waited for rendezvous with Egypt and the Battle of Alexandria.

Sid had swept all our outstanding problems into one big bundle and, since his hand held the joker of the Minor Maintainer, he had settled them all as high-handedly as if they'd been those of a bunch of schoolkids.

It amounted to this:

We'd been Introverted when most of the damning things had happened, so presumably only we knew about them, and we were all in so deep one way or another that we'd all have to keep quiet to protect our delicate complexions.

Well, Erich's triggering the bomb did balance rather neatly Bruce's incitement to mutiny, and there was Doc's drinking, while everybody who had declared for the peace message had something to hide. Mark and Kaby I felt inclined to trust anywhere, Maud for sure, and Erich in this particular matter, damn him. Illy I didn't feel at all easy about, but I told myself there always has to be a fly in the ointment—a darn big one this time, and furry.

Sid didn't mention his own dirty linen, but he knew we knew he'd flopped badly as boss of the Place and only recouped himself by that last-minute flimflam.

Remembering Sid's trick made me think for a moment about the real Spiders. Just before I snuck out of Surgery, I'd had a vivid picture of what they must look like, but now I couldn't get it again. It depressed me, not being able to remember—oh, I probably just imagined I'd had a picture, like a hophead on a secret-of-the-universe kick. Me ever find out anything about the Spiders?—except for nervous notions like I'd had during the recent fracas?—what a laugh!

The funniest thing (ha-ha!) was that I had ended up the least-trusted person. Sid wouldn't give me time to explain how I'd deduced what had happened to the Maintainer, and even when Lili spoke up and admitted hiding it, she acted so bored I don't think everybody believed her—although she did spill the realistic detail that she hadn't used partial Inversion on the glove; she'd just turned it inside out to make it a right and then done a full Inversion to get the lining back inside.

I tried to get Doc to confirm that he'd reasoned the thing out the same way I had, but he said he had been blacked out the whole time, except during the first part of the hunt, and he didn't remember having any bright ideas at all. Right now, he was having Maud explain to him twice, in detail, everything that had happened. I decided that it was going to take a little more work before my reputation as a great detective was established.

I looked over the edge of the couch and just made out in the gloom one of Bruce's black gloves. It must have been kicked there. I fished it up. It was the right-hand one. My big clue, and was I sick of it! Got mittens, God forbid! I slung it away and, like a lurking octopus, Illy shot up a tentacle from the next couch, where I hadn't known he was resting, and snatched the glove like it was a morsel of underwater garbage. These ETs can seem pretty shuddery non-human at times.

I thought of what a cold-blooded, skin-saving louse Illy had been, and about Sid and his easy suspicions, and Erich and my black eye, and how, as usual, I'd got left alone in the end. My men!

Bruce had explained about being an A-tech. Like a lot of us, he'd had several widely different jobs during his first weeks in the Change World and one of them had been as secretary to a group of the minor atomics boys from the Manhattan-Project-Earth-Satellite days. I gathered he'd also absorbed some of his bothersome ideas from them. I hadn't quite decided yet what species of heroic heel he belonged to, but he was thick with Mark and Erich again. Everybody's men!

Sid didn't have to argue with anybody; all the wild compulsions and mighty resolves were dead now, anyway until they'd had a good long rest. I sure could use one myself, I knew.

The party at the piano was getting wilder. Lili had been dancing the black bottom on top of it and now she jumped down into Sid's and Sevensee's arms, taking a long time about it. She'd been drinking a lot and her little gray dress looked about as innocent on her as diapers would on Nell Gwyn. She continued her dance, distributing her marks of favor equally between Sid, Erich and the satyr. Beau didn't mind a bit, but serenely pounded out "Tonight's the Night"—which she'd practically shouted to him not two minutes ago.

[113]

I was glad to be out of the party. Who can compete with a highly experienced, utterly disillusioned seventeen-year-old really throwing herself away for the first time?

Something touched my hand. Illy had stretched a tentacle into a furry wire to return me the black glove, although he ought to have known I didn't want it. I pushed it away, privately calling Illy a washed-out moronic tarantula, and right away I felt a little guilty. What right had I to be critical of Illy? Would my own character have shown to advantage if I'd been locked in with eleven octopoids a billion years away? For that matter, where did I get off being critical of anyone?

Still, I was glad to be out of the party, though I kept on watching it. Bruce was drinking alone at the bar. Once Sid had gone over to him and they'd had one together and I'd heard Bruce reciting from Rupert Brooke those deliberately corny lines, "For England's the one land, I know, Where men with Splendid Hearts may go; and Cambridgeshire, of all England, The Shire for Men who Understand;" and I'd remembered that Brooke too had died young in World War One and my ideas had got fuzzy. But mostly Bruce was just calmly drinking by himself. Every once in a while Lili would look at him and stop dead in her dancing and laugh.

I'd figured out this Bruce-Lili-Erich business as well as I cared to. Lili had wanted the nest with all her heart and nothing else would ever satisfy her, and now she'd go to hell her own way and probably die of Bright's disease for a third time in the Change World. Bruce hadn't wanted the nest or Lili as much as he wanted the Change World and the chances it gave for Soldierly cavorting and poetic drunks; Lili's seed wasn't his idea of healing the cosmos; maybe he'd make a real mutiny some day, but more likely he'd stick to bar-room epics.

His and Lili's infatuation wouldn't die completely, no matter how rancid it looked right now. The real-love angle might go, but Change would magnify the romance angle and it might seem to them like a big thing of a sort if they met again.

Erich had his *Kamerad*, shaped to suit him, who'd had the guts and cleverness to disarm the bomb he'd had the guts to trigger. You have to hand it to Erich for having the nerve to put us all in a situation where we'd have to find the Maintainer or fry, but I don't know anything disgusting enough to hand to him.

I had tried a while back. I had gone up behind him and said, "Hey, how's my wicked little commandant? Forgotten your *und so weiter?*" and as he turned, I clawed my nails and slammed him across the cheek. That's how I got the black eye. Maud wanted to put an electronic leech on it, but I took the old handkerchief in ice water. Well, at any rate Erich had his scratches to match Bruce's, not as deep, but four of them, and I told myself maybe they'd get infected—I hadn't washed my hands since the hunt. Not that Erich doesn't love scars.

Mark was the one who helped me up after Erich knocked me down.

"You got any omnias for that?" I snapped at him.

"For what?" Mark asked.

"Oh, for everything that's been happening to us," I told him disgustedly.

He seemed to actually think for a moment and then he said, "*Omnia mutantur, nihil interit.*"

"Meaning?" I asked him.

He said, "All things change, but nothing is really lost."

It would be a wonderful philosophy to stand with against the Change Winds. Also damn silly. I wondered if Mark really believed it. I wished I could. Sometimes I come close to thinking it's a lot of baloney trying to be any decent kind of Demon, even a good Entertainer. Then I tell myself, "That's life, Greta. You've got to love through it somehow." But there are times when some of these cookies are not too easy to love.

Something brushed the palm of my hand again. It was Illy's tentacle, with the tendrils of the tip spread out like a little bush. I started to pull my hand away, but then I realized the Loon was simply lonely. I surrendered my hand to the patterned gossamer pressures of feather-talk.

Right away I got the words, "Feeling lonely, Greta girl?"

It almost floored me, I tell you. Here I was understanding feather-talk, which I just didn't, and I was understanding it in English, which didn't make sense at all.

For a second, I thought Illy must have spoken, but I knew he hadn't, and for a couple more seconds I thought he was working telepathy on me, using the feather-talk as cues. Then I tumbled to what was happening: he was playing English on my palm like on the keyboard of his squeakbox, and since I could play English on a squeakbox myself, my mind translated automatically.

Realizing this almost gave my mind stage fright, but I was too fagged to be hocused by self-consciousness. I just lay back and let the thoughts come through. It's good to have someone talk to you, even an underweight octopus, and without the squeaks Illy didn't sound so silly; his phrasing was soberer.

"Feeling sad, Greta girl, because you'll never understand what's happening to us all," Illy asked me, "because you'll never be anything but a shadow fighting shadows—and trying to love shadows in between the battles? It's time you understood we're not really fighting a war at all, although it looks that way, but going through a kind of evolution, though not exactly the kind Erich had in mind.

"Your Terran thought has a word for it and a theory for it—a theory that recurs on many worlds. It's about the four orders of life: Plants, Animals, Men and Demons. Plants are energy-binders—they can't move through space or time, but they can clutch energy and transform it. Animals are space-binders—they can move through space. Man (Terran or ET, Lunan or non-Lunan) is a time-binder—he has memory.

"Demons are the fourth order of evolution, possibility-binders—they can make all of what might be part of what is, and that is their evolutionary function. Resurrection is like the metamorphosis of a caterpillar into a butterfly: a third-order being breaks out of the chrysalis of its lifeline into fourth-order life. The leap from the ripped cocoon of an unchanging reality is like the first animal's leap when he ceases to be a plant, and the Change World is the core of meaning behind the many myths of immortality.

"All evolution looks like a war at first—octopoids against monopoids, mammals against reptiles. And it has a necessary dialectic: there must be the thesis—we call it Snake—and the antithesis—Spider—before there can be the ultimate synthesis, when all possibilities are fully realized in one ultimate universe. The Change War isn't the blind destruction it seems.

"Remember that the Serpent is your symbol of wisdom and the Spider your sign for patience. The two names are rightly frightening to you, for all high existence is a mixture of horror and delight. And don't be surprised, Greta girl, at the range of my words and thoughts; in a way, I've had a billion years to study Terra and learn her languages and myths.

"Who are the real Spiders and Snakes, meaning who were the first possibility-binders? Who was Adam, Greta girl? Who was Cain? Who were Eve and Lilith?

"In binding all possibility, the Demons also bind the mental with the material. All fourth-order beings live inside and outside all minds, throughout the whole cosmos. Even this Place is, after its fashion, a giant brain: its floor is the brainpan, the boundary of the Void is the cortex of gray matter—yes, even the Major and Minor Maintainers are analogues of the pineal and pituitary glands, which in some form sustain all nervous systems.

"There's the real picture, Greta girl."

The feather-talk faded out and Illy's tendril tips merged into a soft pad on which I fingered, "Thanks, Daddy Longlegs."

Chewing over in my mind what Illy had just told me, I looked back at the gang around the piano. The party seemed to be breaking up; at least some of them were chopping away at it. Sid had gone to the control divan and was getting set to tune in Egypt. Mark and Kaby were there with him, all bursting with eagerness and the vision of tanks on ranks of mounted Zombie bowmen going up in a mushroom cloud; I thought of what Illy had told me and I managed a smile—seems we've got to win and lose all the battles, every which way.

Mark had just put on his Parthian costume, groaning cheerfully, "Trousers again!" and was striding around under a hat like a fur-lined ice-cream cone and with the sleeves of his metal-stuffed candys flapping over his hands. He waved a short sword with a heart-shaped guard at Bruce and Erich and told them to get a move on.

Kaby was going along on the operation wearing the old-woman disguise intended for Benson-Carter. I got a half-hearted kick out of knowing she was going to have to cover that chest and hobble.

Bruce and Erich weren't taking orders from Mark just yet. Erich went over and said something to Bruce at the bar, and Bruce got down and went over with Erich to the piano, and Erich tapped Beau on the shoulder and leaned over and said something to him, and Beau nodded and yanked "Limehouse Blues" to a fast close and started another piece, something slow and nostalgic.

Erich and Bruce waved to Mark and smiled, as if to show him that whether he came over and stood with them or not, the legate and the lieutenant and the commandant were very much together. And while Sevensee hugged Lili with a simple enthusiasm that made me wonder why I've wasted so much imagination on genetic treatments for him, Erich and Bruce sang:

> *"To the legion of the lost ones, to the cohort of the damned,*
> *To our brothers in the tunnels outside time,*
> *Sing three Change-resistant Zombies, raised from death and*
> *robot-crammed,*
> *And Commandos of the Spiders—*
> *Here's to crime!*
> *We're three blind mice on the wrong time-track,*
> *Hush—hush—hush!*
> *We've lost our now and will never get back,*
> *Hush—hush—hush!*
> *Change Commandos out on the spree,*
> *Damned through all possibility,*
> *Ghostgirls, think kindly on such as we,*
> *Hush—hush—hush!"*

While they were singing, I looked down at my charcoal skirt and over at Maud and Lili and I thought, "Three gray hustlers for three black hussars, that's our speed." Well, I'd never thought of myself as a high-speed job, winning all the races—I wouldn't feel comfortable that way.

Come to think of it, we've got to lose and win all the races in the long run, the way the course is laid out.

I fingered to Illy, "That's the picture, all right, Spider boy."

Try and Change the Past

No, I wouldn't advise anyone to try to change the past, at least not his personal past, although changing the general past is my business, my fighting business. You see, I'm a Snake in the Change War. Don't back off—human beings, even Resurrected ones engaged in time-fighting, aren't built for outward wriggling and their poison is mostly psychological. "Snake" is slang for the soldiers on our side, like Hun or Reb or Ghibbelin. In the Change War we're trying to alter the past—and it's tricky, brutal work, believe me—at points all over the cosmos, anywhere and anywhen, so that history will be warped to make our side defeat the Spiders. But that's a much bigger story, the biggest in fact, and I'll leave it occupying several planets of microfilm and two asteroids of coded molecules in the files of the High Command.

Change one event in the past and you get a brand new future? Erase the conquests of Alexander by nudging a Neolithic pebble? Extirpate America by pulling up a shoot of Sumerian grain? Brother, that isn't the way it works at all! The space-time continuum's built of stubborn stuff and change is anything but a chain-reaction. Change the past and you start a wave of changes moving futurewards, but it damps out mighty fast. Haven't you ever heard of temporal reluctance, or of the Law of Conservation of Reality?

Here's a little story that will illustrate my point: This guy was fresh recruited, the Resurrection sweat still wet in his armpits, when he got the idea he'd use the time-traveling power to go back and make a couple of little changes in his past, so that his life would take a happier course and maybe, he thought, he wouldn't have to die and get mixed up with Snakes and Spiders at all. It was as if a new-enlisted feuding hillbilly soldier should light out with the high-power rifle they issued him to go back to his mountains and pick off his pet enemies.

Normally it couldn't ever have happened. Normally, to avoid just this sort of thing, he'd have been shipped straight off to some place a few thousand or million years distant from his point of enlistment and maybe a few light-years, too. But there was a local crisis in the Change

War and a lot of routine operations got held up and one new recruit was simply forgotten.

Normally, too, he'd never have been left alone a moment in the Dispatching Room, never even have glimpsed the place except to be rushed through it on arrival and reshipment. But, as I say, there happened to be a crisis, the Snakes were shorthanded, and several soldiers were careless. Afterwards two N .C .'s were busted because of what happened and a First Looey not only lost his commission but was transferred outside the galaxy and the era. But during the crisis this recruit I'm telling you about had the opportunity and more to fool around with forbidden things and try out his schemes.

He also had all the details on the last part of his life back in the real world, on his death and its consequences, to mull over and be tempted to change. This wasn't anybody's carelessness. The Snakes give every candidate that information as part of the recruiting pitch. They spot a death coming and the Ressurection Men go back and recruit the person from a point a few minutes or at most a few hours earlier. They explain in uncomfortable detail whats going to happen and wouldn't he rather take the oath and put on scales? I never heard of anybody turning down that offer. Then they lift him from his lifeline in the form of a Doubleganger and from then on, brother, he's a Snake.

So this guy had a clearer picture of his death than of the day he bought his first car, and a masterpiece of morbid irony it was. He was living in a classy penthouse that had belonged to a crazy uncle of his—it even had a midget astronomical observatory, unused for years—but he was stony broke, up to the top hair in debt, and due to be dispossessed next day. He'd never had a real job, always lived off his rich relatives and his wife's, but now he was getting a little too mature for his stern dedication to a life of sponging to be cute. His charming personality, which had been his only asset, was deader from overuse and abuse than he himself would be in a few hours. His crazy uncle would not have anything to do with him any more. His wife was responsible for a lot of the wear and tear on his social-butterfly wings; she had hated him for years, had screamed at him morning to night the way you can only get away with in a penthouse and was going batty herself. He'd been playing around with another woman, who'd just given him the gate: though he knew his wife would never believe that and only add a scornful note to her screaming if she did.

It was a lousy evening, smack in the middle of an August heat wave. The Giants were playing a night game with Brooklyn. Two long-run musicals had closed. Wheat had hit a new high There was a brush fire in California and a war scare in Iran. And tonight a meteor shower was due, according to an astronomical bulletin that had arrived in the mail addressed to his uncle—he generally dumped such stuff in the fireplace unopened, but today he had looked at it because he had nothing better to do, either more useful or more interesting.

The phone rang. It was a lawyer. His crazy uncle was dead and in the will there wasn't a word about an Asteroid Search Foundation. Every penny of the fortune went to the no-good nephew.

This same character finally hung up the phone, fighting off a tendency for his heart to spring giddily out of his chest and through the ceiling.

Just then his wife came screeching out of the bedroom. She'd received a cute, commiserating tell-all note from the other woman; she had a gun and announced that she was going to finish him off.

The sweltering atmosphere provided a good background for sardonic catastrophe. The French doors to the roof were open behind him but the air that drifted through was muggy as death. Unnoticed, a couple of meteors streaked faintly across the night sky.

Figuring it would sure dissuade her, he told her about the inheritance. She screamed that he'd just use the money to buy more other women— not an unreasonable prediction—and pulled the trigger.

The danger was minimal. She was at the other end of a big living room, her hand wasn't just shaking, she was waving the nickle-plated revolver as if it were a fan.

The bullet took him right between the eyes. He dropped down deader than his hopes were before he got the phone call. He saw it happen because as a clincher the Resurrection Men brought him forward as a Doubleganger to witness it invisibly—also standard Snake procedure and not productive of time-complications, incidentally, since Doublegangers don't imprint on reality unless they want to.

They stuck around a bit. His wife looked at the body for a couple of seconds, went to her bedroom, blonded her graying hair by dousing it with two bottles of undiluted peroxide, put on a tarnished gold lamé evening gown and a bucket of make-up, went back to the living room, sat down at the piano, played "Country Gardens" and then shot herself, too.

So that was the little skit, the little double blackout, he had to mull over outside the empty and unguarded Dispatching Room, quite forgotten by its twice-depleted skeleton crew while every available Snake in the sector was helping deal with the local crisis, which centered around the planet Alpha Centauri Four, two million years minus.

Naturally it didn't take him long to figure out that if he went back and gimmicked things so that the first blackout didn't occur, but the second still did, he would be sitting pretty back in the real world and able to devote his inheritance to fulfilling his wife's prediction and other pastimes. He didn't know much about Doublegangers yet and had it figured out that if he didn't die in the real world he'd have no trouble resuming his existence there—maybe it'd even happen automatically.

So this Snake—name kind of suits him, doesn't it?—crossed his fingers and slipped into the Dispatching Room. Dispatching is so simple a child could learn it in five minutes from studying the board. He went back to a point a couple of hours before the tragedy, carefully avoiding the spot where the Resurrection Men had lifted him from his lifeline. He found the revolver in a dresser drawer, unloaded it, checked to make sure there weren't any more cartridges around, and then went ahead a couple of hours, arriving just in time to see himself get the slug between the eyes same as before.

As soon as he got over his disappointment, he realized he'd learned something about Doublegangers he should have known all along, if his mind had been clicking. The bullets he'd lifted were Doublegangers, too; they had disappeared from the real world only at the point in space-time where he'd lifted them, and they had continued to exist, as real as ever, in the earlier and later sections of their lifelines—with the result that the gun was loaded again by the time his wife had grabbed it up.

So this time he set the board so he'd arrive just a few minutes before the tragedy. He lifted the gun, bullets and all, and waited around to make sure it stayed lifted. He figured—rightly—that if he left this space-time sector the gun would reappear in the dresser drawer, and he didn't want his wife getting hold of any gun, even one with a broken lifeline. Afterwards—after his own death was averted, that is—he figured he'd put the gun back in his wife's hand.

Two things reassured him a lot, although he'd been expecting the one and hoping for the other: his wife didn't notice his presence as a Doubleganger and when she went to grab the gun she acted as if it weren't gone and held her right hand as if there were a gun in it. If he'd studied philosophy, he'd have realized he was witnessing a proof of Leibniz's theory of Pre-established harmony: that neither atoms nor human beings really affect each other, they just look as if they did.

But anyway he had no time for theories. Still holding the gun, he drifted out into the living room to get a box seat right next to Himself for the big act. Himself didn't notice him any more than his wife had.

His wife came out and said her piece same as ever. Himself cringed as if she still had the gun and started to babble about the inheritance, his wife sneered and made as if she were shooting Himself.

Sure enough, there was no shot this time, and no mysteriously appearing bullet hole—which was something he'd been afraid of.

Himself just stood there dully while his wife made as if she were looking down at a dead body and went back to her bedroom.

[122]

He was pretty pleased: this time he actually had changed the past. Then Himself slowly glanced around at him, still with that dull look, and slowly came toward him. He was more pleased than ever because he figured now they'd melt together into one man and one lifeline again, and he'd be able to hurry out somewhere and establish an alibi, just to be on the safe side, while his wife suicided.

But it didn't quite happen that way. Himself's look changed from dull to desperate, he came up close...and suddenly grabbed the gun and quick as a wink put a thumb to the trigger and shot himself between the eyes. And flopped, same as ever.

Right there he was starting to learn a little—and it was an unpleasant shivery sort of learning—about the Law of Conservation of Reality. The four-dimentional space-time universe doesn't like to be changed, any more than it likes to lose or gain energy or matter. If it has to be changed, it'll adjust itself just enough to accept that change and no more. The Conservation of Reality is a sort of Law of Least Action, too. It doesn't matter how improbable the events involved in the adjustment are, just so long as they're possible at all and can be used to patch the established pattern. His death, at this point, was part of the established pattern. If he lived on instead of dying, billions of other compensatory changes would have to be made, covering many years, perhaps centuries, before the old pattern could be re-established, the snarled lifelines woven back into—and the universe finally go on the same as if his wife had shot him on schedule.

This way the pattern was hardly effected at all. There were powder burns on his forehead that weren't there before, but there weren't any witnesses to the shooting in the first place, so the presence or absence of powder burns didn't matter. The gun was lying on the floor instead of being in his wife's hands, but he had the feeling that when the time came for her to die, she'd wake enough from the Pre-established Harmony trance to find it, just as Himself did.

So he'd learned a little about the Conservation of Reality. He also had learned a little about his own character, especially from Himself's last look and act. He'd got a hint that he had been trying to destroy himself for years by the way he'd lived, so that inherited fortune or accidental success couldn't save him, and if his wife hadn't shot him he'd have done it himself in any case. He'd got a hint that Himself hadn't merely been acting as an agent for a self-correcting universe when he grabbed the gun, he'd been acting on his own account, too—the universe, you know, operates by getting people to co-operate.

But although these ideas occurred to him, he didn't dwell on them, for he figured he'd had a partial success the second time if he kept the gun away from Himself, if he dominated Himself, as it were, the melting-

[123]

together would take place and everything else go forward as planned.

He had the dim realization that the universe, like a huge sleepy animal, knew what he was trying to do and was trying to thwart him. This feeling of opposition made him determined to outmaneuver the universe—not the first guy to yield to such a temptation, of course.

And up to a point his tactics worked. The third time he gimmicked the past, everything started to happen just as it did the second time. Himself dragged miserably over to him, looking for the gun, but he had it tucked away and was prepared to hold onto it. Encouragingly, Himself didn't grapple, the look of desperation changed to one of utter hopelessness, and Himself turned away from him and very slowly walked to the French doors and stood looking out into the sweating night. He figured Himself was just getting used to the idea of not dying. There wasn't a breath of air. A couple of meteors streaked across the sky. Then, mixed with the upseeping night sounds of the city, there was a low whirring whistle.

Himself shook a bit, as if he'd had a sudden chill. Then Himself turned around and slumped to the floor in one movement. Between his eyes was a black hole.

Then and there this Snake I'm telling you about decided never again to try and change the past, at least not his personal past. He'd had it, and he'd also acquired a healthy respect for a High Command able to change the past, albeit with difficulty. He scooted back to the Dispatching Room, where a sleepy and surprised Snake gave him a terrific chewing out and confined him to quarters. The chewing-out didn't bother him too much—he'd acquired a certain fatalism about things; A person's got to learn to accept reality as it is, you know—just as you'd best not be surprised at the way I disappear in a moment or two—I'm a Snake too, remember.

If a statistician is looking for an example of a highly improbable event, he can hardly pick a more vivid one than the chance of a man being hit by a meteorite. And, if he adds the condition that the meteorite hit him between the eyes so as to counterfeit the wound made by a 32-caliber bullet, the improbability becomes astronomical cubed. So how's a person going to outmaneuver a universe that finds it easier to drill a man through the head that way rather than postpone the date of his death?

A Deskful of Girls

Yes, I said ghostgirls, sexy ones. Personally I never in my life saw any ghosts except the sexy kind, though I saw enough of those I'll tell you, but only for one evening, in the dark of course, with the assistance of an eminent (I should also say notorious) psychologist. It was an interesting experience, to put it mildly, and it introduced me to an unknown field of psycho-physiology, but under no circumstances would I want to repeat it.

But ghosts are supposed to be frightening? Well, who ever said that sex isn't? It is to the neophyte, female or male, and don't let any of the latter try to kid you. For one thing, sex opens up the unconscious mind, which isn't exactly a picnic area. Sex is a force and rite that is basic, primal; and the caveman or cavewoman in each of us is a truth bigger than the jokes and cartoons about it. Sex was behind the witchcraft religion, the sabbats were sexual orgies. The witch was a sexual creature. So is the ghost.

After all, what is a ghost, according to all traditional views, but the shell of a human being—an animated skin? And the skin is all sex—it's touch, the boundary, the mask of flesh.

I got the notion about skin from my eminent-notorious psychologist, Dr. Emil Slyker, the first and the last evening I met him, at the Countersign Club, though he wasn't talking about ghosts to begin with. He was pretty drunk and drawing signs in the puddle spilled from his triple martini.

He grinned at me and said, "Look here, What's-Your-Name—oh yes, Carr Mackay, Mister *Justine* himself. Well, look here, Carr, I got a deskful of girls at my office in this building and they're needing attention. Let's shoot up and have a look."

Right away my hopelessly naive imagination flashed me a vivid picture of a desk swarming inside with girls about five or six inches high. They weren't dressed—my imagination never dresses girls except for special effects after long thought—but these looked as if they had been modeled from the drawings of Heinrich Kley or Mahlon Blaine. Literal vest—

[125]

pocket Venuses, saucy and active. Right now they were attempting a mass escape from the desk, using a couple of nail files for saws, and they'd already cut some trap doors between the drawers so they could circulate around. One group was improvising a blowtorch from an atomizer and lighter fluid. Another was trying to turn a key from the inside, using tweezers for a wrench.

And they were tearing down and defacing small signs, big to them, which read YOU BELONG TO DR. EMIL SLYKER.

My mind, which looks down at my imagination and refuses to associate with it, was studying Dr. Slyker and also making sure that I behaved outwardly like a worshipful fan, a would-be Devil's apprentice. This approach, helped by the alcohol, seemed to be relaxing him into the frame of mind I wanted him to have—one of boastful condescension. Slyker was a plump gut of a man with a perpetually sucking mouth, in his early fifties, fair-complexioned, blond, balding, with the power-lines around his eyes and at the corners of the nostrils. Over it all he wore the ready-for-photographers mask that is a sure sign its wearer is on the Big Time. Eyes weak, as shown by the dark glasses, but forever peering for someone to strip or cow. His hearing bad too, for that matter, as he didn't catch the barman approaching and started a little when he saw the white rag reaching out toward the spill from his drink. Emil Slyker, "doctor" courtesy of some European universities and a crust like blued steel, movie columnist, pumper of the last ounce of prestige out of that ashcan word "psychologist," psychic researcher several mysterious rumored jumps ahead of Wilhelm Reich with his orgone and Rhine with his ESP, psychological consultant to starlets blazing into stars and other ladies in the bucks, and a particularly expert disher-out of that goulash of psychoanalysis, mysticism and magic that is the *chef-d'Oeuvre* of our era. And, I was assuming, a particularly successful blackmailer. A stinker to be taken very seriously.

My real purpose in contacting Slyker, of which I hoped he hadn't got an inkling yet, was to offer him enough money to sink a small luxury liner in exchange for a sheaf of documents he was using to blackmail Evelyn Cordew, current pick-of-the-pantheon among our sex goddesses. I was working for another film star, Jeff Crain, Evelyn's ex-husband, but not "ex" when it came to the protective urge. Jeff said that Slyker refused to bite on the direct approach, that he was so paranoid in his suspiciousness as to be psychotic, and that I would have to make friends with him first. Friends with a paranoid!

So in pursuit of this doubtful and dangerous distinction, there I was at the Countersign Club, nodding respectfully happy acquiescence to the Master's suggestion and asking tentatively, "Girls needing attention?"

He gave me his whoremaster, keeper-of-the-keys grin and said, "Sure,

[126]

women need attention whatever form they're in. They're like pearls in a vault, they grow dull and fade unless they have regular contact with warm human flesh. Drink up."

He gulped half of what was left of his martini—the puddle had been blotted up meantime and the black surface reburnished—and we made off without any fuss over checks or tabs; I had expected him to stick me with the former at least, but evidently I wasn't enough of an acolyte yet to be granted that honor.

It fitted that I had caught up with Emil Slyker at the Countersign Club. It is to a key club what the latter is to a top-crust bar. Strictly Big Time, set up to provide those in it with luxury, privacy and security. Especially security: I had heard that the Countersign Club bodyguarded even their sober patrons home late of an evening with or without their pickups, but I hadn't believed it until this well-dressed and (doubtless well-heeled) silent husky rode the elevator up the dead midnight office building with us and only turned back at Dr. Slyker's door. Of course I couldn't have got into the Countersign Club on my own—Jeff had provided me with my entree: an illustrated edition of the Marquis de Sade's *Justine*, its margins annotated by a world-famous, recently-deceased psychoanalyst. I had sent it in to Slyker with a note full of flowery expression of "my admiration for your work in the psycho-physiology of sex."

The door to Slyker's office was something. No glass, just a dark expanse—teak or ironwood, I guessed—with EMIL SLYKER, CONSULTING PSYCHOLOGIST burnt into it. No Yale lock, but a large keyhole with a curious silver valve that the key pressed aside. Slyker showed me the key with a deprecating smile; the gleaming castellations of its web were the most complicated I'd even seen, its stem depicted Pasiphaë and the bull. He certainly was willing to pay for atmosphere.

There were three sounds: first the soft grating of the turning key, then the solid snap of the bolts retracting, then a faint creak from the hinges.

Open, the door showed itself four inches thick, more like that of a safe or vault, with a whole cluster of bolts that the key controlled. Just before it closed, something very odd happened: a filmy plastic sheet whipped across the bolts from the outer edge of the doorway and conformed itself to them so perfectly that I suspected static electrical attraction of some sort. Once in place it barely clouded the silvery surface of the bolts and would have taken a close look to spot. It didn't interfere in any way with the door closing or the bolts snapping back into their channels.

The Doctor sensed or took for granted my interest in the door and explained over his shoulder in the dark, "My Siegfried Line. More than one ambitious crook or inspired murderer has tried to smash or think his or her way through that door. They've had no luck. They can't. At this moment there is literally no one in the world who could come through that door without using explosives—and they'd have to be well placed. Cozy."

I privately disagreed with the last remark. Not to make a thing of it, I would have preferred to feel in a bit closer touch with the silent corridors outside, even though they held nothing but the ghosts of unhappy stenographers and neurotic dames my imagination had raised on the way up.

"Is the plastic film part of an alarm system?" I asked. The Doctor didn't answer. His back was to me. I remembered that he'd shown himself a shade deaf. But I didn't get a chance to repeat my question for just then some indirect lighting came on, although Slyker wasn't near any switch ("Our talk triggers it," he said) and the office absorbed me.

Naturally the desk was the first thing I looked for, though I felt foolish doing it. It was a big deep job with a dark soft gleam that might have been that of fine-grained wood or metal. The drawers were file size, not the shallow ones my imagination had played with, and there were three tiers of them to the right of the kneehole—space enough for a couple of life-size girls if they were doubled up according to one of the formulas for the hidden operator of Maelzel's chess-playing automaton. My imagination, which never learns, listened hard for the patter of tiny bare feet and the clatter of little tools. There wasn't even the scurry of mice, which would have done something to my nerves, I'm sure.

The office was an L with the door at the end of this leg. The walls I could see were mostly lined with books, though a few line drawings had been hung—my imagination had been right about Heinrich Kley, though I didn't recognize these pen-and-ink originals, and there were some Fuselis you won't ever see reproduced in books handled over the counter.

The desk was in the corner of the L with the components of a hi-fi spaced along the bookshelves this side of it. All I could see yet of the other leg of the L was a big surrealist armchair facing the desk but separated from it by a wide low bare table. I took a dislike to that armchair on first sight, though it looked extremely comfortable. Slyker had reached the desk now and had one hand on it as he turned back toward me, and I got the impression that the armchair had changed shape since I had entered the office—that it had been more like a couch to start with, although now the back was almost straight.

But the Doctor's left thumb indicated I was to sit in it and I couldn't see another chair in the place except the padded button on which he was now settling himself—one of those stenographer deals with a boxing-glove back placed to catch you low in the spine like the hand of a knowledgeable masseur. In the other leg of the L, besides the armchair, were more books, a heavy concertina blind sealing off the window, two narrow doors that

I supposed were those of a closet and a lavatory, and what looked like a slightly scaled-down and windowless telephone booth until I guessed it must be an orgone box of the sort Reich had invented to restore the libido when the patient occupies it. I quickly settled myself in the chair, not to be gingerly about it. It was rather incredibly comfortable, almost as if it had adjusted its dimensions a bit at the last instant to conform to mine. The back was narrow at the base but widened and then curled in and over to almost a canopy around my head and shoulders. The seat too widened a lot toward the front, where the stubby legs were far apart. The bulky arms sprang unsupported from the back and took my own just right, though curving inwards with the barest suggestion of a hug. The leather or unfamiliar plastic was as firm and cool as young flesh and its texture as mat under my fingertips.

"An historic chair," the Doctor observed, "designed and built for me by von Helmholtz of the Bauhaus. It has been occupied by all my best mediums during their so-called trance states. It was in that chair that I established to my entire satisfaction the real existence of ectoplasm—that elaboration of the mucous membrane and occasionally the entire epidermis that is distantly analogous to the birth envelope and is the fact behind the persisted legends of the snake-shedding of filmy live skins by human beings, and which the spiritualist quacks are forever trying to fake with their fluorescent cheesecloth and doctored negatives. Orgone, the primal sexual energy?—Reich makes a persuasive case, still... But ectoplasm?—yes! Angna went into trance sitting just where you are, her entire body dusted with a special powder, the tracks and distant smudges of which later revealed the ectoplasm's movements and origin—chiefly in the genital area. The test was conclusive and led to further researches, very interesting and quite revolutionary, none of which I have published; my professional colleagues froth at the mouth, elaborating an opposite sort of foam, whenever I mix the psychic with psychoanalysis—they seem to forget that hypnotism gave Freud his start and that for a time the man was keen on cocaine. Yes indeed, an historic chair."

I naturally looked down at it and for a moment I thought I had vanished, because I couldn't see my legs. Then I realized that the upholstery had changed to a dark gray exactly matching my suit except for the ends of the arms, which merged by fine gradations into a sallow hue which blotted out my hands.

"I should have warned you that it's now upholstered in chameleon plastic," Slyker said with a grin. "It changes color to suit the sitter. The fabric was supplied me over a year ago by Henri Artois, the French dilettante chemist. So the chair has been many shades: dead black when Mrs. Fairlee—you recall the case?—came to tell me she had just put on mourning and then shot her bandleader husband, a charming Florida tan during the later experiments with Angna. It helps my patients forget themselves when they're free-associating and it amuses some people." I wasn't one of them, but I managed a smile I hoped wasn't too sour. I told myself to stick to business—Evelyn Cordew's and Jeff Crain's business. I must forget the chair and other incidentials, and concentrate on Dr. Emil Slyker and what he was saying—for I have by no means given all of his remarks, only the more important asides. He had turned out to be the sort of conversationalist who will talk for two hours solid, then when you have barely started your reply, give you a hurt look and say, "Excuse me, but if I can get a word in edgewise—" and talk for two hours more. The liquor may have been helping, but I doubt it. When we had left the Countersign Club he had started to tell me the stories of three of his female clients—a surgeon's wife, an aging star scared by a comeback opportunity, and a college girl in trouble—and the presence of the bodyguard hadn't made him hold back on gory details.

Now, sitting at his desk and playing with the catch of a file drawer as if wondering whether to open it, he had got to the point where the surgeon's wife had arrived at the operating theater early one morning to publish her infidelities, the star had stabbed her press agent with the wardrobe mistress' scissors, and the college girl had fallen in love with her abortionist. He had the conversation-hogger's trick of keeping a half dozen topics in the air at once and weaving back and forth between them without finishing any.

And of course he was a male tantalizer. Now he whipped open the file drawer and scooped out some folders and then held them against his belly and watched me as if to ask himself, "Should I?"

After a maximum pause to build suspense he decided he should, and so I began to hear the story of Dr. Emil Slyker's girls, not the first three, of course—they had to stay frozen at their climaxes unless their folders turned up—but others.

I wouldn't be telling the truth if I didn't admit it was a let-down. Here I was expecting I don't know what from his desk and all I got was the usual glimpses into childhood's garden of father-fixation and sibling rivalry and the bed-changing *Sturm und Drang* of later-adolescence. The folders seemed to hold nothing but conventional medico-psychiatric case histories, along with physical measurements and other details of appearance, unusually penetrating précis of each client's financial resources, occasional notes on possible psychic gifts and other extrasensory talents, and maybe some candid snapshots, judging from the way he'd sometimes pause to study appreciatively and then raise his eyebrows at me with a smile.

Yet after a while I couldn't help starting to be impressed, if only by the sheer numbers. Here was this stream, this freshet, this flood of females, young and not-so-young, all thinking of themselves as girls and wearing the girl's suede mask even if they didn't still have the girl's natural face, all converging on Dr. Slyker's office with money stolen from their parents or highjacked from their married lovers, or paid when they signed the six-year contract with semiannual options, or held out on their syndicate boyfriends, or received in a lump sum in lieu of alimony, or banked for dreary years every fortnight from paychecks and then withdrawn in one grand gesture, or thrown at them by their husbands that morning like so much confetti, or, so help me, advanced them on their half-written novels. Yes, there was something very impressive about this pink stream of womankind rippling with the silver and green of cash conveyed infallibly, as if all the corridors and streets outside were concrete-walled spill-ways, to Dr. Slyker's office, but not to work any dynamos there except financial ones, instead to be worked over by a one-man dynamo and go foaming madly or trickling depletedly away or else stagnate excitingly for months, their souls like black swamp water gleaming with mysterious lights.

Slyker stopped short with a harsh little laugh. "We ought to have music with this, don't you think?" he said. "I believe I've got the *Nutcracker Suite* on the spindle," and he touched one of an unobtrusive bank of buttons on his desk.

They came without the whisper of a turntable or the faintest preliminary susurrus of tape, those first evocative, rich, sensual, yet eery chords, but they weren't the opening of any section of the *Nutcracker* I knew—and yet, damn it, they sounded as if they should be. And then they were cut off as if the tape had been snipped and I looked at Slyker and he was white and one of his hands was just coming back from the bank of buttons and the other was clutching the file folders as if they might somehow get away from him and both hands were shaking and I felt a shiver crawling down my own neck.

"Excuse me, Carr," he said slowly, breathing heavily, "but that's high-voltage music, psychically very dangerous, that I use only for special purposes. It is part of the *Nutcracker*, incidentally—the 'Ghost-girls Pavan' which Tchaikovsky suppressed completely under orders from Madam Sesostris, the Saint Petersburg clairvoyant. It was tape-recorded for me by...no, I don't know you quite well enough to tell you that. However, we will shift from tape to disk and listen to the known sections of the suite, played by the same artists."

I don't know how much this recording or the circumstances added to it, but I have never heard the "Danse Arabe" or the "Waltz of the Flowers" or the "Dance of the Flutes" so voluptuous and exquisitely menacing—those tinkling, superficially sugar-frosted bits of music that class after class of little-girl ballerinas have minced and teetered to ad nauseam, but underneath the glittering somber fancies of a thorough-going eroticist. As Slyker, guessing my thoughts, expressed it: "Tchaikovsky shows off each instrument—the flute, the throatier woodwinds, the silver chimes, the harp bubbling gold—as if he were dressing beautiful women in jewels and feathers and furs solely to arouse desire and envy in other men."

For of course we only listened to the music as background for Dr. Slyker's zigzagging, fragmentary, cream-skimming reminiscences. The stream of girls flowed on in their smart suits and flowered dresses and bouffant blouses and toreador pants, their improbable loves and unsus-pected hates and incredible ambitions, the men who gave them money, the men who gave them love, the men who took both, the paralyzing triv-ial fears behind their wisely chic or corn-fed fresh facades, their ravishing and infuriating mannerisms, the trick of eye or lip or hair or wrist-curve or bosom-angle that was the focus of sex in each.

For Slyker could bring his girls to life very vividly, I had to grant that, as if he had more to jog his memory than case histories and notes and even photographs, as if he had the essence of each girl stoppered up in a little bottle, like perfume, and was opening them one by one to give me a whiff. Gradually I became certain that there were more than papers and pictures in the folders, though this revelation, like the earlier one about the desk, at first involved a let-down. Why should I get excited if Dr. Slyker filed away mementos of his clients?—even if they were keepsakes of love: lace handkerchiefs and filmy scarves, faded flowers, ribbons and bows, 20-denier stockings, long locks of hair, gay little pins and combs, swatches of material that might have been torn from dresses, snippets of silk delicate as ghost dandelions—what difference did it make to me if he treasured this junk or it fed his sense of power or was part of his blackmail? Yet it did make a difference to me for, like the music, like the little fearful starts he'd kept giving ever since the business of the "Ghost-girls Pavan," it helped to make everything very real, as if in some more-than-ordinary sense he did have a deskful of girls. For now as he opened or closed the folders there'd often be a puff of powder, a pale little cloud as from a jogged compact, and the pieces of silk gave the impression of being larger than they could be, like a magician's colored handkerchiefs, only most of them were flesh-colored, and I began to get glimpses of what looked like X-ray photographs and artist's transparencies, maybe lifesize but cunningly folded, and other slack pale things that made me think of the ultra-fine rubber masks some aging actresses are rumored to wear, and all sorts of strange little flashes and glimmers of I don't know what, except there was that aura of femininity and I found myself remembering what he'd said about fluorescent cheesecloth and I did seem to get whiffs of very individual perfume with each new folder. He had two file drawers

[132]

open now, and I could just make out the word burnt into their fronts. The word certainly looked like PRESENT, and there were two of the closed file drawers labeled what looked like PAST and FUTURE. I didn't know what sort of hocus-pocus was supposed to be furthered by those words, but along with Slyker's darting, lingering monologue they did give me the feeling that I was afloat in a river of girls from all times and places, and the illusion that there somehow was a girl in each folder became so strong that I almost wanted to say, "Come on, Emil, trot 'em out, let me look at 'em."

He must have known exactly what feelings he was building up in me, for now he stopped in the middle of a saga of a starlet married to a Negro baseball player and looked at me with his eyes open a bit too wide and said, "All right, Carr, let's quit fooling around. Down at the Countersign I told you I had a deskful of girls and I wasn't kidding—although the truth behind that assertion would get me certified by all the little headshrinkers and Viennese windbags except it would scare the pants off them first. I mentioned ectoplasm earlier, and the proof of its reality. It's exuded by most properly stimulated women in deep trance, but it's not just some dimly fluorescent froth swirling around in a dark séance chamber. It takes the form of an envelope or limp balloon, closed toward the top but open toward the bottom, weighing less than a silk stocking but duplicating the person exactly down to features and hair, following the master-plan of the body's surface buried in the genetic material of the cells. It is a real shed skin but also dimly alive, a gossamer mannequin. A breath can crumple it, a breeze can whisk it away, but under some circumstances it becomes startlingly stable and resilient, a real apparition. It's invisible and almost impalpable by day, but by night, when your eyes are properly accommodated, you can just manage to see it. Despite its fragility it's almost indestructible, except by fire, and potentially immortal. Whether generated in sleep or under hypnosis, in spontaneous or induced trance, it remains connected to the source by a thin strand I call the 'umbilicus' and it returns to the source and is absorbed back into the individual again as the trance fades. But sometimes it becomes detached and then it lingers around as a shell, still dimly alive and occasionally glimpsed, forming the very real basis for the stories of hauntings we have from all centuries and cultures—in fact, I call such shells 'ghosts.' A strong emotional shock generally accounts for a ghost becoming detached from its owner, but it can also be detached artificially. Such a ghost is remarkably docile to one who understands how to handle and cherish it—for instance, it can be folded into an incredibly small compass and tucked away in an envelope, though by daylight you wouldn't notice anything in such an envelope if you looked inside. 'Detached artificially' I said, and that's what I do here in this office, and you know what I use to do it with, Carr?" He snatched

[133]

up something long and daggerlike and gleaming and held it tight in his plump hand so that it pointed at the ceiling. "Silver shears, Carr, silver for the same reason you use a silver bullet to kill a werewolf, though those words would set the little head-shrinkers howling. But would they be howling from outraged scientific attitude, Carr, or from professional jealousy or simply from fear? Just the same as its unclear why they'd be howling, only certain they would be howling. If I told them that in every fourth or fifth folder in these files I have one or more ghostgirls."

He didn't need to mention fear—I was scared enough myself now, what with him spouting this ghost-guff, this spiritualism blather put far more precisely than any spiritualist would dare, this obviously firmly held and elaborately rationalized delusion, this perfect symbolization of a truly insane desire for power over women—filing them away in envelopes!—and then when he got bug-eyed and brandished those foot-long stilletto-shears...Jeff Crain had warned me Slyker was "nuts—brilliant, but completely nuts and definitely dangerous," and I hadn't believed it, hadn't really visualized myself frozen on the medium's throne, locked in ("no one without explosives") with the madman himself. It cost me a lot of effort to keep on the acolyte's mask and simper adoringly at the Master.

My attitude still seemed to be fooling him, though he was studying me in a funny way, for he went on, "All right, Carr, I'll show you the girls, or at least one, though we'll have to put out all the lights after a bit—that's why I keep the window shuttered so tightly—and wait for our eyes to accommodate. But which one should it be?—we have a large field of choice. I think since it's your first and probably your last, it should be someone out of the ordinary, don't you think, someone who's just a little bit special? Wait a second—I know." And his hand shot under the desk where it must have touched a hidden button, for a shallow drawer shot out from a place where there didn't seem to be room for one. He took from it a single fat file folder that had been stored flat and laid it on his knees.

Then he began to talk again in his reminiscing voice and damn if it wasn't so cool and knowing that it started to pull me back toward the river of girls and set me thinking that this man wasn't really crazy, only extremely eccentric, maybe the eccentricity of genius, maybe he actually had hit on a hitherto unknown phenomenon depending on the more obscure properties of mind and matter, describing it to me in whimsically florid jargon, maybe he really had discovered something in one of the blind spots of modern science-and-psychology's picture of the universe.

"Stars, Carr. Female stars. Movie queens. Royal princess of the gray world, the ghostly chiaroscuro. Shadow empress. They're realer than people, Carr, realer than the great actresses or casting-couch champions they start as, for they're symbols. Carr, symbols of our deepest longings and—yes—most hidden fears and secretest dreams. Each decade has several who achieve this more-than-life and less-than-life existence, but there's generally one who's the chief symbol, the top ghost, the dream who lures men along toward fulfillment and destruction. In the Twenties it was Garbo, Garbo the Free Soul—that's my name for the symbol she became; her romantic mask heralded the Great Depression. In the late Thirties and early Forties it was Bergman the Brave Liberal; her dewiness and Swedish-Modern smile helped us accept World War Two. And now it's— "he touched the bulky folder on his knees—"now it's Evelyn Cordew the Good-Hearted Bait, the gal who accepts her troublesome sexiness with a resigned shrug and a foolish little laugh, and what general catastrophe she foreshadows we don't know yet. But here she is, and in five ghost versions. Pleased, Carr?"

I was so completely taken by surprise that I couldn't say anything for a moment. Either Slyker had guessed my real purpose in contacting him, or I was faced with a sizeable coincidence. I wet my lips and then just nodded.

Slyker studied me and finally grinned. "Ah," he said, "takes you aback a bit, doesn't it? I perceive that in spite of your moderate sophistication you are one of the millions of males who have wistfully contemplated desert-islanding with Delectable Evvie. A complex cultural phenomenon, Eva-Lynn Korduplewski. The child of a coal miner, educated solely in backstreet movie houses—shaped by dreams, you see, into a master dream, an empress dream-figure. A hysteric, Carr, in fact the most classic example I have ever encountered, with unequaled mediumistic capacities and also with a hypertrophied and utterly ruthless ambition. Riddled by hypochondrias, but with more real drive than a million other avid school-girls tangled and trapped in the labyrinth of film ambitions. Dumb as they come, no rational mind at all, but with ten times Einstein's intuition—intuition enough, at least, to realize that the symbol our sex-exploiting culture craved was a girl who accepted like a happy martyr the incandescent sexuality men and Nature forced on her—and with the patience and malleability to let the feathersoft beating of the black-and-white light in a cheap cinema shape her into that symbol. I sometimes think of her as a girl in a cheap dress standing on the shoulder of a big throughway, her eyes almost blinded by the lights of an approaching bus. The bus stops and she climbs on, dragging a pet goat and breathlessly giggling explanations at the driver. The bus is Civilization.

"Everybody knows her life story, which has been put out in a surprisingly accurate form up to a point: her burlesque-line days, the embarrassingly faithful cartoon-series *Girl in a Fix* for which she posed, her hit parts, the amazingly timed success of the movies *Hydrogen Blonde*

[135]

and *The Jean Harlow Saga*, her broken marriage to Jeff Crain—What was that, Carr? Oh, I thought you'd started to say something—and her hunger for the real stage and intellectual distinction and power. You can't imagine how hungry for brains and power that girl became after she hit the top.

"I've been part of the story of that hunger, Carr, and I pride myself that I've done more to satisfy it than all the culture-johnnies she's had on her payroll. Evelyn Cordew has learned a lot about herself right where you're sitting, and also threaded her way past two psychotic crack-ups. The trouble is that when her third loomed up she didn't come to me, she decided to put her trust in wheat germ and yogurt instead, so now she hates my guts—and perhaps her own, on that diet. She's made two attempts on my life, Carr, and had me trailed by gangsters...and by other individuals. She's talked about me to Jeff Crain, whom she still sees from time to time, and Jerry Smyslov and Nick De Grazia, telling them I've got a file of information on her burlesque days and a few of her later escapades, including some interesting photostats and the real dope on her income and her tax returns, and that I'm using it to blackmail her white. What she actually wants is her five ghosts back, and I can't give them to her because they might kill her. Yes, kill her, Carr." He flourished the shears for emphasis. "She claims that the ghosts I've taken from her have made her lose weight permanently—'look like a skeleton' are her words—and given her fits of mental blackout, a sort of psychic fading—whereas actually the ghosts have bled from her a lot of malignant thoughts and destructive emotions, which could literally kill her (or someone!) if reabsorbed—they're drenched with death-wish. Still, I hear she actually does look a little haggard, a trifle faded, in her last film, in spite of all Hollywood's medico-cosmetic lore, so maybe she has a sort of case against me. I haven't seen the film, I suppose you have. What do you think, Carr?"

I knew I'd been overworking the hesitation and the silent flattery, so I whipped out quickly, "I'd say it was due to her anemia. It seems to me that the anemia is quite enough to account for her loss of weight and her tired look."

"Ah! You've slipped, Carr," he lashed back, pointing at me triumphantly, except that instead of the outstretched finger there were those ridiculous, horrible shears. "Her anemia is one of the things that's been kept top-secret, known only to a very few of her intimates. Even in all the half-humorous releases about her hypochondrias that's one disease that has never been mentioned. I suspected you were from her when I got your note at the Countersign Club—the handwriting squirmed with tension and secrecy—but the *Justine* amused me—that was a fairly smart dodge—and your sorcerer's apprentice act amused me too, and I hap-

[136]

pened to feel like talking. But I've been studying you all along, especially your reactions to certain test-remarks I dropped in from time to time, and now you've really slipped." His voice was loud and clear, but he was shaking and giggling at the same time and his eyes showed white all the way around the irises. He drew back the shears a little, but clenched his fingers more tightly around them in a dagger grip, as he said with a chuckle, "Our dear little Evvie has sent all types up against me, to bargain for her ghosts or try to scare or assassinate me, but this is the first time she's sent an idealistic fool. Carr, why didn't you have the sense not to meddle?"

"Look here, Dr. Slyker," I countered before he started answering for me, "it's true I have a special purpose in contacting you. I never denied it. But I don't know anything about ghosts or gangsters. I'm here on a simple, businesslike assignment from the same guy who lent me the *Justine* and who has no purpose whatever beyond protecting Evelyn Cordew. I'm representing Jeff Crain."

That was supposed to calm him. Well, he did stop shaking and his eyes stopped wandering, but only because they were going over me like twin searchlights, and the giggle went out of his voice.

"Jeff Crain! Evvie just wants to murder me, but that cinematic Hemingway, that hulking guardian of hers, that human Saint Bernard tonguing the dry crumbs of their marriage—he wants to set the T-men on me, and the boys in blue and the boys in white too. Evvie's agents I mostly kid along, even the gangsters, but for Jeff s agents I have only one answer."

The silver shears pointed straight at my chest and I could see his muscles tighten like a fat tiger's. I got ready for a spring of my own at the first movement this madman made toward me.

But the move he made was back across the desk with his free hand. I decided it was a good time to be on my feet in any case, but just as I sent my own muscles their orders I was hugged around the waist and clutched by the throat and grabbed by the wrists and ankles. By something soft but firm.

I looked down. Padded, broad, crescent-shaped clamps had sprung out of hidden traps in my chair and now held me as comfortably but firmly as a gang of competent orderlies. Even my hands were held by wide, velvet-soft cuffs that had snapped out of the bulbous arms. They were all a nondescript gray but even as I looked they began to change color to match my suit or skin, whichever they happened to border.

I wasn't scared. I was merely frightened half to death.

"Surprised, Carr? You shouldn't be." Slyker was sitting back like an amiable schoolteacher and gently wagging the shears as if they were a ruler. "Streamlined unobtrusiveness and remote control are the essence

[137]

of our times, especially in medical furniture. The buttons on my desk can do more than that. Hypos might slip out—hardly hygenic, but then germs are overrated. Or electrodes for shock. You see, restraints are necessary in my business. Deep mediumistic trance can occasionally produce convulsions as violent as those of electroshock, especially when a ghost is cut. And I sometimes administer electroshock too, like any garden-variety headshrinker. Also to be suddenly and firmly grabbed is a profound stimulus to the unconscious and often elicits closely-guarded facts from difficult patients. So a means of making my patients hold still is absolutely necessary—something swift, sure, tasteful and preferably without warning. You'd be surprised, Carr, at the situations in which I've been forced to activate those restraints. This time I prodded you to see just how dangerous you were. Rather to my surprise you showed yourself ready to take physical action against me. So I pushed the button. Now we'll be able to deal comfortably with Jeff Crain's problem...and yours. But first I've a promise to keep to you. I said I would show you one of Evelyn Cordew's ghosts. It will take a little time and after a bit it will be necessary to turn out the lights."

"Dr. Slyker," I said as evenly as I could, "I—"

"Quiet! Activating a ghost for viewing involves certain risks. Silence is essential, though it will be necessary to use—very briefly—the suppressed Tchaikovsky music which I turned off so quickly earlier this evening." He busied himself with the hi-fi for a few moments. "But partly because of that it will be necessary to put away all the other folders and the four ghosts of Evvie we aren't using, and lock the file drawers. Otherwise there might be complications."

I decided to try once more. "Before you go any further, Dr. Slyker," I began, "I would really like to explain—"

He didn't say another word, merely reached back across the desk again. My eyes caught something coming over my shoulder fast and the next instant it clapped down over my mouth and nose, not quite covering my eyes, but lapping up to them—something soft and dry and clinging and faintly crinkled feeling. I gasped and I could feel the gag sucking in, but not a bit of air came through it. That scared me seven-eights of the rest of the way to oblivion, of course, and I froze. Then I tried a very cautious inhalation and a little air did seep through. It was wonderfully cool coming into the furnace of my lungs, that little suck of air—I felt I hadn't breathed for a week. Slyker looked at me with a little smile. "I never say 'Quiet' twice, Carr. The foam plastic of that gag is another of Henri Artois' inventions. It consists of millions of tiny valves. As long as you breathe softly—very, very softly, Carr—they permit ample air to pass, but if you gasp or try to shout through it, they'll close up tight. A wonderfully soothing device. Compose yourself, Carr; your life depends on it."

I have never experienced such utter helplessness. I found that the slightest muscular tension, even crooking a finger, made my breathing irregular enough so that the valves started to close and I was in the fringes of suffocation. I could see and hear what was going on, but I dared not react, I hardly dared think. I had to pretend that most of my body wasn't there (the chameleon plastic helped), only a pair of lungs working constantly but with infinite caution.

Slyker had just set the Cordew folder back in its drawer, without closing it, and started to gather up the other scattered folders, when he touched the desk again and the lights went out. I have mentioned that the place was completely sealed against light. The darkness was complete.

"Don't be alarmed, Carr," Slyker's voice came chuckling through it. "In fact, as I am sure you realize, you had better not be. I can tidy up just as handily—working by touch is one of my major skills, my sight and hearing being rather worse than appears—and even your eyes must be fully accommodated if you're to see anything at all. I repeat, don't be alarmed, Carr, least of all by ghosts."

I would never have expected it, but in spite of the spot I was in (which actually did seem to have its soothing effects), I still got a little kick—a very little one—out of thinking I was going to see some sort of secret vision of Evelyn Cordew, real in some sense or faked by a master faker. Yet at the same time, and I think beyond all my fear for myself, I felt a dispassionate disgust at the way Slyker reduced all human drives and desires to a lust for power, of which the chair imprisoning me, the "Siegfried Line" door, and the files of ghosts, real or imagined, were perfect symbols.

Among immediate worries, although I did a pretty good job of suppressing all of them, the one that nagged at me the most was that Slyker had admitted to me the inadequacy of his two major senses. I didn't think he would make that admission to someone who was going to live very long.

The black minutes dragged on. I heard from time to time the rustle of folders, but only one soft thud of a file drawer closing, so I knew he wasn't finished yet with the putting-away and locking-up job.

I concentrated the free corner of my mind—the tiny part I dared spare from breathing—on trying to hear something else, but I couldn't even catch the background noise of the city. I decided the office must be soundproofed as well as light-sealed. Not that it mattered, since I couldn't get a signal out anyway.

Then a noise did come—a solid snap that I'd heard just once before, but knew instantly. It was the sound of the bolts in the office door

[139]

retracting. There was something funny about it that took me a moment to figure out: there had been no preliminary grating of the key.

For a moment too I thought Slyker had crept noiselessly to the door, but then I realized that the rustling of folders at the desk had kept up all the time.

And the rustling of folders continued. I guessed Slyker had not noticed the door. He hadn't been exaggerating about his bad hearing.

There was the faint creaking of the hinges, once, twice—as if the door were being opened and closed-then again the solid snap of the bolts. That puzzled me, for there should have been a big flash of light from the corridor—unless the lights were all out.

I couldn't hear any sound after that, except the continued rustling of the file folders, though I listened as hard as the job of breathing let me—and in a crazy kind of way the job of cautious breathing helped my hearing, because it made me hold absolutely still yet without daring to tense up. I knew that someone was in the office with us and that Slyker didn't know it. The black moments seemed to stretch out forever, as if an edge of eternity had got hooked into our timestream.

All of a sudden there was a swish, like that of a sheet being whipped through the air very fast, and a grunt of surprise from Slyker that started toward a screech and then was cut off as sharp as if he'd been gagged nose-and-mouth like me. Then there came the scuff of feet and the squeal of the castors of a chair, the sound of a struggle, not of two people struggling, but of a man struggling against restraints of some sort, a frantic confined heaving and panting. I wondered if Slyker's little lump of chair had sprouted restraints like mine, but that hardly made sense.

Then abruptly there was the whistle of breath, as if his nostrils had been uncovered, but not his mouth. He was panting through his nose. I got a mental picture of Slyker tied to his chair some way and eying the darkness just as I was doing.

Finally out of the darkness came a voice I knew very well because I'd heard it often enough in movie houses and from Jeff Crain's tape-recorder. It had the old familiar caress mixed with the old familiar giggle, the naiveté and the knowingness, the warm sympathy and cool-headedness, the high-school charmer and the sybil. It was Evelyn Cordew's voice, all right.

"Oh for goodness sake stop threshing around, Emmy. It won't help you shake off that sheet and it makes you look so funny. Yes, I said 'look,' Emmy—you'd be surprised at how losing five ghosts improves your eyesight, like having veils taken away from in front of them; you get more sensitive all over.

"And don't try to appeal to me by pretending to suffocate. I tucked the sheet under your nose even if I did keep your mouth covered. Couldn't bear you talking now. The sheet's called wraparound plastic—I've got my chemical friend too, though he's not Parisian. It'll be next years number-one packaging material, he tells me. Filmy, harder to see than cellophane, but very tough. An electronic plastic, no less, positive one side, negative the other. Just touch it to something and it wraps around, touches itself, and clings like anything. Like I just had to touch it to you. To make it unwrap fast you can just shoot some electrons into if from a handy static battery—my friend's advertising copy, Emmy—and it flattens out whang. Give it enough electrons and its stronger than steel."

"We used another bit of it that last way, Emmy, to get through your door. Fitted it outside, so it'd wrap itself against the bolts when your door opened. Then just now, after blacking out the corridor, we pumped electrons into it and it flattened out, pushing back all the bolts. Excuse me, dear, but you know how you love to lecture about your valved plastics and all your other little restraints, so you mustn't mind me giving a little talk about mine. And boasting about my friends too. I've got some you don't know about, Emmy. Ever heard the name Smyslov, or the Arain? Some of them cut ghosts themselves and weren't pleased to hear about you, especially the past-future angle."

There was a protesting little squeal of castors, as if Slyker were trying to move his chair. "Don't go away, Emmy. I'm sure you know why I'm here. Yes, dear, I'm taking them all back as of now. All five. And I don't care how much death-wish they got, because I've got some ideas for that. So now 'scuse me, Emmy, while I get ready to slip into my ghosts."

There wasn't any noise then except Emil Slyker's wheezy breathing and the occasional rustle of silk and the whir of a zipper, followed by soft feathery falls.

"There we are, Emmy, all clear. Next step, my five lost sisters. Why, your little old secret drawer is open—you didn't think I knew about that, Emmy, did you? Lets see now, I don't think we'll need music for this—they know my touch; it should make them stand up and shine."

She stopped talking. After a bit I got the barest hint of light over by the desk, very uncertain at first, like a star at the limit of vision, where it keeps winking back and forth from utter absence to the barest dim existence, or like a lonely lake lit only by starlight and glimpsed through a thick forest, or as if those dancing points of light that persist even in absolute darkness and indicate only a restless retina and optic nerve had fooled me for a moment into thinking they represented something real.

But then the hint of light took definite form, though staying at the dim limit of vision and crawling back and forth as I focused on it because my eyes had no other point of reference to steady it by.

[141]

It was a dim angular band making up three edges of a rectangle, the top edge longer than the two vertical edges, while the bottom edge wasn't there. As I watched it and it became a little clearer, I saw that the bands of light were brightest toward the inside—that is, toward the rectangle they partly enclosed, where they were bordered by stark blackness—while toward the outside they faded gradually away. Then as I continued to watch I saw that the two corners were rounded while up from the top edge there projected a narrow, lesser rectangle—a small tab. The tab made me realize that I was looking at a file folder silhouetted by something dimly glowing inside it.

Then the top band darkened toward the center, as would happen if a hand were dipping into the folder, and then lightened again as if the hand were being withdrawn. Then up out of the folder, as if the invisible hand were guiding or coaxing it, swam something no brighter than the bands of light.

It was the shape of a woman, but distorted and constantly flowing,the head and arms and upper torso maintaining more of an approximation to human proportions than the lower torso and legs, which were like churning, trailing draperies or a long gauzy skirt. It was extremely dim, so I had to keep blinking my eyes, and it didn't get brighter.

It was like the figure of a woman phosphorescently painted on a long-skirted slip of the flimsiest silk that had silk-stocking-like sheaths for arms and head attached—yes, and topped by some illusion of dim silver hair. And yet it was more than that. Although it looped up gracefully through the air as such a slip might when shaken out by a woman preparing to put it on, it also had a writhing life of its own.

But in spite of all the distortions, as it flowed in an arc toward the ceiling and dove downward, it was seductively beautiful and the face was recognizably that of Evvie Cordew.

It checked its dive and reversed the direction of its flow, so that for a moment it floated upright high in the air, like a filmy nightgown a woman swishes above her head before she slips into it.

Then it began to settle toward the floor and I saw that there really was a woman standing under it and pulling it down over her head, though I could see her body only very dimly by the reflected glow of the ghost she was drawing down around her.

The woman on the floor shot up her hands close to her body and gave a quick wriggle and twist and ducked her head and then threw it back, as a woman does when she's getting into a tight dress, and the flowing glowing thing lost its distortions as it fitted itself around her.

Then for a moment the glow brightened a trifle as the woman and her ghost merged and I saw Evvie Cordew with her flesh gleaming by its own light—the long slim ankles, the vase-curve of hips and waist, the impudent breasts almost as you'd guess them from the bikini shots, but with larger aureoles—saw it for an instant before the ghostlight winked out like white sparks dying, and there was utter darkness again.

Utter darkness and a voice that crooned, "Oh that was like silk, Emmy, pure silk stocking all over. Do you remember when you cut it, Emmy? I'd just got my first screen credit and I'd signed the seven-year contract and I knew I was going to have the world by the tail and I felt wonderful and I suddenly got terribly dizzy for no reason and I came to you. And you straightened me out for then by coaxing out and cutting away my happiness. You told me it would be a little like giving blood, and it was. That was my first ghost, Emmy, but only the first."

My eyes, recovering swiftly from the brighter glow of the ghost returning to its sources, again made out the three glowing sides of the file folder. And again there swam up out of it a crazily churning phosphorescent woman trailing gauzy streamers. The face was recognizably Evvie's, but constantly distorting, now one eye big as an orange then small as a pea, the lips twisting in impossible smiles and grimaces, the brow shrinking to that of a pinhead or swelling to that of a Mongolian idiot, like a face reflected from a plate-glass window running with water. As it came down over the real Evelyn's face there was a moment when the two were together but didn't merge, like the faces of twins in such a flooded window. Then, as if a squeegee had been wiped down it, the single face came bright and clear, and just as the darkness returned she caressed her lips with her tongue.

And I heard her say, "That one was like hot velvet, Emmy, smooth but with a burn in it. You took it two days after the sneak preview of *Hydrogen Blonde*, when we had the little party to celebrate after the big party, and the current Miss America was there and I showed her what a really valuable body looked like. That was when I realized that I'd hit the top and it hadn't changed me into a goddess or anything. I still had the same ignorances as before and the same awkwardnesses for the cameramen and cutters to hide—only they were worse because I was in the center of the show window—and I was going to have to fight for the rest of my life to keep my body like it was and then I was going to start to die, wrinkle by wrinkle, lose my juice cell by cell, like anybody else."

The third ghost arched toward the ceiling and down, waves of phosphorescence flickering it all the time. The slender arms undulated like pale serpents and the hands, the finger- and thumb-tips gently pressed together, were like the inquisitive heads of serpents—until the fingers spread so the hands resembled five-tongued creeping puddles of phosphorescent ink. Then into them as if into shoulder-length ivory silk gloves came the solid fingers and arms. For a bit the hands, first part to be merged, were brightest of the whole figure and I watched them help fit

[143]

each other on and then sweep symmetrically down brow and cheeks and chin, fitting the face, with a little sidewise dip of the ring fingers as they smoothed in the eyes. Then they swept up and back and raked through both heads of hair, mixing them. This ghost's hair was very dark and, mingling, it toned down Evelyn's blonde a little.

"That one felt slimy, Emmy, like the top crawled off of a swamp. Remember, I'd just teased the boys into fighting over me at the Troc. Jeff hurt Lester worse than they let out and even old Sammy got a black eye. I'd just discovered that when you get to the top you have all the ordinary pleasures the boobs yearn for all their lives, and they don't mean anything, and you have to work and scheme every minute to get the pleasures beyond pleasure that you've got to have to keep your life from going dry."

The fourth ghost rose toward the ceiling like a diver paddling up from the depths. Then, as if the whole room were filled with its kind of water, it seemed to surface at the ceiling and jackknife there and plunge down again with a little swoop and then reverse direction again and hover for a moment over the real Evelyn's head and then sink slowly down around her like a diver drowning. This time I watched the bright hands cupping the ghost's breasts around her own as if she were putting on a luminescent net brassiere. Then the ghost's filminess shrank suddenly to tighten over her torso like a cheap cotton dress in a cloud-burst.

As the glow died to darkness a fourth time, Evelyn said softly, "Ah but that was cool, Emmy. I'm shivering. I'd just come back from my first location work in Europe and was sick to get at Broadway, and before you cut it you made me relive the yacht party where I overheard Ricco and the author laughing at how I'd messed up my first legitimate play reading, and we swam in the moonlight and Monica almost drowned. That was when I realized that nobody, even the bottom boobs in the audience, really respected you because you were their sex queen. They respected the little female boob in the seat beside them more than they did you. Because you were just something on the screen that they could handle as they pleased inside their minds. With the top folk, the Big Timers, it wasn't any better.

To them you were just a challenge, a prize, something to show off to other men to drive them nuts, but never something to love. Well, that's four, Emmy, and four and one makes all."

The last ghost rose whirling and billowing like a silk robe in the wind, like a crazy photomontage, like a surrealist painting done in a barely visible wash of pale flesh tones on a black canvas, or rather like an endless series of such surrealist paintings, each distortion melting into the next—trailing behind it a gauzy wake of draperies which I realized was the way ghosts were always pictured and described. I watched the draperies bunch as Evelyn pulled them down around her, and then they suddenly whipped tight against her thighs, like a skirt in a strong wind or like nylon clinging in the cold. The final glow was a little stronger, as if there were more life in the shining woman than there had been at first.

"Ah that was like the brush of wings, Emmy, like feathers in the wind. You cut it after the party in Sammy's plane to celebrate me being the top money star in the industry. I bothered the pilot because I wanted him to smash us in a dive. That was when I realized I was just property— something for men to make money out of (and me to make money, too, out of me) from the star who married me to prop his box-office rating to the sticks theater owner who hoped I'd sell a few extra tickets. I found that my deepest love—it was once for you, Emmy—was just something for a man to capitalize on. That any man, no matter how sweet or strong, could in the end never be anything but a pimp. Like you, Emmy."

Just darkness for a while then, darkness and silence, broken only by the faint rustling of clothing.

Finally her voice again: "So now I got my pictures back, Emmy. All the original negatives, you might say, for you can't make prints of them or second negatives—I don't think. Or is there a way of making prints of them, Emmy—duplicate women? It's not worth letting you answer— you'd be bound to say yes to scare me.

"What do we do with you now, Emmy? I know what you'd do to me if you had the chance, for you've done it already. You've kept parts of me— no, five real mes—tucked away in envelopes for a long time, something to take out and look at or run through your hand or twist around a finger or crumple in a ball, whenever you felt bored on a long afternoon or an endless night. Or maybe show off to special friends or even give other girls to wear—you didn't think I knew about that trick, did you, Emmy?—I hope I poisoned them, I hope I made them burn! Remember, Emmy, I'm full of death-wish now, five ghosts of it. Yes, Emmy, what do we do with you now?"

Then for the first time since the ghosts had shown, I heard the sound of Dr. Slyker's breath whistling through his nose and the muffled grunts and creakings as he lurched against the clinging sheet.

"Makes you think, doesn't it, Emmy? I wish I'd asked my ghosts what to do with you when I had the chance—I wish I'd known how to ask them. They'd have been the ones to decide. Now they're too mixed in.

"We'll let the other girls decide—the other ghosts. How many dozen are there, Emmy? How many hundred? I'll trust their judgment. Do your ghosts love you, Emmy?"

I heard the click of her heels followed by soft rushes ending in thuds— the file drawers being yanked open. Slyker got noisier.

"You don't think they love you, Emmy? Or they do but their way of showing affection won't be exactly comfortable, or safe? We'll see."

The heels clicked again for a few steps.

"And now, music. The fourth button, Emmy?" There came again those sensual, spectral chords that opened the "Ghostgirls Pavan," and this time they led gradually into a music that seemed to twirl and spin, very slowly and with a lazy grace, the music of space, the music of free fall. It made easier the slow breathing that meant life to me.

I became aware of dim fountains. Each file drawer was outlined by a phosphorescent glow shooting upward.

Over the edge of one drawer a pale hand flowed. It slipped back, but there was another, and another.

The music strengthened, though spinning still more lazily, and out of the phosphorescence-edged parallelogram of the file drawers there began to pour, swiftly now, pale streams of womankind. Ever-changing faces that were gossamer masks of madness, drunkenness, desire and hate; arms like a flood of serpents; bodies that writhed, convulsed, yet flowed like milk by moonlight.

They swirled out in a circle like slender clouds in a ring, a spinning circle that dipped close to me, inquisitively, a hundred strangely slitted eyes seeming to peer.

The spinning forms brightened. By their light I began to see Dr. Slyker, the lower part of his face tight with the transparent plastic, only the nostrils flaring and the bulging eyes switching their gaze about, his arms tight to his sides.

The first spiral of the ring speeded up and began to tighten around his head and neck. He was beginning to twirl slowly on his tiny chair, as if he were a fly caught in the middle of a web and being spun in a cocoon by the spider. His face was alternately obscured and illuminated by the bright smoky forms swinging past it. It looked as if he was being strangled by his own cigarette smoke in a film run backwards.

His face began to darken as the glowing circle tightened against him.

Once more there was utter darkness.

Then a whirring click and a tiny shower of sparks, three times repeated, then a tiny blue flame. It moved and stopped and moved, leaving behind it more silent tiny flames, yellow ones. They grew. Evelyn was systematically setting fire to the files.

I knew it might be curtains for me, but I shouted—it came out as a kind of hiccup—and my breath was instantly cut off as the valves in the gag closed.

But Evelyn turned. She had been bending close over Emil's chest and the light from the growing flames highlighted her smile. Through the dark red mist that was closing in on my vision I saw the flames begin

[146]

to leap from one drawer after another. There was a sudden low roar, like film or acetate shavings burning.

Suddenly Evelyn reached across the desk and touched a button. As I started to red out, I realized that the gag was off, the clamps were loose.

I floundered to my feet, pain stabbing my numbed muscles. The room was full of flickering brightness under a dirty cloud bulging from the ceiling. Evelyn had jerked the transparent sheet off Slyker and was crumpling it up. He started to fall forward, very slowly. Looking at me she said, "Tell Jeff he's dead." But before Slyker hit the floor, she was out the door. I took a step toward Slyker, felt the stinging heat of the flames. My legs were like shaky stilts as I made for the door. As I steadied myself on the jamb I took a last look back, then lurched on.

There wasn't a light in the corridor. The glow of the flames behind me helped a little.

The top of the elevator was dropping out of sight as I reached the shaft. I took the stairs. It was a painful descent. As I trotted out of the building—it was the best speed I could manage—I heard sirens coming. Evelyn must have put in a call—or one of her "friends," though not even Jeff Crain was able to tell me more about them: who her chemist was and who were the Arain—it's an old word for spider, but that leads nowhere. I don't even know how she knew I was working for Jeff; Evelyn Cordew is harder than ever to see and I haven't tried. I don't believe even Jeff' s seen her; though I've sometimes wondered if I wasn't used as a cat's paw.

I'm keeping out of it—just as I left it to the firemen to discover Dr. Emil Slyker "suffocated by smoke" from a fire in his "weird" private office, a fire which it was reported did little more than char the furniture and burn the contents of his files and the tapes of his hi-fi.

I think a little more was burned. When I looked back the last time I saw the Doctor lying in a strait jacket of pale flames. It may have been scattered papers or the electronic plastic. I think it was ghostgirls burning.

Knight to Move

The tall, long-haired girl in the trim olive uniform with the black spiral insignia was tapping very lightly in a dash-dot-dot rhythm on the gallery's golden rail where her elbows rested.

It was her one concession to nervousness. Though Rule Number One of her training had been that even a single such concession can get you killed.

The beautiful hawk face hooded by black bangs searched the golden hall below, where a thousand intelligent beasts from half as many planets were playing chess. The pieces were being moved and the buttons of the time-clocks pressed oftener by tendrils, crablike pincers, and prosthetic devices than by fingers. Dark-clad referees and ushers silently Walked on tentacle tips or soft-shod hooves-or feet—between the tables and among the spectators packed in the stands to either side.

Just an interstellar chess tournament, Swiss system, twenty-four rounds, being conducted on the fifth planet of the star 61 Cygni in the year 5037 A.D., old Earth Time.

Yet inside the girl's mind a muffled alarm bell was ringing, barely in the conscious area.

While outside, a faint whining buzz somewhere far off˜ in the hall reminded her of a wasp in the rafters of the huge dark barn behind the Minnesota farmhouse where she'd been raised. She wondered briefly about the insect life of 61 Cygni 5, then slapped off that train of thought.

First things first!—meaning the alarm bell.

She glanced around the almost empty gallery. At the head of the ramp down to the hall were two robots with a stretcher and a yellow-beaked nurse from a planet of Tau Ceti, who bobbed her red topknot and ruffled her feathers under her white smock. The girl almost smiled-surely chess wasn't that dangerous a game! Still, when a thousand hearts, some old, were pounding with tension...

Only her green eyes moved as she searched out the two players who not only looked human but actually were from Earth—a man and a woman, one currently in thirty-seventh place, still with a chance to end in the money. She felt a small flame of sympathy, but instantly extinguished it.

An agent of the Snakes should never feel sympathy.

Her nervous tapping speeded up as she searched her tidy mind for the cause of her alarm. It did not seem to involve any of the silent furiously thinking beasts, humanoid or inhuman.

Could it be connected with the game of chess itself? With the coming of star-flight, chess had been discovered to exist with almost identical rules on at least half of all intelligent planets, spread by forgotten star-traders, perhaps. There was something about one of the moves in chess...

Under her uniform and lingerie, between her breasts, she felt a large spider moving. No mistaking that quick clingy tread on her naked skin.

She did not flinch. The prickly footsteps were pulses on a narrow metal plate pressing against that sensitive area of her body-pulses which warned of the approach of the body or projection of a friend, a neutral, an unknown, or-in this case-an enemy.

It was a rather common device. For that matter, the being approaching her felt the scaly gliding of a snake high on the inside of his thigh, and he reacted as little.

The girl instantly stopped her dash-dot-dot tapping, although it had been soundless and her other arm had concealed her black-gloved fingers. While watching in the polished black leather of her gauntlet the casual approach of the being along the golden rail, she yawned delicately and tapped her lips with the Cordova-scented-back of her other glove. She knew it was corny, but she loved doing it to enemy agents.

The man stopped a few inches away. He looked twice her age, but fit and youthful. His gray-flecked hair was cut close to his skull. He wore a sharp black uniform with silver insignia that were eight-legged asterisks. He had three times as many silver decorations on his chest as she had black iron ones. To most girls he would have seemed a shining silver knight.

This one ignored his presence. He studied her shoulder-length, gleaming hair, then rested his own arms on the golden rail and gazed down at the chessplayers too. Man and girl were the same height.

"The beasts beat out their brains for an empty title," he murmured.

"It makes me feel delightfully lazy, Erica, sister mine."

"I'd rather you didn't trade on the similarity of our first names, Colonel von Hohenwald," she replied softly.

He shrugged. "Erich von Hohenwald and Erica Weaver—it has always seemed to me a charming coincidence...er," He smiled at her, "...Major. When we meet in the open, in uniform, on a peaceful mission, it seems to me both agreeable and courteous to fraternize. Or sororize? *Geschwis-*

terize? No matter how much throat-cutting in the dark we must do the rest of the time. Now how about a drink?"

"Between Snake and Spider," she answered fiercely, yet still softly and still without looking at him, "there can be nothing but armed truce-with eyes wide open and finger on the trigger!"

The Spiders and the Snakes were the two great warring under-grounds of the Milky Way galaxy. They warred in time, seeking to change the past and future to their advantage, but also in space. Most intelligent planets were infiltrated predominantly by one force or the other, though on some planets, like Earth, they struck a balance and the Unending War was hotter. 61 Cygni 5 was a neutral planet, resembling an open city. Like racketeers turned respectable, the Spiders and Snakes operated here openly-by a mutual agreement which neither side really trusted. Behind the mask of amity, they were competing for such planets; on them the silver asterisk of the Spider and the black spiral of the Snake were recognized, respected, and shunned.

Each underground recruited agents from all times and races—agents who seldom knew the identity of more than a few comrades, a scatter of underlings, and one superior officer. Erica and Erich, though on opposite sides, had both been recruited from Twentieth Century Earth. It was a common experience for an agent to find himself five thousand or many more years in the future, or past. Some agents hated their work, but punishment came swiftly to the traitor or slacker. Others gloried in it.

"*Teufelrot!*—what a murderous slim Amazon you are!" the Spider Colonel commented.

"The Amazons cut off their right breasts to be able to pull their bows to the fullest bend," the Snake Major retorted evenly. "I would do the same if—"

"But—*Gott sei dank!*—you haven't," he cut in. "Erica, they're magnificent! And did they not tauten a trifle when my insignia walked between them? That's where you wear your warning plate, do you not?"

"I hope yours bites you!"

"Don't say it!" he protested. "Then I wouldn't be able to appreciate you with any gusto. Erica, must you hate twenty-four hours a day? It hasn't injured your loveliness yet, not quite, but—"

He laid a scarred hand against her black-gloved one. She snatched it away and sharply slapped his fingers, her face still bland and looking out.

"*Verdammt!*" he cursed lightly, but there was pleasure in his voice.

"My dear green serpent with black fangs, you're much too serious for truce-times. To begin with, you wear too many medals. If I were you, I'd throw away that Ophidian Order of Merit. In fact, if we weren't being watched, I'd rip it off you myself."

"And you with your silver chest-load? Just try it," she breathed, her body poised, her black fingertips hovering on the gold rail.

The other looked oddly, almost worriedly, at her profile, then went on, now banteringly, "My dear Major, how does a firebrand like you—a puritan, yes, but a firebrand also—manage, without going crazy from boredom, to endure *this*?" He spread the fingers of one hand toward the floor below. Played at fifteen moves an hour, chess is a slow game. Not a piece was grasped-by tentacle or other member—not a button was pressed while his fingers stayed out-spread. "And it goes on for a month!" he finished. Then his voice became elaborately sardonic. "For refreshment do you perhaps visit the Rose Hall, where the great bridge tournament is in progress? Or do you recruit your patience in the Black Hall, where they endlessly play that peculiarly intricate Centaurian backgammon?"

"I dislike bridge, I can barely tolerate chess, backgammon I despise," she lied flatly. She was still searching for the thought about chess that his arrival—only a coincidence?—had chased away.

"Perhaps you go too far in undervaluing games," he said, seeming now to shrug off all feeling and become philosophical. "To begin with our own planet and time of recruitment, who can say how much the shared passion for chess had to do with healing the differences between Russia and the West, or how long the whist mind and bridge mentality maintained British might-or what k'ta'hra did for Alpha Centaurus Two?"

She lifted, dropped her shoulders. The alarm bell was still dinning faintly. She must search again, thoroughly, before the elusive thought dived back forever into her deep unconscious.

And the wasp was still faintly whining somewhere, as if in endless search.

The enemy Colonel lectured on: "The games played at the three tournaments here at 61 Cygni 5 represent the three basic types found in the known universe. First, the track games like backgammon and k'ta'hra and parcheesi and dominoes and an American money-fraught monstrosity I remember was called Monopoly. In those games there is a one-dimensional track or trail along which pieces move according to the throws of dice or their equivalents. No matter how much the track curves, or even knots, it remains one-dimensional.

"Second, there are the board games like chess and checkers and Go and Martian jetan—two-dimensional."

Erica put in, frowning slightly, "It's odd that most intelligent planets should be addicted chiefly either to board games or track games. On most planets where chess flourishes, k'ta'hra languishes. And vice versa. I wonder why?"

He shrugged. "Finally, there are the card games, where the essential element is the masked counter, the piece of unknown value, whether it be a card or a hinged Barnardian egg or a bamboo-and-ivory Mah-Jongg block. Hearts, pinochle, skat, and the emperor of them all, contract bridge.

"Then there are the mixed types. Cribbage to some degree mates the card game with the track game, while I recall one named Spy—our game, eh?—in which pieces of masked value are moved on a board. But in the aggregate—"

At that instant the whining buzz grew louder. And louder.

Coming straight at Erica across the hall, increasing in speed every instant, was what looked like a rather large wasp.

The Spider Colonel grabbed at her, but she had moved like a snake away from him down the rail.

The insect shifted its aim, still driving straight at her.

A flat gray gun, snatched from a breakaway pocket at her right hip, was in her hand. She fired.

There was no sound, but the insect veered sharply as the tight inertial beam missed it by a centimeter. It whizzed between them across the golden rail.

The Colonel had his own gun out. He aimed and shot.

The insect veered downward, striking the floor brightly tessellated with red and gold.

There was a sharp explosive *whisht!* A blinding blue stiletto of flame a foot long lanced out.

Then there was only a fuming narrow groove in the gleaming tiles. Across it, Erica's eyes met her adversary's for the first time.

"An assassination missile," she said flatly.

"That's clear enough," he agreed. "Shaped charge."

From the hall below there came a mutter of questions and hushings— gutteral and whistled, musical and atonal. Inhuman dark-clad figures were coming up the ramp.

"And set to home on me," she said.

"I tried to throw you out of the way," he said.

"Or hold me still when it struck. My flesh would have muffled the explosion and the flash. Then your fake nurse and stretcher-bearers—"

She looked around. The two robots and the bird-woman were gone.

The dark figures that had mounted the ramp were moving toward them.

"I can explain—" the Colonel began.

"You can explain this explosion to the tournament officials!"

She darted past the arresting arms of a gold-badged multibrach from Wolf 1 to the express elevator, stabbed the button for Floor 88 and jumped into the empty shaft.

The field seized her and whipped her up. Through the shaft's transparent back she had quick glimpses of scarlet sea and yellow land between the blurs that were downward-whipping passengers. At Floor 43 there was a squeeze. She wondered, *What attack now? A Centipede down my back?* But the field's cybernator juggled the crowding passengers with ease.

At 88 she bounced out. Her door-spy murmured "All clear" so she didn't search her room with its conventional bed, dresser, micro-viewer, and TV-phone with dangling soft-sheathed metal; power-arms, used for long-distance check-signing, handshakes, any-thing else.

She headed for the bathroom, stripping off her uniform. Her Order of Ophidian Merit caught her eye. Her thumbnail dented the black metal. It was the thinnest shell, all right, holding almost certainly the electronic bug on which the assassination missile had homed. When had the switch been made?—and why had von Hohenwald...? She cut off that speculation.

She turned the shower to warm needle and hesitated. Then with a shrug she reached behind her back, loosed the narrow straps of her warning plate, quickly swabbed it and the straps with eau de cologne, and hung it on the towel rack.

Directly the cleansing, mind-clearing tropical rainstorm hit her, the thought about chess she'd been hunting for sprang up crystal clear.

Next instant the bathroom filled with white light flaring in the dot-dot-dash rhythm of the current Snake identification code. It was the TV-phone call-light, which she's earlier set to "dazzle."

She ran to it eagerly. This time her report would knock back their ears. She switched on voice and—after a glance at her dripping nakedness—caller-to-receiver sight only. She could see, but not be seen.

With holographic transmission, the TV screen was like a window into another room. Erich von Hohenwald's scarred face looked through.

She damned herself for her non-reg removal of warning plate.

She said, "How did you break our ID code?"

He grinned, not quite at her. "A stethescope against the gold rail one hundred feet away. You slipped, Major. Sorry to interrupt your bath—that's a shower I hear, isn't it?—but..."

Two of the three dangling power-arms straightened abruptly, swung blindly sideways, hit and imprisoned her wrists. The third fumbled for the button that turned on receiver-to-caller sight.

Without pausing to damn herself this time, she jabbed out a foot and toed off the power in the arms. They fell away. Rubbing her wrists and glancing down at the water pooling on the expensive carpet, she smiled a bit smugly and said, "I'm glad you called, Colonel. I've just had an insight I want to share with you. You were talking about basic games.

Well, the chessboard is clearly a spider's web with crisscross strands—in Go you even put the pieces on the intersections. The object of the game is to hunt down and immobilize the enemy King, just as a spider paralyzes its victim and sometimes wraps it in its silk. But here's the clincher: the Knight, the piece most characteristic of chess, has exactly eight crooked moves when it stands in the clear—the number of a spider's crooked legs, and eyes too! This suggests that all chess-playing planets are Spider-infiltrated from way back. It also suggests that all the chessplayers here for the tournament are Spiders—your shock battalion to take over 61 Cygni 5."

Colonel von Hohenwald sighed. "I was afraid you'd catch on, dear," he said softly. "Now you've signed your abduction warrant at the very least. You may still be able to warn your HQ, but before they can come to your aid, this planet will be in our hands."

He frowned. "But why did you spill this to me, Erica? If you had played dumb—"

"I spilled it to you," she said, "because I wanted you to know that your plot's been blown-and that my side has already taken countermeasures! We've made a crooked Knight's move too. Has the significance of track games never occurred to you, Colonel? The one-dimensional track, sinuously turning, obviously symbolizes the snake. The pieces are the little bugs and animals the snake has swallowed. As for the dice, well, one of the throws is called Snake Eyes. So be assured that all the k'ta'hra players here are Snakes, ready to counter any Spider grab at 61 Cygni 5."

The Colonel's mouth almost gaped. "So you damned Snakes were plotting a takeover too! I must check on this. If you're lying...But even if you are, I'm forced to admit, Major Weaver, that its just about the finest improvised bluff I've ever had thrown at me."

He hesitated a moment, scowling, then snappily lifted his hand to the edge of the close-cropped hair in a congratulatory salute.

She smiled. Now that she'd cut him down to size, she could see that he was quite handsome. And he'd done his best to warn her about the homing bug in her O.O.M.

She said, "Its no bluff, Colonel. And I must admit that this time both you and I, enemies, have worked together to achieve this...stalemate."

While saying that, she found her black lace negligee and fastened it closely around her damp body. Now she stooped to the TV and switched on receiver-to-caller sight.

He smiled at her, a bit foolishly, she thought. A touch of disappointment, a touch of appreciative delight.

She straightened her shoulders, snappily lifted her hand-to her nose, which she thumbed at him.

When the Change Winds Blow

I was halfway between Arcadia and Utopia, flying a long archeologic scout, looking for coleopt hives, lepidopteroid stilt-cities, and ruined villas of the Old Ones.

On Mars they've stuck to the fanciful names the old astronomers dreamed onto their charts. They've got an Elysium and an Ophir too.

I judged I was somewhere near the Acid Sea, which by a rare coincidence does become a poisonous shallow marsh, rich in hydrogen ions, when the northern icecap melts.

But I saw no sign of it below me, nor any archaeologic features either. Only the endless dull rosy plain of felsite dust and iron-oxide powder slipping steadily west under my flier, with here and tere a shallow canyon or low hill, looking for all the World (Earth? Mars?) like parts of the Mojave.

The sun was behind me, its low light flooding the cabin. A few stars glittered in the dark blue sky. I recognized the constellations of Sagittarius and Scorpio, the red pinpoint of Antares.

I was wearing my pilot's red spacesuit. They've enough air on Mars for flying now, but not for breathing if you fly even a few hundred yards above the surface.

Beside me sat my copilot's green spacesuit, which would have had someone in it if I were more sociable or merely mindful of flying regulations. From time to time it swayed and jogged just a little.

And things were feeling eerie, which isn't how they ought to feel to someone who loves solitude as much as I do, or pretend to myself I do. But the Martian landscape is even more spectral than that of Arabia or the American Southwest—lonely and beautiful and obsessed with death and immensity and sometimes it strikes through.

From some old poem the words came, "...and strange thoughts grow, with a certain humming in my ears, about the life before I lived this life."

I had to stop myself from leaning forward and looking around into the faceplate of the green spacesuit to see if there weren't someone there now. A thin man. Or a tall slim woman. Or a black crab-jointed Martian coleopteroid, who needs a spacesuit about as much as a spacesuit does. Or...who knows?

It was very still in the cabin. The silence did almost hum. I had been listening to Deimos Station, but now the outer moonlet had dropped below the southern horizon. They'd been broadcasting a suggestions program about dragging Mercury away from the sun to make it the moon of Venus—and giving both planets rotation too—so as to stir up the thick smoggy furnace-hot atmosphere of Venus and make it habitable.

Better finish fixing up Mars first, I'd thought.

But then almost immediately the rider to that thought had come: *No, I want Mars to stay lonely. That's why I came here. Earth got crowded and look what happened.*

Yet there are times on Mars when it would be pleasant, even to an old solitary like me, to have a companion. That is if you could be sure of picking your companion.

Once again I felt the compulsion to peer inside the green spacesuit.

Instead I scanned around. Still only the dust-desert drawing toward sunset, almost featureless, yet darkly rosy as an old peach. "True peach, rosy and flawless...Peach-blossom marble all, the rare, the ripe as fresh-poured wine of a mighty pulse..." *What was that poem?*—my mind nagged.

On the seat beside me, almost under the thigh of the green spacesuit, vibrating with it a little, was a tape: *Vanished Churches and Cathedrals of Terra*. Old buildings are an abiding interest with me, of course, and then some of the hills or hives of the black coleopts are remarkably suggestive of Earth towers and spires, even to details like lancet windows and flying buttresses, so much so that it's been suggested there is an imitative element, perhaps telepathic, in the architecture of those strange beings who despite humanoid intelligence are very like social insects. I'd been scanning the book at my last stop, hunting out coleopt-hill resemblances, but then a cathedral interior had reminded me of the Rockefeller Chapel at the University of Chicago and I'd slipped the tape out of the projector. That chapel was where Monica had been, getting her Ph.D. in physics on a bright June morning, when the fusion blast licked the southern end of Lake Michigan, and I didn't want to think about Monica. Or rather I wanted too much to think about her.

"What's done is done, and she is dead beside, dead long ago" Now I recognized the poem!—Browning's *The Bishop Orders His Tomb at St. Praxed's Church*. That was a distant cry!—Had there been a view of St. Praxed's on the tape?—The 16th Century...and the dying bishop pleading with his sons for a grotesquely grand tomb—a frieze of satyrs, nymphs, the Savior, Moses, lynxes—while he thinks of their mother, his mistress...

[158]

"Your tall pale mother with her talking eyes...Old Gandolf envied me, so fair she was!"

Robert Browning and Elizabeth Barrett and their great love...

Monica and myself and our love that never got started...

Monica's eyes talked. She was tall and slim and proud...

Maybe if I had more character, or only energy, I'd find myself someone else to love—a new planet, a new girl!—I wouldn't stay uselessly faithful to that old romance, I wouldn't go courting loneliness, locked in a dreaming life-in-death on Mars...

"Hours and long hours in the dead night, I ask, 'Do I live, am I dead?'"

But for me the loss of Monica is tied up, in a way I can't untangle, with the failure of Earth, with my loathing of what Terra did to herself in her pride of money and power and success (communist and capitalist alike), with that unnecessary atomic war that came just when they thought they had everything safe and solved, like they felt before the one in 1914. It didn't wipe out all Earth by any means, only about a third, but it wiped out my trust in human nature—and the divine too, I'm afraid—and it wiped out Monica...

"And as she died so must we die ourselves, and thence ye may perceive the world's a dream."

A dream? Maybe we lack a Browning to make real those moments of modern history gone over the Niagara of the past, to find them again needle-in-haystack, atom-in-whirlpool, and etch them perfectly, the moments of star-flight and planet-landing etched as he had etched the moments of the Renaissance.

Yet—the world (Mars? Terra?) only a dream? Well, maybe. A bad, dream sometimes, that's for sure! I told myself as I jerked my wandering thoughts back to the flier and the unchanging rosy desert under the small sun.

Apparently I hadn't missed anything—my second mind had been faithfully watching and instrument-tending while my first mind rambled in imaginings and memories.

But things were feeling eerier than ever. The silence did hum now, brassily, as if a great peal of bells had just clanged, or were about to. There was menace now in the small sun about to set behind me, bringing the Martian night and what Martian were-things there may be that they don't know of yet. The rosy plain had turned sinister And for a moment I was sure that if I looked into the green spacesuit, I would see a dark wraith thinner than any coleopt, or else a bone-brown visage fleshlessly grinning—the King of Terrors.

"Swift as a weaver's shuttle fleet our years: Man goeth to the grave, and where is he?"

You know, the weird and the supernatural didn't just evaporate when the world got crowded and smart and technical. They moved outward— to Luna, to Mars, to the Jovian satellites, to the black tangled forest of space and the astronomic marches and the unimaginably distant bull's- eye windows of the stars. Out to the realms of unknown, where the unexpected still happens every other hour and the impossible every other day—

And right at that moment I saw the impossible standing 400 feet tall and cloaked in lacy gray in the desert ahead of me.

And while my first mind froze for seconds that stretched toward min- utes and my central vision stayed blankly fixed on that upwardly bifur- cated incredibility with its dark hint of rainbow caught in the gray lace, my second mind and my peripheral vision brought my flier down to a swift, dream-smooth, skimming landing on its long skis in the rosy dust. I brushed a control and the cabin walls swung silently downward to ei- ther side of the pilots' seat, and I stepped down through the dream-easy Martian gravity to the peach-dark pillowy floor, and I stood looking at the wonder, and my first mind began to move at last.

There could be no doubt about the name of this, for I'd been looking at a taped view of it not five hours before—this was the West Front of Chartres Cathedral, that Gothic masterpiece, with its plain twelfth century spire, the *Clocher Vieux*, to the south and its crocketed sixteenth century spire, the *Clocher Neuf*, to the north and between them the great rose window fifty feet across and below that the icon-crowded triple- arched West Porch.

Swiftly now my first mind moved to one theory after another of this grotesque miracle and rebounded from them almost as swiftly as if they were like magnetic poles.

I was hallucinating from the taped pictures. Yes, maybe the world's a dream. That's always a theory and never a useful one.

A transparency of Chartres had got pasted against my faceplate. Shake my helmet. No.

I was seeing a mirage that had traveled across fifty million miles of space...and some years of time too, for Chartres had vanished with the Paris Bomb that near-missed toward Le Mans, just as Rockefeller Chapel had gone with the Michigan Bomb and St. Praxed's with the Rome.

The thing was a mimic-structure built by the coleopteroids to a plan telepathized from a memory picture of Chartres in some man's mind. But most memory pictures don't have anywhere near such precision and I never heard of the coleopts mimicking stained glass, though they do build spired nests a half thousand feet high.

It was all one of those great hypnotism-traps the Arean jingoists are forever claiming the coleopts are setting us. Yes, and the whole universe was built by demons to deceive only me—and possibly Adolf Hitler—as Descartes once hypothesized. *Stop it.*

They'd moved Hollywood to Mars as they'd earlier moved it to Mexico and Spain and Egypt and the Congo to cut expenses, and they'd just finished an epic of the Middle Ages—*The Hunchback of Notre Dame,* no doubt, with some witless producer substituting Notre Dame of Chartres for Notre Dame of Paris because his leading mistress liked its looks better and the public wouldn't know the difference. Yes, and probably hired hordes of black coleopts at next to nothing to play monks, wearing robes and humanoid masks. And why not a coleopt to play Quasimodo?— improve race relations.

Don't hunt for comedy in the incredible.

Or they'd been giving the Martian tour to the last mad president of *La Belle France* to quiet his nerves and they'd propped up a fake cathedral of Chartres, all west façade, to humor him, just like the Russians had put up papier-mâché villages to impress Peter III's German wife. The Fourth Republic on the fourth planet! *No, don't get hysterical. This thing is here.*

Or maybe—and here my first mind lingered— past and future forever exist somehow, somewhere (the Mind of God? the fourth dimension?) in a sort of suspended animation, with little trails of somnambulant change running through the future as our willed present actions change it and perhaps, who knows, other little trails running through the past too?—for there may be professional time-travelers. And maybe, once in a million millennia, an amateur accidentally finds a Door.

A Door to Chartres. But when?

As I lingered on those thoughts, staring at the gray prodigy—"Do I live, am I dead?"—there came a moaning and a rustling behind me and I turned to see the green spacesuit diving out of the flier toward me, but with its head ducked so I still couldn't see inside the faceplate. I could no more move than in a nightmare. But before the suit reached me, I saw that there was with it, perhaps carrying it, a wind that shook the flier and swept up the feather-soft rose dust in great plumes and waves. And then the wind bowled me over—one hasn't much anchorage in Mars gravity—and I was rolling away from the flier with the billowing dust and the green spacesuit that went somersaulting faster and higher than I, as if it were empty, but then wraiths are light.

The wind was stronger than any wind on Mars should be, certainly than any unheralded gust, and as I went tumbling deliriously on, cushioned by. my suit and the low gravity, clutching futilely toward the small low rocky outcrops through whose long shadows I was rolling, I found myself thinking with the serenity of fever that this wind wasn't blowing across Mars-space only but through time too.

[161]

A mixture of space-wind and time-wind—what a puzzle for the physicist and drawer of vectors! It seemed unfair—I thought as I tumbled—like giving a psychiatrist a patient with psychosis overlaid by alcoholism. But reality's always mixed and I knew from experience that only a few minutes an anechoic, lightless, null-G chamber will set the most nomial mind veering uncontrollably into fantasy—or is it always fantasy?

One of the smaller rocky outcrops took for an instant the twisted shape of Monica's dog Brush as he died—not in the blast with her, but of fallout, three weeks later, hairless and swollen and oozing. I winced.

Then the wind, died and the West Front of Chartres was shooting vertically up above me and I found myself crouched on the dust-drifted steps of the south bay with the great sculpture of the Virgin looking severely out from above the high doorway at the Martian desert, and the figures of the four liberal arts ranged below her-Grammar, Rhetoric, Music, and Dialectic—and Aristotle with frowning forehead dipping a stone pen into stone ink.

The figure of Music hammering her little stone bells made me think of Monica and how she'd studied piano and Brush had barked when she practiced. Next I remembered from the tape that Chartres is the legendary resting place of St. Modesta, a beautiful girl tortured to death for her faith by her father Quirinus in the Emperor Diocletian's day. Modesta—Music—Monica.

The double door was open a little and the green spacesuit was sprawled on its belly there, helmet lifted, as if peering inside at floor level.

I pushed to my feet and walked up the rose-mounded steps. Dust blowing through time? Grotesque. Yet was I more than dust? "Do I live, am I dead?"

I hurried faster and faster, kicking up the fine powder in peach-red swirls, and almost hurled myself down on the green spacesuit to turn it over and peer into the faceplate. But before I could quite do that I had looked into the doorway and what I saw stopped me. Slowly I got to my feet again and took a step beyond the prone green spacesuit and then another step.

Instead of the great Gothic nave of Chartres, long as a football field, high as a sequoia, alive with stained light, there was a smaller, darker interior—Churchly too, but Romanesque, even Latin, with burly granite columns and rich red marble steps leading up toward an altar where mosaics glittered in the gloom. One thin stream of flat light, coming through another open door like a theatrical spot in the wings, struck on the wall opposite me and revealed a gloriously ornate tomb where a sculptured mortuary figure—a bishop by his miter and crook—lay above a crowded bronze frieze on a bright green jasper slab with a blue lapislazuli globe of Earth between his stone knees and nine thin columns of peach-blossom marble rising around him to the canopy...

But of course: this was the bishop's tomb of Browning's poem. This was St. Praxed's Church, powdered by the Rome Bomb, the church sacred to the martyred Praxed, daughter of Pudens, pupil of St. Peter, tucked even further into the past than Chartres' martyred Modesta. Napoleon had planned to liberate those red marble steps and take them to Paris. But with this realization came almost instantly the companion memory: that although St. Praxed's Church had been real, the tomb of Browning's bishop had existed only in Browning's imagination and the minds of his readers.

Can it be, I thought, that not only do the past and future exist forever, but also all the possibilities that were never and will never be realized...somehow, somewhere (the fifth dimension? the Imagination of God?) as if in a dream within a dream...Crawling with change too, as artists or anyone thinks of them... Change-winds mixed with time-winds mixed with space-winds...

In that moment I became aware of two dark-clad figures in the aisle beside the tomb and studying it—a pale man with dark beard covering his cheeks and a pale woman with dark straight hair covering hers under a filmy veil. There was movement near their feet and a fat dark sluglike beast, almost hairless, crawled away from them into the shadows.

I didn't like it. I didn't like that beast. I didn't like it disappearing. For the first time I felt actively frightened.

And then the woman moved too, so that her dark wide floor-brushing skirt jogged, and in a very British voice she called, "Flush! Come here, Flush!" and I remembered that was the name of the dog Elizabeth Barrett had taken with her from Wimpole Street when she ran off with Browning.

Then the voice called again, anxiously, but the British had gone out of it now, in fact it was a voice I knew, a voice that froze me inside, and the dog's name had changed to Brush, and I looked up, and the gaudy tomb was gone and the walls had grayed and receded, but not so far as those of Chartres, only so far as those of the Rockefeller Chapel, and there coming toward me down the center aisle, tall and slim in a black academic robe with the three velvet doctor's bars on the sleeves, with the brown of science edging the hood, was Monica.

I think she saw me, I think she recognized me through my faceplate, I think she smiled at me fearfully, wonderingly.

Then there was a rosy glow behind her, making a hazily gleaming nimbus of her hair, like the glory of a saint. But then the glow became too bright, intolerably so, and something struck at me, driving me back through the doorway, whirling me over and over, so that all I saw was swirls of rose dust and star-pricked sky.

I think what struck at me was the ghost of the front of an atomic blast.

In my mind was the thought: St. Praxed, St. Modesta, and Monica the atheist saint martyred by the bomb.

Then all winds were gone and I was picking myself up from the dust by the flier.

I scanned around through ebbing dust-swirls. The cathedral was gone. No hill or structure anywhere relieved the flatness of the Martian horizon.

Leaning against the flier, as if lodged there by the wind yet on its feet, was the green spacesuit, its back toward me, its head and shoulders sunk in an attitude mimicking profound dejection.

I moved toward it quickly. I had the thought that it might have gone with me to bring someone back.

It seemed to shrink from me a little as turned it around. The faceplate was empty. There on the inside, below the transparency, distorted by my angle of view, was the little complex console of dials and levers, but no face above them.

I took the suit up very gently in my arms, carrying it as if it were a person, and I started toward the door of the cabin.

It's in the things we've lost that we exist most fully.

There was a faint green flash from the sun as its last silver vanished on the horizon.

All the stars came out.

Gleaming green among them and brightest of all, low in the sky where the sun had gone, was the Evening Star—Earth.

No Great Magic

CHAPTER I

> To bring the dead to life
> Is no great magic.
> Few are wholly dead:
> Blow on a dead man's embers
> And a live flame will start.
> –Graves

I dipped through the filmy curtain into the boys' half of the dressing room and there was Sid sitting at the star's dressing table in his threadbare yellowed undershirt, the lucky one, not making up yet but staring sternly at himself in the bulb-framed mirror and experimentally working his features a little, as actors will, and kneading the stubble on his fat chin.

I said to him quietly, "Siddy, what are we putting on tonight? Maxwell Anderson's *Elizabeth the Queen* or Shakespeare's *Macbeth*? It says *Macbeth* on the callboard, but Miss Nefer's getting ready for Elizabeth. She just had me go and fetch the red wig."

He tried out a few eyebrow rears—right, left, both together—then turned to me, sucking in his big gut a little, as he always does when a gal heaves into hailing distance, and said, "Your pardon, sweetling, what sayest thou?"

Sid always uses that kook antique patter backstage, until I sometimes wonder whether I'm in Central Park, New York City, nineteen hundred and three quarters, or somewhere in Southwark, Merry England, fifteen hundred and same. The truth is that although he loves every last fat part in Shakespeare and will play the skinniest one with loyal and inspired affection, he thinks Willy S. penned Falstaff with nobody else in mind but Sidney J. Lessingham. (And no accent on the ham, please.)

I closed my eyes and counted to eight, then repeated my question.

He replied, "Why, the Bard's tragical history of the bloody Scot, certes." He waved his hand toward the portrait of Shakespeare that always sits beside his mirror on top of his reserve makeup box. At first that particular picture of the Bard looked too nancy to me—a sort of peeping-tom schoolteacher—but I've grown used to it over the months and even palsy-feeling.

He didn't ask me why I hadn't asked Miss Nefer my question. Everybody in the company knows she spends the hour before curtain-time getting into character, never parting her lips except for that purpose—or to bite your head off if you try to make the most necessary conversation.

"Aye, 'tiz *Macbeth* tonight," Sid confirmed, returning to his frowning-practice: left eyebrow up, right down, reverse, repeat, rest. "And I must play the ill-starred Thane of Glamis."

I said, "That's fine, Siddy, but where does it leave us with Miss Nefer? She's already thinned her eyebrows and beaked out the top of her nose for Queen Liz, though that's as far as she's got. A beautiful job, the nose. Anybody else would think it was plastic surgery instead of putty. But it's going to look kind of funny on the Thaness of Glamis."

Sid hesitated a half second longer than he usually would—I thought, *his timing's off tonight*—and then he harrumphed and said, "Why, Iris Nefer, decked out as Good Queen Bess, will speak a prologue to the play—a prologue which I have myself but last week writ." He owled his eyes. "'Tis an experiment in the new theater."

I said, "Siddy, prologues were nothing new to Shakespeare. He had them on half his other plays. Besides, it doesn't make sense to use Queen Elizabeth. She was dead by the time he whipped up *Macbeth*, which is all about witchcraft and directed at King James."

He growled a little at me and demanded, "Prithee, how comes it your peewit-brain bears such a ballast of fusty book-knowledge, chit?"

I said softly, "Siddy, you don't camp in a Shakespearean dressing room for a year, tete-a-teting with some of the wisest actors ever, without learning a little. Sure I'm a mental case, a poor little A & A existing on your sweet charity, and don't think I don't appreciate it, but—"

"A-*and*-A, thou sayest?" he frowned. "Methinks the gladsome new forswearers of sack and ale call themselves AA."

"Agoraphobe and Amnesiac," I told him. "But look, Siddy, I was going to sayest that I do know the plays. Having Queen Elizabeth speak a prologue to *Macbeth* is as much an anachronism as if you put her on the gantry of the British moonship, busting a bottle of champagne over its schnozzle."

"Ha!" he cried as if he'd caught me out. "And saying there's a new Elizabeth, wouldn't that be the bravest advertisement ever for the

Empire?—perchance rechristening the pilot, copilot and astrogator Drake, Hawkins and Raleigh? And the ship *The Golden Hind?* Tilly fally, lady!"

He went on, "My prologue an anachronism, quotha! The groundlings will never mark it. Think'st thou wisdom came to mankind with the stenchful rocket and the sundered atomy? More, the Bard himself was topfull of anachronism. He put spectacles on King Lear, had clocks tolling the hour in Caesar's Rome, buried that Roman 'stead o' burning him and gave Czechoslovakia a seacoast. Go to, doll."

"Czechoslovakia, Siddy?"

"Bohemia, then, what skills it? Leave me now, sweet poppet. Go thy ways. I have matters of import to ponder. There's more to running a repertory company than reading the footnotes to Furness."

Martin had just slouched by calling the Half Hour and looking in his solemnity, sneakers, levis and dirty T-shirt more like an underage refugee from Skid Row than Sid's newest recruit, assistant stage manager and hardest-worked juvenile—though for once he'd remembered to shave. I was about to ask Sid who was going to play Lady Mack if Miss Nefer wasn't, or, if she were going to double the roles, shouldn't I help her with the change? She's a slow dresser and the Elizabeth costumes are pretty realistically stayed. And she would have trouble getting off that nose, I was sure. But then I saw that Siddy was already slapping on the alboline to keep the grease paint from getting into his pores.

Greta, you ask too many questions, I told myself. *You get everybody riled up and you rack your own poor ricketty little mind*; and I hied myself off to the costumery to settle my nerves.

The costumery, which occupies the back end of the dressing room, is exactly the right place to settle the nerves and warm the fancies of any child, including an unraveled adult who's saving what's left of her sanity by pretending to be one. To begin with there are the regular costumes for Shakespeare's plays, all jeweled and spangled and brocaded, stage armor, great Roman togas with weights in the borders to make them drape right, velvets of every color to rest your cheek against and dream, and the fantastic costumes for the other plays we favor; Ibsen's *Peer Gynt*, Shaw's *Back to Methuselah* and Hilliard's adaptation of Heinlein's *Children of Methuselah*, the Capek brothers' *Insect People*, O'Neill's *The Fountain*, Flecker's *Hassan*, *Camino Real*, *Children of the Moon*, *The Beggar's Opera*, *Mary of Scotland*, *Berkeley Square*, *The Road to Rome*.

There are also the costumes for all the special and variety performances we give of the plays: *Hamlet* in modern dress, *Julius Caesar* set in a dictatorship of the 1920's, *The Taming of the Shrew* in caveman furs and leopard skins, where Petruchio comes in riding a dinosaur, *The Tempest* set on another planet with a spaceship wreck to start it off *Karrumph!*—which means a half dozen spacesuits, featherweight but looking ever so practical, and the weirdest sort of extraterrestrial-beast outfits for Ariel and Caliban and the other monsters.

Oh, I tell you the stuff in the costumery ranges over such a sweep of space and time that you sometimes get frightened you'll be whirled up and spun off just anywhere, so that you have to clutch at something very real to you to keep it from happening and to remind you where you *really* are—as I did now at the subway token on the thin gold chain around my neck (Siddy's first gift to me that I can remember) and chanted very softly to myself, like a charm or a prayer, closing my eyes and squeezing the holes in the token: "Columbus Circle, Times Square, Penn Station, Christopher Street..."

But you don't ever get *really* frightened in the costumery. Not exactly, though your goosehairs get wonderfully realistically tingled and your tummy chilled from time to time—because you know it's all make-believe, a lifesize doll world, a children's dress-up world. It gets you thinking of far-off times and scenes as *pleasant* places and not as black hungry mouths that might gobble you up and keep you forever. It's always safe, always *just in the theatre, just on the stage*, no matter how far it seems to plunge and roam...and the best sort of therapy for a pot-holed mind like mine, with as many gray ruts and curves and gaps as its cerebrum, that can't remember one single thing before this last year in the dressing room and that can't ever push its shaking body out of that same motherly fatherly room, except to stand in the wings for a scene or two and watch the play until the fear gets too great and the urge to take just one peek at *the audience* gets too strong...and I remember what happened the two times I *did* peek, and I have to come scuttling back.

The costumery's good occupational therapy for me, too, as my pricked and calloused fingertips testify. I think I must have stitched up or darned half the costumes in it this last twelvemonth, though there are so many of them that I swear the drawers have accordion pleats and the racks extend into the fourth dimension—not to mention the boxes of props and the shelves of scripts and prompt-copies and other books, including a couple of encyclopedias and the many thick volumes of Furness's *Variorum Shakespeare*, which as Sid had guessed I'd been boning up on. Oh, and I've sponged and pressed enough costumes, too, and even refitted them to newcomers like Martin, ripping up and resewing seams, which can be a punishing job with heavy materials.

In a less sloppily organized company I'd be called wardrobe mistress, I guess. Except that to anyone in show business that suggests a crotchety old dame with lots of authority and scissors hanging around her neck on a string. Although I got my crochets, all right, I'm not that old. Kind of childish, in fact. As for authority, everybody outranks me, even Martin.

Of course to somebody *outside* show business, wardrobe mistress might suggest a yummy gal who spends her time dressing up as Nell Gwyn or Anitra or Mrs. Pinchwife or Cleopatra or even Eve (we got a legal costume for it) and inspiring the boys. I've tried that once or twice. But Siddy frowns on it, and if Miss Nefer ever caught me at it I think she'd whang me.

And in a normaller company it would be the wardrobe room, too, but costumery is my infantile name for it and the actors go along with my little whims.

I don't mean to suggest our company is completely crackers. To get as close to Broadway even as Central Park you got to have something. But in spite of Sid's whip-cracking there is a comforting looseness about its efficiency—people trade around the parts they play without fuss, the bill may be changed a half hour before curtain without anybody getting hysterics, nobody gets fired for eating garlic and breathing it in the leading lady's face. In short, we're a team. Which is funny when you come to think of it, as Sid and Miss Nefer and Bruce and Maudie are British (Miss Nefer with a touch of Eurasian blood, I romance); Martin and Beau and me are American (at least I *think* I am) while the rest come from just everywhere.

Besides my costumery work, I fetch things and run inside errands and help the actresses dress and the actors too. The dressing room's very coeducational in a halfway respectable way. And every once in a while Martin and I police up the whole place, me skittering about with dustcloth and wastebasket, he wielding the scrub-brush and mop with such silent grim efficiency that it always makes me nervous to get through and duck back into the costumery to collect myself.

Yes, the costumery's a great place to quiet your nerves or improve your mind or even dream your life away. But this time I couldn't have been there eight minutes when Miss Nefer's Elizabeth-angry voice came skirling, "Girl! Girl! Greta, where is my ruff with silver trim?" I laid my hands on it in a flash and loped it to her, because Old Queen Liz was known to slap even her Maids of Honor around a bit now and then and Miss Nefer is a bear on getting into character—a real Paul Muni.

She was all made up now, I was happy to note, at least as far as her face went—I hate to see that spooky eight-spoked faint tattoo on her forehead (I've sometimes wondered if she got it acting in India or Egypt maybe).

Yes, she was already all made up. This time she'd been going extra heavy on the burrowing-into-character bit, I could tell right away, even if it was only for a hacked-out anachronistic prologue. She signed to me to help her dress without even looking at me, but as I got busy I looked at *her* eyes. They were so cold and sad and lonely (maybe because they were so far away from her eyebrows and temples and small tight mouth,

[169]

and so shut away from each other by that ridge of nose) that I got the creeps. Then she began to murmur and sigh, very softly at first, then loudly enough so I got the sense of it.

"Cold, so cold," she said, still seeing things far away though her hands were working smoothly with mine. "Even a gallop hardly fires my blood. Never was such a Januarius, though there's no snow. Snow will not come, or tears. Yet my brain burns with the thought of Mary's death-warrant unsigned. There's my particular hell!—to doom, perchance, all future queens, or leave a hole for the Spaniard and the Pope to creep like old worms back into the sweet apple of England. Philip's tall black crooked ships massing like sea-going fortresses south-away—cragged castles set to march into the waves. Parma in the Lowlands! And all the while my bright young idiot gentlemen spurting out my treasure as if it were so much water, as if gold pieces were a glut of summer posies. Oh, alackanight!"

And I thought, *Cry Iced!—that's sure going to be one tyrannosaur of a prologue. And how you'll ever shift back to being Lady Mack beats me. Greta, if this is what it takes to do just a bit part, you'd better give up your secret ambition of playing walk-ons some day when your nerves heal.*

She was really getting to me, you see, with that characterization. It was as if I'd managed to go out and take a walk and sat down in the park outside and heard the President talking to himself about the chances of war with Russia and realized he'd sat down on a bench with its back to mine and only a bush between. You see, here we were, two females undignifiedly twisted together, at the moment getting her into that crazy crouch-deep bodice that's like a big icecream cone, and yet here at the same time was Queen Elizabeth the First of England, three hundred and umpty-ump years dead, coming back to life in a Central Park dressing room. It shook me.

She looked so much the part, you see—even without the red wig yet, just powdered pale makeup going back to a quarter of an inch from her own short dark bang combed and netted back tight. The age too. Miss Nefer can't be a day over forty—well, forty-two at most—but now she looked and talked and felt to my hands dressing her, well, at least a dozen years older. I guess when Miss Nefer gets into character she does it with each molecule.

That age point fascinated me so much that I risked asking her a question. Probably I was figuring that she couldn't do me much damage because of the positions we happened to be in at the moment. You see, I'd started to lace her up and to do it right I had my knee against the tail of her spine.

[170]

"How old, I mean how young might your majesty be?" I asked her, innocently wonderingly like some dumb serving wench.

For a wonder she didn't somehow swing around and clout me, but only settled into character a little more deeply.

"Fifty-four winters," she replied dismally. "'Tiz Januarius of Our Lord's year One Thousand and Five Hundred and Eighty and Seven. I sit cold in Greenwich, staring at the table where Mary's death warrant waits only my sign manual. If I send her to the block, I open the doors to future, less official regicides. But if I doom her not, Philip's armada will come inching up the Channel in a season, puffing smoke and shot, and my English Catholics, thinking only of Mary Regina, will rise and i' the end the Spaniard will have all. All history would alter. That must not be, even if I'm damned for it! And yet...and yet..."

A bright blue fly came buzzing along (the dressing room has *some* insect life) and slowly circled her head rather close, but she didn't even flicker her eyelids.

"I sit cold in Greenwich, going mad. Each afternoon I ride, praying for some mischance, some prodigy, to wash from my mind away the bloody question for some little space. It skills not what: a fire, a tree a-failing, Davison or e'en Eyes Leicester tumbled with his horse, an assassin's ball clipping the cold twigs by my ear, a maid crying rape, a wild boar charging with dipping tusks, news of the Spaniard at Thames' mouth or, more happily, a band of strolling actors setting forth some new comedy to charm the fancy or some great unheard-of tragedy to tear the heart— though that were somewhat much to hope for at this season and place, even if Southwark be close by."

The lacing was done. I stood back from her, and really she looked so much like Elizabeth painted by Gheeraerts or on the Great Seal of Ireland or something—though the ash-colored plush dress trimmed in silver and the little silver-edge ruff and the black-silver tinsel-cloth cloak lined with white plush hanging behind her looked most like a winter riding costume—and her face was such a pale frozen mask of Elizabeth's inward tortures, that I told myself, *Oh, I got to talk to Siddy again, he's made some big mistake, the lardy old lackwit. Miss Nefer just can't be figuring on playing in Macbeth tonight.*

As a matter of fact I was nerving myself to ask *her* all about it direct, though it was going to take some real nerve and maybe be risking broken bones or at least a flayed cheek to break the ice of that characterization, when who should come by calling the Fifteen Minutes but Martin. He looked so downright goofy that it took my mind off Nefer-in-character for all of eight seconds.

His levied bottom half still looked like *The Lower Depths.* Martin is Village Stanislavsky rather than Ye Olde English Stage Traditions. But

[171]

above that...well, all it really amounted to was that he was stripped to the waist and had shaved off the small high tuft of chest hair and was wearing a black wig that hung down in front of his shoulders in two big braids heavy with silver hoops and pins. But just the same those simple things, along with his tarpaper-solarium tan and habitual poker expression, made him look so like an American Indian that I thought, *Hey Zeus!—he's all set to play Hiawatha, or if he'd just cover up that straight-line chest, a frowny Pocahontas.* And I quick ran through what plays with Indian parts we do and could only come up with *The Fountain.*

I mutely goggled my question at him, wiggling my hands like guppy fins, but he brushed me off with a solemn mysterious smile and backed through the curtain. I thought, *nobody can explain this but Siddy,* and I followed Martin.

CHAPTER II

History does not move in one current,
like the wind across bare seas,
but in a thousand streams and eddies,
like the wind over a broken landscape.
–Cary

The boys' half of the dressing room (two-thirds really) was bustling. There was the smell of spirit gum and Max Factor and just plain men. Several guys were getting dressed or un-, and Bruce was cussing Bloody-something because he'd just burnt his fingers unwinding from the neck of a hot electric bulb some crepe hair he'd wound there to dry after wetting and stretching it to turn it from crinkly to straight for his Banquo beard. Bruce is always getting to the theater late and trying shortcuts.

But I had eyes only for Sid. So help me, as soon as I saw him they bugged again. *Greta*, I told myself, *you're going to have to send Martin out to the drugstore for some anti-bug powder.* "For the roaches, boy?" "No, for the eyes."

Sid was made up and had his long mustaches and elf-locked Macbeth wig on—and his corset too. I could tell by the way his waist was sucked in before he saw me. But instead of dark kilts and that bronze-studded sweat-stained leather battle harness that lets him show off his beefy shoulders and the top half of his heavily furred chest—and which really does look great on Macbeth in the first act when he comes in straight from battle—but instead of that he was wearing, so help me, red tights cross-gartered with strips of gold-blue tinsel-cloth, a green doublet gold-trimmed and to top it a ruff, and he was trying to fit onto his front a bright silvered cuirass that would have looked just dandy maybe on one of the Pope's Swiss Guards.

I thought, *Siddy, Willy S. ought to reach out of his portrait there and bop you one on the koko for contemplating such a crazy-quilt desecration of just about his greatest and certainly his most atmospheric play.*

Just then he noticed me and hissed accusingly, "There thou art, slothy minx! Spring to and help stuff me into this monstrous chest-kettle."

"Siddy, what *is* all this?" I demanded as my hands automatically obeyed. "Are you going to play *Macbeth* for laughs, except maybe leaving the Porter a serious character? You think you're Red Skelton?"

[173]

"What monstrous brabble is this, you mad bitch?" he retorted, grunting as I bear-hugged his waist, shouldering the cuirass to squeeze it home.

"The clown costumes on all you men," I told him, for now I'd noticed that the others were in rainbow hues, Bruce a real eye-buster in yellow tights and violet doublet as he furiously bushed out and clipped crosswise sections of beard and slapped them on his chin gleaming brown with spirit gum. "I haven't seen any eight-inch polka-dots yet but I'm sure I will."

Suddenly a big grin split Siddy's face and he laughed out loud at me, though the laugh changed to a gasp as I strapped in the cuirass three notches too tight. When we'd got that adjusted he said, "I' faith thou slayest me, pretty witling. Did I not tell you this production is an experiment, a novelty? We shall but show *Macbeth* as it might have been costumed at the court of King James. In the clothes of the day, but gaudier, as was then the stage fashion. Hold, dove, I've somewhat for thee." He fumbled his grouch bag from under his doublet and dipped finger and thumb in it, and put in my palm a silver model of the Empire State Building, charm bracelet size, and one of the new Kennedy dimes.

As I squeezed those two and gloated my eyes on them, feeling securer and happier and friendlier for them though I didn't at the moment want to, I thought, *Well, Siddy's right about that, at least I've read they used to costume the plays that way, though I don't see how Shakespeare stood it. But it was dirty of them all not to tell me beforehand.*

But that's the way it is. Sometimes I'm the butt as well as the pet of the dressing room, and considering all the breaks I get I shouldn't mind. I smiled at Sid and went on tiptoes and necked out my head and kissed him on a powdery cheek just above an aromatic mustache. Then I wiped the smile off my face and said, "Okay, Siddy, play Macbeth as Little Lord Fauntleroy or Baby Snooks if you want to. I'll never squeak again. But the Elizabeth prologue's still an anachronism. And—this is the thing I came to tell you, Siddy—Miss Nefer's not getting ready for any measly prologue. She's set to play Queen Elizabeth all night and tomorrow morning too. Whatever you think, she doesn't know we're doing *Macbeth*. But who'll do Lady Mack if she doesn't? And Martin's not dressing for Malcolm, but for the Son of the Last of the Mohicans, I'd say. What's more—"

You know, something I said must have annoyed Sid, for he changed his mood again in a flash. "Shut your jaw, you crook brained cat, and begone!" he snarled at me. "Here's curtain time close upon us, and you come like a wittol scattering your mad questions like the crazed Ophelia her flowers. Begone, I say!"

"Yessir," I whipped out softly. I skittered off toward the door to the stage, because that was the easiest direction. I figured I could do with a breath of less grease-painty air. Then, "Oh, Greta," I heard Martin call nicely.

He'd changed his levis for black tights, and was stepping into and pulling up around him a very familiar dress, dark green and embroidered with silver and stage-rubies. He'd safety-pinned a folded towel around his chest—to make a bosom of sorts, I realized.

He armed into the sleeves and turned his back to me. "Hook me up, would you?" he entreated.

Then it hit me. They had no actresses in Shakespeare's day, they used boys. And the dark green dress was so familiar to me because—

"Martin," I said, halfway up the hooks and working fast—Miss Nefer's costume fitted him fine. "You're going to play—?"

"Lady Macbeth, yes," he finished for me. "Wish me courage, will you Greta? Nobody else seems to think I need it."

I punched him half-heartedly in the rear. Then, as I fastened the last hooks, my eyes topped his shoulder and I looked at our faces side by side in the mirror of his dressing table. His, in spite of the female edging and him being at least eight years younger than me, I think, looked wise, poised, infinitely resourceful with power in reserve, very very real, while mine looked like that of a bewildered and characterless child ghost about to scatter into air—and the edges of my charcoal sweater and skirt, contrasting with his strong colors, didn't dispel that last illusion.

"Oh, by the way, Greta," he said, "I picked up a copy of *The Village Times* for you. There's a thumbnail review of our *Measure for Measure*, though it mentions no names, darn it. It's around here somewhere..."

But I was already hurrying on. Oh, it was logical enough to have Martin playing Mrs. Macbeth in a production styled to Shakespeare's own times (though pedantically over-authentic, I'd have thought) and it really did answer all my questions, even why Miss Nefer could sink herself wholly in Elizabeth tonight if she wanted to. But it meant that I must be missing so much of what was going on right around me, in spite of spending 24 hours a day in the dressing room, or at most in the small adjoining john or in the wings of the stage just outside the dressing room door, that it scared me. Siddy telling everybody, "*Macbeth* tonight in Elizabethan costume, boys and girls," sure, that I could have missed—though you'd have thought he'd have asked my help on the costumes.

But Martin getting up in Mrs. Mack. Why, someone must have held the part on him twenty-eight times, cueing him, while he got the lines. And there must have been at least a couple of run-through rehearsals to make sure he had all the business and stage movements down pat, and Sid and Martin would have been doing their big scenes every backstage minute they could spare with Sid yelling, "Witling! Think'st *that's* a wifely buss?" and Martin would have been droning his lines last time he scrubbed and mopped...

Greta, they're hiding things from you, I told myself.

Maybe there was a 25th hour nobody had told me about yet when they did all the things they didn't tell me about.

Maybe they were things they didn't dare tell me because of my top-storey weakness.

I felt a cold draft and shivered and I realized I was at the door to the stage.

I should explain that our stage is rather an unusual one, in that it can face two ways, with the drops and set pieces and lighting all capable of being switched around completely. To your left, as you look out the dressing-room door, is an open-air theater, or rather an open-air place for the audience—a large upward-sloping glade walled by thick tall trees and with benches for over two thousand people. On that side the stage kind of merges into the grass and can be made to look part of it by a green groundcloth.

To your right is a big roofed auditorium with the same number of seats.

The whole thing grew out of the free summer Shakespeare performances in Central Park that they started back in the 1950's.

The Janus-stage idea is that in nice weather you can have the audience outdoors, but if it rains or there's a cold snap, or if you want to play all winter without a single break, as we've been doing, then you can put your audience in the auditorium. In that case, a big accordion-pleated wall shuts off the out of doors and keeps the wind from blowing your backdrop, which is on that side, of course, when the auditorium's in use.

Tonight the stage was set up to face the outdoors, although that draft felt mighty chilly.

I hesitated, as I always do at the door to the stage—though it wasn't the actual stage lying just ahead of me, but only backstage, the wings. You see, I always have to fight the feeling that if I go out the dressing room door, go out just eight steps, the world will change while I'm out there and I'll never be able to get back. It won't be New York City any more, but Chicago or Mars or Algiers or Atlanta, Georgia, or Atlantis or Hell and I'll never be able to get back to that lovely warm womb with all the jolly boys and girls and all the costumes smelling like autumn leaves.

Or, especially when there's a cold breeze blowing, I'm afraid that *I'll* change, that I'll grow wrinkled and old in eight footsteps, or shrink down to the witless blob of a baby, or forget altogether who I am—

—or, it occurred to me for the first time now, *remember* who I am. Which might be even worse.

Maybe that's what I'm afraid of.

[176]

I took a step back. I noticed something new just beside the door: a high-legged, short-keyboard piano. Then I saw that the legs were those of a table. The piano was just a box with yellowed keys. Spinet? Harpsichord?

"Five minutes, everybody," Martin quietly called out behind me.

I took hold of myself. Greta, I told myself—also for the first time, *you know that some day you're really going to have to face this thing, and not just for a quick dip out and back either. Better get in some practice.*

I stepped through the door.

Beau and Doc were already out there, made up and in costume for Ross and King Duncan. They were discreetly peering past the wings at the gathering audience. Or at the place where the audience ought to be gathering, at any rate—sometimes the movies and girlie shows and brainheavy beatnik bruhahas outdraw us altogether. Their costumes were the same kooky colorful ones as the others'. Doc had a mock-ermine robe and a huge gilt papier-mache crown. Beau was carrying a ragged black robe and hood over his left arm—he doubles the First Witch.

As I came up behind them, making no noise in my black sneakers, I heard Beau say, "I see some rude fellows from the City approaching. I was hoping we wouldn't get any of those. How should they scent us out?"

Brother, I thought, *where do you expect them to come from if not the City? Central Park is bounded on three sides by Manhattan Island and on the fourth by the Eighth Avenue Subway. And Brooklyn and Bronx boys have got pretty sharp scenters. And what's it get you insulting the woiking and non-woiking people of the woild's greatest metropolis? Be grateful for any audience you get, boy.*

But I suppose Beau Lassiter considers anybody from north of Vicksburg a "rude fellow" and is always waiting for the day when the entire audience will arrive in carriage and democrat wagons.

Doc replied, holding down his white beard and heavy on the mongrel Russo-German accent he miraculously manages to suppress on stage except when "Vot does it matter? Ve don't convinze zem, ve don't convinze nobody. *Nichevo.*"

Maybe, I thought, *Doc shares my doubts about making Macbeth plausible in rainbow pants.*

Still unobserved by them, I looked between their shoulders and got the first of my shocks.

It wasn't night at all, but afternoon. A dark cold lowering afternoon, admittedly. But afternoon all the same.

Sure, between shows I sometimes forget whether it's day or night, living inside like I do. But getting matinees and evening performances mixed is something else again.

[177]

It also seemed to me, although Beau was leaning in now and I couldn't see so well, that the glade was smaller than it should be, the trees closer to us and more irregular, and I couldn't see the benches. That was Shock Two.

Beau said anxiously, glancing at his wrist, "I wonder what's holding up the Queen?"

Although I was busy keeping up nerve-pressure against the shocks, I managed to think. *So he knows about Siddy's stupid Queen Elizabeth prologue too. But of course he would. It's only me they keep in the dark. If he's so smart he ought to remember that Miss Nefer is always the last person on stage, even when she opens the play.*

And then I thought I heard, through the trees, the distant drumming of horses' hoofs and the sound of a horn.

Now they do have horseback riding in Central Park and you can hear auto horns there, but the hoofbeats don't drum that wild way. And there aren't so many riding together. And no auto horn I ever heard gave out with that sweet yet imperious *ta-ta-ta-TA.*

I must have squeaked or something, because Beau and Doc turned around quickly, blocking my view, their expressions half angry, half anxious.

I turned too and ran for the dressing room, for I could feel one of my mind-wavery fits coming on. At the last second it had seemed to me that the scenery was getting skimpier, hardly more than thin trees and bushes itself, and underfoot feeling more like ground than a ground cloth, and overhead not theater roof but gray sky. *Shock Three and you're out, Greta,* my umpire was calling.

I made it through the dressing room door and nothing there was wavering or dissolving, praised be Pan. Just Martin standing with his back to me, alert, alive, poised like a cat inside that green dress, the prompt book in his right hand with a finger in it, and from his left hand long black tatters swinging—telling me he'd still be doubling Second Witch. And he was hissing, "Places, please, everybody. On stage!"

With a sweep of silver and ash-colored plush, Miss Nefer came past him, for once leading the last-minute hurry to the stage. She had on the dark red wig now. For me that crowned her characterization. It made me remember her saying, "My brain burns." I ducked aside as if she were majesty incarnate.

And then she didn't break her own precedent. She stopped at the new thing beside the door and poised her long white skinny fingers over the yellowed keys, and suddenly I remembered what it was called: a virginals.

She stared down at it fiercely, evilly, like a witch planning an enchantment. Her face got the secret fiendish look that, I told myself, the real

Elizabeth would have had ordering the deaths of Ballard and Babington, or plotting with Drake (for all they say she didn't) one of his raids, that long long forefinger tracing crooked courses through a crabbedly drawn map of the Indies and she smiling at the dots of cities that would burn.

Then all her eight fingers came flickering down and the strings inside the virginals began to twang and hum with a high-pitched rendering of Grieg's "In the Hall of the Mountain King."

Then as Sid and Bruce and Martin rushed past me, along with a black swooping that was Maud already robed and hooded for Third Witch, I beat it for my sleeping closet like Peer Gynt himself dashing across the mountainside away from the cave of the Troll King, who only wanted to make tiny slits in his eyeballs so that forever afterwards he'd see reality just a little differently. And as I ran, the master-anachronism of that menacing mad march music was shrilling in my ears.

CHAPTER III

Sound a dumbe shew. Enter the three fatall sisters, with a
rocke, a threed, and a pair of sheeres.

–Old Play

My sleeping closet is just a cot at the back end of the girls' third of
the dressing room, with a three-panel screen to make it private.

When I sleep I hang my outside clothes on the screen, which is pasted
and thumbtacked all over with the New York City stuff that gives me security: theater programs and restaurant menus, clippings from the *Times*
and the *Mirror*, a torn-out picture of the United Nations building with
a hundred tiny gay paper flags pasted around it, and hanging in an old
hairnet a home-run baseball autographed by Willie Mays. Things like
that.

Right now I was jumping my eyes over that stuff, asking it to keep
me located and make me safe, as I lay on my cot in my clothes with my
knees drawn up and my fingers over my ears so the louder lines from
the play wouldn't be able to come nosing back around the trunks and
tables and bright-lit mirrors and find me. Generally I like to listen to
them, even if they're sort of sepulchral and drained of overtones by their
crooked trip. But they're always tense-making. And tonight (I mean this
afternoon)—no!

It's funny I should find security in mementos of a city I daren't go
out into—no, not even for a stroll through Central Park, though I know
it from the Pond to Harlem Meer—the Met Museum, the Menagerie,
the Ramble, the Great Lawn, Cleopatra's Needle and all the rest. But
that's the way it is. Maybe I'm like Jonah in the whale, reluctant to go
outside because the whale's a terrible monster that's awful scary to look
in the face and might really damage you gulping you a second time, yet
reassured to know you're living in the stomach of that particular monster
and not a seventeen tentacled one from the fifth planet of Aldebaran.

It's really true, you see, about me actually living in the dressing room.
The boys bring me meals: coffee in cardboard cylinders and doughnuts
in little brown grease-spotted paper sacks and malts and hamburgers and
apples and little pizzas, and Maud brings me raw vegetables—carrots and
parsnips and little onions and such, and watches to make sure I exercise

[180]

my molars grinding them and get my vitamins. I take spit-baths in the little john. Architects don't seem to think actors ever take baths, even when they've browned themselves all over playing Pindarus the Parthian in *Julius Caesar*. And all my shut-eye is caught on this little cot in the twilight of my NYC screen.

You'd think I'd be terrified being alone in the dressing room during the wee and morning hours, let alone trying to sleep then, but that isn't the way it works out. For one thing, there's apt to be someone sleeping in too. Maudie especially. And it's my favorite time too for costume-mending and reading the *Variorum* and other books, and for just plain way-out dreaming. You see, the dressing room is the one place I really do feel safe. Whatever is out there in New York that terrorizes me, I'm pretty confident that it can never get in here.

Besides that, there's a great big bolt on the inside of the dressing room door that I throw whenever I'm all alone after the show. Next day they buzz for me to open it.

It worried me a bit at first and I had asked Sid, "But what if I'm so deep asleep I don't hear and you have to get in fast?" and he had replied, "Sweetling, a word in your ear: our own Beauregard Lassiter is the prettiest picklock unjailed since Jimmy Valentine and Jimmy Dale. I'll not ask where he learned his trade, but 'tis sober truth, upon my honor."

And Beau had confirmed this with a courtly bow, murmuring, "At your service, Miss Greta."

"How do you jigger a big iron bolt through a three-inch door that fits like Maudie's tights?" I wanted to know.

"He carries lodestones of great power and divers subtle tools," Sid had explained for him.

I don't know how they work it so that some Traverse-Three cop or park official doesn't find out about me and raise a stink. Maybe Sid just throws a little more of the temperament he uses to keep most outsiders out of the dressing-room. We sure don't get any janitors or scrubwomen, as Martin and I know only too well. More likely he squares someone. I do get the impression all the company's gone a little way out on a limb letting me stay here—that the directors of our theater wouldn't like it if they found out about me.

In fact, the actors are all so good about helping me and putting up with my antics (though they have their own, Danu digs!) that I sometimes think I must be related to one of them—a distant cousin or sister-in-law (or wife, my God!), because I've checked our faces side by side in the mirrors often enough and I can't find any striking family resemblances. Or maybe I was even an actress in the company. The least important one. Playing the tiniest roles like Lucius in *Caesar* and Bianca in *Othello* and one of the little princes in *Dick the Three Eyes* and Fleance and the Gentlewoman in *Macbeth*, though me doing even that much acting strikes me to laugh.

But whatever I am in that direction—if I'm anything—not one of the actors has told me a word about it or dropped the least hint. Not even when I beg them to tell me or try to trick them into it, presumably because it might revive the shock that gave me agoraphobia and amnesia in the first place, and maybe this time knock out my entire mind or at least smash the new mouse-in-a-hole consciousness I've made for myself.

I guess they must have got by themselves a year ago and talked me over and decided my best chance for cure or for just bumping along half happily was staying in the dressing room rather than being sent home (funny, could I have another?) or to a mental hospital. And then they must have been cocky enough about their amateur psychiatry and interested enough in me (the White Horse knows why) to go ahead with a program almost any psychiatrist would be bound to yike at.

I got so worried about the set up once and about the risks they might be running that, gritting down my dread of the idea, I said to Sid, "Siddy, shouldn't I see a doctor?"

He looked at me solemnly for a couple of seconds and then said, "Sure, why not? Go talk to Doc right now," tipping a thumb toward Doc Pyeskov, who was just sneaking back into the bottom of his makeup box what looked like a half pint from the flask I got. I did, incidentally. Doc explained to me Kraepelin's classification of the psychoses, muttering, as he absentmindedly fondled my wrist, that in a year or two he'd be a good illustration of Korsakov's Syndrome.

They've all been pretty darn good to me in their kooky ways, the actors have. Not one of them has tried to take advantage of my situation to extort anything out of me, beyond asking me to sew on a button or polish some boots or at worst clean the wash bowl. Not one of the boys has made a pass I didn't at least seem to invite. And when my crush on Sid was at its worst he shouldered me off by getting polite—something he only is to strangers. On the rebound I hit Beau, who treated me like a real Southern gentleman.

All this for a stupid little waif, whom anyone but a gang of sentimental actors would have sent to Bellevue without a second thought or feeling. For, to get disgustingly realistic, my most plausible theory of me is that I'm a stage-struck girl from Iowa who saw her twenties slipping away and her sanity too, and made the dash to Greenwich Village, and went so ape on Shakespeare after seeing her first performance in Central Park that she kept going back there night after night (Christopher Street, Penn Station, Times Square, Columbus Circle—see?) and hung around the stage door, so mousy but open-mouthed that the actors made a pet of her.

And then something very nasty happened to her, either down at the Village or in a dark corner of the Park. Something so nasty that it blew the top of her head right off. And she ran to the only people and place where she felt she could ever again feel safe. And she showed them the top of her head with its singed hair and its jagged ring of skull and they took pity.

My least plausible theory of me, but the one I like the most, is that I was born in the dressing room, cradled in the top of a flat theatrical trunk with my ears full of Shakespeare's lines before I ever said "Mama," let alone lamped a TV; hush-walked when I cried by whoever was off stage, old props my first toys, trying to eat crepe hair my first indiscretion, sticks of grease-paint my first crayons. You know, I really wouldn't be bothered by crazy fears about New York changing and the dressing room shifting around in space and time, if I could be sure I'd always be able to stay in it and that the same sweet guys and gals would always be with me and that the shows would always go on.

This show was sure going on, it suddenly hit me, for I'd let my fingers slip off my ears as I sentimentalized and wish-dreamed and I heard, muted by the length and stuff of the dressing room, the slow beat of a drum and then a drum note in Maudie's voice taking up that beat as she warned the other two witches, "A drum, a drum! Macbeth doth come."

Why, I'd not only missed Sid's history-making-and-breaking Queen Elizabeth prologue (kicking myself that I had, now it was over), I'd also missed the short witch scene with its famous "Fair is foul and foul is fair," the Bloody Sergeant scene where Duncan hears about Macbeth's victory, and we were well into the second witch scene, the one on the blasted heath where Macbeth gets it predicted to him he'll be king after Duncan and is tempted to speculate about hurrying up the process.

I sat up. I did hesitate a minute then, my fingers going back toward my ears, because *Macbeth* is specially tense-making and when I've had one of my mind-wavery fits I feel weak for a while and things are blurry and uncertain. Maybe I'd better take a couple of the barbiturate sleeping pills Maudie manages to get for me and—but *No, Greta,* I told myself, *you want to watch this show, you want to see how they do in those crazy costumes. You especially want to see how Martin makes out. He'd never forgive you if you didn't.*

So I walked to the other end of the empty dressing room, moving quite slowly and touching the edges here and there, the words of the play getting louder all the time. By the time I got to the door Bruce-Banquo was saying to the witches, "If you can look into the seeds of time, And say which grain will grow and which will not,"—those lines that stir anyone's imagination with their veiled vision of the universe.

The overall lighting was a little dim (afternoon fading already?—a *late* matinee?) and the stage lights flickery and the scenery still a little spectral-flimsy. Oh, my mind-wavery fits can be lulus! But I concentrated on the actors, watching them through the entrance-gaps in the wings. They were solid enough.

Giving a solid performance, too, as I decided after watching that scene through and the one after it where Duncan congratulates Macbeth, with never a pause between the two scenes in true Elizabethan style. Nobody was laughing at the colorful costumes. After a while I began to accept them myself.

Oh, it was a different *Macbeth* than our company usually does. Louder and faster, with shorter pauses between speeches, the blank verse at times approaching a chant. But it had a lot of real guts and everybody was just throwing themselves into it, Sid especially.

The first Lady Macbeth scene came. Without exactly realizing it I moved forward to where I'd been when I got my three shocks. Martin is so intent on his career and making good that he has me the same way about it.

The Thaness started off, as she always does, toward the opposite side of the stage and facing a little away from me. Then she moved a step and looked down at the stage-parchment letter in her hands and began to read it, though there was nothing on it but scribble, and my heart sank because the voice I heard was Miss Nefer's. I thought (and almost said out loud) *Oh, dammit, he funked out, or Sid decided at the last minute he couldn't trust him with the part. Whoever got Miss Nefer out of the ice cream cone in time?*

Then she swung around and I saw that no, my God, it *was* Martin, no mistaking. He'd been using her voice. When a person first does a part, especially getting up in it without much rehearsing, he's bound to copy the actor he's been hearing doing it. And as I listened on, I realized it was fundamentally Martin's own voice pitched a trifle high, only some of the intonations and rhythms were Miss Nefer's. He was showing a lot of feeling and intensity too and real Martin-type poise. *You're off to a great start, kid,* I cheered inwardly. *Keep it up!*

Just then I looked toward the audience. Once again I almost squeaked out loud. For out there, close to the stage, in the very middle of the reserve section, was a carpet spread out. And sitting in the middle of it on some sort of little chair, with what looked like two charcoal braziers smoking to either side of her, was Miss Nefer with a string of extras in Elizabethan hats with cloaks pulled around them.

For a second it really threw me because it reminded me of the things I'd seen or thought I'd seen the couple of times I'd sneaked a peek through the curtain-hole at the audience in the indoor auditorium.

It hardly threw me for more than a second, though, because I remembered that the characters who speak Shakespeare's prologues often stay on stage and sometimes kind of join the audience and even comment on the play from time to time—Christopher Sly and attendant lords in *The Shrew*, for one. Sid had just copied and in his usual style laid it on thick.

Well, bully for you, Siddy, I thought, *I'm sure the witless New York groundlings will be thrilled to their cold little toes knowing they're sitting in the same audience as Good Queen Liz and attendant courtiers. And as for you, Miss Nefer,* I added a shade invidiously, *you just keep on sitting cold in Central Park, warmed by dry-ice smoke from braziers, and keep your mouth shut and everything'll be fine. I'm sincerely glad you'll be able to be Queen Elizabeth all night long. Just so long as you don't try to steal the scene from Martin and the rest of the cast, and the real play.*

I suppose that camp chair will get a little uncomfortable by the time the Fifth Act comes tramping along to that drumbeat, but I'm sure you're so much in character you'll never feel it.

One thing though: just don't scare me again pretending to work witchcraft—with a virginals or any other way.

Okay?

Swell.

Me, now, I'm going to watch the play.

CHAPTER IV

...to dream of new dimensions,
Cheating checkmate
by painting the king's robe
So that he slides like a queen;
–Graves

I swung back to the play just at the moment Lady Mack soliloquizes, "Come to my woman's breasts. And take my milk for gall, you murdering ministers." Although I knew it was just folded towel Martin was touching with his fingertips as he lifted them to the top half of his green bodice, I got carried away, he made it so real. I decided boys can play girls better than people think. Maybe they should do it a little more often, and girls play boys too.

Then Sid-Macbeth came back to his wife from the wars, looking triumphant but scared because the murder-idea's started to smoulder in him, and she got busy fanning the blaze like any other good little *hausfrau* intent on her husband rising in the company and knowing that she's the power behind him and that when there are promotions someone's always got to get the axe. Sid and Martin made this charming little domestic scene so natural yet gutsy too that I wanted to shout hooray. Even Sid clutching Martin to that ridiculous pot-chested cuirass didn't have one note of horseplay in it. Their bodies spoke. It was the McCoy.

After that, the play began to get real good, the fast tempo and exaggerated facial expressions actually helping it. By the time the Dagger Scene came along I was digging my fingernails into my sweaty palms. Which was a good thing—my eating up the play, I mean—because it kept me from looking at the audience again, even taking a fast peek. As you've gathered, audiences bug me. All those people out there in the shadows, watching the actors in the light, all those silent voyeurs as Bruce calls them. Why, they might be anything. And sometimes (to my mind-wavery sorrow) I think they are. Maybe crouching in the dark out there, hiding among the others, is the one who did the nasty thing to me that tore off the top of my head.

Anyhow, if I so much as glance at the audience, I begin to get ideas about it—and sometimes even if I don't, as just at this moment I thought I heard horses restlessly pawing hard ground and one whinny, though that was shut off fast. *Krishna kressed us!* I thought, *Skiddy can't have hired horses for Nefer-Elizabeth much as he's a circus man at heart. We don't have that kind of money. Besides—*

But just then Sid-Macbeth gasped as if he were sucking in a bucket of air. He'd shed the cuirass, fortunately. He said, "Is this a dagger which I see before me, the handle toward my hand?" and the play hooked me again, and I had no time to think about or listen for anything else. Most of the offstage actors were on the other side of the stage, as that's where they make their exits and entrances at this point in the Second Act. I stood alone in the wings, watching the play like a bug, frightened only of the horrors Shakespeare had in mind when he wrote it.

Yes, the play was going great. The Dagger Scene was terrific where Duncan gets murdered offstage, and so was the part afterwards where hysteria mounts as the crime's discovered.

But just at this point I began to catch notes I didn't like. Twice someone was late on entrance and came on as if shot from a cannon. And three times at least Sid had to throw someone a line when they blew up—in the clutches Sid's better than any prompt book. It began to look as if the play were getting out of control, maybe because the new tempo was so hot.

But they got through the Murder Scene okay. As they came trooping off, yelling "Well contented," most of them on my side for a change, I went for Sid with a towel. He always sweats like a pig in the Murder Scene. I mopped his neck and shoved the towel up under his doublet to catch the dripping armpits.

Meanwhile he was fumbling around on a narrow table where they lay props and costumes for quick changes. Suddenly he dug his fingers into my shoulder, enough to catch my attention at this point, meaning I'd show bruises tomorrow, and yelled at me under his breath, "And you love me, our crows and robes. Presto!"

I was off like a flash to the costumery. There were Mr. and Mrs. Mack's king-and-queen robes and stuff hanging and sitting just where I knew they'd have to be.

I snatched them up, thinking, *Boy, they made a mistake when they didn't tell about this special performance*, and I started back like Flash Two.

As I shot out the dressing room door the theater was very quiet. There's a short low-pitched scene on stage then, to give the audience a breather. I heard Miss Nefer say loudly (it had to be loud to get to me from even the front of the audience): "'Tis a good bloody play, Eyes," and some voice I didn't recognize reply a bit grudgingly, "There's meat in it and some poetry too, though rough-wrought." She went on, still

[187]

as loudly as if she owned the theater, "'Twill make Master Kyd bite his nails with jealousy—ha, ha!"

Ha-ha yourself, you scene-stealing witch, I thought, as I helped Sid and then Martin on with their royal outer duds. But at the same time I knew Sid must have written those lines himself to go along with his prologue. They had the unmistakable rough-wrought Lessingham touch. Did he really expect the audience to make anything of that reference to Shakespeare's predecessor Thomas Kyd of *The Spanish Tragedy* and the lost *Hamlet?* And if they knew enough to spot that, wouldn't they be bound to realize the whole Elizabeth-Macbeth tie-up was anachronistic? But when Sid gets an inspiration he can be very bull-headed.

Just then, while Bruce-Banquo was speaking his broody low soliloquy on stage, Miss Nefer cut in again loudly with, "Aye, Eyes, a good bloody play. Yet somehow, methinks—I know not how—I've heard it before." Whereupon Sid grabbed Martin by the wrist and hissed, "Did'st hear? Oh, I like not that," and I thought, *Oh-ho, so now she's beginning to ad-lib.*

Well, right away they all went on stage with a flourish, Sid and Martin crowned and hand in hand. The play got going strong again. But there were still those edge-of-control undercurrents and I began to be more uneasy than caught up, and I had to stare consciously at the actors to keep off a wavery-fit.

Other things began to bother me too, such as all the doubling.

Macbeth's a great play for doubling. For instance, anyone except Macbeth or Banquo can double one of the Three Witches—or one of the Three Murderers for that matter. Normally we double at least one or two of the Witches and Murderers, but this performance there'd been more multiple-parting than I'd ever seen. Doc had whipped off his Duncan beard and thrown on a brown smock and hood to play the Porter with his normal bottle-roughened accents. Well, a drunk impersonating a drunk, pretty appropriate. But Bruce was doing the next-door-to-impossible double of Banquo and Macduff, using a ringing tenor voice for the latter and wearing in the murder scene a helmet with dropped visor to hide his Banquo beard. He'd be able to tear it off, of course, after the Murderers got Banquo and he'd made his brief appearance as a bloodied-up ghost in the Banquet Scene. I asked myself, *My God, has Siddy got all the other actors out in front playing courtiers to Elizabeth-Nefer? Wasting them that way? The whoreson rogue's gone nuts!*

But really it was plain frightening, all that frantic doubling and tripling with its suggestion that the play (and the company too, Freya forfend) was becoming a ricketty patchwork illusion with everybody racing around faster and faster to hide the holes. And the scenery-wavery stuff and the warped Park-sounds were scary too. I was actually shivering by the time Sid got to: "Light thickens; and the crow Makes wing to the rooky wood: Good things of day begin to droop and drowse; Whiles night's black agents to their preys do rouse." Those graveyard lines didn't help my nerves any, of course. Nor did thinking I heard Nefer-Elizabeth say from the audience, rather softly for her this time, "Eyes, I have heard that speech, I know not where. Think you 'tiz stolen?"

Greta, I told myself, *you need a miltown before the crow makes wing through your kooky head.*

I turned to go and fetch me one from my closet. And stopped dead.

Just behind me, pacing back and forth like an ash-colored tiger in the gloomy wings, looking daggers at the audience every time she turned at that end of her invisible cage, but ignoring me completely, was Miss Nefer in the Elizabeth wig and rig.

Well, I suppose I should have said to myself, *Greta, you imagined that last loud whisper from the audience. Miss Nefer's simply unkinked herself, waved a hand to the real audience and come back stage. Maybe Sid just had her out there for the first half of the play. Or maybe she just couldn't stand watching Martin give such a bang-up performance in her part of Lady Mack.*

Yes, maybe I should have told myself something like that, but somehow all I could think then—and I thought it with a steady mounting shiver—was, *We got two Elizabeths. This one is our witch Nefer. I know. I dressed her. And I know that devil-look from the virginals. But if this is our Elizabeth, the company Elizabeth, the stage Elizabeth...who's the other?*

And because I didn't dare to let myself think of the answer to that question, I dodged around the invisible cage that the ash-colored skirt seemed to ripple against as the Tiger Queen turned and I ran into the dressing room, my only thought to get behind my New York City Screen.

[189]

CHAPTER V

Even little things are turning out to be great things and becoming intensely interesting.
Have you ever thought about the properties of numbers?
–The Maiden

Lying on my cot, my eyes crosswise to the printing, I looked from a pink Algonquin menu to a pale green New Amsterdam program, with a tiny doll of Father Knickerbocker dangling between them on a yellow thread. Really they weren't covering up much of anything. A ghostly hole an inch and a half across seemed to char itself in the program. As if my eye were right up against it, I saw in vivid memory what I'd seen the two times I'd dared a peek through the hole in the curtain: a bevy of ladies in masks and Nell Gwyn dresses and men in King Charles knee-breeches and long curled hair, and the second time a bunch of people and creatures just wild: all sorts and colors of clothes, humans with hoofs for feet and antennae springing from their foreheads, furry and feathery things that had more arms than two and in one case that many heads— as if they were dressed up in our *Tempest, Peer Gynt* and *Insect People* costumes and some more besides.

Naturally I'd had mind-wavery fits both times. Afterwards Sid had wagged a finger at me and explained that on those two nights we'd been giving performances for people who'd arranged a costume theater-party and been going to attend a masquerade ball, and 'zounds, when would I learn to guard my half-patched pate?

I don't know, I guess never, I answered now, quick looking at a Giants pennant, a Corvette ad, a map of Central Park, my Willie Mays baseball and a Radio City tour ticket. That was eight items I'd looked at this trip without feeling any inward improvement. They weren't reassuring me at all.

The blue fly came slowly buzzing down over my screen and I asked it, "What are you looking for? A spider?" when what should I hear coming back through the dressing room straight toward my sleeping closet but Miss Nefer's footsteps. No one else walks that way.

She's going to do something to you, Greta, I thought. *She's the maniac in the company. She's the one who terrorized you with the boning knife in the shrubbery, or sicked the giant tarantula on you at the dark end of the subway platform, or whatever it was, and the others are covering up for. She's going to smile the devil-smile and weave those white twig-fingers at you, all eight of them. And Birnam Wood'll come to Dunsinane and you'll be burnt at the stake by men in armor or drawn and quartered by eight-legged monkeys that talk or torn apart by wild centaurs or whirled through the roof to the moon without being dressed for it or sent burrowing into the past to stifle in Iowa 1948 or Egypt 4,008 B.C. The screen won't keep her out.*

Then a head of hair pushed over the screen. But it was black-bound-with-silver, Brahma bless us, and a moment later Martin was giving me one of his rare smiles.

I said, "Marty, do something for me. Don't ever use Miss Nefer's footsteps again. Her voice, okay, if you have to. But not the footsteps. Don't ask me why, just don't."

Martin came around and sat on the foot of my cot. My legs were already doubled up. He straightened out his blue-and-gold skirt and rested a hand on my black sneakers.

"Feeling a little wonky, Greta?" he asked. "Don't worry about me. Banquo's dead and so's his ghost. We've finished the Banquet Scene. I've got lots of time."

I just looked at him, queerly I guess. Then without lifting my head I asked him, "Martin, tell me the truth. Does the dressing room move around?"

I was talking so low that he hitched a little closer, not touching me anywhere else though.

"The Earth's whipping around the sun at 20 miles a second," he replied, "and the dressing room goes with it."

I shook my head, my cheek scrubbing the pillow, "I mean...shifting," I said. "By itself."

"How?" he asked.

"Well," I told him, "I've had this idea—it's just a sort of fancy, remember—that if you wanted to time-travel and, well, do things, you could hardly pick a more practical machine than a dressing room and sort of stage and half-theater attached, with actors to man it. Actors can fit in anywhere. They're used to learning new parts and wearing strange costumes. Heck, they're even used to traveling a lot. And if an actor's a bit strange nobody thinks anything of it—he's almost expected to be foreign, it's an asset to him."

"And a theater, well, a theater can spring up almost anywhere and nobody ask questions, except the zoning authorities and such and they can always be squared. Theaters come and go. It happens all the time. They're transitory. Yet theaters are crossroads, anonymous meeting places, anybody with a few bucks or sometimes nothing at all can

[191]

go. And theaters attract important people, the sort of people you might want to do something to. Caesar was stabbed in a theater. Lincoln was shot in one. And..."

My voice trailed off. "A cute idea," he commented.

I reached down to his hand on my shoe and took hold of his middle finger as a baby might.

"Yeah," I said, "But Martin, is it true?"

He asked me gravely, "What do you think?"

I didn't say anything.

"How would you like to work in a company like that?" he asked speculatively.

"I don't really know," I said.

He sat up straighter and his voice got brisk. "Well, all fantasy aside, how'd you like to work in this company?" He asked, lightly slapping my ankle. "On the stage, I mean. Sid thinks you're ready for some of the smaller parts. In fact, he asked me to put it to you. He thinks you never take him seriously."

"Pardon me while I gasp and glow," I said. Then, "Oh Marty, I can't really imagine myself doing the tiniest part."

"Me neither, eight months ago," he said. "Now, look. Lady Macbeth."

"But Marty," I said, reaching for his finger again, "you haven't answered my question. About whether it's true."

"Oh that!" he said with a laugh, switching his hand to the other side. "Ask me something else."

"Okay," I said, "why am I bugged on the number eight? Because I'm permanently behind a private 8-ball?"

"Eight's a number with many properties," he said, suddenly as intently serious as he usually is. "The corners of a cube."

"You mean I'm a square?" I said. "Or just a brick? You know, 'She's a brick.'"

"But eight's most curious property," he continued with a frown, "is that lying on its side it signifies infinity. So eight erect is really—" and suddenly his made-up, naturally solemn face got a great glow of inspiration and devotion—"Infinity Arisen!"

Well, I don't know. You meet quite a few people in the theater who are bats on numerology, they use it to pick stage-names. But I'd never have guessed it of Martin. He always struck me as the skeptical, cynical type.

"I had another idea about eight," I said hesitatingly. "Spiders. That 8-legged asterisk on Miss Nefer's forehead—" I suppressed a shudder.

"You don't like her, do you?" he stated.

"I'm afraid of her," I said.

"You shouldn't be. She's a very great woman and tonight she's play-ing an infinitely more difficult part than I am. No, Greta," he went on as I started to protest, "believe me, you don't understand anything about it at this moment. Just as you don't understand about spiders, fear-ing them. They're the first to climb the rigging and to climb ashore too. They're the web-weavers, the line-throwers, the connectors, Siva and Kali united in love. They're the double mandala, the beginning and the end, infinity mustered and on the march—"

"They're also on my New York screen!" I squeaked, shrinking back across the cot a little and pointing at a tiny glinting silver-and-black thing mounting below my Willy-ball.

Martin gently caught its line on his finger and lifted it very close to his face. "Eight eyes too," he told me. Then, "Poor little god," he said and put it back.

"Marty? Marty?" Sid's desperate stage-whisper rasped the length of the dressing room.

Martin stood up. "Yes, Sid?"

Sid's voice stayed a whisper but went from desperate to ferocious. "You villainous elf-skin! Know you not the Cauldron Scene's been playing a hundred heartbeats? 'Tis 'most my entrance and we still mustering only two witches out of three! Oh, you nott-pated starveling!"

Before Sid had got much more than half of that out, Martin had slipped around the screen, raced the length of the dressing room, and I'd heard a lusty thwack as he went out the door. I couldn't help grinning, though with Martin racked by anxieties and reliefs over his first time as Lady Mack, it was easy to understand it slipping his mind that he was still doubling Second Witch.

CHAPTER VI

I will vault credit
and affect high pleasures
Beyond death.
–Ferdinand

I sat down where Martin had been, first pushing the screen far enough to the side for me to see the length of the dressing room and notice anyone coming through the door and any blurs moving behind the thin white curtain shutting off the boys' two-thirds.

I'd been going to think. But instead I just sat there, experiencing my body and the room around it, steadying myself or maybe readying myself. I couldn't tell which, but it was nothing to think about, only to feel. My heartbeat became a very faint, slow, solid throb. My spine straightened.

No one came in or went out. Distantly I heard Macbeth and the witches and the apparitions talk.

Once I looked at the New York Screen, but all the stuff there had grown stale. No protection, no nothing.

I reached down to my suitcase and from where I'd been going to get a miltown I took a dexedrine and popped it in my mouth. Then I started out, beginning to shake.

When I got to the end of the curtain I went around it to Sid's dressing table and asked Shakespeare, "Am I doing the right thing, Pop?" But he didn't answer me out of his portrait. He just looked sneaky-innocent, like he knew a lot but wouldn't tell, and I found myself think of a little silver-framed photo Sid had used to keep there too of a cocky German-looking young actor with "Erich" autographed across it in white ink. At least I supposed he was an actor. He looked a little like Erich von Stroheim, but nicer yet somehow nastier too. The photo had used to upset me, I don't know why. Sid must have noticed it, for one day it was gone.

I thought of the tiny black-and-silver spider crawling across the re-membered silver frame, and for some reason it gave me the cold creeps.

Well, this wasn't doing me any good, just making me feel dismal again, so I quickly went out. In the door I had to slip around the actors coming back from the Cauldron Scene and the big bolt nicked my hip.

Outside Maud was peeling off her Third Witch stuff to reveal Lady Macduff beneath. She twitched me a grin.

"How's it going?" I asked.

"Okay, I guess," she shrugged. "What an audience! Noisy as high-school kids."

"How come Sid didn't have a boy do your part?" I asked.

"He goofed, I guess. But I've battened down my bosoms and playing Mrs. Macduff as a boy."

"How does a girl do that in a dress?" I asked.

"She sits stiff and thinks pants," she said, handing me her witch robe. "'Scuse me now. I got to find my children and go get murdered."

I'd moved a few steps nearer the stage when I felt the gentlest tug at my hip. I looked down and saw that a taut black thread from the bottom of my sweater connected me with the dressing room. It must have snagged on the big bolt and unraveled. I moved my body an inch or so, tugging it delicately to see what it felt like and I got the answers: Theseus's clew, a spider's line, an umbilicus.

I reached down close to my side and snapped it with my fingernails. The black thread leaped away. But the dressing room door didn't vanish, or the wings change, or the world end, and I didn't fall down.

After that I just stood there for quite a while, feeling my new freedom and steadiness, letting my body get used to it. I didn't do any thinking. I hardly bothered to study anything around me, though I did notice that there were more bushes and trees than set pieces, and that the flickery lightning was simply torches and that Queen Elizabeth was in (or back in) the audience. Sometimes letting your body get used to something is all you should do, or maybe can do.

And I did smell horse dung.

When the Lady Macduff Scene was over and the Chicken Scene well begun, I went back to the dressing room. Actors call it the Chicken Scene because Macduff weeps in it about "all my pretty chickens and their dam," meaning his kids and wife, being murdered "at one fell swoop" on orders of that chickenyard-raiding "hell-kite" Macbeth.

Inside the dressing room I steered down the boys' side. Doc was putting on an improbable-looking dark makeup for Macbeth's last faithful servant Seyton. He didn't seem as boozy-woozy as usual for Fourth Act, but just the same I stopped to help him get into a chain-mail shirt made of thick cord woven and silvered.

In the third chair beyond, Sid was sitting back with his corset loosened and critically surveying Martin, who'd now changed to a white wool nightgown that clung and draped beautifully, but not particularly enticingly, on him and his folded towel, which had slipped a bit.

From beside Sid's mirror, Shakespeare smiled out of his portrait at them like an intelligent big-headed bug.

Martin stood tall, spread his arms rather like a high priest, and intoned, "*Amici! Romani! Populares!*"

I nudged Doc. "What goes on now?" I whispered.

He turned a bleary eye on them. "I think they are rehearsing *Julius Caesar* in Latin." He shrugged. "It begins the oration of Antony."

"But why?" I asked. Sid does like to put every moment to use when the performance-fire is in people, but this project seemed pretty far afield—hyper-pedantic. Yet at the same time I felt my scalp shivering as if my mind were jumping with speculations just below the surface.

Doc shook his head and shrugged again.

Sid shoved a palm at Martin and roared softly, "'Sdeath, boy, thou'rt not playing a Roman statua but a Roman! Loosen your knees and try again."

Then he saw me. Signing Martin to stop, he called, "Come hither, sweetling." I obeyed quickly. He gave me a fiendish grin and said, "Thou'st heard our proposal from Martin. What sayest thou, wench?"

This time the shiver was in my back. It felt good. I realized I was grinning back at him, and I knew what I'd been getting ready for the last twenty minutes.

"I'm on," I said. "Count me in the company."

Sid jumped up and grabbed me by the shoulders and hair and bussed me on both cheeks. It was a little like being bombed.

"Prodigious!" he cried. "Thou'lt play the Gentlewoman in the Sleepwalking Scene tonight. Martin, her costume! Now sweet wench, mark me well." His voice grew grave and old. "When was it she last walked?"

The new courage went out of me like water down a chute. "But Siddy, I can't start *tonight*," I protested, half pleading, half outraged.

"Tonight or never! 'Tis an emergency—we're short-handed." Again his voice changed. "When was it she last walked?"

"But Siddy, I don't *know* the part."

"You must. You've heard the play twenty times this year past. When was it she last walked?"

Martin was back and yanking down a blonde wig on my head and shoving my arms into a light gray robe.

"I've never studied *the lines*," I squeaked at Sidney.

"Liar! I've watched your lips move a dozen nights when you watched the scene from the wings. Close your eyes, girl! Martin, unhand her. Close your eyes, girl, empty your mind, and listen, listen only. When was it she last walked?"

In the blackness I heard myself replying to that cue, first in a whisper, then more loudly, then full-throated but grave, "Since his majesty went into the field, I have seen her rise from her bed, throw her nightgown upon her, unlock her closet, take forth—"

"Bravissimo!" Siddy cried and bombed me again. Martin hugged his arm around my shoulders too, then quickly stooped to start hooking up my robe from the bottom.

"But that's only the first lines, Siddy," I protested.

"They're enough!"

"But Siddy, what if I blow up?" I asked.

"Keep your mind empty. You won't. Further, I'll be at your side, doubling the Doctor, to prompt you if you pause."

That ought to take care of two of me, I thought. Then something else struck me. "But Siddy," I quavered, "how do I play the Gentlewoman as a boy?"

"Boy?" he demanded wonderingly. "Play her without falling down flat on your face and I'll be past measure happy!" And he smacked me hard on the fanny.

Martin's fingers were darting at the next to the last hook. I stopped him and shoved my hand down the neck of my sweater and got hold of the subway token and the chain it was on and yanked. It burned my neck but the gold links parted. I started to throw it across the room, but instead I smiled at Siddy and dropped it in his palm.

"The Sleepwalking Scene!" Maud hissed insistently to us from the door.

CHAPTER VII

I know death hath ten thousand several doors
For men to take their exits, and 'tis found
They go on such strange geometrical hinges,
You may open them both ways.
–The Duchess

There is this about an actor on stage: he can see the audience but
he can't *look* at them, unless he's a narrator or some sort of comic. I
wasn't the first (Grendel groks!) and only scared to death of becoming
the second as Siddy walked me out of the wings onto the stage, over the
groundcloth that felt so much like ground, with a sort of interweaving
policeman-grip on my left arm.

Sid was in a dark gray robe looking like some dismal kind of monk,
his head so hooded for the Doctor that you couldn't see his face at all.

My skull was pulse-buzzing. My throat was squeezed dry. My heart
was pounding. Below that my body was empty, squirmy, electricity-
stung, yet with the feeling of wearing ice cold iron pants.

I heard as if from two million miles, "When was it she last walked?"
and then an iron bell somewhere tolling the reply—I guess it had to be
my voice coming up through my body from my iron pants: "Since his
majesty went into the field—" and so on, until Martin had come on stage,
stary-eyed, a white scarf tossed over the back of his long black wig and
a flaring candle two inches thick gripped in his right hand and dripping
wax on his wrist, and started to do Lady Mack's sleepwalking half-hinted
confessions of the murders of Duncan and Banquo and Lady Macduff.

So here is what I saw then without looking, like a vivid scene that
floats out in front of your mind in a reverie, hovering against a background
of dark blur, and sort of flashes on and off as you think, or in my case act.
All the time, remember, with Sid's hand hard on my wrist and me now
and then tolling Shakespearan language out of some lightless storehouse
of memory I'd never known was there to belong to me.

There was a medium-size glade in a forest. Through the half-naked
black branches shone a dark cold sky, like ashes of silver, early evening.

The glade had two horns, as it were, narrowing back to either side
and going off through the forest. A chilly breeze was blowing out of them,
almost enough to put out the candle. Its flame rippled.

[198]

Rather far back in the horn to my left, but not very far, were clumped two dozen or so men in dark cloaks they huddled around themselves. They wore brimmed tallish hats and pale stuff showing at their necks. Somehow I assumed that these men must be the "rude fellows from the City" I remembered Beau mentioning a million or so years ago. Although I couldn't see them very well, and didn't spend much time on them, there was one of them who had his hat off or excitedly pushed way back, showing a big pale forehead. Although that was all the conscious impression I had of his face, he seemed frighteningly familiar.

In the horn to my right, which was wider, were lined up about a dozen horses, with grooms holding tight every two of them, but throwing their heads back now and then as they strained against the reins, and stamping their front hooves restlessly. Oh, they frightened me, I tell you, that line of two-foot-long glossy-haired faces, writhing back their upper lips from teeth wide as piano keys, every horse of them looking as wild-eyed and evil as Fuseli's steed sticking its head through the drapes in his picture "The Nightmare."

To the center the trees came close to the stage. Just in front of them was Queen Elizabeth sitting on the chair on the spread carpet, just as I'd seen her out there before; only now I could see that the braziers were glowing and redly high-lighting her pale cheeks and dark red hair and the silver in her dress and cloak. She was looking at Martin—Lady Mack— most intently, her mouth grimaced tight, twisting her fingers together.

Standing rather close around her were a half dozen men with fancier hats and ruffs and wide-flaring riding gauntlets.

Then, through the trees and tall leafless bushes just behind Elizabeth, I saw an identical Elizabeth-face floating, only this one was smiling a demonic smile. The eyes were open very wide. Now and then the pupils darted rapid glances from side to side.

There was a sharp pain in my left wrist and Sid whisper-snarling at me, "Accustomed action!" out of the corner of his shadowed mouth.

I tolled on obediently, "It is an accustomed action with her, to seem thus washing her hands: I have known her continue in this a quarter of an hour."

Martin had set down the candle, which still flared and guttered, on a little high table so firm its thin legs must have been stabbed into the ground. And he was rubbing his hands together slowly, continually, tormentedly, trying to get rid of Duncan's blood which Mrs. Mack knows in her sleep is still there. And all the while as he did it, the agitation of the seated Elizabeth grew, the eyes flicking from side to side, hands writhing.

He got to the lines, "Here's the smell of blood still: all the perfumes of Arabia will not sweeten this little hand. Oh, oh, oh!"

[199]

As he wrung out those soft, tortured sighs, Elizabeth stood up from her chair and took a step forward. The courtiers moved toward her quickly, but not touching her, and she said loudly, "'Tis the blood of Mary Stuart whereof she speaks—the pails of blood that will gush from her chopped neck. Oh, I cannot endure it!" And as she said that last, she suddenly turned about and strode back toward the trees, kicking out her ash-colored skirt. One of the courtiers turned with her and stooped toward her closely, whispering something. But although she paused a moment, all she said was, "Nay, Eyes, stop not the play, but follow me not! Nay, I say leave me, Leicester!" And she walked into the trees, he looking after her.

Then Sid was kicking my ankle and I was reciting something and Martin was taking up his candle again without looking at it saying with a drugged agitation, "To bed; to bed; there's knocking at the gate."

Elizabeth came walking out of the trees again, her head bowed. She couldn't have been in them ten seconds. Leicester hurried toward her, hand anxiously outstretched.

Martin moved offstage, torturedly yet softly wailing, "What's done cannot be undone."

Just then Elizabeth flicked aside Leicester's hand with playful contempt and looked up and she was smiling the devil-smile. A horse whinnied like a trumpeted snicker.

As Sid and I started our last few lines together I intoned mechanically, letting words free-fall from my mind to my tongue. All this time I had been answering Lady Mack in my thoughts, *That's what you think, sister.*

CHAPTER VIII

God cannot effect that anything which is past should not have been.

It is more impossible than rising the dead.

–Summa Theologica

The moment I was out of sight of the audience I broke away from Sid and ran to the dressing room. I flopped down on the first chair I saw, my head and arms trailed over its back, and I almost passed out. It wasn't a mind-wavery fit. Just normal faint.

I couldn't have been there long—well, not very long, though the battle-rattle and alarums of the last scene were echoing tinnily from the stage—when Bruce and Beau and Mark (who was playing Malcolm, Martin's usual main part) came in wearing their last-act stage-armor and carrying between them Queen Elizabeth flaccid as a sack. Martin came after them, stripping off his white wool nightgown so fast that buttons flew. I thought automatically, *I'll have to sew those.*

They laid her down on three chairs set side by side and hurried out. Unpinning the folded towel, which had fallen around his waist, Martin walked over and looked down at her. He yanked off his wig by a braid and tossed it at me.

I let it hit me and fall on the floor. I was looking at that white queenly face, eyes open and staring sightless at the ceiling, mouth open a little too with a thread of foam trailing from the corner, and at that ice-cream-cone bodice that never stirred. The blue fly came buzzing over my head and circled down toward her face.

"Martin," I said with difficulty, "I don't think I'm going to like what we're doing."

He turned on me, his short hair elfed, his fists planted high on his hips at the edge of his black tights, which now were all his clothes.

"You knew!" he said impatiently. "You knew you were signing up for more than acting when you said, 'Count me in the company.'"

Like a legged sapphire the blue fly walked across her upper lip and stopped by the thread of foam.

"But Martin...changing the past...dipping back and killing the real queen...replacing her with a double—"

His dark brows shot up. "The real—You think this is the real Queen Elizabeth?" He grabbed a bottle of rubbing alcohol from the nearest table, gushed some on a towel stained with grease-paint and, holding the dead head by its red hair (no, wig—the real one wore a wig too) scrubbed the forehead.

The white cosmetic came away, showing sallow skin and on it a faint tattoo in the form of an "S" styled like a yin-yang symbol left a little open.

"Snake!" he hissed. "Destroyer! The arch-enemy, the eternal opponent! God knows how many times people like Queen Elizabeth have been dug out of the past, first by Snakes, then by Spiders, and kidnapped or killed and replaced in the course of our war. This is the first big operation I've been on, Greta. But I know that much."

My head began to ache. I asked, "If she's an enemy double, why didn't she know a performance of Macbeth in her lifetime was an anachronism?"

"Foxholed in the past, only trying to hold a position, they get dulled. They turn half zombie. Even the Snakes. Even our people. Besides, she almost did catch on, twice when she spoke to Leicester."

"Martin," I said dully, "if there've been all these replacements, first by them, then by us, what's happened to the *real* Elizabeth?"

He shrugged. "God knows."

I asked softly, "But does He, Martin? Can He?"

He hugged his shoulders in, as if to contain a shudder. "Look, Greta," he said, "it's the Snakes who are the warpers and destroyers. We're restoring the past. The Spiders are trying to keep things as first created. We only kill when we must."

I shuddered then, for bursting out of my memory came the glittering, knife-flashing, night-shrouded, bloody image of my lover, the Spider soldier-of-change Erich von Hohenwald, dying in the grip of a giant silver spider, or spider-shaped entity large as he, as they rolled in a tangled ball down a flight of rocks in Central Park.

But the memory-burst didn't blow up my mind, as it had done a year ago, no more than snapping the black thread from my sweater had ended the world. I asked Martin, "Is that what the Snakes say?"

"Of course not! They make the same claims we do. But somewhere, Greta, you have to *trust*." He put out the middle finger of his hand.

I didn't take hold of it. He whirled it away, snapping it against his thumb.

"You're still grieving for that carrion there!" he accused me. He jerked down a section of white curtain and whirled it over the stiffening body. "If you must grieve, grieve for Miss Nefer! Exiled, imprisoned, locked forever in the past, her mind pulsing faintly in the black hole of the dead and gone, yearning for Nirvana yet nursing one lone painful patch of consciousness. And only to hold a fort! Only to make sure Mary Stuart is executed, the Armada licked, and that all the other consequences flow on. The Snakes' Elizabeth let Mary live...and England die...and the Spaniard hold North America to the Great Lakes and New Scandinavia."

Once more he put out his middle finger.

"All right, all right," I said, barely touching it. "You've convinced me."

"Great!" he said. "'By for now, Greta. I got to help strike the set."

"That's good," I said. He loped out.

I could hear the skirling sword-clashes of the final fight to the death of the two Macks, Duff and Beth. But I only sat there in the empty dressing room pretending to grieve for a devil-smiling snow tiger locked in a time-cage and for a cute sardonic German killed for insubordination that *I* had reported...but really grieving for a girl who for a year had been a rootless child of the theater with a whole company of mothers and fathers, afraid of nothing more than subway bogies and Park and Village monsters.

As I sat there pitying myself beside a shrouded queen, a shadow fell across my knees. I saw stealing through the dressing room a young man in worn dark clothes. He couldn't have been more than twenty-three. He was a frail sort of guy with a weak chin and big forehead and eyes that saw everything. I knew at one he was the one who had seemed familiar to me in the knot of City fellows.

He looked at me and I looked from him to the picture sitting on the reserve makeup box by Siddy's mirror. And I began to tremble.

He looked at it too, of course, as fast as I did. And then he began to tremble too, though it was a finer-grained tremor than mine.

The sword-fight had ended seconds back and now I heard the witches faintly wailing, "Fair is foul, and foul is fair—" Sid has them echo that line offstage at the end to give a feeling of prophecy fulfilled.

Then Sid came pounding up. He's the first finished, since the fight ends offstage so Macduff can carry back a red-necked papier-mache head of him and show it to the audience. Sid stopped dead in the door.

Then the stranger turned around. His shoulders jerked as he saw Sid. He moved toward him just two or three steps at a time, speaking at the same time in breathy little rushes.

Sid stood there and watched him. When the other actors came boiling up behind him, he put his hands on the doorframe to either side so none of them could get past. Their faces peered around him.

And all this while the stranger was saying, "What may this mean? Can such things be? Are all the seeds of time...wetted by some hell-trickle...sprouted at once in their granary? Speak...speak! You played me a play...that I am writing in my secretest heart. Have you disjointed the frame of things...to steal my unborn thoughts? Fair is foul indeed. Is all the world a stage? Speak, I say! Are you not my friend Sidney James Lessingham of King's Lynn...singed by time's fiery wand...sifted over with the ashes of thirty years? Speak, are you not he? Oh, there are more things in heaven and earth...aye, and perchance hell too...Speak, I charge you!"

And with that he put his hands on Sid's shoulders, half to shake him, I think, but half to keep from falling over. And for the one time I ever saw it, glib old Siddy had nothing to say.

He worked his lips. He opened his mouth twice and twice shut it. Then, with a kind of desperation in his face, he motioned the actors out of the way behind him with one big arm and swung the other around the stranger's narrow shoulders and swept him out of the dressing room, himself following.

The actors came pouring in then, Bruce tossing Macbeth's head to Martin like a football while he tugged off his horned helmet, Mark dumping a stack of shields in the corner, Maudie pausing as she skittered past me to say, "Hi Gret, great you're back," and patting my temple to show what part of me she meant. Beau went straight to Sid's dressing table and set the portrait aside and lifted out Sid's reserve makeup box.

"The lights, Martin!" he called.

Then Sid came back in, slamming and bolting the door behind him and standing for a moment with his back against it, panting.

I rushed to him. Something was boiling up inside me, but before it could get to my brain I opened my mouth and it came out as, "Siddy, you can't fool me, that was no dirty S-or-S. I don't care how much he shakes and purrs, or shakes a spear, or just plain shakes—Siddy, that was Shakespeare!"

"Aye, girl, I think so," he told me, holding my wrists together. "They can't find dolls to double men like that—or such is my main hope." A big sickly grin came on his face. "Oh, gods," he demanded, "with what words do you talk to a man whose speech you've stolen all your life?"

I asked him, "Sid, were we *ever* in Central Park?"

He answered, "Once—twelve months back. A one-night stand. They came for Erich. You flipped."

He swung me aside and moved behind Beau. All the lights went out.

Then I saw, dimly at first, the great dull-gleaming jewel, covered with dials and green-glowing windows, that Beau had lifted from Sid's reserve makeup box. The strongest green glow showed his intent face, still framed by the long glistening locks of the Ross wig, as he kneeled before the thing—Major Maintainer, I remembered it was called.

[204]

"When now? Where?" Beau tossed impatiently to Sid over his shoulder.

"The forty-fourth year before our Lord's birth!" Sid answered instantly. "Rome!"

Beau's fingers danced over the dials like a musician's, or a safecracker's. The green glow flared and faded flickeringly.

"There's a storm in that vector of the Void."

"Circle it," Sid ordered.

"There are dark mists every way."

"Then pick the likeliest dark path!"

I called through the dark, "Fair is foul, and foul is fair, eh, Siddy?"

"Aye, chick," he answered me. "'Tis all the rule we have!"

Guide to the Change World

Abbreviations

BT *The Big Time* (1958)
CW *When the Change Winds Blow* (1964)
DG *A Deskfull of Girls* (1958)
DM *Damnation Morning* (1959)
KM *Knight to Move (1965)*
NM *No Great Magic* (1960)
OS *The Oldest Soldier* (1960)
TP *Try and Change the Past* (1958)

61 Cygni 5 – An inhabited planet. By treaty it is a neutral area in the Change War. *KM*

Alpha Centauri 2 – An inhabited planet. *KM*

Alpha Centauri 4 – A planet under open contention in the change war. *TP*

Assassination Missile – A robotic weapon that moves on insect-like wings. It can be fitted with a variety of munitions and set to track an electronic signal. *KM*

Atropos – A hand-held device used to cut people out of their life lines. It can be used to create doublegangers or to kill them. *BT, DM*

Benson–Carter – A spider change soldier. His specialty is atomic technology. *BT*

Big Time, The – Spider slang term for the Change War. *BT*

Black Dog – A genetically altered monster used to hunt change soldiers. Reasonably intelligent but poorly disciplined. It has shaggy black fur, glowing red eyes, and body elements that resemble those of a hound, a panther, a bat, and a man. *OS*

Bournemann, Max – A veteran change soldier who specializes in operations in active war zones. *OS*

Caller – An electrically–powered portable communications device carried by change soldiers. Most frequently used to signal friendly places and request doors for extraction of personnel. *BT, OS*

Change Death – The phenomenon where a doubleganger ceases to exist because the timeline changes such that their zombie self's death occurs before the time of their resurrection. *BT*

Change Soldier – A time traveler in the service of one of the principal factions of the Change War. *BT, DM, NM, OS, TP*

Change War – Eternal and universal conflict between the Snakes and Spiders, fought both planet–side and in space on battlegrounds throughout all of space and time, both covertly and openly. Most worlds in the universe are permanently aligned with one faction or another. Others, such as Earth, are being actively contended for. A few are neutral areas, established by treaty, on which both sides refrain from active operations (in theory). *BT, DM, NM, OS, TP*

Change Winds – An atmospheric phenomenon native to The Void. *BT*

Cordew, Evelyn (a.k.a. Eva-Lynn Korduplewski) – A zombie film star on 20th century Earth with some interesting connections. *DG*

Countersign Club – An extremely exclusive gentlemens club on 20th century Earth. *DG*

Crain, Jeff – A zombie film star on 20th century Earth. Formerly married to Evelyn Cordew. *DG*

Davies, Maud – A Spider entertainer. Originally a psycho-medical professional. Born on 23rd century Ganymede. *BT, NM*

Demon – A doubleganger who is temporally aware and capable of independant action and is thus able to make use of time travel technology and retain memories from timelines which have ceased to exist. Only a minority of people are capable of becoming demons, even with the help of a resurrectionist. *BT*

Dispatching Room – A facility with equipment for rapidly opening doors to various times and places. The controls are so simple a child could use them. *TP*

Door – A portal, only visible to doublegangers, between the regular time-space continuum and an artificially constructed place outside the time-space continuum. See also *place*. *BT, DM*

Doubleganger – A copy of a person, able to exist outside of normal space-time. Doublegangers are either demons or ghosts depending on the degree of self awareness and independent existance they retain. Multiple doublegangers can be cut from the same person. See also *demon, ghost, zombie. BT, NM, TP*

Earth – Third planet of the star Sol. An active battleground in the Change War. Also known as Terra. *BT, DM, OS*

Entertainer – A doubleganger charged with staffing recuperation stations and otherwise providing rear-area support for change soldiers. *BT*

Express Room – A place which is equiped to transport change soldiers to and from action. *BT*

Forzane, Greta – A spider entertainer, originally from mid-20th century Chicago. "29 and a party girl". *BT, NM*

Foster, Lilian – A Spider entertainer. Originally from early-20th century Britain. *BT*

Foxholing – Change soldiers' term for cutting off communication and going into deep cover in a particular era, sometimes for years at a time. *BT, NM*

Fred – A clerical worker in mid–20th century Chicago with an interest in war and military history. *OS*

Ghost – A type of doubleganger which is essentially an animated record of a persons physical appearance and emotions, capable of limited thought and independent action. Can be stored indefinitely but, once activated, fade away if no one pays attention to it. All known ghosts are made from human females. See also *demon BT, DG*

Ghost-Girls Pavan – A lost movement of Tchaikovsky's *Nutcracker Suite* that was suppressed because it was too erotic.

Heat Ray – A squad-level weapon that projects beams of coherent thermal energy. *BT*

High Command – Each faction of the Change War's supreme headquarters, the exact location of which in time and space are closely guarded secrets. Most of each high command is given over to data processing and storage; Snake high command is said to possess archives totaling "several planets of microfilm and two asteroids of coded molecules." *BT, TP*

Illhilihis – A Spider change soldier. Originally a Lunan "thinger"—a profession which is impossible to explain in English. *BT*

Introversion – A mode on a major maintainer which takes a place out of phase with the rest of the time–space continuum, so that other places are completely unable to detect, communicate with, or interact with it in any way. Introverting is incredibly dangerous without support from headquarters and is only used as a last–ditch gambit to escape destruction. The void equivalent of dropping a submarine onto the bottom and turning off the engines. *BT*

Invertor – A medical device which harnesses the power of the void to turn patients' bodies inside–out for surgery. *BT*

K'ta'hra – A backgammon-like game native to the Alpha Centauri system. *KM*

Labrys, Kabysia – Spider field officer. She was born into the matriarchal warrior aristocracy of ancient Crete. *BT*

Lassiter, Beauregard – Spider entertainer, originally from 19th century Louisiana. A man of many skills including gambling, playing piano, and picking locks. *BT, NM*

Late Cosmicians – A hypothetical far-future society that will be able to use its advanced technology to limit the spread of the Change War beyond the start of its own era. The relationship between the Late Cosmicians and the original Snakes and Spiders is a source of conjecture. *BT*

Law of the Conservation of Reality – The principle that the universe resists changes to the timeline and heals itself in the way that requires the least net energy, however improbable. *BT, TP*

Lessingham, Sidney James – Spider officer in command of a recuperation station. Born in King's Lynn, England, in 1564, he attended Cambridge and knew a young William Shakespeare personally. *BT, NM*

Leutnant, The – A former soldier in mid–20th century Chicago. *OS*

Lili – Traditional Spider nickname for the most junior female entertainer in a recuperation station. *BT*

Luna – The single moon of Earth. Luna was formerly habitable but lost its biosphere and atmosphere millions of years ago in a nuclear holocaust. *BT*

Lunans – The dominant race of Luna, which perished millions of years before the rise of humanity. Adult Lunans are covered with silver fur and have six tentacles and two legs, giving them an appearance to humans as "a Persian cat crossed with an octopus" They stand over 2 meters tall but have very little mass for their size. *BT*

Mackay, Carr – A zombie private investigator on mid-20th century Earth. *DG*

Maintainer, Major – A device used to create and communicate between places. *BT, NM*

Maintainer, Minor – A device used to provide life support and artificial gravity inside a place. *BT*

Marchant, Bruce – A Spider change soldier. Formerly a British officer and poet whose zombie self was killed in World War I. *BT, NM*

Marcia – A Spider entertainer. Deceased. *BT*

Mars – The fourth planet in the Sol system. At multiple points in history it has evolved sentient native races. It will also be colonized by humans during their own spacefaring age. *BT, OS*

Martians – One of multiple intelligent races which have inhabited the planet Mars including the Coleopts (a race of telepatic social insects), a race with highly assymetric anatomy, and the humans who will colonize Mars beginning in the 21st century. *BT, CW*

Martin – A Spider change soldier. *NM*

Mind Bomb – A weapon of mass destruction from the far future. *BT*

Needle Gun – A squad level automatic weapon which is practically silent. Normally crewed by two people. *BT*

Nefer, Iris – A Spider deep-cover agent. *NM*

Niger, Marcus Vipsaius (Mark) – Spider change soldier. Originally a Roman officer whose zombie self died in 10 A.D. *BT, NM*

Now – A concept of understandable confusion to time travelors since Change World or Void time moves distinctly from that in regular space-time and even regular time is relative. "Now" in the Change World is believed by Spider High Command to roughly correspond to a point in the second half of Earth's 20th century, an assertion which is not only hard to proove but may be academic. *BT*

Place – An artificial bubble of space–time created by a major maintainer. Used as bases and time-space vehicles by doublegangers. *BT*

Pyeskov, Doc – A Spider physician, originally from Czarist Russia. A low-bottom alcoholic. *BT, NM*

Recuperation Station – A place outfitted with medical and entertainment facilities where change soldiers go to rest between missions. *BT*

Refresher – A high tech personal hygiene device that serves much the same role as a shower. *BT*

Resurrectionist – A temporal agent charged with recruiting new time travelers by cutting them out of the timeline shortly before they are destined to die. *BT, DM, TP*

Sevensea – A Spider change soldier, native to far-future Venus. *BT*

Sigil – A permanent, tattoo-like mark which many (possibly all) change soldiers bear on their foreheads. The Spider sigil resembles an asterisk with eight points. The Snake sigil resembles a stylized 'S' shaped like an unconnected yin yang symbol. *DM*

Slyker, Dr. Emil – A zombie psycho-physiologist to the stars from mid 20th century Earth. *DG*

Snakes – One of the two major factions struggling for control of the time-space continuum. Snake dress uniforms are green. Their symbol is a a stylized 'S' shaped like an unconnected yin yang symbol. See also *Spiders*. *BT, DM, KM, NM, TP*

Sol – A former soldier who operates a liqueur store in mid-20th century Chicago. *OS*

Spiders – One of the two major factions struggling for control of the time-space continuum. It is frequently conjectured, but not confirmed, that the Spider leadership is drawn from a race of super-intelligent arachnoids. Spider dress uniforms are black with silver hardware. Their symbol is an eight-pointed asterisk. See also *Snakes*. *BT, DG, DM, KM, NM, TP*

Stun Gun – A sidearm carried by change soldiers. Usually camouflaged as a period weapon. Direct hits cause unconsciousness whereas near misses cause confusion and/or temporary partial paralysis. *BT*

[211]

Suzaku – A Spider resurrectionist, originally a samurai from feudal Japan. *BT*

Tau Ceti – A star system with at least one inhabited planet, inhabited by an intelligent avian race. *KM*

Thought Writing – A system of communication used by change soldiers in which specially treated paper is made to display words from a distance. It is unknown whether the words themselves are transmitted or simply written invisibly and then activated remotely. *OS*

Unborn – A person potentially destined to live in a future (as referenced by doublegangers living outside of normal time) timeline. The exact distinction between zombies and unborn is often unclear, given the relative nature of timekeeping in a time traveling organization. *BT*

Venus – The second planet of the star Sol. During the time of humanity Venus is uninhabitable to most races due to high heat and extreme weather. *BT*

Venusians – The dominant race of Venus in the far future. Somewhat resemble that satyrs of Earth mythology. They possess an advanced technology which allows them for warp time and space more or less at will. *BT*

Void – An infinite expanse of nothingness which exists outside the time-space continuum. Conditions in the void are cyclical, so that places traversing the void can only make contact with normal space-time during certain windows. *BT*

von Hohenwald, Colonel Erich Friederich – A Spider field officer. Originally a Nazi SS officer from 20th century Earth. His zombie self lives to become commandant of Toronto after the Nazi conquest of North America. *BT, KM, NM*

Warning Plate – A device worn by change soldiers to warn of the presence of nearby doublegangers. It is worn next to the skin and creates distinctive sensations based on whether it detects Snake or Spider doublegangers. *KM*

Weaver, Major Erica – A Snake field officer, originally from 20th century Minnesota. *KM*

Wolf 1 – An inhabited planet. It's sentient inhabitants have several arms.

Woody – A former soldier in mid-20th century Chicago. *OS*

Zombie – Slang term for an ordinary person who is unable to travel in time and unaware of the existence of the Change War. Also used by change soldiers as a general derogatory term. See also *doubleganger, unborn. BT, DM*

Fritz Leiber Chronology

Titles of works are listed in the year they where originally published. Many of Leiber's stories were later reprinted in anthologies and/or translated to other languages. For an exhaustive bibliography the reader is directed to the *Internet Speculative Fiction Database* at http://isfdb.org.

1910

Born December 24 in Chicago, IL

1928

First tour with parents' theater company

1932

Graduated with honors from University of Chicago

1932

Spent one year at General Theological Seminary

1934

Second tour with parents' theater company
Wrote first known short stories

1936

Married Jonquil Stevens

1938

Justin Leiber born

1939

Two Sought Adventure

1940

The Automatic Pistol, The Bleak Shore

1941

Began teaching speech and drama at Occidental College

The Howling Tower, The Power of the Puppets, Smoke Ghost, They Never Came Back

1942

The Hill and the Hole, The Hound, The Phantom Slayer, Spider Mansion, The Sunken Land

1943

Conjure Wife, Gather Darkness!, The Mutant's Brother, Thieves' House, To Make a Roman Holiday

1944

Business of Killing, Sanity, Taboo, Thought

1945

Destiny Times Three, The Dreams of Albert Moreland, Wanted: An Enemy

1946

Alice and the Allergy, Mr. Bauer and the Atoms

1947

Adept's Gambit, Diary in the Snow, The Man Who Never Grew Young

1949

The Girl with the Hungry Eyes, In the X-Ray

1950

The Black Ewe, Coming Attraction, The Dead Man, The Enchanted Forest, Later Than You Think, Let Freedom Ring, The Lion and the Lamb, Martians Keep Out!, The Ship Sails at Midnight, You're All Alone

1951

Appointment in Tomorrow, Cry Witch!, Dark Vengeance, Nice Girl with Five Husbands, A Pail of Air, When the Last Gods Die

1952

Dr. Kometevsky's Day, The Foxholes of Mars, I'm Looking for 'Jeff', The Moon is Green, Yesterday House

1953

A Bad Day for Sales, The Green Millennium, The Sinful Ones, The Big Holiday, The Night He Cried, The Seven Black Priests

1954

The Mechanical Bride, The Silence Game

1954-1956

Slid into an alcoholic haze and was unable to write for three years.

1957

The Big Trek, Femmequin 973, Friends and Enemies, Last, Time Fighter, Time in the Round, What's He Doing in There?

1958

Began writing full-time
The Big Time (Magazine Version), Bread Overhead, Bullet With His Name, A Deskful of Girls, The Last Letter, Little Old Miss Macbeth, Rump-Titty-Titty-Tum-TAH-Tee, Space Time for Springers, Try and Change the Past

1959

Damnation Morning, The House of Mrs. Delgado, The Improper Authorities, Lean Times in Lankhmar, The Number of the Beast, The Mind Spider, MS Found in a Maelstorm, Our Saucer Vacation, Pipe Dream, Psychosis from Space, The Reward, The Silver Eggheads (Magazine Version), Tranquility. Or Else!

1960

Deadly Moon, Mariana, The Night of the Long Knives, The Oldest Soldier, Rats of Limbo, Schizo Jimmie, When the Sea-King's Away

1961

All the Weed in the World, The Beat Cluster, The Big Time (Novel), The Goggles of Dr. Dragonet, Hatchery of Dreams, Kreativity for Kats, Scream Wolf, Scylla's Daughter, The Silver Eggheads (Novel), A Visitor from Back East

1962

The 64-Square Madhouse, The Big Engine, A Bit of the Dark World, The Creature from the Cleveland Depths, The Man Who Made Friends with Electricity, Mirror, The Moriarty Gambit, The Secret Songs, The Snowbank Orbit, The Thirteenth Step, The Unholy Grail

1963

237 Talking Statues, Etc., Bazaar of the Bizarre, The Casket-Demon, The Cloud of Hate, Crimes Against Passion, Dr. Adams' Garden of Evil, Game for Motel Room, A Hitch in Space, Kindergarten, Myths my Great-Granddaughter Taught Me, No Great Magic, The Spider, Success, X Marks the Pedwalk

1964

Be of Good Cheer, The Black Gondolier, Lie Still, Snow White, The Lords of Quarmall, Midnight in the Mirror World, When the Change-Winds Blow, The Wanderer

1965

Cyclops, Far Reach to Cygnus, Four Ghosts in Hamlet, The Good New Days, Knight to Move, Moon Duel, Stardock

1966

The Crystal Prison, Sunk Without Trace, Tarzan and the Valley of Gold, To Arkham and the Stars

1967

Answering Service, Black Corridor, Gonna Roll the Bones, The Inner Circles

1968

Crazy Annaoj, In the Witch's Tent, One Station of the Way, A Specter is Haunting Texas, The Square Root of Brain, Their Mistress, the Sea, The Turned-off Heads, The Two Best Thieves in Lankhmar, When Brahma Wakes, The Wrong Branch

1969

Jonquil died. Leiber stayed drunk for the next three years.

Endfray of the Ofay, Richmond, Late September, 1849, Ship of Shadows, When They Openly Walk

[216]

1970

*America the Beautiful, The Circle Curse, Ill Met in
Lankhmar, The Price of Pain-Ease, The Snow Women*

1971

Gold, Black, and Silver

1972

*Another Cask of Wine, The Bump, Dry Dark, Night
Bright, The Lotus Eaters, You're All Alone*

1973

*The Bait, Cat Three, The Sadness of the Executioner,
Trapped in Shadowland*

1974

*Beauty and the Beasts, Cat's Cradle, Do You Know
Dave Wenzel, Midnight by the Morphy Watch,
Mysterious Doings in the Metropolitan Museum,
WaIF*

1975

*Belsen Express, Catch That Zeppelin, The Glove,
Night Passage, Trapped in the Sea of Stars, Under the
Thumbs of the Gods*

1976

*Dark Wings, The Death of Princes, The Eeriest
Ruined Dawn World, The Frost Monsteme, The
Terror from the Depths*

1977

*Our Lady of Darkness, The Princess in the Tower
250,000 Miles High, Rime Isle, A Rite of Spring, Sea
Magic*

1978

Black Glass, The Mer She

1979

*The Button Molder, The Man Who Was Married to
Space and Time*

1980

The Repair People

1981

The Great San Francisco Glacier

1982

Horrible Imaginings, The Moon Porthole

1983

The Cat Hotel, The Curse of the Smalls and the Stars, Quicks Around the Zodiac: A Farce

1984

Black Has Its Charms, The Ghost Light

1988

The Mouser Goes Below

1990

Replacement for Wilmer: A Ghost Story

1992

Married Margo Skinner
Died September 5

1993

Thrice the Brinded Cat

1997

The Dealings of Daniel Kesserich

2002

The Enormous Bedroom

List of Change War Apocrypha

The following stories are sometimes considered to be part of the Change War series but, while the tone and style are similar, they do not directly reference any characters or other elements from the Change War universe.

The Haunted Future (aka *Tranquility or Else*), 1959
The Number of the Beast, 1959
The Mind Spider, 1959
Black Corridor, 1959

Index

About the Author

Picture by Will Hart [CC-BY]

Fritz Leiber (1910-1992) was one of the most beloved science fiction and fantasy writers of the 20th century. Over the course of his career he earned an astounding total of six Hugo Awards, three Nebula Awards, two World Fantasy Awards, and two Locus Awards, as well as many minor honors. He also earned SFWA Grand Master, World Fantasy, Bram Stoker, and Forry awards for lifetime achievement and was posthumously inducted to the Science Fiction Hall of Fame.

Besides his well known *Swords* and *Change War* series and other short stories he published numerous novels and collections as well as screen and stage plays. A quarter century after his death his work continues to provide entertainment and inspiration to millions of fans.

About the Editor

Kevin A. Straight lives in Los Angeles County, California with his partner, a cat, and a turtle. He has previously published short stories and an academic monograph and has been blogging since 2008. Kevin also hosts a streaming television show, *Handyman Kevin*, on YouTube in which he teaches ordinary people how to be master handy-people.

Kevin holds an MBA degree from the University of California, Riverside and undergraduate degrees from Western Governors University and Flathead Valley Community College, and suspects that his educational journey is far from over.

For news about Kevin and his upcoming projects, please visit http://www.kevinastraight.com.

Also from CMP

ISBN
978-1-944327-01-9 (paperback)
978-1-310285-01-1 (ebook)

The story of the University is the story of Western Civilization itself. Newman's classic work traces the history of higher education from its beginnings in ancient Greece, through the turbulent years of the Dark Ages, and up to his own day in Victorian England. Includes a new forward and copious foot notes by Kevin A. Straight. Available from Amazon.com and other bookstores and ebook platforms worldwide.

Short Fiction by Kevin A. Straight

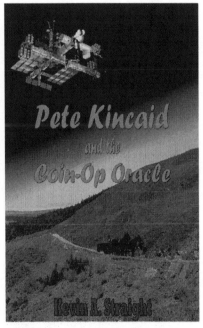

Available from the Amazon Kindle Store

Made in the USA
San Bernardino, CA
15 March 2018